EVEN A~~MERICA'S TV DARLINGS~~
HAVE THEIR SHARE OF SECRETS
. . . AND SINS.

From the white-hot lights of Hollywood studios to the
TV screens of suburban living rooms, they personified the
American dream — three loving, mischievous children,
models of a generation of complacent prosperity.

Dubbed "The Glitter Gang" by delighted publicists, the
young actors of "Charlie's Gang" worked carefully to cover
their tracks. No one would ever suspect that the sugar-
coated family they portrayed masked a tangle of lies, ob-
sessions, and raging sexual appetites.

No one would ever guess that America's darlings were
the objects of abuse, torment, and jealous rage. No one . . .
except one man.

Never to be forgotten, never to be forgiven, the actors
of the glitter gang followed their stars around the world,
from L.A. to Paris to Palm Springs. But someday, somehow, they would return to the scene of the crime.

He would make sure of it.

Also by Dona Vaughn:

ROYALE

DONA VAUGHN

THE GLITTER GANG

TUDOR PUBLISHING COMPANY
NEW YORK CITY

A TUDOR BOOK

October 1989

Published by

Tudor Publishing Company
276 Fifth Avenue
New York, NY 10001

Printed in the United States of America.

For David

Contents

"There are secrets in all families."
—George Farquhar

PROLOGUE

BUCKY'S BACK: AMERICA'S FAVORITE TV KID RETURNS

In spite of the poor track records of recent one-shot revivals, another favorite from TV's golden age of nostalgia will be returning this fall. Plans are underway for a two-hour prime time network reunion movie which will answer the question, *"Whatever Happened to Charlie's Gang?"* This latest entry in the resurrection sweepstakes arouses more interest than most, since the former stars of *Charlie's Gang* need no where-are-they-now buildup. Negotiations are underway for the Glitter Gang of actresses Victoria Carr, Sharon Bradford, and Oscar-winning actor/director Daniel Garrick to play grown-up versions of Nan, JoJo, and Bucky Weston, the characters they made famous during the five-year run of the series. The original *Charlie's Gang* ceased production abruptly in 1961 in a welter of off-camera scandal that failed to dim the popularity of the series itself. *Charlie's Gang* has *never* gone off the air. Reruns of the original episodes have played in continual syndication for almost thirty years.

TV GUIDE, January 14, 1989

1989

Three of them.

Crude human figures of twisted wire, no taller than a man's hand. Each one unmistakably male with its grotesquely large penis protruding like an extra arm.

The wire circles of their rib cages, the loops of their legs, the pointed towers of their penises, held nothing but air yet.

Hollow men. Like the poem. He still remembered the poem. But the poem reminded him of other things. Bad things he didn't want to think about now. It was the betrayers who mattered now.

He stood the three figures in a line on the desk like obscene toy soldiers and marched them over to stand against a book. Frowning, he knocked them flat, one by one. They lay on their backs, their foolishly large weapons pointing at the ceiling.

Three wire men.

But wire would not burn, and they had to burn. Three flaming men. Three human torches. One for each of the betrayers.

For over thirty years, the betrayers had whispered together on the flickering black and white screen, ignoring him. His family. The only family that he had, but for them he didn't exist.

He stood the figures up against the book again.

Three wire men.

They *had* to burn. *Had to*.

He yanked a sheet from the bed and tried to rip it, but the

4

firm weave of the material resisted him. He went to the kitchen for a knife, but there he found too many choices: steak knives, bread knives, paring knives, butcher knives. He lingered over the selection, running his thumb down each blade until his flesh was marked with crisscrosses of red. Enjoying it, until he remembered the three hollow men.

He took a small, sharp-pointed paring knife back to the bedroom and stabbed it into the sheet to start the tear.

Now he could rip the material. He shredded it into smaller and smaller strips, until the widest were a little less than an inch across.

Carefully he forced the material into the wire men, filling their bodies, their heads, their legs, and even the tiny loops of their feet with tight wads of it. He saved the penises for last, packing them until they bulged with the fabric, until he couldn't jam another piece of it within the wire forms. Then he began to wind each figure with long strips of cloth, giving them a smooth outer skin.

Did they know, the betrayers, that he had discovered their treachery? He had learned they were going to be together again. All three of them. His family.

But not him. He would be alone. Nothing had changed. He had kept their secret for almost thirty years, but nothing had changed. His family, but they acted as though he were a stranger. Laughing and talking with each other, but never with him.

Today he would change that.

He bound off the last of the strips and propped the three figures against the book once more. The wire skeletons stuffed with tight balls of fabric had vanished beneath the winding strips of cloth. Now the three wire men looked like round little mummies, their exaggerated penises pointing at him like bold cotton fingers.

He smiled at his handiwork.

Then he went to get the gasoline.

"Darling!"

Hug. Kiss. Smile for the cameras.

A pause while makeup was repaired.

"This time, Miss Carr, you stand beside Mr. Garrick while Miss Bradford greets you both."

"Darling!"

Hug. Kiss. Smile for the cameras.

Daniel Garrick stood with his arm around first one, then the other of the two women, changing partners as the press demanded, a job any man in the country would have killed for.

The photographers gave equal time to both women, and each of them was equally striking in her own way. At forty-six, Victoria Carr was still a brunette masterpiece, still the woman Daniel had been in love with since he was fourteen years old. Seven years younger, Sharon Bradford, with her tousled blonde hair and unbelievably green eyes in that perfect oval face remained—at least in Daniel's mind—the little sister she had played for the five years of *Charlie's Gang*.

This afternoon, Victoria was wickedly lovely in an elegant tube of black silk crepe that slid down her perfect body like a second skin, sheering off just above her knees, while Sharon was casually beautiful in a mid-calf-length dress of pure white silk, neckline open nearly to the wide leather belt tightly cinched at her waist.

Perfect complements to each other.

And between them, as always, Daniel. The Golden Boy, the trades called him, for his golden tan, his golden hair and for the two Oscars that graced his mantelpiece.

The Glitter Gang, the publicists had christened them.

The press *loved* it.

"Mr. Garrick? Now put your arm around Miss Bradford, while Miss Carr greets you."

"Darling!"

Hollywood hugs. False kisses. Then the questions, the endless questions that all boiled down to the same thing in the end. *Why* rephrased in every imaginable way. Why are you doing this? Three brilliant people at the height of their professional careers. None of you need this reunion special.

Do you?

The three of them were veterans of the media event since childhood. They fielded the questions like the pros they were, laughing and joking with the press while they presented the image they were hired to deliver: America's best-loved family reunited again.

But every time their eyes met, messages flashed between the three of them.

Did you get one?

I got one too.

We all did. A flaming wire reminder of the sins of our youth.

Someone knows!

We have to talk!

When the first wave of questions subsided, Daniel commandeered a vacant office, promising the crowd they would be back after a five-minute break. "A private reunion," he told them, letting his famous charm wash over the press.

What a poignant paragraph that would make! Satisfied, the men and women of the press scribbled wildly or muttered into their tape recorders.

Daniel closed the door behind him, alone with the two most beautiful women in America. As always his glance went first to Victoria.

"Now what?" she asked, killing the daydream before it could begin.

Daniel shrugged. "Pay the bastard."

"What if it's not money he wants?" Sharon demanded.

Daniel took a good look at her for the first time that afternoon and he didn't like what he saw. There was a funny wild light in those brilliant green eyes, almost as though she might be on the verge of hysteria. Drugs? he wondered.

Victoria chuckled, a rich vibrant sound that stirred up feelings in Daniel's groin and made him forget everything else. "Out of the mouths of babes."

"Don't do that to me, Victoria!" Sharon snapped. "I won't be treated like a child anymore! I'm thirty-nine years old, for God's sake!"

Daniel glanced from one to the other. "Sibling rivalry already?"

Sharon looked sullen, Victoria thoughtful. "Maybe that's just want he wants," Victoria said slowly. "To drive us apart."

Someone banged on the door. "Can we get started again, Mr. Garrick?"

"In a minute," he yelled.

"We have to find out who it is," Victoria said. "When we know who it is, then we'll know what to do."

"But what does he want?" Sharon demanded.

"To punish us," Victoria said slowly. "Don't we deserve it?" The terrible vulnerability in that beautiful face Daniel had worshiped for over thirty years made him want to scoop her into his arms and hold her so closely he could feel her heart beat. "After all, we *are* murderers."

"Victoria, don't—"

"Not me!" Sharon cried.

"All three of us," Victoria insisted. "Murderers. And I think someone has decided that we should die for our sins."

BOOK ONE:
Nan, Bucky, and JoJo

CHARLIE'S GANG

Situation Comedy

First Telecast: October 3, 1957

Last Telecast: November 9, 1961

Cast:

Charlie Weston	Nick Hanson
Mary Weston	Miranda Patton
Nan Weston	Victoria Carr
Bucky (Charles, Jr.) Weston	Daniel Garrick
JoJo (Joan) Weston	Sharon Bradford
Stevie Phillips	Theodore Kuhn
Henry Kaiser	Rudy Haynes
Miss Rand	Sue Crossman

Producer: Emery Friedman

Director: Owen Knox

Since *Charlie's Gang* ran from Dwight D. Eisenhower's second time in office to the first term of John F. Kennedy, this series has been repeatedly hailed by social historians as the primary symbol of this era of innocence. Nan, Bucky, and JoJo were *Charlie's Gang*, the three perfect children of the idealized family of Charlie Weston and his wife, Mary, ordinary people living in an ordinary Midwestern community. Like the Andersons on *Father Knows Best* and the Cleavers on *Leave It to Beaver*, the Westons were accepted without question as the typical, middle-class American family by television viewers of the late fifties and early sixties. Bucky Weston, a classic, all-American boy played by Daniel Garrick (son of swashbuckling movie actor, Leif Garrick), was the focal point of the series. The contrasts between Bucky, entering, experiencing, and trying to survive his turbulent teen years, Nan, the generally serene older sister, and precocious little sister, tomboy JoJo, were what gave the show its endearing charm. When *Charlie's Gang* began in 1957, Bucky Weston was 12, Nan Weston was 14, and JoJo was 7. As the show's fifth and last season began, Nan had just graduated from high school and was attending college, although still living at home. *Charlie's Gang* ceased production in 1961 at the height of its popularity due to off-camera problems, including the tragic and untimely death of Nick Hanson. Reruns of *Charlie's Gang* have played in syndication continuously for nearly thirty years.

The TV Nostalgia Handbook, Lyles and Martin, Curtis Press, 1989

Chapter One

1957

This was Nan Weston's refuge, the place she loved best in all the world. Victoria Carr let that love flow into her voice as she called gaily, "Mom? I'm home. What's for dinner?"

The roar of the surf answered.

Victoria sighed and leaned back to squint at the sea gulls gliding over the deserted beach. This was hopeless! How would she ever make a television audience believe she was part of a typical happy family like the Westons on *Charlie's Gang*? She didn't have the slightest idea what a typical family was like. She had no brothers, no sisters, her mother died when she was three, and she had never known her father! That stupid Elinor Donahue probably grew up in the same kind of perfect family she was part of on *Father Knows Best*. That's not fair, Victoria told herself. That's not even acting. A gull landed on the sand near her toes and she blew an unladylike raspberry at it. "Take that, Princess!" she told the startled bird as it departed in a flurry of wings.

What would it be like to be her father's Princess, the apple of his eye? She had no idea. Victoria Carr had never been anyone's favorite in the whole fourteen years of her life and she knew it. But somehow she was going to have to learn, because that was what Nan Weston was, according to the script: Charlie Weston's favorite. It just wasn't fair! Why did her big chance have to be something like this?

She had come down to the beach this afternoon so she could study the script for *Charlie's Gang* without one ear cocked for the whine of her grandfather's wheelchair. The strip of sand below the house was the only place on the whole property that was not accessible to him. Eleven years ago the automobile accident that killed Victoria's mother had paralyzed him, leaving him mute. Since then Vincent Stanton had spent a fortune remodeling the huge old house with elevators and ramps, so that there was nowhere in it, from the attic to the basement, that he could not penetrate. Victoria felt guilty for sneaking away, but she knew she would never be able to learn her lines with her grandfather watching her like a stern silent statue.

Besides, this sandy, isolated strip of beach really was her favorite place. She had hoped coming to this spot to read over her lines would give her an insight into Nan's character. Victoria could dimly remember being here with her mother, laughing and splashing in the surf, rolling and giggling on the warm sand. She treasured those fleeting memories because they were all she had. She had no recollection at all of her mother in the huge old house on the cliff above or of the car crash which killed Thea Stanton Carr and paralyzed her grandfather, even though there was a thin white scar on her left thigh to prove she had been there too. Victoria's life had begun the day her grandmother brought her home from the hospital. The only rip in that black curtain before the accident was the memory of salt and sand and her mother's arms here on this beach. She had hoped that just being here would get the right tone in her voice, the sound of a much-loved daughter in a very happy family.

The stiff sea breeze caught the cover of the script and ruffled through the pages. Victoria snatched it up and brushed the sand away, smoothing out the rumpled corners. She hugged the script to her meager chest and told herself that it was the wind off the sea and not utter despair that made her eyes tear.

She had been shaken to learn last week that one of the other child actors who was going to be on the show was a real pro. Danny Garrick was the son of a film star and the little twirp had already been in over a hundred TV shows and several feature films. The only professional work Victoria had ever done was two shampoo commercials and her grandparents had almost refused to let her do those.

It had been sheer luck that she was chosen for the part of the older sister on *Charlie's Gang*, since the network had wanted a blonde to match the coloring of the actress who would play the mother. But then someone had made the decision that Nan Weston would not only be her father's favorite, she would also have the dark hair and fair complexion of the actor chosen to play that part, a description which fit Victoria with her blue-black hair and milky white skin. Just after that decision was made, the show's producer, Emery Friedman, had gone to watch his niece in her eighth grade class play and spotted Victoria when she came on stage for her sole, two-sentence-long speech. She hadn't even known he was in the audience until two weeks later when her grandmother had told Victoria with great reluctance that she and Victoria's grandfather *might* allow Victoria to take the part. The realization that this chance could have been turned down without her ever even knowing it was offered nearly drove Victoria wild. Her grandparents didn't understand at all. They had no idea what acting really meant to her.

"You want to act because Thea was an actress," her grandmother insisted, disapproving of that as she had everything else about her daughter. But it just wasn't true. Young as she was, Victoria knew that one season of summer stock and the pregnancy, hasty marriage, and hastier divorce that resulted from it had not been enough to make Thea Stanton Carr an actress. Perhaps if she had continued her career . . .

However Thea's pregnancy and then the accident when Victoria was three had sniffed out whatever bright spark of talent Thea might have had. Maybe her mother's acting had been the reason she had volunteered for her first class play, Victoria conceded. Nevertheless, when she stepped out on the stage on opening night, she realized she felt truly alive for the first time. When she walked into the wings again, she knew she would never be able to bear an existence where she could not experience that exhilarating sense of aliveness over and over, the joy of being someone other than herself.

Victoria jumped to her feet, leaving the script behind her on the blanket, and raced across the sand to the water, scattering the gulls before her. She plunged into the surf, letting the battering waves pound against her as she dove and swam, until all her melancholy had washed away. She was bone weary with the effort before she came trudging out of the water toward the blanket. But happy. It didn't matter what kind of home life she *really* had, she could *be* Nan Weston. "I'm an actress!" she whooped to the gulls overhead. "I can be *anybody*!"

Peeling out of the wet swimsuit, she dropped it on the sand and lay back on the blanket, letting the slanting rays of the late afternoon sun dry the water from her skin. Her body wasn't *too* bad, Victoria thought, propping herself up on her elbows to take inventory. Tall and slender with long legs and a slim waist, she was not to be sniffed at. But the fact that she had no breasts yet was a major flaw and Victoria knew it. The sparse little triangle of dark pubic hair glistened damply in the sunlight. Victoria looked away, embarrassed by how little hair there was between her legs. Some of the girls at school had regular *jungles* down there. Idly she wondered what her mother had been like at her age. Had Thea Stanton had breasts at fourteen? And what about her father, the elusive Mr. Carr? What had he been like? Victoria had never even seen a photograph of him.

She rolled over to give the sun a chance at her backside, and a movement at the top of the cliff caught her eye. It was her grandfather in his wheelchair, a black silhouette against the clear blue of the sky.

She grabbed her swimsuit. The sandy fabric gritted against her skin as she squirmed into the clammy suit without rising from the blanket. When her nakedness was covered, she looked up at the top of the cliff again.

Vincent Stanton was no longer in view.

Danny Garrick made a running dive off the high board: Tarzan from the top of the cliff. He knifed down through the water until he touched the bottom of the pool and then shot toward the surface, lungs bursting. Just like my dad, he thought proudly as he cut through the water with strong, clean strokes to the other end of the Olympic-sized pool. He scrambled up the ladder and stood beside it, head cocked to one side, listening. The same faint sound still came from the house and the boy wondered what it was.

Instead of going back to the cabana to change, Danny
followed the golden sunlight through the French doors into
the cavernous, cathedral-ceilinged family room and held his
breath, trying to identify the noise he had heard. It came
again, floating down from upstairs, and now he recognized it:
laughter. It was the sound of women laughing.

The clear sharp laughter rose and fell and rose again.
Danny frowned at the ceiling. He hadn't heard that sound in
the house for a long time, not since before his father died.
Before his father's death, for as far back as Danny could
remember, the house had been full of women. Women talking
to his mother. Women ruffling his hair and telling him how
cute he was. Women asking him if he knew when his father
would be home. Women who wanted to hold him on their lap
so that when Leif Garrick walked in the room his eyes would
go directly to them. Because everyone in Hollywood knew
that the one thing that kept Leif Garrick coming back to the
mansion and his third wife was not her beauty or sex appeal,
but the son she had borne him.

But when Leif Garrick died, so did the laughter. The
women no longer came. No one was interested in a dead
star's third wife and her seven-year-old son anymore.

Now the women were back. Danny wondered why.

A sudden rivulet of water ran from his hair into his eyes.
Danny shook himself vigorously, spraying the rosewood desk
beside him with a fine mist of water droplets.

Rosita, the plump little maid, rushed toward him, scolding
in Spanish. Last year, when he was eleven, she had been
taller than Danny. Now he was twelve and taller than she
was. Rosita babbled something about *agua*. Danny glanced
down at the water pooling around his feet. "*Agua*," he
agreed. "Mop it."

Rosita kept chattering. Danny stepped around her and
went up to the wide, winding staircase, leaving slim, high-
arched footprints on the polished hardwood treads. Upstairs,
the thick carpeting on the hall dried the last traces of the
swimming pool from his feet and muffled his steps. He
paused outside the door of the master bedroom suite, listening
to the laughter rising and falling. For some reason, it reminded him of waves on gold sand and a huge white sail
billowing in the wind. He frowned, trying to understand why,

and then he remembered. There was a scene like that in *King of the Pirates*. Danny and his mother had run the movie dozens of times in the projection room downstairs along with all the other Leif Garrick movies. In *King of the Pirates*, his father played Blackbeard. The women in the movie had laughed like the women in the bedroom were laughing now. Danny pushed through the door without knocking.

Both of the women lolling on the huge bed were drunk, but the blonde was drunker than the brunette. She sprawled, legs apart, on the mauve satin, her dress hiked up past the tops of her hose. Danny stepped over the three discarded pairs of high heels just inside the door and maneuvered through the stunted forest of bulging shopping bags scattered across the floor. He was beside the bed before either of the women saw him.

The brunette noticed him first, but it was the blonde who reached out to slip her hands beneath his damp swimsuit, closing her warm fingers around the cool skin of his penis. "So this is the world-famous prick you inherited." She flashed a quick, surprised smile at the other woman. "Not bad, Danny." Her hand slipped further down the shaft until she was massaging the boy's testicles. After the first shudder of surprise, Danny stood quite still, the breath caught somewhere deep in his throat.

"For God's sake, Lena!" the brunette said. "Cut it out. He's just a kid." Her eyes narrowed. Danny did not move away from the caressing hand as it found his penis again. He stared down at the blonde with a dreamy, contented look. "Besides, Beth'll be back in a minute. She's only taking a pee, for Crissake."

"I was too young for your father, Danny," the blonde said, her hand moving faster. "And now I'm too old for you. Isn't life a bitch!" The sound of the toilet flushing came from the bathroom, and the blonde jerked her hand away.

Danny stood where he was, looking down at the two drunken women on the mauve satin of his mother's bed, his swollen penis an emphatic line up the front of his swimsuit. He didn't turn around when his mother called his name.

"You remember my friends," Beth Garrick told him with a careful enunciation that sent the blonde off into helpless laughter. "Lena Booth and Paula Nelson. Lena gave you a beautiful silver rattle when you were born." The blonde laughed even harder. Danny watched as her dress climbed further up her legs. Now he could see the pale blue crotch of her panties and the dark mat of hair behind it.

Beth Garrick put her arms around her son's shoulders in a clumsy drunken embrace and hugged him to her body. "Danny's going to be in a new TV series," she said proudly. "*Charlie's Gang*. They say he's going to be the star. He's my little man now," she told the women. "This past five years he's been the breadwinner. Ever since Leif . . ." Her voice trailed off with a hiccup that turned into a sob.

The blonde sobered for a moment. Then she caught the direction of Danny's glance and a new fit of giggles shook her.

"Lena and Paula and I ran into each other while we were shopping and decided to have lunch. Just like old times," Beth Garrick told her son with a desperate gaiety. The blonde giggled again, but the brunette had the grace to blush when Danny looked at her.

He shrugged out of his mother's grasp and turned to face her. Their eyes were almost level. Soon he would be taller than her, too. Already he felt older. Her wispy blonde hair was wild and unkempt looking, her lipstick smeared, her face puffy. Both of the other women had a smooth, polished look that Beth Garrick had lost. She would never have let herself go like this if Leif Garrick were still alive. The thought angered him. "Did you eat lunch?" he asked roughly. "Or drink it?"

Beth staggered back a step as though he had struck her. "Danny," she said pleadingly. "Please don't—"

"Whoops," the blonde said, a look of surprise on her face. She pressed her hand to her mouth and scrambled off the bed, staggering into the bathroom. In a moment there was a horrible retching sound that made Danny's stomach lurch.

Beth Garrick looked across at Paula Nelson. "I'm no good with sick people."

The brunette shrugged. "It's your john."

Beth followed the blonde into the bathroom, closing the door behind her.

"Danny?"

He turned.

Paula Nelson swung her feet off the bed and stood up in one graceful movement that made her breasts jiggle beneath her dress. They were bigger and fuller than the blonde's breasts or his mother's. She came toward him, her stockinged feet making no sound on the carpet. When she stopped in front of him, the print of her nipples through the fabric of her dress was exactly level with his eyes. "You got anything to eat in this place, Danny?" Her voice had changed somehow, but Danny couldn't figure out what the difference was.

"Downstairs," he told her.

She took his arm, holding it close to her body, so that the warmth of her left breast burned against it. "Show me the way," she said, with a husky little undertone, and he knew what it was that was different about her voice now. She was no longer talking to him as though he were a twelve-year-old kid. This was the way women had talked to Leif Garrick in his movies. The realization both excited and terrified him.

All at once his mouth was so dry he could hardly speak. "Okay," he said, and blushed when his voice cracked. But he led her through the door and out into the hall.

At the top of the stairs, she paused and turned so that she was looking straight down into his eyes. "You know, Danny," she said softly. "You and I are going to be great friends."

"Friends?" he repeated doubtfully. He knew about friends. They were the people who disappeared when you were no longer important. He had been old enough when Leif Garrick died to understand what happened to Beth. Friends were the people who never called, never invited you anywhere, and never spoke to you in restaurants when you were no longer married to a star.

"Friends," Paula Nelson said firmly. "And friends share secrets with each other."

Danny gazed at her silently.

"I'm going to share one with you." She moved closer, so close that he could smell the musky female scent of her beneath her perfume. "Unlike that stupid drunken cow in the bathroom, *I* was not too young for your father." She reached forward and traced the outline of his lips with one lazy finger, brushing against the faint promise of a moustache that shadowed his upper lip. The gesture made his penis tighten as though she had taken it in her hands as the blonde had. "Do you know what that means, Danny?"

He shook his head.

"It means I may not be too old for you."

                    *   *   *

They both knew what each other was thinking. They had always known, in some way beyond words. They clung to that wordless communication because it, and each other, was all they had. No one else had ever wanted them, not from the first moments of their lives. Even their mother's body had tried to reject them. They had clung, first to her and then to life when they were thrust from the security of the womb to meet the outside world prematurely. Now they clung to each other.

The two pairs of green eyes, so alike and yet so vastly different, exchanged glances. *Nurse has been bad*, was the frantic message that flashed from one set of green eyes to the other. *Nurse will be punished*, was the comforting reply.

Nurse had been very bad. Nurse made Andrew wait and wait for dry pants while she talked on the phone. Then she smacked him for wetting in the first place when she knew that sometimes he was just too excited or too frightened to hold it. Today he had been both.

"Ah, the little actress," Nurse said when she turned and caught Sharon Bradford watching her as she dressed Sharon's sobbing twin. "Enjoyed yourself, did you?"

Sharon stared at her stonily. It had been a nurse like this one who was in charge of the twins when Andrew hit his head so hard an ambulance had to come and take him away. Andrew stayed in the hospital for weeks. That was the first time the twins had ever been separated. When he finally came home Sharon found out that they were separated in a way that was almost as final as death itself. Something had changed inside of Andrew. It seemed as though his words could no longer keep up with his thoughts. The twins still knew what each other was thinking, but Andrew no longer shared as many words aloud with his sister. "Don't hit Andrew again," Sharon told Nurse. "You'll be sorry if you do."

Nurse chuckled. "Isn't she the little priss?" she asked Andrew. "Seven years old and she thinks she rules the roost. Stand still, Mister!"

Nurse gave Andrew a shake as he tried to squirm away from her, and then zipped his fly so roughly that he yelped.

"Shut up, you little bastard!" Nurse told him. "If it weren't for you, I'd be the one going to the studio with your sister. I have a fancy to see a TV show made."

"Mother wouldn't let you go anyway," Sharon taunted.

"Of course not. I have to take care of this brat."

That wasn't the real reason and Sharon knew it. But she wasn't going to give fat, slobbery old Nurse a hint of what the real reason was. But that reason was why Mother was even at the Beverly Hills house in the first place. Otherwise she would have been in Washington with Father where he worked for the government, or else traveling with him to New York, or Paris, or London, or somewhere—anywhere—else. Anywhere except for where her twins were. Other people had mothers and fathers; she and Andrew had nurses and nannies.

This one was better than most, Sharon thought as she watched the fat old woman run a comb through the tangle of Andrew's blonde curls. She was slow and stupid and lazy. That meant she couldn't catch the twins if they ran from her, couldn't figure out where they would hide, and didn't exert herself to complain to their mother. She could be worse. There had been worse, so Sharon knew the difference. But today Nurse was in a foul mood. She had learned she would not be the one to take Sharon to the television studio everyday, so she was taking out her disappointment on Andrew. She would have to be punished.

"Any trouble, Nurse?" Cynthia Bradford paused in the doorway of the children's playroom, slim and graceful in a black linen sheath, her platinum hair piled high on her head.

"Mrs. Bradford!" Nurse dropped the comb with a clatter and scrambled to her feet. "You gave me a start, Mrs. Bradford. I thought you had already left."

Cynthia Bradford extracted a cigarette from her evening bag and lit it with a delicate gold lighter, observing her children with a cool smile through the veil of smoke.

Andrew stared back, open-mouthed. It was the first time he had seen his mother in three weeks. Even while she was here in Beverly Hills, she seldom came into the children's area of the house. Andrew was never allowed out of it.

Sharon resentfully watched the coolly elegant figure in the doorway. She'd had a taste of something completely different today at the audition for *Charlie's Gang*. There, Cynthia Bradford had been determinedly maternal, pushing and clawing a way for herself and her daughter through the crowd of mothers with little girls vying for the part of JoJo. She had held Sharon on her lap and hugged her tenderly while the director and producer interviewed them. She had acted like a real mother to Sharon for the first time ever, and it had lasted until they climbed into the limousine afterwards. Riding home, Cynthia was as remote and unapproachable as ever. But at least Sharon had those few hours with a real mother. She knew what it was like now. Andrew had nothing, and the guilt over that settled in Sharon's stomach like a heavy weight.

"How are the twins behaving, Nurse?" Cynthia asked with no real interest.

"They're doing just fine, Mrs. Bradford," the woman assured her as Sharon had known she would. Nurse was too lazy to admit her charges were more than she could control. "They've been perfect little angels."

Cynthia's smile did not warm the malachite of her eyes. "I doubt that."

Andrew was trembling. Sharon could read his thoughts as though they were her own; she knew exactly what her twin wanted. "Mother!" she said quickly, as Cynthia dropped her lighter into the purse and closed it with a snap.

"Yes?" Cynthia glanced down at her diamond-encrusted wristwatch.

"Andrew wants to hug you, Mother."

"Don't be ridiculous," Cynthia told her daughter. "He'll muss my hair."

"He'll be careful, Mother," Sharon pleaded. "Won't you, Andrew?"

Cynthia was already walking away. She didn't look back as Andrew began to sob. But when the sobs rose to a wail, she spun around furiously. "Do something about that," she told the nurse. "Or I'll find someone who can!"

Andrew flung himself on the floor and began to scream in earnest. Sharon ran after her mother. She caught up with Cynthia just as her mother reached the doorway that separated the children's wing from the rest of the house. She was sobbing herself now with half-anger and half-terror. "Mother, please!" she cried.

Cynthia never paused. She disappeared through the doorway, slamming the door behind her. Sharon dropped down on the floor, staring at the door, tears trickling down her face. She couldn't go through that door. She didn't dare. She and

Andrew were never allowed in the rest of the house without permission.

A smack of flesh against flesh sounded in the playroom. Andrew's wails cut off abruptly.

Sharon scrambled to her feet and raced back down the hall. When she reached the playroom, she saw Andrew trying desperately to cut off the flow of tears as Nurse smacked him again across the face.

"Stop that!" Sharon yelled at her.

"You shut up, Miss, and go straight to your room." Nurse yanked Andrew up by his collar and dragged him toward the closet.

Terrified, Andrew started to wail again, kicking at the woman's fat, purple-lined legs. Nurse lifted him higher, by his collar, so that his feet dangled. His face began to turn blue.

Andrew thrashed wildly, and she smacked him again, harder than before.

Sharon lunged at the woman, burying her sharp little teeth in Nurse's flabby forearm. The woman howled and released Andrew, who scrambled out of her reach. Nurse grabbed Sharon by her long blonde curls, yanking violently until Sharon opened her mouth to scream with the pain. Before she could clamp her teeth into Nurse's forearm again, Nurse threw her into the closet with such force that Sharon struck the rear wall of the cubicle and slumped down to the floor.

Nurse was sobbing now herself as blood welled up out of the bite. "You little savages," she muttered as she caught Andrew by the collar and the back of his pants and threw him into the closet too.

Sharon was just scrambling to her feet when Andrew's body struck hers, knocking the breath from her lungs. She was unable to move or breath as the door slammed shut, leaving them in total darkness.

Crying hysterically now, Andrew flung himself at the door, kicking it and hitting it with his small fists. Sharon dragged herself up into a sitting position and tried to think while Andrew howled. Nurse had been very, very bad this time. She would definitely have to be punished.

Nurse slapped Andrew in the face all the time, but she never hit Sharon's face and Sharon knew why. Because Sharon was an actress and her face was her fortune. That was what Mr. Friedman told her when he called Sharon and her mother into his office and told Sharon she had the part of JoJo Weston on *Charlie's Gang*.

Sharon felt around on the closet floor, fingering and identifying each object as she came to it. At last her hand closed on a handle and she knew she had located a ping pong paddle. She took a deep breath as she raised it up and then slapped herself on the right cheek with it.

The blow stung, but she knew it wasn't hard enough. Sharon began to cry silently, the tears running down her cheeks as she raised the paddle again and hit her cheek as hard as she could.

She shrieked with the pain of the blow, and Andrew sobbed louder in the darkness. Sharon let the paddle drop and cradled her face in her hands, sobbing as loud as Andrew. The warm taste of blood was in her mouth as she slumped back against the wall. Already she could feel the puffy swelling of her cheek and jaw. Sharon hiccuped as her sobs died away and then grinned in the darkness. Nurse would really be punished this time. Rehearsals started Monday and by then her face would be awful, all black and blue like Andrew's.

"Nurse did it," she said aloud, practicing. "Nurse did it," she said again, this time with the pathetic little catch in her voice that had caught Mr. Friedman's attention at the audition.

Satisfied, she crawled forward and grabbed Andrew by the waist, pulling him down beside her. His sobs dwindled off as he laid his head against her shoulder. Andrew was the oldest, by three whole minutes, but all of her life, it was she who had taken care of him. Now Sharon held him close, breathing shallowly as a strong acrid smell flooded the closet, nearly choking her.

Andrew had wet his pants again.

Tina Sawyer pouted. Nude, her magnificent creamy breasts jutting out like melons, the redhead sat in the welter of sheets watching Emery Friedman, equally nude, pace and curse. His thing had been nice and hard when he started to climb on top of her, but now it was small and shriveled. It bounced against his balls like a pathetic little worm as he stormed around the apartment. Tina was just as hot as she had been when the fight started. Maybe even more so, since Emery was especially good when he was mad. She knew just what tantalizing tricks to play with her mouth and her hands to get him up again. She wanted to get all the silly talk out of the way and start working at it. "Really, Emery," she complained. "You're being tiresome."

"Tiresome? I saw the way that doorman looked at you." Emery bounced back on his heels and ran his hands through hair already graying at thirty-five. "You've probably had him up here already, you stupid cunt. You haven't been in this goddamned apartment six days yet and I'll bet you've already fucked everything in the building but the fire hose."

Emery was always full of nervous energy, but right now, caught up in the excitement of the new television show he was producing, he fairly crackled with it. It was his nervous energy that Tina liked best about him. The only way he could get rid of all that energy was by screwing, and since he had so much of it, he always wanted to screw. This week had been the best ever. Emery had thrown himself on top of her, fucking like a madman, at least twice a night all week long. If any one man could have satisfied her, it would have been Emery, Tina thought wistfully. They would be perfect together if he weren't so wildly jealous when she even smiled at a man. If he suspected a tiny fraction of the things she really did, he would go insane. "That's not even the regular doorman, Emery," she said soothingly. "He's a replacement for a couple of days. That's the only reason I stopped to talk to him. Just to find out who he was." She clenched handfuls of the sheet around her and looked at Emery pleadingly. If she didn't get him back on the bed with her soon, she was going to be just as crazy as he was. This morning's session with the doorman had only whetted her appetite. Now she needed Emery and she needed him badly. Emery could give her an orgasm that could keep her satisfied for simply hours. If he just would! "It's a lovely apartment, Emery. I like it much better than my old place."

"Sure you do," he snarled. "You probably fucked everyone in your old building fifty times apiece. You were tired of them, right? You wanted fresh cock, right?"

Tina just smiled. Never admit names or numbers to a man. Especially numbers. Tina had learned that long ago. She swung her feet off the bed and stood up, wrapping a sheet around her.

"What do you think you're doing?" Emery demanded.

"I'm going to take a shower," she said innocently. "There's nothing else to do here." She walked closer to him and took a wicked delight in seeing his penis stir and start to lengthen. Cover it up and a man always wanted it twice as bad. It never failed. Tina almost giggled at the thought as she paused right in front of Emery and reached up to caress his cheek, keeping the sheet wrapped tightly around her. "I've been thinking about getting another job, Emery. I'm bored here and you don't even care. You just want me to be available whenever you're in the mood. I need something to keep me busy."

"I want you with me," he said hoarsely. "Not out fucking the rest of the city." He reached out and pulled her against him. His erection poked at her through the sheet.

She made a mock show of pushing him away. "But I get bored here," she complained again, giving the words a special twist, a hidden meaning. Hinting at something wasn't the same thing as admitting it; you could always say that you had been teasing, or that he had misunderstood. "I'm a good secretary, Emery. You know that. If I had something to do . . ." She let her voice trail away while she kept her torso twisted just enough that his strengthening erection kept missing his target as he jabbed against her.

"We talked about this before. I told you I don't want you working again. You're getting a fortune in expenses from me!" He was weakening. Tina could tell. Weakening everywhere but his cock, which was getting harder by the moment.

She grinned up at him as she took him in her hand and guided him close to his target. She let him almost reach it before she twisted away once more. "I could work with you."

"What?" he muttered, his attention completely centered between her legs.

"I could be your personal secretary." His penis poked inside the sheet, brushing across her public hair. She squirmed away again.

"I *have* a secretary, Tina. She's been with me for ten years."

Tina yanked back out of his arms, dropping the sheet to the

floor. "Then go fuck her," she said coldly. "I'm going to take a shower."

"You crazy cunt! I'm not stupid. You'd be fucking everyone in the studio while my back was turned."

Tina was instantly wet at the thought. Thank God it didn't show on a woman like an erection on a man! "Think how much fun we would have in your office, Emery. In your private office." She smiled up at him with warm blue eyes. "Anytime you got a little tense or uptight, I'd be right there to help you work out your problems." She stepped closer. "Right there, Emery," she said softly as his cock bobbed against her.

"Tina! Please!" Tina had to fight to keep from grinning at the ragged desperation in Emery's voice. She had already won and they both knew it. "It's a family show," he pleaded. "There'll be kids on it! Little kids!"

She tossed her hair back from her face and gave him a long sultry look from beneath her lashes. "I love kids," she told him, making her voice drip with unspoken promises. Variety was what she really loved and the set of *Charlie's Gang* was where she was going to find it. Tina had discovered her sexuality late. She was eighteen before she went on her first date, twenty before she had her first sexual experience. She had spent the four years since then making up for lost time. The memory of those last four years made her lick her lips in an unconsciously provocative gesture.

"All right," Emery said suddenly, reaching for her again.

"All right, what?" Tina asked suspiciously, but letting him pull her closer.

"All right, you're my new secretary." He grabbed her with both hands, pulling her onto his erection like a glove. Still holding her there, he fell backwards across the bed.

Tina just had time to check the clock across the room as he rolled her over, underneath him, and began to pound away at her furiously. She thrust herself up to meet each lunge, knowing she could bring both him and herself to the brink in minutes. Emery would be through in plenty of time for dinner at home with his wife and kids.

And the new doorman got off duty in forty-five minutes.

Owen Knox went through the list of the cast for *Charlie's*

Gang again. He had really fucked up on this one and he knew it.

When the talk about the new television series Emery Friedman was producing first surfaced, Owen would have sworn there wasn't a snowball's chance in hell he would be the director on it. He hated Friedman's guts too much to ever work with him. Not that anyone else knew that. Owen was far too clever to let anyone guess how he really felt about that self-important bastard. So clever that he had wound up with his balls in a trap. Because Friedman's first two choices for director on *Charlie's Gang* had fallen through, Owen had finally gotten a look at what the producer planned for the show. *Charlie's Gang* had all the earmarks of a hit, and Owen wasn't about to let Emery Friedman cheat him out of his chance at the big one.

Owen stared at the cast list again and then crumpled it up and flung it across his office. For the past ten years he had watched Emery Friedman rise from boy wonder director to important television producer. Friedman's awesome temper was legendary. But as long as he kept coming up with winning projects, no one was willing to make an issue of it. Whatever Friedman wanted, he got. That didn't surprise Owen a bit. He'd known all along that the business was all family ties. Friedman had them. Owen didn't.

But Owen had been content to watch and smolder until Friedman waltzed in and stole lush Tina Sawyer right out of Owen's office without even an apology for leaving him without a secretary. What Friedman *did* leave him with was the worse case of blue balls he'd ever had.

So when someone had asked Owen for a suggestion for an actor to play the father's part on *Charlie's Gang*, he had recommended Nick Hanson in glowing terms. Then he followed up with a quick call to Nick's agent to let him know his client had a very good chance at the part. Because Owen knew something about Nick Hanson few people in Hollywood were aware of. Something that was guaranteed to scuttle Emery Friedman's new show in the worst possible way and make him an anathema in this town for years to come.

Owen Knox's hobby was gathering information. Gossiping, some people called it, but with Owen, it was beyond gossip. It was information-gathering elevated to a fine art. He didn't need anything as crude as private detectives or phone taps. He had a network of sources all over town that he checked and rechecked with the vigilance of a gardener caring for his prize roses. His reward was stray bits and pieces of information that other people would have discarded as worthless. However Owen knew that information correlated correctly would gain him what his talent would not in this crazy business. It wasn't anything as crude as blackmail. Just small hints, insinuations, and whatever Owen wanted was granted. It had always worked like a charm.

But then Friedman appropriated Tina, setting her up in an apartment, and Owen lost his perspective. For the first time he had used his information not to gain something for himself but to revenge himself against someone else. It would have worked beautifully, too. Nick Hanson was a fine actor, perfect for the part of Charlie Weston, an idealized father figure the whole country would be looking up to as soon as the show went on the air. No one suspected Nick's taste for young girls, the younger the better, or he would never have been offered the part of the father on a family show like this one. Predictably, Nick jumped at the chance to do the series. He had known with an instinct born of twenty years in show business that *Charlie's Gang* was going to be a big hit. If Nick's sexual proclivity had not come out without Owen's help, Owen had planned to launch a few subtle rumors. Nothing that could be traced to him, of course.

Jail bait made for bad publicity at any time, but the resulting furor over *Charlie's Gang* would have roasted Emery Friedman's career. If Owen hadn't been offered the chance to direct the show, he would have been more than happy to see the bastard crash and burn.

But not now.

It was too late to get Nick Hanson off the show. The prank Owen had tried to play on Friedman had backfired, and he was just going to have to live with it. But he would make sure Nick Hanson kept his dick out of anything underage. Not that Owen cared what Nick did in his private life, but he didn't want to lose his own chance at a hit series.

Nick tried to lie his way out of it when Owen confronted him yesterday about Nick's affair with the twelve-year-old last summer. However, Owen had come down on him hard with the evidence: all the facts and figures, right down to the girl's hospital bills and the adoption papers on the kid. The whole affair had cost Nick a bundle to keep quiet. Nick broke down and blubbered like a baby when Owen confronted him. He had sworn he would never do it again.

A sense of unease made Owen reach for the phone. He was relieved when Nick answered on the second ring. "I just wanted to remind you that the first rehearsal is set for Monday, Nick."

"I'm looking forward to it." Nick's voice faded and came back, as though he had moved away from the phone.

"What are you doing?" Owen asked him quickly.

"Getting dressed," Nick told him. "I've got a hot date tonight."

Owen rubbed his bald spot nervously. "Ah . . . what's she like Nick?"

The warm fatherly chuckle that came over the line reassured Owen. Nick was perfect for the part. Just perfect! "Don't get in an uproar, Owen. She's an older woman."

Owen realized he had been holding his breath. "Great, Nick! See you on Monday."

Owen hung up and leaned back in his chair. Things were going to be just fine. *Charlie's Gang* would be a hit and Owen would be a part of it. And maybe, just maybe, along the way, he'd get another chance to stick it to that bastard Friedman.

Nick Hanson hung up the phone and went back to adjusting his tie. A calm, competent actor, Nick left his problems on the set and never let them interfere with his personal life. He didn't have a doubt in the world that he would play the part of Charlie Weston to perfection. He couldn't understand what Owen Knox was so hot and bothered about.

Nick gave his tie one final tug and grinned at himself in the mirror. Tonight was his first date with Mindy and he wanted everything to be just right. He certainly didn't want to start off their relationship by being late. A glance at his watch told him he should be on his way to the high school right now. Cheerleader practice ended at six o'clock.

He just hoped Mindy would remember to bring her pom-poms.

Chapter Two

Florence Stanton's voice darted all around Victoria like a fluttering, panicked bat in the closed passenger compartment of the Rolls. "It was a terrible thing Thea did." Her daintily gloved hands gripped each other in her lap. "A terrible thing!"

Victoria leaned back, trying to ignore her. She never knew what set her grandmother off. Most of the time Florence Stanton was quiet, withdrawn. But once or twice a month she would break out in one of these tirades, denouncing her dead daughter for some terrible dark deed. Victoria had no idea what the ancient sin was. Florence Stanton never answered her granddaughter's questions when she was having one of these seizures, never even seemed to realize that anyone else existed while she mumbled her terrifying litany of blame. When she was herself, calm and self-contained, she refused to discuss her daughter with her daughter's child.

Florence Stanton's voice dropped to an indistinguishable mumble that was in its own way more frightening than the words which had gone before.

"What was it that Mother did?" Victoria asked her. "Was it the accident? Was that what she did wrong?" Thea Stanton Carr had been driving that awful night that left her dead, her father paralyzed, and her three-year-old daughter stunned and bleeding beside the highway. That much Victoria knew. Had Thea planned to crash the car? Had she taken her own life on purpose? Victoria had wondered that ever since she had been old enough to understand the concept of suicide.

"No one must find out," Florence Stanton said abruptly, with frightening desperation.

"Find out what?" Victoria demanded. When there was no response, she leaned over and grasped her grandmother's thin shoulder. "Grandmother!"

Florence Stanton seemed to wake from a dream. "What is it, Victoria?"

The words caught in Victoria's throat. Florence Stanton was herself again, a trim, elegant woman in command of her emotions. "Nothing, Grandmother," Victoria said quietly. She leaned back and closed her eyes wearily, letting herself drift off into the world of *Charlie's Gang*. Too bad the Weston family was only a dream, a fantasy, because Victoria would have loved nothing better than to lose herself in that make-believe family.

She wondered if the rest of the cast felt that way. Miranda Patton was such a mess off the set, chain-smoking, cursing like a sailor when there were no outsiders around, throwing tantrums if she didn't get the lines she wanted in the script, ignoring the three child actors as though they didn't exist aside from the characters they played. However when the cameras rolled, Miranda Patton *was* Mary Weston. When she opened her arms and hugged Victoria to her bosom, Victoria felt as though she really was the much-treasured daughter of a loving family. Miranda's portrayal of Mary Weston was the way Thea would have been if she had lived; Victoria was sure of it.

Nick Hanson was different. Even though he fit the part of Charlie Weston to perfection, Victoria couldn't seem to lose herself in the illusion of Nick as her parent as she could with Miranda. When Nick became Charlie Weston for the camera, Victoria remained wary. There was something about him, some strange watchfulness, which reminded Victoria in a weird way of her grandfather even though the two men looked nothing alike.

But Danny and Sharon tumbled so easily into their roles as the younger Weston children that Victoria found herself forgetting that they were not actually her brother and sister. Yesterday she absentmindedly reached over to ruffle Danny's hair as he stood beside her waiting to be called back on to the set. It was only when his startled expression sunk in that she remembered who he really was and snatched her hand away. That must mean that she was a pretty good actress after all, Victoria thought with a great deal of satisfaction.

Victoria looked forward to the time when she could spend more than four hours a day working. Some shows turned out two episodes a week, but with so many child actors involved that was impossible for *Charlie's Gang*. All of the young performers were required by California law to spend three hours a day with the studio teachers. That was time stolen from her acting as far as Victoria was concerned.

The rhythm of the show was the same each week. She didn't mind Mondays when all the actors sat around the table in the rehearsal hall, reading their parts aloud for Owen Knox. Especially since the director spent a lot of time changing lines so that they were clearer and easier to say. Some of the dialogue that looked just fine on paper turned out to be ridiculous when spoken aloud. A lot of things which were funny on the page went flat in the rehearsal, and Owen Knox worked with the writers on adjustments to the script when that happened.

But as far as Victoria was concerned, Tuesdays were the best days. On Tuesdays they moved to the soundstage for the rehearsal of that week's script. They wore the clothes they would wear for the actual filming and moved through the sets as though they were rooms in real buildings. It was easier to lose herself in the fiction of the Weston family on Tuesdays.

Wednesdays through Fridays when the actual filming was done, the story was interrupted too many times to seem real anymore. Scenes were shot out of order, in bits and pieces. It wasn't that she didn't enjoy the acting on those days; she did. But it was harder to hold on to the feeling that the Westons were an actual family of which she was an important part.

When she watched the films of the first scripts, her favorite scenes were the opening ones which would be repeated each week at the beginning of the show while the theme song played. The establishing shot of the exterior of the Westons' comfortable two-story house looked so real it was hard to believe that it sat on the studio's back lot instead of a residential street in a Midwestern town. Even the sets themselves had a wonderful, lived-in look. Sometimes she wandered through them alone—through Nan Weston's bedroom, Mary Weston's kitchen, Charlie Weston's study—and they seemed more real than the rooms in her grandparents' house.

Until she looked up.

None of the rooms had real ceilings. The dangling chandelier in the Weston's dining room hung from a rafter at the top of the soundstage. When the show was being filmed, lighting men crouched with their huge lights on the catwalks high on the soundstage's crossbeams to light the set below. Anytime Victoria glanced up, she could see that the Weston family was a fake.

The blare of the Silver Wraith's car-horn punctured her reverie.

Florence Stanton stared straight ahead, her lips moving silently as she repeated the same phrase over and over to herself.

Victoria knew what it was without hearing it spoken aloud: *Thea did a terrible thing!*

"Lesbians!"

Mike Nelson heaved his glass at the bathroom door. It shattered, sending a shower of bourbon and glass shards everywhere. He looked at the mess blearily for a moment and then lurched over to the bed and sat down heavily. Six weeks on location, six miserable weeks in the Mojave, letting himself be ordered back for take after take by that fag director, and he had come home to this. "A bunch of fucking dykes," he muttered, and then raised his voice to shout at the closed door, "Why else would you spend all your time over there?"

The bathroom door opened. "Why, indeed?" Paula Nelson said with icy indifference as she stepped across the mess on the carpet. "It's so pleasant here."

Mike didn't answer. Instead, he watched her legs as she moved around the room. Long-stemmed American beauty, he had called her when he first met her. Paula's long beautiful legs were her best feature and she knew it. Why else would she be walking around the bedroom in bra, panties, and garter belt, stooping now and then to smooth her hose? Mike thought about Elizabeth Garrick's hands running up those legs, cradling that tight little ass of Paula's, and he nearly puked. "How do you do it?" he asked bitterly. "Dildos? Or do you just tongue each other?"

Paula swung around to give him a cold little stare and then went back to combing her hair.

Her silence stung. "Hell, what do you expect me to think? You've spent every waking hour over there for the past three weeks."

"Beth Garrick is a friend of mine," Paula said, keeping her eyes on her reflection in the mirror.

"You told me you couldn't stand the bitch."

"That was a long time ago. I really didn't know her then." Paula turned suddenly, dark eyes flaming. "Besides, what do you expect me to do? You're gone on location half the time. Aren't I entitled to have friends? To see people?"

"Sure, Baby." Mike stood up and tried to embrace her, but she moved away. He watched as she slipped her dress over her head. "Only I'm home now. Don't I deserve a little attention?"

Paula buttoned the dress and then picked up her purse. "Sure you do." She patted his cheek and turned away, her perfume trailing after her. "Only right now I'm late."

"Late for what?"

"I'm taking Danny over to the studio for Beth."

Mike Nelson followed his wife downstairs. "That's the third time this week you've taken the goddamned kid to the studio. Let Beth take care of the little bastard herself."

"I don't mind." Paula paused for a last glimpse of herself in the hall mirror. "He's a nice kid."

Mike reached for her and pulled her back against him. He nuzzled her right earlobe. "We could have a nice kid of our own, Baby. We could start to the process right now."

Paula jerked away from him. "I wouldn't want to spoil the beautiful affair you have going with your bottle." She reached for the door handle.

He moved more swiftly than she had anticipated, grabbing her by the arm and swinging her around to face him. Her bag went sailing across the hall. "My affair? Or yours?" Mike tightened his grip, enjoying the wince of pain that flashed across her face, the little flicker of fear in those dark eyes. "Don't try playing around again, Baby. I warned you last time I wouldn't put up with it. Even with a dyke. Especially with a dyke!"

"What about you?" Paula said through clenched teeth. "I

know all about you and that little hot-pants starlet, Mike. You may have tried to keep it a secret, but she didn't.''

He shrugged, still holding her arm. "So what? I pay the bills in case you've forgotten." His eyes narrowed. "I remember you and Leif Garrick, Baby. That's not why you're hanging around with Beth, is it? Does the kid have a cock like his dad's?''

Paula jerked away and rubbed her wrist. "Don't be stupid! Danny's twelve years old, for God's sake."

"I knew Leif better than you did. He always claimed he was fucking before he was ten. Maybe the kid's following in his old man's footsteps."

"You have a filthy mind!''

"Right, Baby. That's why you love me," he said as Paula knelt and scooped up her purse. She left without replying and in a few minutes, he heard her car roar to life in the drive.

Mike walked into the den and straight to the bar. He grabbed himself a fresh glass and poured a hefty slug of bourbon. Outside this house he might be an overage, overweight actor who had peaked and started the long slide into obscurity, but not inside it. No way. He was going to stay the number one priority in Paula's life, whatever it took. That ten thousand dollar, powder blue Mark II she had just burned out in was one way. Jake Moriarty was another.

Something was going on between Paula and Beth Garrick, and Mike as going to get to the bottom of it. Jake Moriarty was a damned good private detective. Paula didn't know it, but Mike had used Jake to break up her affair with Leif Garrick twelve years ago. Jake was fast and discreet. One phone call to Jake and Mike knew that he'd find out who Paula was balling this time.

If it was Beth Garrick, then those two dykes would have a surprise in store for them the next time they climbed in bed together.

Paula Nelson stood to one side watching the lumbering television camera move in for a close-up on Danny's face.

"But why, Dad?" he asked Nick Hanson. Real tears ran down his cheeks. "He was just a puppy. Why did he have to go and die like that?''

"The kid's not bad, is he?" a female voice commented right beside Paula.

Paula turned. The redheaded, full-bodied woman looked vaguely familiar, but Paula couldn't place her immediately.

"Are you his mother?" the redhead asked, her eyes still on the scene being filmed between Danny and Nick Hanson.

"I'm Paula Nelson, a friend of the family. I brought Danny in today."

"I'm Tina Sawyer, the producer's secretary." The redhead looked at Paula curiously for a moment. "Nelson? Sure! You're the muscleman's wife, aren't you?"

Paula nodded, taking a certain pleasure in the recognition this morning. Mike hated the three muscleman pictures that had brought him his fame. He had tried his best to forget them and hoped everyone else had also. After the scene he threw this morning, it did Paula good to find out they were still Mike's chief claim to fame. She'd be sure to repeat the redhead's comment to Mike this evening. That was, if she could catch him sober enough to understand it, she thought bitterly. She wrenched her thoughts away from Mike. "He looks like his father, doesn't he?" she said softly, as her glance sought out Danny again.

"Does he?" the redhead asked curiously. "I never watched any of Leif Garrick's old movies. I'll have to catch one sometime."

Paula glanced at the woman, annoyed for Leif's sake. What was she? Twenty-four? Twenty-five? She wasn't too young to be familiar with Leif's movies. "Do that," she said dryly.

"I heard Leif was quite a man with the ladies in his time," the redhead said.

"His time lasted right up until the day he died," Paula said with more force than she had intended. "He was hell on wheels with anything female between the ages of twelve and dead."

She didn't look away as the redhead's glance swept over her. "How about the kid?" the woman asked. Paula saw something besides idle curiosity in the redhead's eyes as Tina Sawyer looked back at the living room set. "Does he have any of his old man's characteristics?"

"Danny's a good kid," she blurted with an instant protectiveness that made her feel ashamed of her own intentions.

"Too bad," the redhead said with real regret in her voice

and Paula remembered where she had seen the woman before. It had been at a party several months ago. Someone asked Mike if he'd ever met a real nymphomaniac and then dragged him across the room to meet the redhead. Mike disappeared right after that, Paula remembered, and she had driven herself home.

She owed the woman her thanks for giving her a night off from Mike's attentions. Did a nympho find Mike Nelson's harsh pounding more acceptable than a woman of normal appetites? Paula curbed the impulse to ask. Besides, the redhead had already lost interest in both Paula and Danny. Her warm blue eyes were on the cameraman as the scene broke off. She drifted over to his side and began to talk to him, her hand resting lightly on his thigh.

Paula glanced around for Danny and was amused to see that the redhead's conversation with the cameraman was the object of intense interest to at least two other men on the set. Owen Knox, the director, was staring across at Tina Sawyer like a kid with his nose pressed to the candy store window, and Emery Friedman, the show's producer, was storming over to the couple, oblivious to anyone else on the crowded set.

Paula cut through actors and technicians and grabbed Danny by the hand. "Ready to go?" she asked him. "It looks like stormy weather in here."

"Mr. Friedman's always yelling at Tina for talking to people," Danny said as he followed Paula outside. "He's not very nice, is he?"

Paula considered explaining the situation to Danny and then decided not to. Learning about nymphomaniacs was not part of the education she had in mind for Leif Garrick's son.

Taking Danny back to Beth's, Paula battled the traffic in silence. The memories of Leif that came flooding back every time she looked at his son were taking their emotional toll. Paula had been twenty when she met Leif Garrick in the flesh for the first time, but she already knew everything there was to know about the actor. She had watched each of his films dozens of times in the movie house in Sacramento, memorizing his voice, his mannerisms, his walk. She had scanned newspapers and magazines for any mention of him. Her father brought Paula and her mother from Sacramento to Los

Angeles to live with her grandparents when he enlisted in 1942, and Paula had been forever grateful to World War II. Her life began the day she and her mother moved into the bungalow with her grandparents. By the end of the day, she had unpacked and had also managed to learn the location of three personal appearances Leif Garrick would be making that week to publicize *King of the Pirates*. By the end of the week, she was in his bed. Her eventual marriage to his buddy Mike Nelson had been Leif's way of keeping their affair under wraps. Too bad Mike had finally figured out what was going on.

"Paula?"

"What is it, Danny?" Paula braked for a light and reached over to ruffle his hair. Her hand lingered on his brow, toying with the thick gold locks that had fallen across it. His hair was as unruly as his father's had been, she thought with nostalgic fondness, and his eyes were the same golden brown.

Danny watched her steadily, not moving away from her hand. "You're not mad at me, are you, Paula? You've been very quiet."

"No, I'm not mad. I was just thinking." She threaded her fingers through his hair and smiled at him. "In fact, I'm very happy today, Danny. My husband's going out of town Friday and your mom invited me to spend the weekend at your place so I won't have to stay by myself." She could feel the faint film of perspiration that dampened his forehead abruptly.

"She . . . she likes the company," he managed to say, almost choking on the words.

Paula leaned closer. "We're going to be great friends, Danny." The words were a husky whisper against his ear. "You'll see."

Horns honked behind them as the light changed. Paula straightened and accelerated into the intersection. She risked a quick glance at Danny. His head was turned toward the window. All she could see was his faint reflection in the glass. Leif's smile was on his lips.

Emery Friedman leaned over to pat Sharon on the cheek. "I'm glad to see you're taking better care of that pretty face."

Sharon smiled up at him happily. The purple bruise was barely visible now behind the makeup, but it had been bad enough the first two weeks of filming that it had been necessary to write her injury into the opening episodes of *Charlie's Gang*. JoJo was a tomboy, her TV father had explained, and she had fallen out of a tree. Sharon liked the sound of that so much she had wanted to climb a tree herself. But everyone from Mr. Friedman and Mr. Knox to her mother vetoed the idea. Everyone but Nurse. "Nurse was awful to Andrew," Sharon told Emery Friedman. "But now she's gone for good."

"Yes, well, take care of yourself," Emery Friedman said absently as he straightened, his eyes on the red-haired woman approaching them on the almost deserted set. "Ready to go, Tina?" he called.

Sharon scuffed the toe of her shoe absently as she waited for the redhead to say something to her. But both Miss Sawyer and Emery Friedman seemed to have forgotten she existed. Mr. Friedman was talking about different restaurants they could go to after they left the studio. Then Miss Sawyer leaned over and whispered in his ear, and he turned all red as he glanced down and caught Sharon watching them with great interest. Mr. Friedman grabbed Tina Sawyer's hand and hurried her away.

"I wonder where they're going," Owen Knox said as he walked over to Sharon.

Sharon looked at him doubtfully. She never knew what to make of the director. When he was on the set, he was always picking at her: straighten up, turn this way, turn that way, talk louder, talk softer, talk slower, talk faster. But when she wasn't playing JoJo, he was the only one of the adults who talked to her, really talked to her. He was always asking her questions about the rest of the cast and crew. It was like playing a game with Andrew. "I know where they're going," she bragged now, knowing that Owen Knox would keep after her until she told.

He was just as interested as she had known he would be. "Where?" he demanded.

"It's stupid, though," Sharon told him, scorn for adults' weird ways coloring her seven-year-old voice. "They're going to go home and go to bed before they go to dinner. Why would anyone take a nap if they didn't have a nurse to make them do it?"

Owen Knox didn't reply.

Sharon was disappointed. Usually when she told him a little bit about someone, he would tease her until she told him everything. Now he seemed to have forgotten that she was there. She searched desperately for something else to catch his interest. "Are Mr. Friedman and Miss Sawyer going to make a baby and get married?"

She had caught Mr. Knox's attention with that. His lips moved but he didn't say anything.

A hand closed on Sharon's shoulder like a claw as Cynthia Bradford's laughter sounded beside her. "Kids say the cutest things, don't they?" Sharon tried to squirm away from her mother's hand, but Cynthia held on firmly. "We better be going, Sharon Darling."

Sharon Darling! Her mother had taken to calling her Sharon Darling whenever they were on the set of *Charlie's Gang*, but never anywhere else. "I don't want to go anywhere," Sharon said angrily. "I want to talk to Mr. Knox."

"Mr. Knox is a busy man. He doesn't have time to talk to you. Come along, Sharon Darling," she said, as she led her daughter away.

Sharon looked back over her shoulder. Mr. Knox was still just standing there with the strangest expression on his face. He hadn't said anything else. "I wanted to talk to him about Andrew," she whined.

Cynthia stopped abruptly and grabbed Sharon by the shoulders. "You keep your mouth shut about Andrew!"

"Andrew could be on the show with me," Sharon told her. "He could be my brother just like Danny. Mr. Knox would let him if I asked."

For a moment Sharon thought her mother was going to slap her. "Mr. Friedman won't like it if you hit me," she said desperately. "He'll make you go away like Nurse did!"

Cynthia gave her a rough shake. "Shut up, you little monster. He didn't make Nurse go away. I did. And I'll make Andrew go away if you talk to anyone about him." She shook Sharon again. "Do you understand me?"

Sharon was so terrified that she flopped around like a rag doll in her mother's hands. Never, never, not even in her worst nightmares, had it occurred to her she and Andrew might be separated.

"Do you understand?" her mother demanded again. When Sharon remained silent, Cynthia gave her another shake.

Sharon began to sob. "I don't want Andrew to go away!" she screamed through her tears.

"Then don't mention his name here! Don't say anything at all about him. If you do, I'll make sure you never see him again!"

Sharon shook with terror. "I won't," she promised through her tears. "Please don't send him away. I'll be good."

Cynthia scanned her face and gave a satisfied nod. "See that you are," she said. "Or you'll be responsible for what happens to Andrew." She grabbed Sharon's arm and pulled her daughter along behind her.

Sharon stumbled, unable to see where she was going through her tears. *It wasn't fair!* It wasn't fair that Mother should be able to make Andrew go away if she wanted to. Mother was the one who should go away. Things were always better when Mother was away. Andrew had been so happy when Sharon made Nurse go away. His happiness made up for the pain she had endured. If only there were some way to make Mother go away too.

Cynthia Bradford pulled her sobbing daughter past a man and a woman. When Sharon saw who the woman was, she managed to break free of her mother's grip and run to her. "Mom!" she wailed, throwing her arms around Miranda Patton's waist.

"Isn't that cute?" the actress said grimly to her companion. "She thinks I really am Mary Weston." She peeled Sharon's arms free and thrust the child away. "But then you're just as confused as she is, aren't you, Henry? You think her mother is your wife."

Cynthia hurried up and grabbed Sharon's hand again, ignoring the child's attempt to escape.

"I believe you know my husband, Harry," Miranda Patton said to Cynthia. "As a matter of fact, I believe you know each other *very* well." She turned and stalked away.

Cynthia and Harry Patton exchanged a complicated look, and then Harry Patton hurried after his wife.

"Come on, you little monster," Cynthia told Sharon and jerked her in the opposite direction.

Sharon followed, her sobs now low whimpers. She knew that man. He was the one her mother had stayed in Beverly Hills to be with. But Sharon hadn't known until just now that he was Miranda Patton's husband. She wondered if her mother would make a baby with Harry Patton and then immediately dismissed the thought. Cynthia had told her more than once that if she and Andrew hadn't come at the same time there would be only one of them. Cynthia didn't like having babies at all.

But even if they weren't making babies together, Miranda Patton didn't seem very happy about Cynthia being with her husband. Sharon wondered if her father would be unhappy about it too, if he found out. Maybe if Sharon told him that Cynthia spent almost every night out with Harry Patton, Father would make Cynthia go away, just like Nurse. Maybe he would be so happy when Sharon told him that he would come and live with Sharon and Andrew.

If Mother went away, Sharon could take care of Father and Andrew herself. Then they wouldn't need any more nurses *ever*.

Sharon smiled through her tears.

Beth Garrick twisted her hands nervously as she paced. She had long beautiful hands, she thought dispassionately. Long and slender with long graceful fingers and perfect nails. Perfection brought on by idleness.

There were too many idle days behind her, long days when all she had to think about was the shape of her nails, the color of her polish. Beth didn't want to spend any more days like that.

Paula would be bringing Danny home soon. Beth cast her mind about frantically, trying to decide what to do. Offer Paula a drink? Invite her to stay for dinner? Offer to take her out for dinner? Beth felt totally at a loss. She was still feeling her way along in this new friendship and terrified that something might happen to sour it.

She had to stay on Paula's good side. Paula had the power to bring Beth's days to life again.

It was unfair really, Beth thought bitterly. Paula's husband wasn't half the actor Leif Garrick had been. But Mike Nelson was still alive and Leif was dead. Paula still had a place in Hollywood's social life, while Beth had been a nonentity for the five miserable years since Leif's death.

Beth wondered sometimes about Leif's other wives. She

never saw their names in print anymore. Did they suffer as much in their obscurity as she had in hers? There had been three of them before her, each of them glamorous actresses who had put the naive little Minnesota girl she had been to shame. The magazines had a field day when Leif married her. What did the girl from Minnesota have that the glamour queens of Hollywood lacked? That was the question the headlines asked over and over.

It was nine months into the marriage before Beth figured it out for herself. The key to her attraction for Leif Garrick had been the press release that preceded her when she won the talent contest in Minnesota. The first prize had been a two week stay in Hollywood, a tour of a major studio, and a glamorous evening out with one of the studio's top stars. When she arrived in Los Angeles, Beth found out that the top star was someone she had never heard of and had resigned herself to being shunted to one side for the rest of the trip. It was something she had grown used to in her own family, as the only girl out of eight children. But then she was told there had been a mix-up. Leif Garrick himself was going to be her escort. They had stayed out all night and by the end of the week she had given up all thoughts of returning to Hibbing. By the end of the month they were united in a storybook wedding that broke the hearts of girls all across the United States.

Months later, Beth, huge with child, was searching through a drawer in Leif's desk for an extra set of car keys and discovered instead the press release that had been sent to the studio by the talent contest organizers in Minnesota. One phrase had been circled in red. ''Miss Ford is the only girl in three generations of Fords.'' Leif's other wives had given him only daughters; he had been certain that she would give him a son.

She had.

And that son had been Beth's assurance that no matter how far Leif strayed, no matter whom he ended up in bed with, no matter how glamorous that partner might be, he would always be hers.

Now Danny had given her a second chance to enter that fairy-tale world of Hollywood society. She had lost her place as Leif Garrick's wife. Perhaps there was another niche waiting for her as Daniel Garrick's mother.

And just as she hadn't let herself dwell on Leif's activities when he was away from her, she wouldn't allow herself to wonder just what it was that interested Paula Nelson in a boy twenty-three years her junior.

Danny cut through the house without stopping to speak to his mother or to Rosita, heading through the family room and out to the terrace into the evening darkness. He walked over and dropped down on one of the loungers beside the pool, listening to the lap-lap of the water as the faint breeze stirred up little wavelets.

Beth called his name through the French doors and he sank down lower into the lounger. She called once more and then gave up. He heard Paula's high laughter distracting Beth, and then the voices of both women faded away.

Paula was coming to stay this weekend.

Danny didn't know exactly what that meant, but he knew that something important was about to happen. Something that had to do with him and his father and the things that men and women did when they were alone together. The thought made him excited and nauseous by turns.

Everything had changed in his life since the day his mother came home from shopping with Paula and the drunken blonde woman. Paula and her husky, whispered promises had become a part of his life. She was always close to him, touching him, watching him. She had taken to showing up at the house at odd times to chat with Beth. She drove him to the studio over Beth's faint protests. She took him shopping for clothes "to save Beth the bother."

Danny blushed in the darkness, remembering how Paula had come into the dressing room to check the length of his new dress pants and caught him standing there with nothing on but his undershorts and socks. Her glance had lingered on the bulge in his underwear that grew as she watched it.

The only place he could forget her was on the set of *Charlie's Gang*. At twelve he was a veteran actor. He had gotten his start at age three-and-a-half on live television commercials, and then he had gone on to television shows and feature films. But in all that time and in all the different roles he had played, there had never been any confusion in his mind as to what was real and what was merely playacting.

Until now.

Now he felt like the role on *Charlie's Gang* was going to swallow him up.

Sometimes he hoped it would.

Bucky Weston was the boy he had always wanted to be. Spunky, brave, adventurous, he was the son that Leif Garrick would have wanted. Bucky had a loving mother, a proud father, and two sisters who, although they teased and tormented him, made him feel a part of the family. A real family. A family like he had never known before. Line by line, it was exactly what the script called for.

Yet somehow, it was also real.

On the set, Danny would forget for long periods of time that it was all an act. He would forget that Miranda Patton was a nervous, chain-smoking ex-model with no use for children at all. That Nick Hanson was so driven by his need to give his performance and get it over with so he could escape from the studio for the day, that he never wasted any time talking to the other actors. "Get on with it. Get on with it," he was always saying.

But when the television camera was rolling, those two people no longer existed. Instead they were Charlie and Mary Weston, a real mother and a real father who were never too busy to give a few minutes of total attention to their children, to comfort and console with a hug or loving words. It was so easy to wish that they actually were his parents, that his life could be as normal and uncomplicated as Bucky Weston's life. Even when Danny was just watching the two girls who played his sisters act out their own parts, he could slip effortlessly into the daydream that the Weston family was real and Danny Garrick didn't exist at all.

Then he would look up and catch Paula's hungry eyes on him, and the fantasy of the Weston family would be stripped away.

Something was going to happen this weekend. The thought made his heart race and his stomach lurch.

He reached down to feel his stiffening penis through the fabric of his trousers. Since the day the blonde had touched him beneath his swimsuit, he kept wondering what it would be like if Paula touched him there.

Was that what was going to happen this weekend?

Danny rubbed himself through his trousers, enjoying the feeling building within him. His penis poked against the front of his trousers, straining against the fabric. Danny reached for his zipper . . . and the world exploded into blinding incandescence as all the lights around the pool came on at once.

"There you are," Beth Garrick called as she hurried across the terrace toward him, her heels clicking on the flagstones. "Paula and I were wondering what had happened to you."

Danny stood up and dived, fully-clothed, into the pool.

Owen Knox rang the bell and moved to the right of the doorway. Emery Friedman was descending in the elevator on the first leg of the nightly journey back to his wife and kids. Owen was counting on that. Tina would think Emery had forgotten something and come back for it.

He was right.

"Oh, for God's sake, Emery," Tina said crossly as she threw open the door. "Can't you even—" She halted in mid-sentence when she saw Owen.

"Hello, Tina. Aren't you going to invite me in?" He let his glance drift down to the cleavage her white satin wrap revealed.

"No, I'm not," she said flatly. "If you're not away from here in two seconds flat, I'm calling the police." She started to slam the door, her breasts bobbing beneath the wrap, but he moved his body and blocked it with his shoulder.

"You're so friendly to everyone else, Tina." His voice was half-caress, half-complaint. "Why not to me?"

"Because I don't like you, Owen."

"How can you know that? You've never let me show you what I can do. I can be very good, Tina." He reached out to stroke the bobbing breast through the white satin, and she jerked backwards so quickly that he grazed his knuckles against the door frame. Anger began to rise within him.

As if she could sense the rage, Tina leaned forward. "Do you ever wonder what Emery and I do in bed, Owen?" she asked him in a husky whisper. "Would you like for me to tell you?" Her tongue flicked out to wet her full lips.

His groin tightened and he licked his own suddenly dry lips. He leaned closer, his hand on the door frame. "Tell me!"

"We laugh, Owen," she said triumphantly. "We laugh at you."

Blood pounded in his temples with murderous violence.

She had been waiting for that moment.

Tina slammed the door as hard as she could.

Owen screamed when the wood bit into his fingers and continued to bite as she threw her weight against the inside of the door.

He thought he was going to lose his goddamned fingers. He thought he was going to pass out from the pain. He screamed again as she slammed against the inside of the door once more with her body.

When she released the pressure for a moment, Owen yanked his hand free and staggered backwards, holding the bloody mess to his chest.

He threw up in the doorway of the apartment across the hall from Tina's and twice more in the elevator as the security guard escorted him down to street level.

"You do that in the lobby, motherfucker, and I call the police regardless of what Miss Sawyer says," the security guard told him.

Owen clamped his teeth against the nausea until the man had shoved him past the doorman and out the entrance onto the sidewalk. He staggered a few feet away, out of the glare of the streetlight, and leaned against the gritty side of the building. He had jammed his ruined hand into the front of the jacket, and he could feel the blood soaking through his shirt front.

"Oh, Friedman," he moaned. "You bastard! You're going to pay for this."

Chapter Three

Her hair turbaned in a thick towel, a bulky white terry cloth robe wrapped tightly around her slim young form, Nan Weston hurried down the hall toward her bedroom door. Frowning intently, her mind on the evening ahead and her date with a handsome young man, she failed to see her sister, JoJo, emerge from her own room, with her pet mouse clutched in her chubby little hands.

They collided.

Nan jerked back, tearing at her turban, screaming, "Don't let it touch my hair!"

"Don't step on Herman!" JoJo cried.

Further down the hall Bucky Weston stuck his head out of his bedroom doorway. "What's up?" he called to JoJo.

"She's so silly," JoJo told him. "It's only Herman."

Together, she and Bucky dropped to their knees and scrambled after Herman the mouse, while Nan continued to shriek.

"Cut!" Owen Knox yelled.

Sharon rushed up to Victoria. "Did I really scare you that time, Nan?"

Victoria smiled down at the seven-year-old, amused. "Now I'm not Nan, remember. Now I'm Victoria again."

"I like it better when you're Nan," Sharon pouted. "And when Danny is Bucky. Don't you?"

"Well . . . sometimes," Victoria admitted. She looked around to see what Danny Garrick thought of that, but he had already vanished. Sometimes, when they were acting, he really did seem like her brother, but most of the time—like now—he ignored both girls.

49

Sharon tugged at her hand. "Wouldn't you like to have a real little sister just like me?"

"Sure I would." Victoria unwrapped the towel around her head and shook her hair free. Mr. Knox would complain, but the towel was too hot to wear for long under the lights. "I don't have any brothers or sisters."

"I do," Sharon said softly, so softly that Victoria almost missed the words.

"A brother or a sister?"

Sharon shook her head, her lips pursed.

"You're not going to tell me?"

"I'm not supposed to talk about him."

"This sounds like a game JoJo would play. Have you been reading next week's script?"

Sharon sucked in her breath. She stared beyond Victoria with round eyes. "Who's that?" she breathed. "He's scary!"

Victoria turned.

Bearing down on them was Vincent Stanton in his motorized wheelchair.

"It's my grandfather," she told Sharon. "He wanted to see how the series was filmed. Would you like to meet him?"

Sharon shook her head and backed up. When Vincent Stanton was less than twelve feet away, she took to her heels.

She couldn't really blame Sharon. The stern, stone-visaged man in the wheelchair would seem frightening to a seven-year-old. Victoria wiped her own damp palms against the terry cloth robe as the wheelchair halted three feet away, barricaded from the set by the thick cables that lay on the floor in front of it.

"Hello, Grandfather. Did you enjoy the filming?" Victoria asked politely.

His eyes bothered her. On the outside he was glacier-like, but some secret fire burned deep inside those gray eyes. His lip twitched slightly as if there was something he wanted to say to her. Some word he needed to force past the immobile barrier of flesh.

She clutched the robe more tightly around her as she watched the infinitesimal movements of his finely-shaped mouth. It was an aristocrat's mouth, the same mouth as on the portrait of Great-Grandfather Stanton, the black-sheep of a wealthy old Boston family who had come to California to start again.

For the past few months Victoria had the strangest feeling that her grandfather wanted to tell her something about herself. She wondered what it was. She leaned forward to touch the lifeless arm strapped to the wheelchair's armrest. "Grandfather?"

"There you are, Vincent!" Florence Stanton hurried up to her husband. Twin spots of red dotted her pale cheeks. "I wondered where you had gotten off to." She grasped the back of his chair as though she needed the support herself. "I was afraid all this was going to be too much for him," she told Victoria, as she wheeled the chair around.

"Grandmother! Wait! I think he wanted to tell me something."

Florence Stanton's stricken glance flew from her granddaughter's face to her husband's. "No," she said firmly. "He just wants something to drink. Don't worry about it, Victoria. I'll find him something."

Before Victoria could protest, her grandmother pushed the silent, staring man in the wheelchair away.

"All right, everybody," Owen Knox called. "Back on the set."

Danny lay in his bed, watching the patterns of leaf shadows dancing on the ceiling.

Waiting.

Somewhere in the midnight silence of the big house, Paula Nelson was awake, too. He could sense her presence.

And she knew it.

A strange new form of communication developed between them when Paula arrived with her overnight bag for the weekend. He was achingly aware of her every movement, her every breath. Danny knew that she was just as aware of him and his movements as he was of her.

It had been sheer agony this evening, waiting for Beth to tire of her houseguest. He felt a small twinge of guilt as he watched his mother glowing with pleasure while she sipped her drink and chatted with Paula, guilt because he knew Paula's thoughts as though they were his own. He knew Paula seethed with the desire to get away from Beth's overeager smile and her sappy conversation, knew that the only reason that Paula was in the house that night or any other time was because of him.

When he couldn't stand it anymore, he came upstairs to bed. Beth had been so caught up in her guest that she hadn't noticed her son's abrupt departure, but Rosita had. The maid came in to check on him, feeling his forehead with her work-calloused hand to see if he were coming down with something. Then she squawked in outrage when she jerked the covers down and found him stripped to his briefs beneath them.

Danny let himself be ordered out of the bed and into the bathroom to put on his pajamas. Then he suffered the further indignity of warm milk and cookies before the little maid bustled out, satisfied that her charge would make it through the night.

Danny lay there listening to the sounds of Paula and Beth moving around downstairs: laughter, music, and the clink of ice in glasses. Then the French doors creaked open and more laughter drifted up through his window, followed by a gigantic splash from the pool.

He rose and looked out the window.

The pool light were on and he could see two nude female forms frolicking in the aquamarine waters below. He watched as they dove and surfaced and dove again, rolling and twisting agilely in a graceful game of tag, flashing him tantalizing glimpses of pubic hair and the secrets that it hid.

Paula had long, lovely legs and small high breasts. Danny's penis pushed through the fly of his pajamas as he watched her dive and surface. Slowly, guiltily, he let his glance seek out his mother at the other end of the pool.

Funny. He had always believed Beth to be a thick, stocky woman. That was the message sent by the clothes she wore. The truth of her figure had been hidden. Now the transparent glow of the pool's waters revealed it.

She was lovely. Shorter than Paula, but with larger breasts and a tinier waist that swelled out into full, firm hips. He forgot all about Paula as he watched his mother splash in the water.

The throb in his groin frightened him.

He turned away from the window and went back to bed. He slipped beneath the sheets and pulled the pillow over his head, blocking out the sounds of female laughter from the pool.

He had no idea how long he had lain there like that when someone tugged the pillow away from his head.

"Danny?"

It was Paula's husky whisper. Elation and disappointment warred within him.

She slipped into the bed beside him, joining him beneath the sheets. She was warm and dry and he could feel the silky fabric of her gown against his forearm as she snuggled closer. Her hand crept into the tent his erection had formed beneath the sheet and when she touched him, he groaned.

She hugged him to her fiercely. "Oh, Danny," she whispered as he buried his face in the valley between her breasts, inhaling the warmth of her scent, "We've got all the time in the world."

Drawing back, she unbuttoned his pajama top, one slow tantalizing button at a time. When it hung open, she pushed it off his slender shoulders.

Impatiently, he jerked his arms free and threw the top to the floor.

Paula laughed and caught his hands as he reached for the snap at his waist. "Slowly, Darling," she cautioned. She leaned over to kiss him on the mouth, her tongue seeking his, and the silken globes of her breasts moving across his bare chest.

Something in him raged out of control. He thrust upward, futilely, separated from the target he still only dimly understood by both his pajamas and the gossamer fabric of her gown. But his fire ignited her and she retreated only long enough to pull her gown up and over her head and then leaned forward to tug his pajamas down and off.

His penis bobbed like a pole and she moved quickly to settle herself on it, driving them both to a crashing climax with only a few sharp thrusts of her pelvis.

She slumped forward against his chest, gasping for breath. As the wonderment of the strangely violent sensation subsided, Danny lay quietly beneath her, assimilating one by one all the various new sensations.

There was the distinctive yet not unpleasant smell that now surrounded them, a mingling of both their secrets, and more.

He liked it, he decided.

There was the feeling of her, all soft and silky and pulsing with little aftershocks, around his now deflated maleness. The beating of her heart against his. The curve of her stomach against his stomach. The feel of her breasts mashed against his chest. Her soft breath stirring against the hollow at the base of his neck.

Paula snuggled closer, raising her head just enough to capture his earlobe between the velvet of her lips, then began to trace the shape of his ear with her warm, wet tongue.

Danny lay passively, letting each new sensation she aroused wash over him like the waves at the beach until a sharp knock on the door of his bedroom made Paula jerk upright. He caught her around the waist, holding her lower body to his so that she could not dislodge him from inside her and roll away.

"Danny!" his mother called. "Are you all right?"

He could feel Paula's panicky breathing against the side of his neck and the warmth of her embarrassment on her soft skin. "I'm fine, Mother," he called out. "Go back to bed." Paula trembled in surprise at the new male firmness in his voice.

"Danny? Are you sure—"

"Go back to bed, Mother."

Paula tried to pull away again. He pressed her closer as he began to grow within her, lengthening, hardening. She made one more half-hearted attempt to escape his grasp, and then sighed her surrender.

Still buried in her softness, Danny rolled her over on her back. Her eyes flew open. He stared into them as he pulled slowly back until only the tip of his penis remained within her and kept watching as he plunged into the very center of her. Paula cried out once, and then muffled her moans against his chest. Danny continued to thrust, growing with each stroke.

The bouncing of the mattress drowned out the footsteps retreating down the hall.

Sharon hid under the cloth-draped table on the empty living room set and listened to the mother call her name. Sometimes she found it hard to remember which mother was the real one.

She tried to talk to Andrew about it, but he just cried. He was lonely when she was gone all day filming *Charlie's Gang* and going to school on the set. When they watched the show together on television instead of making him happy, it only made him cry more. He wet his bed every single night, and another nurse had already come and gone. Now they had a new nurse who wrinkled her nose every time she had to touch Andrew. Sharon knew she wouldn't be there much longer either.

Andrew begged and begged Sharon to let him come and play with her and the Weston children. But Mother had said if Sharon talked to anyone about him, she would make Andrew go away. Sharon hugged her knees to her chest. She had been afraid to tell Andrew that; she didn't even want to think about it herself.

Miranda Patton was closer now. She had given up calling for Sharon. Now she called JoJo.

Sharon almost came crawling out from under the table. Hearing JoJo's name called made her want to run to the woman and throw her arms around her. It made her think that Miranda was really Mary Weston, and that she was really JoJo. When she was JoJo, Sharon felt all warm and loved.

But Sharon remembered the last time she had tried to hug Miranda when it hadn't been in the script, and she stayed beneath the table.

Besides, she knew what Miranda wanted. Harry Patton had been standing beside Cynthia Bradford, talking to her while Miranda finished up a scene with Nick Hanson and Victoria. Miranda would want to know what the two of them talked about.

Sharon wasn't going to tell her. She would remember every single word and tell her father about it, her real father. When Keith Bradford came home, Sharon would tell him everything. Then he would make Mother go away, and Mr. Knox would let Andrew be on *Charlie's Gang* with her.

Miranda Patton gave up finally. Sharon waited until the click-click of her heels died away. But before she could scramble out from beneath the table, she heard someone else come in and sit down on the living room sofa. She listened as hard as she could, but she couldn't hear any voices, only wet, sticky sounds and soft, breathy moans. Curious, she lifted the edge of the tablecloth and peeked out.

Mr. Friedman's secretary, Tina, was stretched out on the sofa. The tall blonde cameraman named Mike was laying right on top of her. Sharon almost snorted. That was the

funniest way to take a nap she ever saw. Besides, they were
wiggling as bad as Andrew did when he had to lay down for a
nap in the middle of the afternoon. They would never go to
sleep like that.

She scrambled out from under the other side of the table
and tiptoed away so they wouldn't hear her.

She was watching Owen Knox direct a scene in Charlie
Weston's study when the mother grabbed her by the collar of
her dress. "There you are, you little monster! I've been
looking all over for you. It's time to go home!"

Sharon twisted around. This mother was Cynthia. "I want
to stay and watch," she protested.

Cynthia Bradford paid no attention to her daughter. She
simply pulled Sharon along behind her as she stalked away.

Sharon tried dragging her heels but it did no good. Cynthia
gave her a jerk that nearly dislocated her shoulder. The howl
Sharon would have loosed died on her lips when she caught
sight of the grim-lipped expression on her mother's face.
Even in public, tears did no good when her mother looked
like that.

Sharon glanced back over her shoulder. Mr. Knox was
breaking off the filming, but now she would have to wait
until tomorrow to talk to him. He liked for her to tell him
about the cast and crew. Sometimes, when she made him
laugh, he gave her a candy bar. She knew he would laugh
when she told him about Tina Sawyer's funny nap time.

1958

"This fucking loincloth is driving me crazy," Mike Nelson
complained as he opened the trailer door. "My balls can't
breathe. The family jewels are drowning in their own sweat."
In full Apache war paint and warbonnet he was an awesome
sight, even with sweat beginning to blur the bands of paint
across his face. "How come every fucking picture I make has
to be in the fucking desert?"

"Maybe they could rewrite Cochise as an Eskimo chief,"
Jake Moriarty suggested as he dropped into a chair.

"You wouldn't think that crap is so funny if you had to eat
sand ten hours a day, Buster." He took two cold bottles of
beer from the refrigerator, opened them and handed one over

to the private detective. He kicked a pair of lacy black panties under the sofa. "Shit! You can't have a broad in place for two minutes before they start dropping their crap everywhere."

"That how long it takes you these days, Mike? Two minutes?"

Mike chuckled. "You've got to do it fast in the desert or you'll die of heat stroke before you get your rocks off." He switched on a fan and pulled a straight chair over into the stream of air before he straddled it, facing the back. "Got to give my balls a break for a few minutes," he told Jake. "Big scene coming up."

"In here or out there?"

"Both, friend." Mike sighed with relief. The fan and the ice cold beer were beginning to revive him. He raised an eyebrow at Jake. "So why are you here? You got something for me finally? I expected to hear from you months ago."

Jake passed across a manila envelope.

Mike hefted it. "What's this?"

"Look it over," Jake told him.

"You like the mystery crap, don't you, Jake?" Mike set the beer aside and opened the envelope. Inside was a thick stack of photographs. He slipped them out.

The one on top was an eight by ten glossy of Paula and Beth Garrick swimming naked in that big motherfucker of a pool that asshole Leif had built for himself.

"That dyke!" he howled. "I was right. I'm going to strangle that goddamned bitch!"

He looked up and caught a strange expression on Jake Moriarty's face. "That's what I thought at first, too," Jake said. "But I was wrong."

Mike shuffled rapidly through the rest of the photos. There were no more of Paula and Beth together. The rest were all Paula and Leif's kid. "All right, she's babysitting the Garrick kid. I already knew that. So who's she fucking?"

"Look again, Mike," Jake said patiently.

Mike went through the photographs one by one, really looking at them this time. Now he could see it. Not Paula cuddling Leif's kid. It was Leif's little bastard fucking his wife!

Mike's hands were trembling by the time he got to the last photograph. Paula knelt in front of Danny Garrick, the kid's prick in her mouth. The kid, his hands tangled in Paula's hair, gazed down at the top of her head, an expression of rapturous delight on his face.

The cunt!

She wouldn't do it for him, but she would do it for a twelve-year-old jerk-off.

Mike crumpled the photograph.

Jake Moriarty shifted in his chair.

Mike looked up. The expression on Jake's face diminished him. He could feel his balls shriveling up. His rage vanished. Fear replaced it.

If word of this got out, he would never live it down. The wife of tough-guy Mike Nelson so hard up that she had to go to a twelve-year-old kid for satisfaction.

Paula would pay for setting him up like this.

But he could tell from the expression on Jake Moriarty's face that he would have to proceed very carefully.

"The negatives?" The way his voice cracked you'd think he'd swallowed the whole fucking desert.

Silently, Jake handed over a smaller envelope.

"How are they getting together?"

"She takes him to the studio to film *Charlie's Gang*." Jake's expression lightened. "It's a real good show. I watch it myself."

"What else?"

"She spends weekends at the Garrick place. She takes Beth Garrick with her to parties and shopping, but it's just a front to be with the kid."

"I'll kill the little prick." It was an unadorned statement of fact.

"That's not the way, Mike. Filming's almost over on *Charlie's Gang* for the season. Let it ride, for Crissake."

"No!" He stood up, kicking the chair away.

"Cool down," Jake told him. "She's not doing anything you're not doing."

"She's doing it with a fucking kid!"

Owen fumbled with his fly. He no longer wore the cast on his right hand, but the fingers were still stiff.

"Must have been hell jerking off with all that plaster in the way," Emery Friedman said genially from the next urinal.

Owen had lost the urge to piss, but he went grimly ahead with the motions. As far as he could tell, Tina hadn't said anything to Emery about that little incident at her doorway.

Emery zipped up with a flourish and strolled out, whistling.

He wouldn't be whistling if he knew what that redheaded cunt of his was up to, Owen thought. She had screwed almost everybody on the set this season. Even the delivery boy who showed up with flowers for Miranda Patton, a peace offering from the lady's husband. Tina had seen to it that the kid was amply consoled for having two dozen red roses shoved down his shirt front.

She's fucked everyone except me, Owen thought.

If there was any way he could see clear to tell that bastard Emery what Tina was up to, he'd do it. But no telling how that goddamned wild man would react.

Two more weeks and filming was over for this season. He could hang on for two more weeks.

After all, there was more than one diversion on the *Charlie's Gang* set.

Miranda was waiting for him outside his office. Thin, nervous, twitchy Miranda. She didn't look like much on the outside, but she was a regular dynamo in the sack. She had ignored Owen before her husband started wandering. Now she was anxious to pay Harry back in kind.

Owen was just the kind of generous guy who'd help out a lady in a situation like that.

"Mike Nelson's here," Tina told Emery when he strolled into his office, Tuesday morning.

Emery looked blank for a moment.

"You know," Tina prompted. "The muscle man?"

"Oh, him." Emery looked puzzled. "Why does he want to see me?"

"He wouldn't say. It's something private he wanted to talk to you about in person."

"I used to watch his pictures when I was a kid," Emery mused. "Oh, hell. Give him five minutes with me and then put through a call." He felt generous this morning. Riding a successful TV series did wonderful things for a man's ego, he decided as he sat down behind his desk. Not to mention his love life. At home, Margaret was warm and attentive, never upset if he had to work late, because she knew the burdens of producing a hit like *Charlie's Gang*. And Tina . . . Tina was available anytime in his office, just like she'd promised. For a moment he regretted telling her to show Nelson in. There would have been time for a quick romp this morning.

But the big man was already looming through his doorway.

Emery stood and took Mike Nelson's hand. He was immediately sorry. Nelson had no conception of his own strength. "I've always admired your movies, Mr. Nelson," he said as he rescued his injured fingers. "What can I do for you?"

"Christ! You make me sound ancient. Call me Mike."

The voice was hearty, but the big man was sweating. What the fuck was going on? "Mike it is. Call me Emery." Was the big bastard hoping for a guest shot?

"I've got a little personal problem I hoped you might help me with, Emery." Mike Nelson took the chair in front of the desk and it creaked in protest.

Emery sat down. "What kind of a problem, Mike?" he said cautiously. Just because he'd liked this old bruiser's movies as a kid didn't mean he owed the man anything.

"You probably know that Leif Garrick and I were pretty good pals for a long time before he kicked off?"

Emery nodded.

"I promised Leif I'd check up on his kid from time to time. Only Beth Garrick is a batty broad. She won't let any of Leif's old friends have anything to do with the kid. I was wondering if you could let me have a few minutes with Danny in private somewhere, so I could just check up on him. For Leif's sake."

Emery nodded, bemused. Incredible! The man was a worse actor in person than on film. The whole town knew that all Leif's buddies dropped Beth like a hot potato when Leif died. So what did Mike Nelson want to talk to Leif's kid about? Emery's curiosity was definitely piqued. "No problem at all," he told Mike Nelson. "You can use this office. I'll have Danny up here in just a few minutes."

"I . . . ah . . . I'd rather no one knew about this," Mike said quickly. "I wouldn't want . . . Beth to find out."

"I'll handle it myself," Emery assured him. *Curiouser and curiouser.*

He stepped out in to the outer office. "I'll get rid of Nelson myself," he told Tina. "But I just remembered that I need to talk to Danny Garrick a few minutes. Run down to the set and tell him to come up. Then you can have the morning off."

She moved closer, until her breasts were brushing his chest. "And the afternoon, too, Lover. I've got some shopping to do. I want to look good for you."

No office high jinks today. "If you save me a couple of hours out of your busy schedule tonight at your place. Around eight?"

"Won't Margaret mind?" Tina asked coyly.

"It takes a lot of late night work to keep a success like this rolling."

"So what will you tell her when the season ends?"

"I have to get ready for next season. What else?"

"You'd think with her old man in the business, she'd see right through you."

Emery patted her shapely ass. "You let me worry about Margaret and my father-in-law. Just send Danny on up and then spend your afternoon getting beautiful for me, okay?"

"Right," she said with a smart salute. She exited with a wiggle that made him wish it were eight already.

When Danny appeared, Emery took the time to give him a good once-over. In spite of what he told Margaret, he really hadn't been spending that much time on the set of *Charlie's Gang*. The post-production supervisor had quit last month and Emery was keeping a closer eye on that end of things until he was sure how the new one would work out. It had been several weeks since he had seen Danny or the other kids in the flesh. Now he could discern something different about Danny, something that didn't show up on film, but was definitely there. A new air of maturity maybe? He hoped not. He didn't want his kiddy stars growing up too fast.

"You wanted to see me, Mr. Friedman?" the kid asked.

"An old friend of your dad's would like to talk to you for a few minutes." Emery took the boy's shoulder and ushered him into the inner office. He felt the start of surprise when the kid caught sight of Mike Nelson's hulking figure in front of the desk.

"Danny Garrick, Mike Nelson," Emery said heartily, ignoring the charged atmosphere in the room. "Danny, Mike just wanted to chat with you for a few minutes."

Mike Nelson stood up, towering over the boy. He did not extend a hand. Danny had moved around Emery so that the desk was between himself and Mike Nelson.

"I'll just gather up a few papers and let you two visit in peace." Emery leaned across the desk to grab a folder and unobtrusively switched on the intercom. "I'll be at my secretary's desk," he told Mike. "I'll see that you're not disturbed."

"Thanks," the man said heavily, his attention centered on Leif Garrick's son.

Emery closed the door to his office firmly behind him.

". . . who I am?" Mike Nelson's voice thundered from the intercom on Tina's desk as Emery sat down in her chair.

"Mr. Friedman said you were a friend of my dad's." Danny sounded very young and very frightened over the intercom.

"Cut the crap, you little asshole. I'm Paula's husband and I'm going to cut off your dick if I find you within a hundred yards of her again."

"I don't know what you're talking about, Mr. Nelson," the kid blustered.

"I'm talking about you fucking my wife, you little shithead. I've got pictures of the two of you."

"Then you know I wasn't fucking her," Danny Garrick said calmly. "She was fucking me."

Something crashed in the inner office and the intercom went dead.

Emery lunged for the door.

Mike Nelson had the kid by the shirt collar and his ham-like fist was drawn back, ready to take Danny Garrick's head off.

"Hold it!" Emery shouted. He slammed the door behind him. "You touch that kid and I'll personally see to it that everyone in town knows that big Mike Nelson can't take care of his homework."

Nelson's murderous glance shifted to him and for a moment Emery knew what it felt like to be standing in the path of a bull about to charge. "Do you want that, Mike?" he said desperately. "Do you want everyone to know you were beat out by a twelve-year-old?"

"I'm going to kill the little motherfucker," Mike Nelson said.

Danny took a futile swing at the big man.

"Cut it out, kid," Emery ordered. He grabbed the boy's arm. "Let go of him, Mike!"

The muscle man released Danny.

Emery shoved the kid behind him. "So long, Mike."

"Not so fast." The big man glowered at Danny. "You make sure that brat stays away from my wife or I'll take care of him personally. And I won't care how many people know about it."

"Don't worry," Emery said grimly. The negative publicity that would break over this would kill the show instantly, no matter how big a hit it was. "I'll take care of it."

"I don't have to—" Danny began.

"Shut up, kid," Emery said without turning around. "You have my word, Mike. Now get the hell out of here."

When that man-mountain moved out the door, Emery felt like he had gained a new lease on life. Even a hit series wouldn't be worth being on the receiving end of Mike Nelson's big, broken-knuckled fists. He leaned down and picked up his intercom and replaced it on the desk top.

Danny for all his bluster of a moment before looked like death warmed over. Emery shook his head and chuckled. "Honest to God, kid! Were you really screwing Mike Nelson's wife?"

The kid looked at him stonily.

"Even if your old man *was* the greatest stud in town, don't you think twelve years old is—"

"I'm thirteen now."

"Big fucking deal." Emery's temper, always unstable, got the better of him. "You keep your prick in your pants, kid. Bucky Weston won't be screwing anyone until he's a married man and as far as the public is concerned, you're Bucky. Keep the fuck away from Paula Nelson."

Something in the kid's stance reminded Emery of Leif Garrick. "Fine," the kid said. "Who's gonna keep her away from me?"

Tina dug a long crimson nail into Emery's ribs. "I know it was good, but was it that good?"

The grin on Emery's face widened. He reached out and pulled her closer. "Oh, it was good all right. It's always good."

Tina poked harder.

"Ouch!" He scooped her up and rolled her over on top of him.

She threatened his bare chest with all ten nails. "What's so funny, Emery?"

"It's a secret," he said blandly.

She wiggled her pelvis against him and received a faint stir of acknowledgement for her efforts. "Ve have vays of making you talk," she threatened, enjoying the game.

"You wouldn't believe it anyway."

She leaned forward so that her breasts were hanging just above Emery's face. "Try me," she whispered huskily.

He strained upward, seeking her right breast with his lips.

Tina straightened a fraction, moving the prize just out of his reach. "Talk first. Then you get your reward."

He shifted, letting her feel the effect her teasing was having on him. "And you get yours."

"Maybe," she taunted. "If what you're grinning about is good enough."

"Oh, it's good enough," Emery assured her. "You know what that big bruiser Mike Nelson wanted today?"

"A part as a weight lifter?" she said nastily, feeling a return of the irritation she had felt when Nelson came storming into Emery's office this morning. She wasn't used to going unrecognized by former bed partners, not even after a one-night stand. Especially not after one as satisfying as she and Mike had. But this morning he had been too distracted to pay any attention to anything. And it hadn't seemed like a good place to refresh his memory of their little interlude, not with Emery due at any moment.

Emery just shook his head, chuckling.

Tina poked him again with her sharp fingernail.

"Ouch! I'll talk! He wanted to warn Danny Garrick to stay away from his wife."

"What?"

"Oh, yes. I know it's hard to believe, but it turns out that the kid has been having a hot and heavy affair with Nelson's wife for the past few months. The little bastard must have been trying to live up to his father's reputation."

"Leif Garrick was quite a lover?" Now she remembered Paula Nelson saying something like that one day on the set.

"He made Errol Flynn look like a fairy."

"So what are you going to do about Danny?"

"I already did it. Read the kid the riot act. He'll either be a choirboy or he'll be a soprano for real." Tiring of the conversation, Emery reached up and seized her breast with his lips.

Tina leaned forward, enjoying the sensation. Emery was almost ready for another bout. His poor wife wouldn't have any fun at all tonight.

Too bad the season was almost over, Tina thought, as Emery began to thrust upward. It would be interesting to find out what a thirteen-year-old kid had that a woman like Paula Nelson would risk her marriage over.

Tina wasn't worried, though. *Charlie's Gang* was a hit. There was always next season.

It was happening again!

Beth Garrick slammed down the phone. Paula was home. She had to be! Yet that stupid maid kept lying through her teeth every time Beth called. Saying Paula was out. Saying she would have Paula return Beth's calls.

Only Beth's phone hadn't rung for a week.

She had tried talking about it to Danny, to find out what had gone wrong, but he had been sullen and uncommunicative.

It wasn't fair! For a while she had really begun to believe she belonged again. Now what was she going to do?

Beth stared down at her long perfect fingernails and began to cry.

Chapter Four

The lid of the battered leather trunk gave an enormous creak as Victoria lifted it, and the sound echoed through the silent attic. She sighed heavily when she saw that this trunk, like the other two she had rifled through this morning, contained only ancient clothing packed carefully away with mothballs.

Before she could investigate further, the door behind her opened with a crash. The whine of Vincent Stanton's wheelchair filled the attic like an angry insect.

Without stopping to think, Victoria darted behind the trunk, flattening herself against the splintery wood of the floor. She prayed that the dust she had stirred up wouldn't make her sneeze. The wheelchair came no closer. The hum of its motor reminded her of a fly caught in a spider's web.

Shame washed over Victoria as she lay there. What impulse had led her to hide like that? What would Grandfather think if he had seen her trying so hard to avoid him? It wasn't because of him exactly; she just wanted to be alone.

Even after the sound of his wheelchair dwindled away, she continued to lie there, staring up at the cobweb-covered rafters above her. It was so seldom that she could be by herself, and she treasured every moment of solitude. Everywhere she went, it seemed there was someone watching her.

Here it was Grandfather; on the set of *Charlie's Gang* it was Danny Garrick.

Sometime during the first few weeks of this third season of the show, Victoria realized that Danny was always looking at

her. In the classroom while their teacher from the Los Angeles Board of Education droned on or when they passed in the
studio corridors or on the set, his glance followed her. He
never spoke to her, though, except when it was in the script.

At first she was annoyed, thinking that he was trying to
irritate her on purpose, teasing her like his character teased
hers in the scripts. She hated to admit that she found him kind
of cute. Especially since he was only fourteen. She had
turned sixteen last month and had her driver's license and her
own checking account. She was no longer a child. Girls her
age were supposed to fall in love with older men, not little
boys, any dope knew that. Only there weren't any older men
around for her to fall in love with. Sometimes there would be
a new teenage actor on the show playing Nan's boyfriend, but
never for more than one show. They came and vanished so
quickly that more than once she never even caught their real
names.

Sometimes she found herself watching Danny Garrick back,
wondering what she could say to him that would break the
deadly silence between them. She could never think of anything brilliant, though, not without a scriptwriter to write it
down for her!

Besides, even if she had, Tina Sawyer, the producer's
secretary, was always fussing around Danny every time she
got the chance. Almost, Victoria realized, as though the
redhead were Danny's girlfriend.

Not that she *could* be, of course. Danny was just a kid and
Tina had to be at least twenty-four or twenty-five.

Still, when Victoria looked up and realized that Danny was
staring at her and Tina was staring at him, she got the
strangest feeling about the two of them.

It bothered her more than she cared to admit. Of course,
she would never let Danny know that. She treated him like
the young twirp he was. Served him right, too!

She sat up, brushing the dust from her hands, and began
searching through the trunk she had just opened. This time
she was rewarded with a small cardboard box tied with twine
tucked in with the old dresses. She worried the string off and
lifted the lid. Inside were dry papers, crackly with age:
letters, bills, circulars, and bent old photographs of people
she did not recognize. She looked at each one of them

carefully before she laid them aside. None of them were what she was searching for and a couple of letters in the bottom of the box with thirty-year-old dates confirmed it. There was nothing of her mother in this box. Nothing that would explain the dark secret her grandmother kept hinting at.

Victoria shoved the box back in the trunk and slammed the lid on it, sending a cloud of dust swirling everywhere. Why couldn't there at least be a photograph of her father somewhere in this huge attic? A girl shouldn't have to grow up not knowing what her father looked like.

It just wasn't fair!

A giant insect whined to life behind her.

Victoria scrambled to her feet and backed away in terror before she realized that it was the wheelchair. Her grandfather had not left. He had just been waiting until she came out of her hiding place.

"I'm sorry," she said swiftly, worried that she had hurt his feelings. "You frightened me. I had no idea anyone else was up here."

His eyes were the only thing alive in his face.

"I . . . I was just looking around," she said with a gaiety that rang false in the dusty silence of the attic. "I hope you don't mind."

The corner of his mouth moved the merest fraction of an inch. For him it was the equivalent of a shout.

"You're angry," she said. "I'm sorry, Grandfather. I won't do it again."

She tried to edge past him and the wheelchair swung around to block her path.

It was so unexpected that she couldn't help giving a little shriek as she jumped back.

He edged the chair closer, until it nudged against her leg.

Victoria took an involuntary step backwards, her glance held by his, by the urgent look in those gray eyes.

Once more he edged the chair closer.

Once more she stepped backwards.

He pushed her across the attic that way, to the far side, where another jumble of trunks lay piled. Until she could go no further, her retreat blocked by the wall behind her.

Victoria thrust her trembling hands in her pockets. She had no idea what he was going to do. She wondered if she should try to dart around him and escape.

The chair moved again and she gasped in fright for there was nowhere else to go as it came to her.

But this time she was not the target. He crashed into one of the smaller trunks.

He's confused, she thought, and reached for his shoulder to turn him around. But as she did the wheelchair roared backwards, and then accelerated once more, smashing into the same trunk again.

"Grandfather!"

He pulled back once more. He could not turn his head, so she moved around to face him. The gray eyes were fastened, not on her now, but on the trunk.

With tantalizing slowness, he edged the wheelchair forward once more until he just tapped the trunk. Then before she could say or do anything, he whirled the chair around and was gone.

Victoria stood there for a moment, staring after him. Then, her heart beating rapidly, she dropped to her knees in front of the trunk. She fumbled with the catch and then eased the lid back.

The small trunk was crammed full of books, thin volumes with identical leather bindings. She picked up one and opened it.

Inside the cover was her mother's name.

If Emery found out he would kill her.
If she didn't get hold of herself, Emery would find out.

Tina paced around nervously, listening to the murmur of Emery's voice on the phone in the inner office. He was supposed to have left already for a ten o'clock meeting, but so far she hadn't been able to budge him.

She had to get him out of here before Danny showed up.

Sometimes Tina's head cleared and she knew she was a fool to take such outrageous chances just to be with Danny, but she didn't care. All her life she had fascinated men; now she was totally fascinated by this fourteen-year-old boy. There was no way she could get enough of him.

It had all started as a lark. Last year, when *Charlie's Gang* began its second season, she hadn't forgotten the amusing little tidbit Emery had passed on about Danny screwing Big Mike Nelson's wife. Naturally she couldn't resist finding out for herself what Paula Nelson had found so interesting about the kid. After all, when had she ever resisted anything?

It had taken her less than a week after the hiatus ended to escape Emery's eagle eye and get Danny alone long enough to ball him.

Now she knew what Paula Nelson had found worth risking her marriage for, Tina thought grimly. She'd spent all last season and well into this one trying to balance Emery's excessive jealousness against her intense need to be with Danny every possible moment.

For the first time in her life she had no need for—no desire for—other men. Only Danny.

Maybe a shrink could tell her why. Maybe a shrink could have told her why she'd been the way she was before Danny. Tina herself didn't stop to analyze this new compulsion. She was too busy scheming up ways to be alone with Danny.

If there had been any way in the world she could have dumped Emery and still had access to Danny she would have done it in a minute.

But there wasn't. Besides, being the personal secretary to the producer of a very successful TV show well into its third season gave her carte blanche around the studio. She could even summon Danny to Emery's office as she had done this morning, and no one would question her.

No one except Emery.

She had to get him out of here in the next ten minutes. Otherwise he'd want to know just why she scheduled an appointment for him with Danny at a time when he was supposed to be in a meeting with one of the network vice presidents.

Thankfully, she heard him hang up the phone at last. She stepped into his office. "You're going to be late for your meeting, Lover," she prompted, leaning back against the door frame, so that her blouse strained against her breasts.

Emery glanced at her appreciatively. "You're so right," he murmured as he shoved his chair back from the desk and unzipped his fly.

He leaned back in the black leather hair, his legs spread, and Tina hurried over to kneel between them, before he could change his mind and decide to ball her on the sofa instead. With any luck at all, she'd have him out of here in five minutes.

Emery was going to think he'd met a vacuum cleaner.

"You're crazy, Tina," Danny said roughly, as the redhead pulled him into Emery Friedman's private office. He was sick of this, sick of Tina always hanging around, always asking him what he was thinking, always touching him, handling him.

"Crazy for you," she agreed, pushing him down into the producer's black leather chair.

There must be something wrong with him, Danny thought. He didn't want to do this, didn't want to be with her. But one touch of her hands and he was rock hard and aching for relief, unable to shove her away as her mouth closed around him.

Why was he here when where he really wanted to be was back in the studio classroom watching Victoria with her head bent over her lessons? Why had he even bothered to answer Tina's summons? He had known it was her, even though the memo said Emery Friedman wanted to see him.

What a laugh. Friedman had no time for the child actors on his series, unless there was a problem like season before last.

Danny had missed Paula at first. He had also resented Friedman's ultimatum. And it wasn't just him. His mother plummeted into a deep depression when her "friend" dropped her again. Danny wondered if Beth Garrick had any idea why Paula stopped returning her calls.

God! He felt so awful! It was twice as bad watching his mother being ostracized for the second time. Especially since this time it was partly his fault.

But the first day Victoria walked in to the soundstage this season, Danny forgot everything else. She had changed so much during the hiatus he hardly recognized her. She was sixteen, all grown up. And beautiful! He could spend hours just gazing at the curve of her cheek. Or watching the soft flutter of her long eyelashes.

He had never been in love before, but he knew he was in love now.

Victoria ignored him completely. He might as well be her pesky little brother for real for all the attention she gave him. He was only fourteen, a kid to her, and he knew it.

If she knew the truth about him, would that make her see

him differently? She was a virgin, he was sure of that. Sure that she was nothing like Tina.

Or Paula.

But he knew instinctively that he shouldn't mention his sexual adventures to her or anyone. He'd been lucky that nothing had happened after Mike Nelson threatened him, lucky that Emery Friedman had kept Nelson from beating him. He realized that he might not be that lucky again.

Then he could think of nothing else as Tina settled herself on him and began to pump up and down.

Owen waited in his office, and he was never good at waiting. Especially not now. Not when his networks of informants had brought him so much disturbing news at one time. First there was Emery's red-headed whore. He had wanted Tina for a long time, since before Emery snatched her away. Every day that passed only made him want her more. But without her cooperation, he hadn't dared make a move in her direction. She might tell Emery, and Emery's jealousy and his awesome temper were legendary.

However, what Friedman would do to Owen was nothing compared to what he would do to Danny Garrick if what Owen suspected was true: Tina was screwing the Garrick boy.

Owen was beside himself with jealousy, but there was nothing he could do about it. Not yet. Any move he made to stop that affair might bring it to Emery's attention and he couldn't risk that.

All he could do was watch in total frustration as Tina made a fool of herself over a fourteen-year-old boy.

There was one situation he could do something about, though, Owen thought grimly. He intended to take care of it. Today.

"Nick Hanson's here, Mr. Knox," the secretary said.

"Show him in, and then you can take off," Owen told her. He had planned this little get-together so he and Nick could have all the privacy they needed.

The secretary smiled her gratitude and then showed Nick in.

Owen waved Nick toward a chair. Nick started to speak, but Owen shook his head. Nick watched him, one eyebrow raised in inquiry, but Owen just sat there silently, staring at the warm fatherly face with real loathing, until he heard the door of the outer office close. Then he said, "What are you trying to do? Fuck up both of our careers?"

Nick chuckled, and that familiar paternal sound made Owen's blood start to boil.

"You son of a bitch. How long do you think you can get away with it and not get caught?"

"I don't know what you're—"

"For God's sake, what kind of a pervert are you? Why can't you ball a woman your own age?"

"Owen, I haven't—"

"The rumor is that you're back to your old tricks. Dating jailbait again. If the network finds out we'll be off the air faster than those damn quiz shows!" It was no idle threat. Last season everything from *Dotto* to *The $64,000 Question* to *Twenty-One* had been kicked off the air after charges they were rigged had surfaced. Already there was talk of the payola scandal dislodging some of the big-name radio deejay's.

"I swear to you, I'm not," Nick said fervently. "I wouldn't do that. Not after I promised you."

Owen rubbed his bald spot. It would be so easy to believe that honest, sincere voice, the voice that got *Charlie's Gang*— instead of the oater opposite it—invited into American living rooms this season. "God help you, you better not be lying about this, Nick. If you are, it won't be just me you'll have to deal with. Emery will cut off your dick and feed it to you if you screw up his show."

The pallor in Nick's face reassured Owen. No one wanted that wild man Friedman after them. "You don't have to worry about me, Owen," he promised and Owen leaned back, relieved.

Mission accomplished, he thought proudly, as Nick left hastily. Even if the actor *was* screwing young stuff again, this little interview would put a stop to it.

If only there were something as effective he could use to manipulate Tina. He wondered what the record was for the world's longest case of blue balls.

Sharon paused in the hallway outside Miranda Patton's dressing room and looked both ways. No one was watching her, so she opened the door and darted inside. She was supposed to be doing her lessons. Pretty soon Mrs. Frank, the studio teacher, would notice Sharon was gone and tell her nanny. Then they would both start looking for her and she would get in trouble again. Sharon didn't care, though. She had to talk to Miranda alone.

Sharon would be ten on her birthday. Last year she was a baby. Last year she still confused the mothers with each other sometimes. This season when *Charlie's Gang* started filming, she knew which mother was the real one. She realized Miranda was only a pretend mother for when the cameras were running. The rest of the time she was an actress. But now Sharon knew something else, something that she had to tell Miranda.

She wrinkled her nose at the stale tobacco smell of Miranda's room. On the dressing table were all sorts of bottles. Sharon picked up one and sprayed a cloud of perfume around herself. That was better, she decided. She sniffed another bottle of perfume, and then sprayed it into the air liberally. She inhaled, satisfied. That would be enough if Miranda didn't take too long to come back to her dressing room.

She crawled into the chair in front of the dressing table and gazed around the room. For a while she sat there expectantly, her knees together, her hands folded primly in her lap, waiting. When Miranda didn't appear, she grew bored. Finally, she slipped down from the chair and began looking through the clothes hanging across one end of the room.

An emerald dress slipped off the hanger and slithered to the floor. Instead of putting it back, Sharon slipped it over her head instead, turning this way and that to see it in Miranda's full length mirror.

Then she climbed back up on the chair in front of the dressing table and began putting Miranda's makeup on her face, humming to herself. This was what it would be like when she was all grown up, she thought happily. She would get ready and then she and Andrew would go out to a restaurant.

The thought of Andrew made her frown at her reflection. Andrew was so unhappy that he hardly ever talked to anyone but her. The nurses and nannies came and went, never staying for more than a month or two, and each one was worse than the last. Their mother never even came to see Andrew any-more. She was too busy for him, and that was what Sharon wanted to talk to Miranda Patton about. She painted thick red lips on her face with Miranda's lipstick and smiled at herself.

She turned this way and that, admiring her glamorous makeup. Why didn't they ever let her dress up like this for *Charlie's Gang*? She would have to tell Andrew how good she looked.

She told her twin everything about the show. She even read her scripts to him. The first season the show was on, Andrew cried when he saw her on the screen with the other children. But now, every week, he sat with Sharon in front of the television and they watched together. Sometimes Andrew would reach over and grab her hand and squeeze it, just to make sure she was really there beside him.

What she wanted most of all was to have Andrew come to the studio and see how the shows were made, but Mother wouldn't even talk about it. It wasn't fair! Even Victoria's grandfather, that scary old man, had gotten to come, but not Andrew.

Mother had to be punished, and Sharon knew there was only one person who could punish Mother.

She picked up a tube of mascara and leaned closer to the mirror as she applied it to her lashes, knocking over several of the beautiful bottles.

"What in the hell do you think you're doing, you little brat? That's my best dress!"

Sharon jumped, jabbing herself in the eye with the mascara wand and knocking over still more bottles.

Miranda Patton grabbed Sharon around the waist and tried to pull the dress over her head. Sharon, terrified, fought to free herself and Miranda drew back her hand to slap her.

"I'll tell!" Sharon shrieked, and Miranda hesitated.

Sharon took advantage of that to squirm away and run to the door. But there, one hand on the knob, she paused.

"Go on, you little hellion! And stay out of here if you know what's good for you."

It was all Sharon could do to keep from bolting, but the thought of Andrew and what she was trying to do for him, made her stand there shivering as she faced Miranda's rage.

Miranda had turned to her ruined dressing table, muttering under her breath as she replaced the overturned bottles. She stopped suddenly, realizing Sharon had not left. "I said get out. Do you want me to call your mother?"

Sharon puffed out her chest bravely. "I want you to call my father."

"What?"

"Mother's been bad. She doesn't take good care of me. She's with your husband all the time instead of with . . ." Mad as she was, she still didn't risk saying Andrew's name. She remembered too well her mother's promise to make Andrew go away if she talked about him. "I want you to call my father and tell him. He'll make her behave."

"I doubt if anyone could make that whore behave," Miranda countered.

Sharon did not know what a whore was, but she did know that her mother would do what her father said. He wasn't around them much, but when he was, *everyone* did what he said. "Just try," she told Miranda Patton eagerly. "Please."

Miranda looked at her strangely. "I could almost think that you hate her as much as I do. Anyway, I don't know how to get in touch with your father. God knows, I've tried. I've tried everything to get that bitch out of my life. He's harder to get to than the President."

Sharon couldn't explain to Miranda that she didn't hate Mother; she really loved her. But it was Andrew she had to think of. Nobody cared about Andrew but her. She reached under the green dress and found the piece of paper she had stuffed into her own dress pocket. "Here," she said. "This is my father's private number in Washington. You can get him there." She had overheard her father tell her mother that the last time he was home. She had copied down the number from her mother's purse carefully so that all the numbers were legible, just like the studio teacher was always telling her.

Miranda took the piece of paper and looked at it thoughtfully. "Thank you, kid," she said, "I think you might have just saved my marriage."

"Tell him she has to be punished. Tell him she has to take care of us."

"Jesus, don't tell me there're more like you at home!" Miranda reached for a cigarette. "You've done me a favor, kid. Now I'm going to do you one. I'm not going to tell anyone, including your father, how I got this number and if you're smart, you won't either. That vindictive bitch would . . . Just keep your mouth shut, that's all.''

Miranda turned around and started straightening the dresser. She looked so much like the mother she played on *Charlie's Gang* that it made Sharon sad she had caused so much damage. She hadn't meant to. ''Miranda?''

''What, kid?'' Miranda said, without turning back.

''Would you hug me like the mother would?''

Miranda turned around then and looked at Sharon for several seconds in silence, cigarette smoke curling around her. ''You have a rough life, don't you, kid?''

Sharon just stood there watching her. She didn't know why, but it was very important that Miranda hug her.

After a moment, Miranda stubbed out her cigarette and held her arms open. Sharon ran to her and Miranda held her tightly for a moment.

When she released Sharon, Miranda gave her a shove and turned back to the mirror. ''Now take off that dress and get lost, kid,'' she said hoarsely. ''I've got things to do.''

Sharon slipped out of the dress, laid it aside, and let herself out quickly. As she hurried back down the hall, she realized that there was several things she couldn't tell Andrew about today. She couldn't tell him what she had asked Miranda to do, and she couldn't tell him that Miranda had hugged her like a real mother. But most of all she couldn't tell him that Miranda had been crying when Sharon left her dressing room.

It would make him too sad if he heard she had made Mary Weston cry.

The peculiar thing was, she had no idea how she had done it.

A circus, that's what it was!

Upstairs in one of the guestrooms of her parents' spacious Bel Air home, Margaret Friedman was crying her eyes out. Downstairs, Emery's daughters, unattended, shrieked with laughter as they pulled the wagon with their baby brother inside around and around the massive dining room table, making little Winston scream with delight every time the wagon careened against an ornate mahogany leg.

In the den, Emery faced the firing squad.

"Some son-in-law you turned out to be!" Benjamin Ledermann roared at Emery. "You let this red-headed whore lead you around by your—"

"Benjamin!" Fay Ledermann, interrupted. "The children will hear you!"

"Let them hear! Poor innocent babes! Let them hear what kind of man their father is!"

Fay burst into tears.

Great, Emery thought. Crying women all over the house. "Look Ben, can't we discuss this reasonably?"

"I'll give you reasonable! Every door in this town will be shut to you tomorrow."

"People change," Emery said stubbornly. "A man's needs change."

"You have needs my daughter isn't filling? I'll have her mother talk to her."

"It has nothing to do with Margaret! She's . . . she's been a wonderful wife." That was true. What was happening had nothing to do with Margaret. She had been a perfect wife, a perfect mother, a perfect hostess, an amiable bed partner. He still loved her.

But all that just wasn't enough. Not when the alternative was Tina.

Ledermann lit up one of his fat cigars.

Fay broke off her bawling long enough to shriek, "Ben! Remember what the doctor said!"

"What does the doctor know about disloyalty?" He inhaled deeply. "That will kill a man faster than a good cigar." He scowled at his son-in-law. "Your father and I were in business together from 1919 until the day he died, Emery. We never even had a contract! He would turn over in his grave if he knew you wanted to dump my daughter and abandon his grandchildren!"

"I'll meet my financial responsibilities."

"How? One phone call from me and you're unemployed."

"You can make your phone call or not, as you prefer. I'm going to marry Tina." Emery stood up, towering over his red-faced father-in-law. "Tell Margaret she can stay here or move back home. It's up to her. I'll be out of the house by tomorrow."

He stopped in the dining room door. "Bye, Kids. See you later," he called.

Rachel, at six the oldest, threw him a kiss. Little Linette was too busy making the baby squeal.

In the entry hall, he paused, listening to the sound of his wife weeping upstairs. He wanted to go to her, comfort her, but that would mean giving up the one thing he couldn't: Tina.

He squared his shoulders and left, slamming the door behind him. That particular bridge was burned. It would be tricky managing without Ben Ledermann's money and power behind him, but it could be done. The prize, if he succeeded, was worth any sacrifice.

Tina would be his, all his. He didn't know what had come over her this past year; he only knew that she was faithful at last. There were no other men in her life now, only him.

As soon as the divorce went through, they would marry. That thought, and that thought alone, made the scene he had just gone through almost bearable.

He climbed into his sleek little BMW convertible. Last year when he brought it home there had been another tear-filled crisis. Only a few of the Type 507s had been imported into the U.S. He was damned lucky to get one. But Ben Ledermann had objected to the car on both moral and financial grounds.

"It was cheap at the price," Emery had bragged to his father-in-law. "It's practically handbuilt."

"In Munich, by Nazis!" Ben had roared back. Any German car would have been an affront to him, but the price made it ten times worse.

Margaret refused to ride in a two-seater. "There's no room for the children," she had complained the first time she set eyes on it and that had been that.

But Emery loved the racy little car. Its spectacular styling suited him.

Like Tina.

And it was Tina he was thinking of when he roared down the drive, leaving the Ledermann mansion, his career, his wife, and his children behind him.

Sharon brought her arithmetic book over to Danny between scenes. "Danny?"

Danny didn't respond. She followed his gaze and saw that
he was watching Owen Knox scold Victoria again.

Sharon tugged at his shirt. "Danny, could you help me
with this problem?"

In the past, he had often helped her with her homework,
teasing her and ruffling her hair. Lately, he had ignored her.
Today, he just muttered, "Not now, Sharon."

It made her feel like crying. Except for the studio teacher,
no one had even talked to her today. Soon they would be
through filming for the season, and she wouldn't even have
the studio teacher to talk to. She would be back in regular
school with a lot of strangers. At home, there was only her
and Andrew and still another new nanny.

Nothing had worked out like she had hoped. Miranda must
have called Father, because *he* called Mother. Sharon and
Andrew could hear her screaming at him over the phone,
even in their bedroom. The silence afterward was even more
scary. Andrew had been so frightened he slept in Sharon's
bed that night. She didn't like for him to do that because he
always wet. This time she let him, because she knew it was
her fault he had gotten scared.

In the morning was worse, because Cynthia Bradford had
left without a word to the nanny or anybody. Andrew hadn't
even gotten to look out the window and see her car drive
away. When he found out that she was gone, he had cried so
hard that the nanny let him stay home from the special
school that day. He hadn't been any fun since then, just
moping around.

Danny was like her brother in some ways, she thought.
That was the part he played on the show and until recently,
that was the way he had treated her off the set, too. Not that
she was confused about brothers. She knew that Andrew was
her really-true brother. Nothing would ever change that.

But Danny had been nice to her, nicer than anyone except
Andrew.

Until recently.

Now all he did was hang around Victoria. He never talked
to Victoria, not like he had talked to Sharon. He just watched
her. If Sharon tried to talk to him while he watched Victoria,
he would shush her.

Grown-ups were mean, Sharon thought. Mother had been

mean to leave her and Andrew like that. Father was mean not
to come home and see them sometimes. The nurses and
nannies were always mean.

The only people who had been nice to her were Victoria
and Danny. Now they both acted like she didn't even exist.
Like they were grown-ups, too.

When she was a grown-up, she wasn't going to be mean to
anyone. Especially Andrew. She would always be nice to
Andrew.

She studied Victoria thoughtfully. She could be more grown
up if she wore dresses like Victoria's instead of the stupid
kiddy dresses that were like JoJo's.

Sharon wondered if she could get the new nanny to take
her shopping for clothes.

"Well, Miss Carr. Are we ready to concentrate?" Owen
Knox asked nastily.

"Yes, Mr. Knox," Victoria told the director meekly. This
was the third time he had stopped the whole crew to admon-
ish her and she was near tears. "I'm sorry. I just forgot the
line."

"It wasn't just any line of dialogue, Miss Carr. It was your
brother's name. You've only been calling him Bucky for
three years now. I can see how a little thing like that might
slip your mind."

Danny clenched his fists, wishing Knox would ease off. He
called them by their last names when he was mad at them:
"Miss" Carr, "Mr." Garrick, "Miss" Bradford. Somehow it
made them seem even more like kids when he did it and
Danny hated that.

And he hated to see Victoria's eyes so wet and shiny with
unshed tears. Owen Knox was a real bastard when he wanted
to be. No one who wasn't on the set would understand. How
could you complain to someone that the creep was too polite
to the three of them?

Now as Owen gave the signal for them to take their places
once more, Danny could see that the director was just waiting
for Victoria to goof up one more time so that he could come
at her again with his sadistic politeness.

Of course, she was going to forget her lines again. She was
worrying too much about the director. Danny could see it

coming as he sat back down in Charlie Weston's chair and
Victoria leaned across the desk. Nan was supposed to explain
to Bucky how he had screwed up *this* week. They must have
played variations on that scene a million times by now. But as
she said her lines, he could see the glazed look of fear starting
to build in her eyes, and he knew she was going to stumble
again.

No one else had seen it yet and Danny knew he had to
make sure they wouldn't. He didn't plan what happened next.
He just did it.

He leaned back far enough to tilt the desk chair over and
went crashing to the floor with a tremendous thud.

Danny lay there moaning as the crew ran on to the set.
When they helped him to his feet, he clutched his left arm
with his right.

It really *did* hurt, as a matter of fact, but he found he could
stand the pain. The flash of gratitude in Victoria's eyes made
it worthwhile.

Then Tina was there, her hand on his arm, and nothing had
changed.

Victoria held a damp cloth to her face, trying to cool the
embarrassed flush. It had been so sweet of Danny to pull
Owen Knox's attention away from her for a few minutes. But
it was only a few minutes, and then she would have to go
back and try to pretend she was a normal person.

Normal!

She didn't know if she would be able to go on with acting,
with this series. Remembering how much she had wanted to
be an actress, Victoria couldn't believe she felt this way now.

But that had been before she found the diaries. Thea's
diaries. Thea Stanton Carr.

What a joke!

She had carried the slim, leather-bound volumes down
from the attic and hidden them in her closet. Any time she
could steal a few minutes, she read them feverishly. She
stayed up far into the night, every night. She had practically
quit studying her scripts. The diaries were all that mattered.
Volume after volume of them in Thea's graceful handwriting.
The entries started when Thea was twelve and ended the day
before her death.

Victoria was no fool; she understood exactly what she was reading. The only thing she couldn't understand was why her grandfather had *wanted* her to find them. Why had he wanted her to know that he had molested his own daughter, over and over, year after year? Why did he want her to learn that when Thea discovered she was pregnant by her own father, he had insisted that she keep the baby, and created the fictitious Carr out of forged documents so no one would know his secret. For a while it had stopped, until after the baby was born. After *she* was born, Victoria thought. Then, it had started again.

And when Thea realized that it would never stop, that she would never be free of him, she had decided to kill him, herself, and the baby in an automobile accident.

Only it didn't work.

Thea alone died. He was still alive.

And *me*!

Every time she thought of it, thought of what she really was, the bile rose in Victoria's throat. Why had he wanted her to know that?

Why?

"Victoria? Are you all right?"

Florence Stanton had decided Victoria's strange behavior meant she was coming down with something and had driven in with her this morning. Now, she peered at her granddaughter worriedly.

"I'm fine," Victoria said hastily. She had to get hold of herself. She couldn't let her grandmother know the truth about her husband and her daughter.

She would do anything to prevent that.

Sharon sat by the stage pouting. Everyone was still gathered around Danny, except for Owen Knox, who was yelling for Victoria. No one talked to *her*, Sharon thought. No one paid any attention to her. She was so bored she could scream.

Then she heard a heavy sigh beside her. Someone else was bored, too.

She glanced up to find Nick Hanson standing there, watching everyone mill around on the set. Sharon hesitated. He almost never talked to her off the set. But today she was so bored that she would try to talk to anyone. "I hate to wait," she said. "Don't you?"

"Why, young Miss Bradford," Nick Hanson said as though he had just noticed her sitting there. He gave her last name a teasing twist that didn't make it sound like it did when Owen Knox was angry with her. "You look very pretty today, Miss Bradford. I'm sure you'll get your turn in front of the cameras before long."

"I know *my* lines," she told him proudly. "And I would never fall out of my chair."

"Of course not. Pretty little girls like you have to take good care of themselves."

He looked at her more closely. "Your hair is different, isn't it?"

Sharon beamed. He was the first person to notice! "The hairdresser combed it just like Victoria's for me. Do you like it?"

"I certainly do. You look very attractive, very grown-up."

Nick gave her shoulder a squeeze, just one, as though it were a secret just between the two of them.

Someone called his name on the set then, and he walked away.

Sharon smoothed her hair back from her ears. Maybe Victoria would loan her some of her makeup, she thought. If she asked nicely.

Chapter Five

1960

"You were *seen*, goddamn it!" Owen Knox, nose to nose with Nick Hanson, recovered himself enough to lower his voice. "Why did you have to go with her?"

Nick shrugged helplessly. "She was afraid. She didn't want to go through with it by herself."

"At fourteen? I don't blame her."

"Besides, I didn't go inside. I'm not that big a fool. I just waited in the car while she—"

Owen slammed him back against the wall. "Haven't you ever heard of rubbers, you ignorant bastard? It's bad enough that you're a pervert. Why do you have to keep getting them pregnant?"

"You can't feel anything with rubbers."

"You won't feel anything dickless, either." Owen had forgotten to lower his voice on that one. A passing script girl giggled. He leaned forward, whispering hoarsely. "Do you realize what Friedman will do to you—to both of us—if he finds out about this?"

"I paid a great deal of money to keep the girl and her parents quiet, I assure you. There's nothing for him to find out," Nick said, projecting a calmness he did not feel.

"You're right. And there won't be. I've hired a private

detective firm to keep an eye on you. They're going to follow you everywhere. You won't even be able to piss in private. One report to me that you're involved with anyone under the age of twenty-one, and I'll take the information straight to Friedman. If you think I'm going to screw up my career because of your cock, you're wrong, Buster.''

"Really, Owen! This is a violation of my privacy. You can't—''

"You stupid son of a bitch! Don't you realize this is not some wet dream! We're playing for real with big bucks here. This is the fourth season of a guaranteed winner. If you fuck it up, Friedman will have both of our hides. Your jailbait days are over, Nick.''

Owen stormed off down the corridor without waiting for Nick's reply. What reply could there be, after all, Nick thought reasonably. But reason couldn't fight off the panic beating in his chest. Owen didn't understand. No one understood. This infatuation with young girls wasn't something he could control; it controlled him. Ruled him.

If he couldn't see anyone—

He turned blindly in the direction of the set and bumped into little Sharon Bradford.

"Why, Miss JoJo, '' he exclaimed. "How you've grown.''

Owen slammed the door of his inner office and then picked up the phone to tell the secretary he had just stomped past to hold all of his calls.

Christ! What was happening to the world?

Superman had killed himself. Lucy was divorcing Desi. There were rumors *Howdy Doody* was going off the air this fall, for God's sake.

Everything was changing. It felt like a whole way of life was coming to an end. Who knew how long a family show like *Charlie's Gang* would remain a hit?

The quiz show scandals were having a profound effect on the American public. Television viewers felt betrayed by their heroes. By television itself.

What would Mr. and Mrs. John Q. Public think if they found out the truth about Nick Hanson? Charlie Weston fucking young girls! They'd probably lynch him.

And kill the show.

There were precedents Owen thought glumly. Look what happened to *Mr. Lucky* last season. The show was a hit from the start. It had a great premise: a suave gambler and his sidekick on their own floating casino/yacht, cruising the Pacific coast. Only when the quiz show scandals broke, the sponsor got moral and demanded that the floating casino become a floating restaurant. Of course, the show was axed.

He just hoped that Nick believed him about the private detectives. He didn't dare have Nick followed for real. Someone would find out and start asking why. Then the digging and the prying would start. It wouldn't take long for the truth about Nick to surface if someone put their mind to it. Then the scandal rags would be full of it, and good-bye *Charlie's Gang*.

At least Emery's divorce had been put on hold for a season. Owen had found out from a friend of the Ledermanns that Emery was wildly impatient to divorce Margaret and marry Tina. But Ben Ledermann had used financial pressure on Emery to delay the proceedings, at least until next year. Owen was unaccountably relieved at that. The thought of Tina marrying Emery, of belonging to Emery permanently, was enough to drive Owen crazy.

Thank God Ledermann had flexed his financial muscles. There were only so many crises a man could handle in one year.

He caught himself rubbing his bald spot again and jerked his hand away. Much more of this shit and he wouldn't have a sprig of hair left by the time he was thirty-five.

Danny and Victoria were alone in the classroom. Sharon, in hot water for wandering around the sets alone again, had left with the teacher to be turned over to her nanny in person. Danny watched Victoria gathering up her school books. He wondered why she bothered. She always finished the homework assignments in class. Danny cleared his throat. "Victoria?"

When she paused and turned his way, he came very close to blurting out "Excuse me" and bolting from the classroom. As it was, he had to clear his throat twice before he could force the words out. "I was wondering if you'd have time to go over a scene with me," he said hoarsely, trying to ignore the blush he could feel building. It had taken him two days to build up the courage to speak to her. You'd think he was asking her for a date, instead of to read a couple of pages of a crappy TV script.

"I don't feel like it right now," she said absently. "Get somebody else."

She picked up the rest of her things and left the studio classroom. Danny dropped back into his seat and stared at his notebook. She thinks you're a jerk, he told himself. She's right, too.

As if that wasn't enough to ruin his day, Tina was waiting for him when he came out of the classroom. Danny tried to brush past her, but she caught his arm. "I almost feel like you've been avoiding me, Danny. I couldn't even get you on the phone during the hiatus. Now you've been back two whole days and you didn't even try to see me."

"I've had things to do." His voice was lower, more masculine now; Owen Knox had already been on his case about it, telling him that wasn't the way Bucky was supposed to sound.

"And one of them is supposed to be me, Bucky."

"Don't call me that!"

Tina glanced around quickly. There was no one else in the corridor. She stepped forward, pressing herself against him. 'What's wrong with that?"

"I just . . . don't like it." How could he explain that he didn't want her intruding into that fantasy world of *Charlie's Gang* where he was safe and secure, healthy and normal? Above all, normal. Bucky Weston didn't have to deal with things like the way Danny's cock was beginning to bulge against his pants.

Of course Tina had noticed. "Well, part of you likes it," she pointed out with a seductive little giggle. Then she pulled him back into the empty classroom.

And, disgusted with himself, he went.

Nick gave Sharon a quick hug. "That was very good, Miss JoJo."

Sharon beamed up at him. Nick was the only one who paid any attention to her these days. Victoria and Danny were no fun at all. Victoria, quiet and withdrawn, barely spoke to anyone.

Danny kept mooning around, staring at Victoria or hiding from Tina Sawyer.

But Nick was always there, teasing Sharon, hugging her, asking her to sit on his lap as he did now. "We'll go over that next scene while we're waiting," he told her.

Sharon let him lift her into his lap, and leaned back against his chest as he opened his script to the right page so she could read it too. She felt a little strange being so close to an adult male, hearing the starchy crinkle of his shirt as she wiggled into a more comfortable position. Her father had never been around the twins much and there had been no other men in her life.

Owen Knox paused in his instructions to the cameraman. "That looks so damned good I ought to get a photographer up here for a few publicity shots," he told Nick. "You're making quite a difference in her delivery, too."

"What does that mean?" she asked Nick when Owen walked away.

"It means, young Miss Bradford, that you are a charmer and quite a good little actress too."

"What's a charmer?"

"A very beautiful young lady," Nick told her. He gave her a hug, holding her close for a moment, and at the same time shifting her so that she was over something hard in his lap. She tried to squirm away, but he held her there. "Comfortable?" he murmured.

She nodded wordlessly, afraid to deny it, afraid he might push her off his lap and ignore her like everyone else in her life.

"Good," he said softly. Then he was all business once more. "Let's hear you on that first line again."

Victoria stood at the edge of the set, gnawing on her lower lip, as she watched Nick and Sharon.

Owen Knox paused for a moment. "It wouldn't hurt you to go over your lines again, too, Victoria," he said nastily. "You're going through your scenes like a sleepwalker."

She barely heard him. There was another voice in her head, a voice from Thea's diaries:

At first, I thought he was just being fatherly. He would

*hold me on his lap and read to me, wonderful stories from
the thick books in the library, the ones I was never allowed
to touch myself. As he talked he would hold me close with
one hand, stroking my shoulder, my arm, sometimes my
leg. I was twelve the summer he touched me* there *for the
first time. Looking back, I'm surprised he waited so long.*

She looked around the set. Nobody else was paying any
attention to Nick and Sharon. Was it her imagination? She
couldn't be sure of anything anymore. Ever since she had
discovered Thea's diaries she had felt like such a freak. She
was terrified everyone could see her shameful secret.

It had never been easy for her to make friends. All her life
she had felt so different from other children. No one else had
a dead mother or a mystery father. Switching back and forth
between high school and the studio school, she'd lost what
few friends she'd had before *Charlie's Gang*.

For that she was glad. She didn't want friends, didn't want
anyone to share her thoughts. In spite of her grandmother's
protests, she had her own car now, a white Ford Thunderbird.
She drove it to the studio every day, enjoying the time alone
and the wonderful freedom of not having to pretend to her
grandmother that everything was wonderful.

Everything was *not* wonderful.

Everything was awful.

Thea's diaries were hidden in her room. Victoria had read
them over and over until she had practically memorized them.
She would be doing something else, walking on the beach,
practicing a scene, trying to learn her lines, and a phrase from
one of Thea's entries would float up out of her memory,
blocking out the reality around her. She felt as though she
were living in two different worlds at once.

Why had her grandfather led her to the diaries? Why had
he wanted her to know his shameful secret? Those were
questions she could not answer.

Nor the other one which troubled her: If he had not been
paralyzed in that terrible accident would he have done to her
what he did to Thea? Was that why his chair followed her
everywhere? Why did he keep staring at her?

God! She felt so unclean!

The deep murmur of Nick's resonant voice floated across the set, followed by Sharon's high childish giggle.

Victoria knew she couldn't wait any longer. Someone had to stop this.

"Can I talk to you for a minute?" Victoria asked Miranda Patton and then followed the actress into her dressing room without waiting for a reply.

Miranda tossed her script across the room and then sat down in front of the mirror. "Can't it wait till tomorrow?" she asked peevishly as she lit a cigarette. "I really need to get out of this place." She began to tissue off her makeup.

"It will only take a minute," Victoria blurted. She didn't dare wait. She was afraid she'd never be brave enough to broach the subject again if she walked away now.

Miranda sighed dramatically. "All right. Make it quick, though."

Victoria hesitated, finding it hard to frame the words.

"Really, Victoria, I'm in a hurry," Miranda complained as she began to apply her street face.

"It's . . . it's about Sharon," Victoria blurted, and then blushed.

Miranda swung around to regard her with a jaundiced eye, and then turned back to the mirror. "It's taken you long enough to catch on," she said to her reflection. "But there's nothing you can do about it. God knows, I've tried. If you stay in this business, it's just something you have to get used to."

"I'll never get used to it!" Victoria said violently. "Never in a hundred years!"

"Kids and dogs," Miranda mused to the mirror. "Dogs are the worst, you know."

Victoria blinked. "Dogs?"

"Real scene stealers. Between Danny and Sharon, you and I don't have a chance. Nick knows how to keep himself in the scene, though. I'll have to give him that. There's never been a kid who could upstage him."

"I—You don't understand, Miranda." Victoria blushed again, but she was determined to get it out. "Don't you think Nick is too friendly with Sharon? Always holding her—"

"That's what I'm telling you, kid. He knows how to play

both ends against the middle. He know he looks so damn good sitting around holding her on his lap. Why do you think Owen keeps having the scripts changed so there's more of that? And less of me and you," she added bitterly.

"I didn't know Mr. Knox was doing that."

Miranda stood up and took off her robe. She wasn't wearing anything under it. Victoria had never seen a grown woman naked before and she was amazed. If Miranda was model-thin in her clothes, she was scrawny without them. Every rib, every bone made a separate and distinct lump beneath her skin.

"This is a rough career for a woman, kid," Miranda put on panties, bra, and then reached for her suit. "Nick will still be working when he's seventy and I'll be washed up in ten more years." She paused and leaned forward to give herself a long critical look in the mirror. "Maybe five," she said, gently caressing the drooping skin beneath her eyes. "Get it while you can. That's all you can do." She picked up her purse and lit another cigarette, leaving a half-finished butt smouldering in the ashtray.

"Wait, Miranda!" Victoria cried, desperate to make her TV mother understand. "Don't you think someone should do something about Sharon and Nick?"

"Kids and dogs," Miranda said as she started for the door. 'There's not a damn thing you can do about them."

"What are these contortions supposed to mean?" Owen Knox asked nastily.

"I . . . nothing, Mr. Knox," Victoria said quickly. "I just thought if I turned my head, I would be able—"

"Don't think, Miss Carr. You're obviously not equipped for it. Just sit in that chair and try to act like a normal teenager and not the rubber man at the circus."

Victoria dropped back into the chair, fighting the urge to turn and glance at the edge of the set where Nick Hanson stood, his arm around Sharon's shoulders. Phrases from Thea's diaries kept floating up into her consciousness, and her stomach lurched.

Was everyone else blind?

"Are we ready, Miss Carr?" Owen Knox asked sharply.

She nodded meekly and made an effort to throw herself

into the scene, but she couldn't stop the warning voice—Thea's voice—in her head.

It wasn't working! Victoria had made herself Sharon's bodyguard. Whenever Sharon was on the set, she was, too. They walked the corridors together, ate lunch together. Victoria had even taught the little girl how to put on makeup.

What a mistake that had been, she thought dismally. It had only served to make Nick Hanson more interested in Sharon.

If only there were someone she could talk to. She had thought about approaching the studio teacher, but she didn't dare. She would do anything to keep Sharon from harm, anything but reveal her own terrible secret.

Hard as she tried, she couldn't be with Sharon every minute of the day. There were just too many scenes she played without Sharon, and Nick pounced on every opportunity to be alone with the little girl. There was only one thing left to do, Victoria realized. She *was* an actress, after all.

It was a dangerous game he was playing, Nick admitted to himself, as he waited for Sharon to complete her scene. But it was a game Owen Knox had forced him into with his private detectives and his threats.

"Nick?"

He turned to find Victoria beside him. My God, but she was a lovely thing. She looked so young, so vulnerable, standing there, that he could feel an erection starting. The teasing smile on her face only made it worse.

"I'm really jealous, Nick. You're always helping Sharon with her lines." She took a step closer, looking up into his face. "What about me? Don't you think I need some coaching, too?"

Sharon came bouncing over, delighted with the praise she had gotten from Mr. Knox for her last scene. Nick and Victoria were deep in conversation, but she couldn't contain her joy. "Nick?" She tugged at his sleeve. "Will you help me some more now?"

"Not now," he said impatiently. "Can't you see I'm talking to Victoria?"

He turned away too quickly to see the hurt on Sharon's face.

"Victoria?" she appealed.

"Go sit down," Victoria ordered.

Sharon was so startled that she retreated to a nearby chair and sat there impatiently, waiting for the two of them to stop talking and notice *her*.

Instead, after a few more moments of conversation, Nick and Victoria left the set together.

Sharon had never felt so betrayed in her life. Nick was her best friend after Andrew, and Victoria was trying to steal him. She knew Victoria was doing this on purpose.

What a meany!

The hands of the clock on her nightstand crawled past midnight, but Victoria found herself unable to sleep. She rose and took one of the leather-bound diaries from its hiding place in the closet and carried it back to her bed. She had read through the entire series more than once, but something still puzzled her.

In the beginning, there was indignation in Thea's words as she described her seduction at the hands of her own father. Towards the end, after Victoria herself was born, there was desperation as Thea realized that nothing would end, and that her baby daughter might one day be at risk also.

But in the middle, the vast, vast middle, there was the description of what could only be called a long and satisfying love affair.

> *Today he brought me roses. A dozen red and a dozen white. I understood the symbolism. Tonight I scattered rose petals, red and white, over my sheets and lay on them naked, waiting for him to come to me.*

And:

> *No one knows my body as well as he does. He brings me such pleasure that I weep.*

Nowhere, in all the diaries, was there a mention of Florence Stanton.

Victoria closed the book.

What would it be like to lay on rose petals, waiting for your lover to come to you?

Your lover.

Your father.

Nick had put his arm around her shoulder today. Accidently, it had seemed at the time, his hand had brushed her right breast.

Victoria caressed her breast with her hand through the fabric or her gown, feeling it grow taunt. Then she slipped her hand beneath her gown, between her legs, letting her fingers search for the hard little button hidden there.

She had almost reached release when she heard the sound of her grandfather's wheelchair passing in the hallway outside her room.

Victoria jerked her hand away and lay there panting.

When the house was silent again, she returned the diary to its hiding place and went to take a shower.

"Need any help with those lines?" Nick asked, standing too close to her.

"Not today." Victoria shifted her weight to her other foot, leaning away from him, and flipped nosily through the script, not meeting his glance.

Rebuffed he wandered away and she breathed a sigh of relief.

Throughout the next scene, she kept her mind on her work, but when it ended, she realized Nick had disappeared.

So had Sharon.

Victoria asked Miranda Patton where Nick had gone, and she mumbled something about his dressing room.

Victoria all but ran down the corridor. When she reached the door of Nick's dressing room, she paused. What if she was wrong?

But she wasn't. Sharon was inside. Victoria could hear her voice through the closed door, but not the words. She pressed her ear against the wood.

"Sit on my lap," she heard Nick urging.

Victoria stepped back and knocked loudly on the door. There were brief, furtive sounds from the dressing room. Then Nick answered the door, his face pale and nervous looking. When he saw Victoria standing, he took a deep breath.

"I should have taken you up on your offer," Victoria

said softly, smiling up into his eyes. "I'm really having a lot of trouble with my lines."

Sharon had followed Nick to the door. Now she leaned forward and gave Victoria a shove. "You go away. Nick is helping me."

"I'm sure Nick would rather help me," Victoria said, without looking down at the little girl. Instead she kept her gaze trained on Nick, and the smile she gave him seemed to help him make his decision.

"Now, Sharon," Nick said quickly. "Everybody gets their turn. You run along." He took Victoria's arm, pulling her into the dressing room.

Sharon stood there defiantly for a moment, until Nick ushered her out. "Now," he said to Victoria when he had closed the door, "Let's look at that script." He sat down on the couch and patted the space beside him.

Victoria had not allowed herself to think beyond this moment. If she didn't make at least a pretense of going along with him, she knew he would just lure Sharon back in here. And Sharon was all too willing to be lured. But to take one more step might put her into a situation she could not control.

A frown crossed Nick's handsome face and his next words confirmed her fears. "I hope you were serious, Victoria," he said sharply. "I wouldn't want to think you were just teasing me. Little Sharon actually needs help with her lines." He sounded so much like Charlie Weston at that moment it was scary.

"Oh, I do, too, Nick," she assured him in a breathy, seductive voice. "I really want your help." Before she could lose her nerve, she moved quickly across the room to sit beside him. All she had to do was keep him occupied until Sharon had left for the day. Then she would make her escape.

How?

And how not to anger him when she did?

She would worry about that later.

I'm an actress, she told herself. I'll think of something. And he'll believe me. Because I'm a *good* actress.

At first, in spite of her fears, Nick was all business. He ran through the scene she had chosen with a brisk professionalism, questioning her motivation. The reason she had come to Nick's dressing room drifted to the back of her mind and

Victoria found she was actually learning something about the craft of acting.

It came as a shock to her when a glance at her wristwatch made her realize that Sharon must be leaving the studio by now. She was sitting side by side on the couch with Nick, their shoulders touching. She shifted slightly away from him, and he responded by putting his arm around her shoulder.

"Nick, I really have to go now." She kept her eyes trained on the page they had been going over.

"You drive yourself to the studio now. No one is waiting for you." He was rubbing her shoulder, her upper arm, stroking her hair.

What a strange feeling it was to have someone stroking her hair. It came to Victoria in a blinding flash that no one ever touched her except when she was acting. She had the brief faraway memory of her mother hugging her, holding her, as they played together on the beach below the house. But after her mother's death, after she left the hospital, there had been no one to cuddle her. Certainly not Vincent Stanton, in the hospital for months and then confined to his wheelchair after that. And, curiously, not her grandmother either. Victoria couldn't remember a single instance of Florence Stanton putting her arms around her. But the Westons were huggers, touchers. On the set, she was constantly cuddled, hugged, *loved*, by her make-believe parents and siblings.

Now with Nick holding her close, she was able, for the first time off the set, to recapture the warm, wonderful feeling of being part of a real family.

That feeling was so warm, so wonderful, that when he touched his lips to hers, her mouth opened to him like a rose. His slow, soft kiss was only a continuation of that wonderful feeling, and she was not alarmed.

He was a good kisser. Not that she'd had that many others with which to compare him. Her only experiences had been with the actors on the show who portrayed her boyfriends. This was so much better. She found herself responding to Nick as the kiss intensified, enjoying the strange lazy warmth the movement of his mouth on hers caused to shoot through her body. His tongue intruded delicately between her lips, and at the same time Nick began to caress her breasts, shaping their firmness with his fingers. She murmured a

protest into his mouth, trying to draw away, trying to hold the
warm feeling intact.

In answer, he increased his assault on her mouth, his
tongue probing deeper and deeper, until she pressed against
his hand, instead of withdrawing, until her own tongue sought
his.

The script slipped from her hand to the floor, forgotten.
She scarcely realized that he was unbuttoning her blouse. Or
that he had reached behind her to unhook her bra. Not until
he pushed the fabric aside and broke off his kiss to take her
left nipple in his mouth, rolling the tender bud between his
lips, and then sucking it until it hardened. The sensation that
began between her legs and flashed through her body was so
intense that she could not tell if it was pleasure or pain.

Nick found her lips again, and still kissing her, leaned her
back on to the couch. His fingers searched for the warmth of
her and when they took possession of that hard little button
she had already found for herself the pleasure that flooded
through her was like nothing she had ever known before. The
intensity of it kept her pinned there, like a butterfly to
the collector's display. Each moment was so much better
than the last that she couldn't move away or rescue herself
from his hands. To do so would be to miss the next wave
of pleasure he might release.

In the process she lost her panties, lifting first one hip and
then the other, to aid their removal. Without the intrusion of
the nylon, the sensations Nick released within her became
infinitely better. She clung to him, trembling, as his mouth
caressed her breast once more, connecting all the pleasure
points of her body simultaneously.

He raised himself over her, freeing his rigid penis from his
trousers, and now he guided her hand to it. Curiosity kept her
from jerking her hand back. It was the strangest feeling in the
world to be holding that piece of him. It seemed so *alive*, as
though it were a creature in its own right.

She moved her hand tentatively, feeling the strength of it
and Nick groaned. "Nan," he whispered into her hair, his
breath hot against her ear. "Nan!"

Victoria jerked her hand away, terror starting up inside her
as his penis poked against her belly. His kisses teased her

mouth again and his fingers sought the warm cleft of her once more, but her legs were drawn tightly together.

"No!" she cried, but Nick forced her thighs apart with his knee with a firmess just short of violence, pushing himself into her only a little way before her virginity resisted him. Efficient in sex as in everything else, he drew back and rammed himself home, catching her gasp of pain with his mouth, probing deeply with his tongue, trying vainly to rekindle the fire within her.

But it was dead. Killed, not by the pain of his penetration or the rhythmic thrusts that followed, but by the realization that she—just as surely as Thea—had committed incest.

The full force of the shower rained down while Victoria scrubbed at her skin, trying to wash away the traces of something that wasn't visible in the first place. She let the water strike her skin like thousands of tiny darts, running it so long until at last her grandmother banged on the bathroom door and asked if she was all right.

She turned the shower off then, but she remained in the stall, leaning her cheek against the cold tile. When she finally stepped out of the shower and wrapped herself in a huge towel, she still felt unclean.

At last she climbed into bed, but she could not sleep. How could she live with herself knowing what kind of vile and disgusting person she really was? What would she do tomorrow? How could she run through a scene with Nick Hanson and pretend that none of this had happened?

And more important than any of that, much more important, what could she do to protect Sharon in the days to come?

Victoria hurried to her dressing room, terrified that someone would be able to read on her face what had happened the day before. Once inside the door, she froze in amazement, staring at the chaos.

Her personal possessions had been scattered everywhere. Her makeup and perfume had been opened and dumped on top of her books, her clothes. Across the mirror of her dressing table, in Sharon's childish scrawl, was the word

"Meany." The ruined remains of Victoria's favorite lipstick lay on the dressing table.

Victoria cleaned up the mess herself, hurriedly, so that no one else would see it and question her about what had happened.

But as the day went on, things got worse. Sharon spilled a cold drink on her between scenes and pinched Victoria, hard, when Victoria hugged her for the camera.

When Victoria tried to talk to her between takes, Sharon said, "I hate you," and danced away, out of Victoria's reach.

Owen Knox noticed the byplay and as usual blamed it on Victoria, spitefully calling her "Miss Carr," and asking her if she had time to go through the next scene or did she plan to keep the whole cast waiting.

Halfway through the scene, Nick, in his character of Charlie Weston, leaned over and hugged Victoria. "I'm proud of you, Nan," he said. Victoria, in her character of Nan, smiled up at her seducer and said, "Thanks, Dad." And no one on the set of *Charlie's Gang* questioned that scene.

So that's what actors are, Victoria thought, as Owen Knox congratulated both of them for a good take. *We're liars!* And she knew that the part of her that played Nan was another person, separate and distinct from the real Victoria.

A different person.

A better person.

1961

Victoria lay with her cheek against the cold porcelain of the toilet bowl. This was the third morning in a row that she had thrown up. She could no longer ignore the evidence. She was pregnant.

Sharon had made her life miserable the last four weeks, harrassing Victoria during filming with childish tricks, making her life miserable. She acted as though Victoria had stolen her only friend.

The only bright spot Victoria could see was that Sharon was just as mad at Nick Hanson as she was at Victoria. She refused to have anything to do with him off the set, and Owen Knox had been forced to speak to the little girl quite sharply to get her to climb into Nick's lap for publicity photos.

Victoria had done everything she could to save Sharon, and it had apparently worked.

What could she do now to save herself?

The white Ford T-Bird sitting all by itself caught Danny's eye as he came out of the studio. He planned to get a neat car like that himself one of these days. A "Squarebird" they called it in the car magazines he devoured every month. This model was a jewel, he realized, one of the limited-production hardtops with sliding steel sunroof. He sauntered over to admire its boxy lines firsthand. When he saw someone inside—a woman, sobbing—Danny started to back away. Then he realized that the figure hunched over the steering wheel was Victoria, and he couldn't leave her like that. He tapped on the glass.

She looked up, startled, tears still streaming down her cheeks. When she recognized him, she rolled the window down.

"Is something wrong with your car, Victoria?"

"Oh, Danny." She hesitated for a moment, and then the words tumbled out. "I don't know what to do. Someone's supposed to go with me, to drive me, but there's no one I can ask."

"I'll drive you."

"You can't. You're only fifteen. You don't have your license yet."

The reference to his age annoyed him. "You don't need a license to drive, stupid. You just have to know how and not get stopped by a cop."

Victoria smiled through her tears. "I can't imagine Bucky Weston ever saying anything like that."

"Bucky's just a kid. I'm not."

Victoria looked at him uncertainly, but she relinquished her place behind the wheel to him.

Danny slid into the bucket seat and glanced over at her. "So where to?"

She just looked at him in silence.

"Home? The beauty salon? To meet your boyfriend?" The last had a bitter sound to it he hadn't intended. He hadn't realized that Victoria *had* a boyfriend until the words popped out, but one look at her face now and he was sure of it.

She looked down at her hands, clenched in her lap, hiding her face from him. "You don't want to go with me, Danny. I've got to get an abortion."

He stared at her, stunned.

She still didn't look up. "I was supposed to find someone to drive me there and drive me home. But I don't know anyone to ask." Tears fell on her clenched hands, but she wasn't making any sobbing sounds. "I'm so afraid."

Something twisted inside Danny's chest. "Who's the guy? Why isn't he here with you?"

"He arranged everything. It's all paid for."

"He should be here!"

She looked up then. "I don't want him here," she said fiercely. Then the fierceness burned away, "Besides, he wouldn't come. He can't afford to be seen with me. It would ruin him." Now she did sob aloud. "You can't either. It could ruin you, too."

Danny turned the key in the ignition. "What's the address?"

There was a small room to wait in, clean but sparsely decorated. Danny sat in a pink plastic chair and tried not to think about what they were doing to Victoria beyond that door.

Someone had left a pack of cigarettes laying on a table. He took one and then searched for matches. He finally found a folder wedged down behind the cushions in the sofa. The first drag burned his throat and lungs. He smoked a little occasionally, when he wanted to look older. But instead of inhaling again, he just held the cigarette, watching the smoke spiral toward the ceiling, and thought about what he had tried not to think about until now.

Who was the man?

Images of Victoria leaped into his mind, vivid pictures of Victoria doing the things Tina did. Danny had never thought of Victoria in that way. She had always seemed above all that.

This evening he had learned she was not. That she was, in fact, no better than himself.

It only made him love her more.

Victoria was bundled through the door, pale as death. Danny supported her out to the car, helping her into the seat on the passenger side as though she were made of fragile crystal.

When he got behind the wheel, he said, "Do you want me to drive you home? Or is there someone you can stay with?"

"Home," she said. He drove carefully, without looking at her. There were so many things he wanted to say to her, to ask her, that he couldn't say anything at all.

"Danny," she said suddenly. "Pull over." Her face was stark white.

He pulled over to the side of the street, leaving the motor running.

She leaned toward him and he put his arms around her. He had wanted to do this for so long that he almost wept with pleasure to feel her cheek against his.

"Oh, Danny," she said, softly, so close that her breath caressed his ear. "Oh, Danny, I'm bleeding. I'm going to die."

Chapter Six

Danny stood in front of the pay phone in the hospital waiting room and patted his pockets for change.

Nothing.

It was a good thing he had hung onto Victoria's slim navy leather purse when they wheeled her into the emergency room, because he didn't have a cent.

He glanced around nervously. The hospital waiting room was a vastly different place than the clinic had been. There were people everywhere. He turned his back, shielding the purse with his body as he pawed through it, trying to ignore the faint elusive scent of Victoria's perfume that rose from its interior.

Mature Victoria. Of course she'd have enough change for a phone call.

Mad money.

Too bad she hadn't used it a couple of months ago.

Danny dropped the coins into the pay phone. Thank heaven Owen Knox was listed with information. He had no idea who else to call. He blurted it all out in a rush, giving Owen no time to interrupt.

When he ran down, Owen said, "Did you give her real name?"

"I haven't given any name yet, but I told them she's my sister. They'll be tracking me down in a few minutes. I haven't filled out any paperwork."

"Put them off until I get there."

"What will I tell them?"

Owen hesitated. "Did they recognize either one of you?"

"Christ, Owen! You wouldn't have recognized her! I think she's dying!"

"Calm down, Danny. Tell them you called you called your father and he's on his way down. Just don't answer any questions at all, and try to stay out of sight. If someone should recognize you—"

Danny glanced around the waiting room. Everyone there was caught up in their own personal misery. "No one's paying any attention to me."

"Good. Keep it that way."

When Owen broke the connection, Danny hung up the phone, but he remained standing there, with his back to the room, rifling through Victoria's purse. Quickly he emptied it of everything with her name on it: her driver's license, checkbook, credit cards, stuffing them all in his shirt.

"There you are," an official-sounding woman's voice said. "We need some information about your sister."

Danny turned, trying to look younger than his fifteen years, trying to look scared. This was no problem; he was panic-stricken. "My dad's on his way down. He'll give you all the information you need."

"Is that her purse?" the nurse said. She took it from him without waiting for his answer and began to go through it. "Were you with her when she had the abortion?"

"Gee, is that what's wrong with her?"

The nurse gave him a quick look, as though she couldn't quite believe he was for real. "Are you sure she's your sister and not your girlfriend?"

"Of course she's my sister."

"Let me see your driver's license," the woman said.

"I'm too young to drive," Danny protested.

"Then how did you get here?"

"We took a cab."

"From where?"

"My dad will be here soon." He tried to edge away.

"Oh, no you don't!" The woman grabbed his arm and marched him into her office. "You just wait right here until he shows up." She looked at him sharply. "If he shows up."

"He'll show up," Danny insisted.

He took the chair beside her desk and sat there trying not to acknowledge her eyes, studying him.

"I know you," she said suddenly.

Danny sucked in his breath, dreading her next words. He and Victoria would both be ruined.

"You've been in here before, haven't you?" the woman said. "Tonsils, I bet. I never forget a face."

"Tonsils," Danny agreed quickly. Then he sank back in the chair, lowering his voice to a whisper. "That was before my mom died. Dad's all we have now. This will just kill him." Danny started to cry, silently, letting the tears trickle down his cheeks.

"You poor thing," the woman said. She came around to kneel beside him and gave him a hug.

Danny let her crush him against her. She smelled like rubbing alcohol. Where the fuck was Owen? he wondered.

"Son!"

Danny had nodded off to sleep, sitting erect in the chair. Owen's voice woke him. "Dad?" he said, staying in character.

Owen looked at the woman and then back to Danny. "Could we be alone for a few minutes?" he asked her.

"Certainly," she said warmly. "I understand."

"What did you tell her?" Owen said when the door had closed behind the woman. "She acted like I was a saint."

"That my mom died and you were trying to hold the family together."

"Good work." Owen sat down behind the desk and dialed a number.

"How's Victoria?"

"No names," Owen said sharply. "It's me," he said into the phone. "The package is ready for transport. Yes. Yes. I'll meet you there later. I have to deliver the other package and talk to her grandparents." He listened for a moment. "Are you kidding? Sure they will. Think they want a story like this getting out?" He looked up at Danny and Danny realized that whoever was on the other end of the phone had asked about him. "No problem there," Owen said into the phone. "He handled it like a real pro. Right. See you there."

He hung up and hustled Danny out of the office. "How did you get here?" he asked when they reached the hospital entrance.

"I drove her Thunderbird."

Owen held out his palm. "Keys."

Danny handed them over. "Wait a minute." He fished in his shirt and brought out Victoria's IDs and checkbook, dropping those in Owen's palm also.

"That was smart," Owen told him. "Come on." He hurried across the parking lot.

"What about Victoria?" Danny asked, following him.

"She's being picked up by an ambulance. They'll transport her to a private clinic."

"Owen, wait!"

Owen waited.

"Is she going to die?"

"I don't think so. She lost a lot of blood, though. If you hadn't gotten her here right away, she would have. Get in the car, Danny."

Danny got in. Owen started the motor.

"They saw the T-Bird," Danny said suddenly. "I pulled up by the emergency room door and honked for them to come out."

"I'll take care of a couple of guys after I get you home. There won't be any problem." He paused. "Level with me, Danny. Was it you?"

Danny looked at him, stunned.

"I didn't think so. Did she say who it was?"

"She just said that he had arranged everything, but he wouldn't go with her." Danny clenched his fists. "I'd like to kill the son of a bitch."

"You and me both," Owen said wearily. "But you're out of this now. You haven't seen Victoria tonight. You went for a little joy ride with some friends."

"What about Victoria? Will this be in the papers?"

"Poor Victoria. She had an appendicitis attack. They barely got her to the clinic in time. If she pulls through there won't be any problems. Otherwise . . ." He shrugged. "I'll take you home and then I'm going to the clinic."

"I want to go with you to the clinic."

"No."

"Come on, Owen. If she didn't have an abortion, then there's no reason I can't go to the clinic. Round up Sharon, too. Take some pictures. I can see the caption: "*Charlie's Gang* Co-stars Worry about Nan."

Owen thought about it, rubbing his bald spot. He smiled suddenly. "That's good, Danny. That'll make it look more legit with Sharon there, too. Okay."

Danny slumped down in his seat, almost too weary to appreciate his small victory.

Dear God, please don't let Victoria die.

Emery inserted his key into Tina's lock, but found the night chain on. He slammed his shoulder against the door, but the chain held. "Tina!" he bellowed.

"Emery? Is that you? Are you trying to knock the door down? You scared me to death."

"Let me in," he told her.

She removed the chain and he shouldered his way through. "You don't have to be so rough, Emery," she protested. She wore a robe and nothing else.

"Who's here?" He looked around wildly and started for the bedroom.

"Nobody's here. I was painting my toenails. What's wrong with you?"

He looked in the bedroom anyway. He even stooped to look under the bed and checked the closet, shoving her clothes aside to make sure no one was hidden behind them.

"Emery?" Tina said from the doorway. "What are you looking for?"

"Your boyfriend," Emery said. He shoved past her to the bar and poured himself a shot of bourbon, downing it in one gulp.

"What the hell are you talking about?" She pulled her robe together. "You're my boyfriend, Emery, when you're not being tiresome."

"Here I thought you had reformed, you stupid cunt. I thought—" He broke off abruptly and poured himself another shot of bourbon. "I'm getting a divorce to marry you. I'll probably never see my kids again. Doesn't that mean anything to you?"

"Emery! I don't understand what's wrong."

"My father-in-law doesn't think I should divorce his daughter."

"So what else is new?"

"He especially doesn't think I should divorce her for a promiscuous bitch who's sleeping with Danny Garrick behind my back."

"Danny!" Tina's wide-eyed look of innocence was perfection itself. "Don't be stupid."

"Stupid!" He slapped her so hard her head snapped back.

She cringed, and he realized his hand was raised to slap her again. He clenched his jaw, trying to hold on to the ragged edges of his temper. "Don't lie to me, Tina," he said after a moment. "I'm risking my marriage and my career for you."

"Emery, I swear I'm not—"

The phone rang.

She stared at him.

"Let it ring," he said.

He poured himself another shot of bourbon, and tried to steady his breathing, to calm himself. To damp down the hot rage that had consumed him since the moment Ben Ledermann had told him Danny Garrick was fucking Tina. "And for that whore, you want to divorce my daughter?" Ledermann had screamed at him.

The phone continued to ring.

"Answer the fucking thing!" Emery bellowed.

Owen waited impatiently for Tina to put Emery on the line. Everything was under control. Nothing could go wrong. He wasn't going to let the fact that she had almost hung up on him bother him. But then when Emery came on the line, breathing hard, Owen knew what he had interrupted. Emery was fucking her. Danny was fucking her. There was no one that bitch wouldn't put out for.

Except him.

"Victoria Carr had an abortion tonight. It went wrong and she's in the hospital." He listened to Emery curse on the other end of the line. "I took care of everything," Owen said and covered the steps he had taken. He made sure to give himself credit for Danny's PR idea. No use letting it go to waste. The photographer had arrived before Owen left the hospital and Sharon was supposed to be on her way over.

"Fine," Emery muttered. "You stay on top of it. I've got to go now. I'm busy."

At what Owen could imagine, and the thought of that made him do something outside his ordinarily cautious character. This was a chance to break off the affair between Danny and Tina Sawyer—and get the little prick in trouble in the bargain. "What do you want me to do about Danny?"

"Danny? What about him?"

"He's the father." Owen smiled to himself. "We better put him under guard. No telling who he'll get to next," he added slyly.

"Where is he now?"

The strange note in Emery's voice chilled Owen, but he had said too much to back down. "He's still at the clinic. I'm going back there in a little while."

Owen heard a crash on the other end and then his call was disconnected.

The sweat started in his armpits, cold and clammy. He redialed Tina's number, and got a busy signal. He slammed down the receiver and dialed again, over and over, listening to the eternal busy signal, his terror mounting. When his call finally went through and Tina answered, he knew by her voice that his panic was justified.

"Owen, my God! I've been trying and trying to get you. What did you tell Emery? He left here saying he was going to kill Danny. I think he means it."

Of all the waiting rooms Danny had been in tonight, the clinic's was the nicest. There was real money here, and Danny wondered cynically if it was all payoff money like Owen's.

Danny had to admit Owen was certainly getting his money's worth. Sharon had shown up thirty minutes after the director left, looking wide-eyed and alarmed, and the two of them had their pictures taken just as Danny had suggested. Then he listened to a starched nurse give Sharon a lesson about appendixes with the aid of a three-dimensional figure, while the studio photographer again snapped photos. After that Sharon was sent home. The photographer left too.

He wished Owen would show up. He had no idea if the nurse on duty was in on the fake appendicitis story. When he asked her how Victoria was doing, she just said, "Fine, dear," and went back to her paperwork.

"Can I see her now?"

"Hadn't you better go home, Mr. Garrick?" the nurse asked, her voice as cool and starched as her uniform.

"Not until I've seen Victoria."

"She's not allowed any visitors tonight."

"Don't you understand? I brought her in."

"No, Mr. Garrick. You didn't. She came in by ambulance from her home." She lowered her glance to her paperwork once more.

He slammed his fist against the desk. "I want to see her! I want to make sure she's all right."

"She's receiving the best of care, Mr. Garrick. You can be sure of that."

"I won't be sure of anything until I see her myself."

"I'm afraid that's impossible."

"You better get somebody up here right now that can say it is possible or I'll tear this place apart."

Someone grabbed Danny's arm from behind. "Stow it, Garrick. What are you trying to do?"

He turned. The two men behind him looked vaguely familiar. He had seen them hanging around the producer's office before. "They won't tell me how Victoria's doing."

"Friedman wants to see you."

"Not now," Danny protested. "I want—"

They were on either side of him and his arm was twisted up behind his back in a way that made it extremely painful to move in any direction but the one they indicated.

"You're coming with us, Garrick."

He went.

"I don't care what you're doing," Owen threatened from the gate house. "You open this gate right now, Albert. Or you'll be sorry."

He didn't have to be more specific than that. Al knew exactly what Owen had on him. But neither of them had ever expected Owen to be so terrifyingly blunt about it. Hints, innuendos, suggestions, insinuations; that was Owen's way.

But not now, Owen thought, as the gate swung open and he burned up the drive with a shriek of rubber. There wasn't time for that now. How could he have been such a fool? He was the director of the most popular show on television and tonight he had managed to put his fifteen-year-old star in mortal danger.

Fat little Albert Wallace was the best Owen could do on short notice, but he should be good enough. Al Wallace was high enough up in the network hierarchy that Emery would have to listen to him. Luckily, Owen was in possession of some very titillating details of Al's financial life, enough to assure that Al would keep his mouth shut about whatever happened tonight.

He pulled up in front of the house just as Al emerged, tucking his shirt tail into his pants. Owen leaned across and unlocked the passenger door. Al barely had it closed before Owen put the car into gear and sped down the drive.

The studio was deserted. Danny had never seen it like this. He had stopped struggling, but the two men still held his arms. Their three pairs of footsteps echoed and reechoed through the empty soundstage.

The lights were on in Charlie Weston's study on the set of *Charlie's Gang*. It was eerie, Danny thought, to see Emery Friedman sitting behind Charlie Weston's desk. Almost as if he, Danny, were really Bucky after all, and his dad was about to administer punishment.

Friedman looked up at the sound of the footsteps, shielding his eyes from the glare of lights, as he peered into the darkness.

"It's us, Mr. F," one of the men called out.

"What's up?" Danny asked.

Friedman charged from behind the desk.

Danny tried to jerk away from the two men holding his arms, but they hung on. Then Friedman was on top of him.

His first blow caught Danny in the stomach. The second landed beneath his chin, snapping his head back.

Danny's knees folded. The two men pulled him erect and held him there.

Friedman continued to hammer on Danny's ribs and his belly. One rib went with a crack.

Now a blow landed on Danny's face, just above the eyebrow, and another on the right cheekbone.

"Not his face, Mr. F!" one of the men warned. But Friedman kept pounding.

The men released Danny.

He slumped to the floor, groaning, and Friedman followed him down, still hammering into Danny's unprotected flesh.

He didn't know when the blows stopped.

After a time, Danny realized that Friedman was no longer punishing him with his fists. He couldn't see anymore, but he could hear Friedman raging at his henchman for pulling him off.

"You'll kill him, Mr. F!" one of them said.

"I want to kill him," Friedman screamed, enraged. "But first I'm going to castrate the little bastard."

There wasn't a doubt in Danny's mind that was exactly what Emery was going to do.

Owen and Al Wallace tried the *Charlie's Gang* set last. They had tried half a dozen other places first, and now Owen was terribly afraid they were too late.

Al stopped when he saw Emery struggling with the two men. "Thugs," he whispered. "They're beating him up. We've got to get out of here, Owen."

Owen shoved Al on into the light. He had already realized that the two men were trying to hold that wild man off the boy. "Talk to the son of a bitch," he told Al. "Calm him down. Tell him what we're going to do."

They had worked it all out as they searched for Emery and Danny. All they needed was Danny alive and Emery's cooperation. Owen wondered if they would get either.

He almost puked when he saw Danny lying there on the floor of the *Charlie's Gang* set. If the boy was still alive, it would be a miracle. His face looked like he had gone through a meat grinder. Two stars in one night, he thought. That fucks the show.

And it's your own stupid fault, you meathead.

You and that bastard Emery.

Owen bent over the boy. Thank God there was still a pulse. Maybe, just maybe, things weren't entirely fucked.

There were other voices now, only Danny couldn't make out what they were saying through the bloody haze. He had never been hurt before—not so much as a sprained ankle— but he knew he was hurt now.

One of the voices came closer, and he finally recognized it as Owen Knox's. Making arrangements. Something about an automobile accident to cover things up. Of course. If anyone found out that the producer had beaten a kid star, they would all be up the creek.

Was it Tina, Danny wondered, or was it something else?

Money would smooth this over, he thought. Big money could hide anything. Just as it had turned Victoria's abortion into an appendicitis attack, it would turn this beating into an automobile accident.

". . . money," he moaned aloud.

Knox bent over him. "It's all right, Danny. We're going to get you to a hospital."

"And I end up in jail for beating up the little prick. No way." Emery Friedman's voice was jarringly close.

"Don't be stupid," Owen said. "We'll pay them off for this just like we did for Victoria."

". . . pay me, too." Danny fought to stay conscious while he forced the words out. "Cash."

"He's delirious," Al said.

". . . in a safe deposit box . . . key to my mother."

"The little son of a bitch," Friedman howled with rage. "I'm not paying him a dime."

"How much?" Owen asked him.

Figures kept dancing through his head. He wasn't sure which of them was real. Nausea churned in his belly. ". . . hundred thousand dollars . . . cash . . . when she gives me the key . . . I'll know . . . won't say anything to anyone. . . ."

"I don't have that kind of cash," Friedman snapped.

"You better get it," Owen told him.

"And if he dies?"

"Then the payoff will be the least of your concerns, Emery. You'll need a good criminal lawyer." Owen bent over Danny once more. "The money's yours, Danny. You can trust me. I'll get the key to your mother."

Danny grabbed Owen's arm. ". . . have to know," his voice trailed off and he was terrified he wouldn't get the words out.

The director leaned closer. "What do you want to know?"

"Victoria . . . is she okay?"

"She's going to be all right," Owen told him. "Just hang

on a little while longer, Danny. We have to get you in the car. Then we can call the ambulance."

". . . car?"

"Listen, Danny. You have to remember this. You were so upset over Victoria's appendicitis operation, that Friedman brought you to the studio to let you drive his car, to help you get your mind off her. He knew you were too young to get your license yet, but this was private property, so he didn't think there would be a problem. Only something went wrong with the car. The accelerator hung. You crashed it into a wall. That's how you got all banged up."

"Not my BMW," Emery howled. "It's handbuilt! Do you know how much that fucker's worth?"

"About five years in prison and never working in television again," Owen said calmly.

Danny was only dimly aware as they carried him out into the night air. One of Emery's men helped Al Wallace tie down the accelerator and then they sent the beautifully-engineered machine crashing into a wall. Danny almost passed out when they picked him up to load him into the ruined front seat. But he held on long enough to reach out and grabbed Owen's shirt. ". . . money . . ." he mumbled. "Don't forget the money. If my mother doesn't get the key, I blab."

"She'll get it," Owen promised. "Call the ambulance," he shouted to Al.

Nothing would be the same again, Emery thought, watching the dancing lights of the ambulance reflecting off the wreckage of the 507. In a funny way the convertible reminded him of Tina. Of himself and Tina. He had been such a fool to believe that she was finally all his, fool enough to wreck his marriage over her.

"Are you coming to the hospital with us?" Al asked him as the ambulance doors were slammed shut.

Friedman shook his head.

"It would be better if you do, Emery," Owen told him. "Stifle any rumors before they get started."

"Later," he said so softly that Owen had to lean forward to catch the words. "I'll be there later."

The ambulance left.

"We have to talk, Emery. You have to get the crash together."

"How am I going to get that kind of money?"

"Ledermann. He'll give it to you."

For a price. Emery ran his hand over the crumpled fender. The price would be that he dropped the divorce. Wily old Ben Ledermann would pay anything to keep his daughter from being dumped. Ben would also try to force him to fire Tina, to never see her again.

Emery looked down at his bloody knuckles. That price he couldn't pay. He had been a fool to believe she would ever be faithful. And to cuckold him with a kid!

But he wouldn't give her up, couldn't give her up.

He stroked the ruined metal. It could be repaired, repainted, but he would always know what lay beneath the restoration.

Emery sank down beside the fender and began to cry.

There was a woman weeping in the hospital bed. For a moment, Owen thought he had let himself into the wrong room. Then he realized that the woman was Victoria, and he was transfixed at the sight of her. The blue-black hair, the milky white skin were the same. But something had happened to her. Her face was thinner. Her cheekbones more prominent. Overnight she had changed from a girl to a woman and she was beautiful!

His first thought was what that might do to the show. She was, what, seventeen now? Next season it would be time for the writers to send her to college. Nan would still live at home, of course, but they could introduce new story lines about her problems with university life and that would give Charlie Weston plenty of opportunity to wax philosophic, something that Nick could really get his teeth into.

The thought of Nick reminded Owen why he had come. So far she hadn't cracked, hadn't told anyone, as far as he knew, that it was Nick Hanson who'd knocked her up. She hadn't even admitted it to Owen himself. Not that she needed to; he knew Nick's modus operandi far too well.

But he kept remembering how Danny looked, beaten to a pulp by that wild man Friedman. He didn't want Friedman's rage turned against him. *Especially* Owen didn't want Friedman finding out that he had recommended Nick for the show in spite of knowing Nick's hang-up.

Owen cleared his throat.

Victoria started, and then hurriedly daubed at her eyes. "I didn't hear you come in," she said quickly.

He walked over to the bed and took her hand in his. "Why are you crying, Victoria? There's nothing to worry about. I've taken care of everything."

A delicate flush spread over her skin. ". . . I appreciate what you've done . . . Owen." She stumbled over the name. He had asked her to call him by his first name, and she was making an effort. "I'm so glad no one knows the truth. It would just kill my grandparents."

So Florence Stanton hadn't told her granddaughter that it was mostly her money that went into the substantial payoffs required to keep this juicy little tidbit quiet. If the old lady wanted to keep it like that, it was fine with Owen. He didn't mind taking more credit than he deserved from Victoria. It would make the girl—the woman, he corrected himself, as he surreptitiously watched her breasts rise and fall beneath the bed jacket—that much easier to control. "No one has to know, Victoria. I told you that. Just as no one has to know the father's name," he hinted.

"I won't tell anyone. I promised you that, and I meant it."

"So why are you crying, Victoria? What's wrong? You can tell me."

The lovely dark eyes brimmed over with tears. "It's Danny."

"Danny?"

"I know what happened to him. I heard some of the nurses talking. It's not fair, Mr. . . . Owen. He was only trying to help me. Someone beat him up for that, didn't they?"

Christ, the money he had paid, and the nurses stand around gossiping. As soon as he left this room, he'd talk to the administrator about that one. But right now, he had to make sure this question didn't come up again. He frowned. "I had hoped to spare you this, Victoria. But it seems I can't. Danny isn't what you think."

"What do you mean?" Her voice climbed toward hysteria. "He was wonderful to me!"

"You're a big girl now, old enough to have a little dalliance of your own. You have to realize Danny is, too."

"Is too, what?" she whispered.

"Danny took a chance by making love to the producer's mistress. He's been having an affair with Tina for over a year. Friedman found out." Owen shrugged, trying to look casual while hoping to God he wasn't making a mistake. "You might say that Danny only got what he deserved. A kid like that . . ." He shook his head. 'Who would have thought it?"

Victoria's face had gone dead white.

"You won't repeat any of this, I know, Victoria. You and I have to have our little secrets. To look out for each other. Right?"

"Right," she whispered, and turned her face to the wall.

Owen stood up. He could see the silent tears trickling down her face. "I'll be in to see you tomorrow, Victoria."

Victoria kept her face to the wall until the door had closed behind Owen Knox. Somehow the news about Danny was the worst thing that had happened to her. It was crazy. After all the years of thinking of Danny as a little kid, when he came to her rescue she had seen him in an entirely new light. Lying here, thinking how wonderful he had been to her that awful night, she had been stupid enough to think she was falling in love with him! And for over a year, he and Tina . . .

For a brief moment in time, she had felt that she knew Danny, really knew him. Now, she realized he was a complete stranger.

She blotted her tears on the sheet, gently so her eyes wouldn't puff, and took a deep breath. Then she eased herself out of bed and walked slowly over to the mirror. Ever since that awful experience, and the way her body had reacted— had *betrayed* her!—she had treated herself as though she were made of fragile porcelain and might shatter at the slightest jar.

Cautiously, she began to brush her hair. Her grandmother was coming at 2 P.M. She had less than half an hour to hide the traces of her tears. She stopped brushing and leaned forward to study her eyes in the mirror.

So much for romantic novels. There was nothing in that clear gaze to indicate what she had gone through. Thank goodness her grandparents had not been told the truth of Victoria's hospital stay. They, and the public, thought it was an emergency appendectomy, just as Owen had arranged. Not by a single glance or gesture had Florence Stanton indicated to her that it might be anything else. Victoria was determined to do everything she could to shelter her grandmother from the real reason she was here.

There were so many things she needed to shelter Grandmother from, she thought desperately. The terrible secret of her own birth, the botched abortion, and then the awful thing the doctor had told her this morning. The thing she couldn't bear to repeat, even to Owen Knox.

"You'll never have children, Miss Carr. The damage was just too extensive," he had said in his cold, clinical voice, wiping out dreams she never realized she had until they were gone forever.

But it was a good thing, Victoria had told herself, as she lay with the silent tears trickling down her face after the doctor left. She couldn't tell him or anyone that she was the product of incest. Who knew what genetic problems might be lurking if she'd had children of her own?

As she lay alone in the hospital bed after the doctor left, she had made a vow to herself. Somehow she would manage to become financially independent. The most important thing in the world to her now was to get her grandmother out of Vincent Stanton's control. To accomplish that she would need cash.

Hurriedly, she applied makeup, trying to bring a healthy glow back to her pale cheeks, and then climbed back into bed. When her grandmother's tentative knock sounded on the door to her room, Victoria smiled to herself. Vincent Stanton had made his wife afraid of life itself; Victoria would try to change all that.

Florence Stanton pushed into the room, followed by Joseph Moretti, Vincent Stanton's lawyer. "Your grandfather just didn't feel like getting out," she explained to her granddaughter. "You know how much he hates hospitals. Ever since . . ." Her voice dwindled away. Victoria knew. Ever since the accident that paralyzed him, Vincent Stanton had an almost unreasoning hatred of hospitals. "Joseph drove me."

Joseph Moretti was a handsome and distinguished man in his early forties. A widower, Victoria remembered, and her smile glowed warmer.

Moretti had a sudden dazed look on his face, as though he had just looked directly into the sun. He leaned across the bed to take the hand she offered.

"Mr. Moretti," she said warmly. "How nice to see you again. It's been years." It had, too. At least, ten. She wondered if he watched her on television, because he obviously did not expect to see someone quite so grown-up lying in the hospital bed.

"My God!" he said abruptly. "You're a woman, Victoria!" Then he remembered himself abruptly. "Sorry, Florence," he told her grandmother. "It's just that I remember her as a tyke, racing through the house on her tricycle."

"I have a Thunderbird now." Victoria smiled again, putting more into it this time. It had just occurred to her that if anyone would know how to take control of her grandfather's finances, it would be Joseph Moretti.

Chapter Seven

Owen rifled through the sheaf of clippings on his desk. They couldn't be better if he'd staged the events of last season himself. The series had gone into early reruns because of the accidents, and the public clamor for new episodes was gratifying. The news stories on Victoria's "appendicitis attack" and Danny's "accident" had roused public interest in the show to a fever pitch. Even Sharon had gotten her share of attention. "*Charlie's Gang* Troubles To Come In Threes?" one headline worried, and another asked "Is Little JoJo Next?"

Charlie's Gang was the one bright spot in Newton Minow's "vast wasteland." The new FCC chairman had just sent the industry reeling with that phrase in his speech to the National Association of Broadcasters. But Newton's complaint about "formula comedies with unbelievable families" had gladdened Owen's heart. Because if *Charlie's Gang* had one overwhelming trait, it was the complete believability of the Weston family.

They were your next door neighbors, the family across the street. They were the family you wished *yours* was. The show grabbed people where they lived.

Sometimes it even got to him.

Who had a perfect family anyway? His wasn't.

No cookies-and-warm-milk mom for him. His mother had been an elusive redheaded beauty, never home for her three children. Her drab bookkeeper husband was certainly no Charlie Weston. He was too busy making money to have time for the kids. Too busy to notice that only Owen, the oldest, looked at all like him. Too busy to notice his old lady was fucking half of Winnetka.

Owen never got back to Illinois anymore. It depressed him too much. The gorgeous redhead had been replaced by a shriveled old prune. His sister and brother still squabbled like children. His dad was completely bald now, his scalp as pink as a baby's butt.

Owen found himself rubbing his own bald spot and jerked his hand away.

He sifted through the clippings again. This fifth year of *Charlie's Gang* would be the show's best season ever. He couldn't wait to begin production. But this year he would stay on top of things. Nothing, absolutely nothing, would happen on this show that he didn't know about. And he wouldn't be stupid again.

He had been stupid twice. Once when he put Nick Hanson up for the part of Charlie Weston. And once when he lied to Emery about Danny Garrick.

Owen grinned with spiteful delight. He had relished forcing Emery to wreck that cocky little sports car more than anything he had in a long time. He knew at the time there were alternative ways to cover up Danny's beating, but nothing else would have given Owen quite so much malicious pleasure as seeing Emery's shiny toy crumpled against that wall.

He hadn't dared to approach Nick Hanson about his involvement with Victoria. He was terrified Emery might find out he'd lied, that he'd known all along that Danny wasn't really responsible for Victoria's problem. Owen had no desire to have that wild man after him!

Danny Garrick's every move was going to be watched; Owen had already taken care of that. The only fly in the ointment he could see was that Emery was giving every indication of acting like a real producer this season. Having Friedman hanging around the set was the last thing Owen wanted. There was no way in the world that Tina could get to Danny this year, and Owen knew that she wouldn't go without a man for long.

This time maybe he had a chance with her.

That redheaded slut!

Only not slut enough to sleep with you, a little voice taunted in his brain.

When he daydreamed about Tina's lush body, Owen knew he would do anything to get her into the sack.

Anything.

He realized he had crumpled the sheaf of clippings in his clenched fist. Owen smoothed them flat again.

"*Charlie's Gang* Troubles To Come In Threes?" the top headline warned.

And Owen knew he couldn't afford to be stupid for the third time.

He caught himself rubbing the bald spot again and swore loudly enough to bring his secretary running in.

Victoria pulled four of the diaries from their hiding place in her closet and carried them back to bed with her. Somehow just seeing her mother's handwriting scrawled on these pages gave her courage to face tomorrow, the start of the new season. She wasn't sure she could have gone through with it otherwise.

She wondered how many of the people on *Charlie's Gang* knew the truth. That her "appendicitis attack" had really been an abortion. That Danny's "car accident" had actually been a brutal beating. Brutal enough that Danny's crutches would have to be written into the first scripts as a high school football injury.

What liars adults were.

Thea had known that too.

Victoria hugged the thin leather-bound book to her chest. Thea had been fifteen when she wrote in this volume so long ago. Three years younger than Victoria, but already old enough to wonder why no one realized what was going on between Vincent Stanton and his daughter.

Victoria read the diaries until nearly midnight, dipping into one after the other, hoping to find a courage that would help her to face tomorrow.

She had no idea anyone else was up in the still, silent house until her grandmother opened the door and walked in without knocking. "Why haven't you gone to bed?" Florence Stanton demanded.

"I was just about to, Grandmother." Victoria tried to slip the diaries she'd been reading under the covers. The movement caught Florence's eye. She grabbed one from Victoria's hands and opened it.

Victoria had never seen that look on her grandmother's face before.

"Where are the rest?" Florence asked in a quiet, terrible voice.

"Grandmother . . ."

"Where are they?"

Victoria got up and showed her the hiding place. Florence scooped up the rest of the diaries.

"Grandmother, please don't . . ." Victoria faltered. How could she say it aloud? Don't open those diaries. If you do, you'll find out that your husband and your daughter committed incest. That your granddaughter . . . "Please don't read those," she begged.

"*He* gave you these, didn't he?" her grandmother screamed in sudden rage. "I told him we should burn them! Years ago! I told him!"

Before Victoria could react, Florence Stanton had carried the diaries away.

It wasn't the loss of her mother's words that held her immobile, gasping short panicky breaths. It was the sudden revelation that Florence Stanton had known all along what was happening. That the grandmother Victoria had thought she was protecting had actually been a silent accomplice to the seduction of her own daughter by her husband.

What liars adults were!

Sharon hid in the closet and plotted murder. Ever since Inga Lindholm had come to take care of Andrew things had been different.

For the first time that Sharon could remember she and Andrew had separate nurses. Hers was a young nervous woman named Marilyn, whose main job consisted of driving Sharon back and forth to the studio.

Andrew's companion was Inga. A blonde, statuesque Swede, 5'10" tall and muscled like a man, Inga had come back with Cynthia and Keith Bradford after their last trip to England. She had high, hard cheekbones and deep-set pale blue eyes that watched everything, especially Sharon. Every time Sharon tried to talk to Andrew, Inga pounced on her, shoving her away.

Marilyn would have been easy to elude if it were not for

Inga. Inga continually scolded the other girl, telling her how lazy she was, making her watch Sharon's every action.

That was mean enough. But the worse part was that Sharon was no longer allowed to play with Andrew. To tell him about her day, she had to wait until everyone else was asleep and then sneak into his room.

And every time Sharon tried to talk to her father about Inga, he brushed her off.

These days, he was here at the Beverly Hills house most of the time. It seemed as though her mother and father had come to some kind of agreement, because they were always together now. Somehow that seemed like Inga's fault.

For a while Sharon had been sure that her mother and father would get a divorce. Mother had come back to Los Angeles. Then Father had shown up and there had been yelling and screaming. The two of them had gone off to England together, still fighting. They were gone for a whole month and when they returned Inga Lindholm was with them.

That was when things had changed.

Now there were new rules, Inga's rules. And there was no way around them. Inga was bright and young. Unlike her old nurses and nannies Sharon could neither outthink her nor outrun her.

Her parents would do nothing to change the rules. Andrew was doing better they said, meaning that he didn't cry as much, or break his toys. That was all they cared about; that they weren't bothered. They were so pleased with Inga that they were going to help her get her citizenship. That meant she would never go away!

It had been so easy to get rid of other nurses. It would have been so easy to get rid of Marilyn if Inga weren't around to coach her.

So Sharon sat in the closet of the playroom and tried to think of ways to murder Inga.

Only she wasn't sure Andrew would still love her if she did. Sometimes it seemed like he loved Inga more than he did her now. Maybe what she should do was ask Andrew to help her murder Inga. Then she would know that he really loved her the most.

Satisfied with that, Sharon opened the door a crack and peeked out. Andrew sat across the room, playing quietly with a set of blocks.

Sharon hissed at him, but her twin didn't look up.

She stuck her head further through the opening and some-one seized her by the hair, yanking her forward.

"Andrew!" she screamed, but he wouldn't even look her way as Inga pulled her across her knee and began to paddle her bottom.

She was more angry than hurt when Inga finally released her. She sprang away, tears of rage streaming down her face. "I'll tell!" she threatened.

"And who will you tell, little Sharon?" Inga asked with a grin. 'You're parents have told me I should do what I must to keep Andrew improving. You're a bad influence on him and they know it."

"I'm not," Sharon screamed. "Andrew! Tell her you love me best!"

He did look up then and she could see the silent tears that had been running down his face too. She darted toward him, but Inga was too fast for her.

The girl grabbed Sharon. Clamping her hand firmly over Sharon's mouth, Inga hustled her from the room and down the hall to Sharon's own bedroom. There Marilyn sat reading, and Inga berated her for being so stupid and lazy. "Ameri-cans!" she muttered as she dumped Sharon on the bed.

"If you don't leave me alone, I'm going to cut off my hair and say you did it," Sharon screamed at Inga. "Then my father will make you go away!"

"You are a spoiled brat, which your father knows. If you cut off your hair, they will make you wear a hot scratchy wig." Inga moved closer and there was a definite threat in those pale blue eyes. "I might just cut off your hair myself," she threatened. 'You would hate the wig every day. It would remind you not to cross me."

"No," Sharon screamed and scrambled across the bed to Marilyn. "Marilyn won't let you."

Marilyn giggled. "I think I'll help her," she said. "All you do is try to get us both in trouble."

"Get out!" Sharon screeched at them. "Both of you. Just get out of my room."

"Come, Marilyn," Inga said, and added slyly, "There's a wig catalog in my room. We'll see if we can find a really scratchy one for our little angel."

"You won't! You won't! My father won't let you!" Sharon screamed at them. But deep down she wasn't sure that was true.

Flashbulbs popped as Victoria walked into the soundstage. The press shoved forward, enclosing her in their midst as they clamored their questions. Danny, on his crutches, was surrounded by his own group of reporters, and the third knot must be encircling little Sharon, although Sharon herself wasn't visible in the crush.

Extraordinary, Victoria thought as the media people hammered at her with their questions. Not a single one of them appeared to doubt the PR stories they had been fed. It was amazing what money could do, she realized. Unbelievable what power it could give one. She hadn't forgotten that vow she had made to herself in her hospital bed: to become financially independent of her grandfather. Then she had been thinking solely of getting her grandmother out of Vincent Stanton's control. Now, for the first time, it occurred to her that she could use the power of money in her own behalf.

But that thought fled as Danny looked up and caught her eye. Quickly she turned away to answer a reporter's question. She couldn't stand to see that yearning look in his eyes. Couldn't bear to think what he knew about her. Neither could she stand to think what she knew about herself. Of what she knew about her family.

She had felt like a sleepwalker ever since last night.

She thought of all the lies, all the convoluted explanations she had come up with to protect her grandmother.

What a *fool* she had been!

Danny leaned on his crutches and watched Victoria deal with the press. He couldn't believe how much she had changed. She was thinner and paler, but the thinness made the delicate bones of her face more prominent. The photographers kept exclaiming over her. She had always been beautiful. Now she was extraordinary.

When the crowd around Victoria began to thin, he started toward her. He hadn't really made any kind of conscious decision about what he would say to her, or what he would do. He just wanted to be with her, to talk to her.

A stagehand stepped in front of him, blocking his way.

"Excuse me," Danny muttered, trying to maneuver around him. But the man stuck out his foot, blocking Danny's left crutch.

Angrily, Danny shoved past him, but it was too late. Victoria had already moved away.

Twenty minutes later he spotted her again, talking to the studio teacher. He had almost reached her, when a stagehand, a different one this time, set a chair right in front of him.

"Hey!"

"You look tired, Garrick. Have a seat."

"Get out of my way."

"Sure." The stagehand moved the chair, but Victoria had strolled off with the teacher, and the opportunity was lost.

The stagehand was still watching him and Danny realized suddenly that the man was ready to move in front of him with the chair again if necessary. He also realized that none of this had been accidental.

Someone, probably Owen Knox or Emery Friedman, was making sure he had no time alone with Victoria. But there were ways around anything.

Danny made his way laboriously to the classroom. By the time someone finally came in search of him, a note to Victoria was hidden in his pants' pocket. All he needed was a change to pass it to her.

The chance came later that afternoon when the whole *Charlie's Gang* cast was called back on to the set for a group photograph. Danny was shoved in between Victoria and Sharon, and he took that moment to surreptitiously slip the note into Victoria's hand.

When the photographer finished, Danny glanced over at Victoria. She looked him right in the eyes as she opened her hand and dropped the unopened note, letting it flutter to the floor. She turned and walked swiftly away.

A stagehand hovered near him, but Danny didn't try to follow her. He wouldn't be allowed near her, he could see that now. The only way he'd be able to talk to her would be with her cooperation.

It was obvious he wasn't going to get it.

Sharon waited patiently after the photographer had finished

taking pictures of everyone, hoping that Danny or Victoria would say something to her. Neither one of them did. They had changed so much she felt like she hardly knew them anymore, and they didn't act like they wanted to know her. Eleven probably seemed like too much of a baby to them. At any rate, Victoria at eighteen and Danny at sixteen seemed like distant grown-ups to her. And these days she hated grown-ups.

Grown-ups never wanted to talk to you, never had any time for you.

She was sure Inga was being mean to Andrew! She had tried and tried to talk to her father about it, but he wouldn't listen. Mother never had, but in the past Keith Bradford had at least pretended to be interested in the twins. But not any more.

"Andrew is Inga's responsibility now," Keith Bradford had told his daughter. "Your mother and I are leaving everything to her. We won't interfere."

And stupid Marilyn wouldn't listen. She acted like she admired Inga, but Sharon could tell she was afraid of the tall Swedish girl too.

So was Andrew.

Sharon was desperately afraid that Inga was hurting him when no one was looking.

But who could she talk to about it?

"Miss JoJo! Why so sad?"

Sharon turned around quickly to find Nick Hanson smiling at her.

She almost walked away.

She hadn't forgotten last year and how mean Nick and Victoria had been to her.

She hadn't forgotten that Nick was a grown-up. One of the enemy.

But he was smiling at her.

Tentatively she smiled back.

No more bullshit, Emery swore to himself, as he went back to his office. The producer was supposed to be responsible for the style of the show. Not the fucking director. Not the fag story editor. Not the asshole writers. Some people had forgotten that quintessential fact of life, and it was time they were

reminded of it. *Charlie's Gang* was his show and he was
taking control of it.

As far as Emery was concerned, Owen Knox's days were
numbered. So were Danny Garrick's. Emery was not reconciled to losing his BMW so that a teenage prick could get
away with screwing half the world. Somehow, someway, he
would remove both those bastards from his show.

The only good thing that had come out of last season's
fiasco was that Tina had at long last settled down. She never
would admit she'd been screwing the Garrick kid. But if she
had, beating the shit out of the kid had put an end to it.

Unfortunately, Ben Ledermann had indeed used the loan of
the payoff money to force Emery to drop the divorce proceedings. Just the whisper of a story that Friedman had beaten his
child star would put *Charlie's Gang* off the air. So Emery had
knuckled under to most of Ledermann's demands in order to
come up with the money to keep Danny Garrick's mouth
buttoned. But not all of them.

Margaret and the kids had come back home, and they were
all living there like polite strangers. He and Margaret never
discussed any of it. Tina's name wasn't mentioned between
them. But Margaret must have known that Emery had refused
to let Ledermann pressure him into firing Tina or agreeing not
to see her again.

You could only push a man so far. Eventually, in spite of
Ledermann's money and influence, Emery planned to divorce
Margaret and make Tina his wife.

Step one in that direction was to make *Charlie's Gang* the
best goddamned show on television. He had to make himself
known as Emery Friedman, producer of one of the top-rated
shows of the season, not Emery Friedman, Ben Ledermann's
son-in-law.

Because that last was a temporary state, one he intended to
end by the time this season was over.

Victoria overheard Nick Hanson say a cheerful good morning to Sharon as he walked into the rehearsal hall. Sharon
beamed up at their television father.

Victoria dug her fingernails into her palms to keep herself
from screaming at the two of them. How could it be starting
again? Not after all she'd sacrificed. It just wasn't fair!

She wanted to weep when she saw Sharon thawing toward Nick Hanson. There wasn't a thing she could do about it. Sharon was far too young to understand what was going on and far too wary of Victoria after last season to listen to anything she might say.

She and Sharon and Danny must be wonderful actors, Victoria thought sullenly. To be so estranged in private and still manage to come across as warm, loving siblings on the television screen.

She didn't want to worry about Sharon, not now. She didn't want to think about anything at all. Her whole world had been turned upside down.

But she couldn't ignore Sharon and the situation she could see developing between Sharon and Nick Hanson.

Victoria understood exactly what Nick was trying to do. The thought of Sharon having to endure the same degrading mental anguish she suffered made Victoria decide to act. But once that decision was made, she found herself stymied. What could she actually do? Who could she turn to?

Briefly the thought of Danny surfaced. She pushed it away. The memory of how she had misjudged him was too humiliating.

But what had happened to Danny at Emery Friedman's hands gave her an idea.

It was a cruel idea, something she wouldn't have done previously. But the revelation of Florence Stanton's guilt gave her the strength to carry it out.

"Victoria!" Owen's voice right beside her made her jump. "I said we're ready to begin now."

Victoria took her place at the table.

Nick sat beside Sharon.

I'll do what I have to do, Victoria vowed to herself. Whatever I have to do.

Bored! Bored! Bored!

Tina was about to go out of her mind with boredom.

She drummed a pencil on her clipboard and watched the actors on the kitchen set. That wonderful time with Danny was over. It might as well have never existed. She wasn't fool enough to try and bring it back either. Tina knew that Emery was having Danny watched. He wasn't entirely sure whether to believe his father-in-law or not, and she wasn't going to give the old bastard any ammunition.

But she craved variety again, and variety was what she was definitely *not* getting just now. She looked around, frowning. There wasn't a single new cock in sight.

She'd already bedded almost everyone on *Charlie's Gang* during the first weeks of the new season's filming. Danny, her sweet, wildly impressive Danny, was watched too closely for them to get together any more. And although Owen had been trying wildly for four—no—five years to get her into bed, Tina couldn't stand him.

That left Nick Hanson.

Everybody liked Nick. Even Emery. And Emery didn't suspect that she'd love to see what Nick was like in the sack. "Everybody's father figure," one of the trades had called him and she guessed that was true.

Not that *her* father had been like Nick. No, her dad was a fat-bellied slob who cared more for a televised baseball game and a six-pack than a daughter.

She really wondered, given his inattention and her mom's wispy grasp on reality, why she'd waited so long to start screwing around.

Oh, well, thank God for slow starters. They ended up with a fast finish.

Nick walked by her when she left the set, and she gave him a slow sensual smile guaranteed to delight.

Nick noticed the redheaded charmer smiling at him as he left the set. He smiled back, but he kept walking. Nick hadn't gotten as far as he had by being incautious, and he was one of the few people who knew the real story behind what happened to Danny Garrick. A delightful little nurse had told him all about it.

But that was only part of the reason he avoided Tina Sawyer. She was too old to still possess that virginal purity that turned Nick on. He wouldn't have been able to get it up for her if he tried, and he had no intention of revealing his sexual leaning to a woman who was intimate with half of Hollywood.

Victoria was a different story. She had always been a lovely young girl; now she was something spectacular. Their little tryst last season hadn't marred her innocence. If any-thing, it had only enhanced it. This year, she was truly Nan Weston, schoolgirl virgin.

And she had proven to be the soul of discretion as well. He'd been apprehensive that Owen Knox might find out he was the cause of Victoria's little problem. But Owen had remained silent on the subject, so Nick knew he'd gotten away free on that one.

He hoped very much that he might be able to renew his friendship with Miss Carr.

But in the meantime, he would amuse himself by trying to lure Sharon, wary little fawn that she was, back into his life.

Tina had never thought she'd be bored enough to enjoy lunching with a female, but Victoria Carr had turned out to be something entirely different from what she'd imagined. They'd fallen into the habit of eating their cottage cheese and carrot sticks together each day. Tina found herself enjoying the fact that every male eye was on them. And she positively relished the fact that Emery was so pleased about her new buddy.

"What do you two find to talk about?" he kept asking her.

She'd lower her glance demurely and say, "Girl stuff."

God knows what Emery thought that meant, but he was satisfied. As for Tina, Victoria was sort of a little sister that she had to clue in on how the world worked. After all, Victoria had already learned quite a bit about it. Tina knew all about the abortion. Frankly, she'd never thought the kid had it in her. Just went to show you how deep still waters ran.

She'd even gotten the name of the guy out of Victoria. Something even Emery hadn't been able to do.

And who would have thought it!

Talk about hidden talent in your own backyard!

Tina had always been kind of interested in Nick Hanson. Now she was practically frothing at the mouth to get at him. But he was turning out to be skittish as a virgin.

"I'm going to die if I don't get him into bed with me," she whispered to Victoria for the fifth time that week. "I can't even get him to stop and talk."

"Men," said Victoria with disgust. "The ones you don't want are always after you and the ones you want are always running away."

"That's the truth."

"Too bad we can't . . ." She trailed off, blushing.

"We can't what?" Tina demanded.

"You know, trick him. Not that he wouldn't want to go to bed with you," she added in a rush, as though she feared she might have hurt her new friend's feelings. "He's asked me to meet him a couple of times, but I . . ."

"You're like me," Tina sympathized. "Always wanting what you can't have."

"You could have it," Victoria said cautiously. "If you did want to play a trick on Nick."

"And he was good, right? You really enjoyed it?"

"Sure." Victoria's smile wavered. "But . . . but it wouldn't really be honest, Tina."

"Honest! You think the male animal is honest with us?"

It took exactly fifteen minutes for Tina to talk Victoria into the scheme, but that was all right because Victoria had allowed thirty.

It took only a couple of seductive looks and a short whispered conversation to convince Nick Hanson she was as desperate to get together with him as he was with her. "But not here, Nick. Some place where we can really be alone."

Nick suggested a motel's name with such alacrity that she knew he must have used it many times before.

Tina was overjoyed when Victoria told her it was all set. Nick would arrive at the motel and find Tina there instead of Victoria. Tina had unlimited self-confidence. "He won't be able to resist me," the redhead bragged. "No one ever has. It will be a good joke on Nick, and he'll *love* the punch line."

Victoria didn't contradict her. It really didn't matter what happened after Nick and Tina arrived at the motel. The fact that they were there together would be enough to arouse Emery Friedman's well-known temper.

That was what she was counting on.

"I know something you don't know," Victoria taunted Sharon. They were alone in the classroom.

"What?" Sharon asked warily. She hadn't forgotten that Victoria was a meany, but it was hard to keep a little thrill of pleasure from rising up inside her. Victoria sounded like big sister Nan when she said that, and it would be so much fun to play Nan and JoJo without the scripts, just like they really were sisters. "What, Victoria?" she demanded when the other girl remained silent.

"It's about Tina Sawyer and Nick Hanson."

Sharon lost interest. This wasn't going to be any fun.

"Mr. Friedman would like to know what I heard," Victoria went on. "But then Tina would find out I told and I'd get in trouble."

Sharon considered this. Mr. Friedman never talked to her, not since the first season when he picked her for the show. If she told him something interesting, he might pay more attention to her. Besides, she didn't like Tina Sawyer very much. Tina had been Danny's friend and now she was Victoria's friend, but she had never tried to be Sharon's friend. "I could tell Mr. Friedman for you," she offered.

"You'd tell him I told you and then I'd get in trouble."

"No I won't. I swear I won't, Victoria."

"Swear then."

"Cross my heart and hope to die, I won't tell anyone you told me."

"But you're such a baby. You'll forget to tell him. Or you'll get it wrong."

"I won't. I'll write it down," she said. "You tell me what to say."

Sharon had to beg and beg to get Victoria do it, but finally Victoria agreed. Sharon sat there happily copying down what Victoria said in big neat letters so Mr. Friedman wouldn't have any trouble reading it at all.

But after Victoria finished, Sharon was disappointed. "Is that all? He won't care about this."

"Yes he will," Victoria told her. "You'll see. He's in his office now. You go ahead and take it to him. And don't show it to anyone else."

Victoria almost lost her nerve when she saw Sharon trudge off in the direction of Emery Friedman's office with the note. If her plan worked, Friedman would beat Nick Hanson to a bloody pulp. Did she want to be responsible for that?

She thought about Sharon and what Nick planned to do to her.

And she knew she had to do whatever it took to keep Nick away from Sharon.

Mr. Friedman's office was scary. It reminded Sharon of when she sneaked out of the children's wing at home. She knew she didn't belong here, and she worried that someone would suddenly appear and order her out.

She could hear Mr. Friedman in the inner office, talking on the phone, but she couldn't decide whether or not she should go on in and give him the note. What if it was a trick? What if Victoria was just trying to get her in trouble?

As far as Sharon knew, Victoria had never told anyone about all the mean things Sharon had done to her last season. At the time, Sharon had been so mad she didn't care whether Victoria told or not. But then, after Victoria got sick and Danny got hurt, Sharon was so worried about them both that she was sorry she had been so awful. She would hate it if she couldn't play JoJo anymore. If she couldn't be with Nan and Bucky, it would be almost as bad as losing Andrew.

But maybe Victoria was still mad about last season. The note crinkled in Sharon's pocket, but she couldn't decide what to do.

Framed photographs of all the *Charlie's Gang* stars hung on one of the office walls. Sharon walked down the line until she found her picture. She could tell by the dress she wore that these were the new photographs that had been taken only a few weeks ago.

Miranda Patton's photograph drew her attention because there wasn't a single wrinkle on Miranda's face. Sharon wondered how they did that, because the real Miranda was as wrinkly as she could be.

Danny's picture smiling at her made her smile back. She wished there was a picture of Andrew here, too. Maybe if the note made Mr. Friedman happy, he'd put a picture of Andrew right beside hers.

Thinking about Andrew helped her decide. She took a deep breath and then walked into Emery Friedman's private office.

Mr. Friedman raised his eyebrows in surprise when he saw her. "I'll get back to you later," he said into the phone and hung up. "What is it, Sharon?"

It was a good thing Victoria had made her write it down,

because when he said that, Sharon couldn't think of a single thing to say. She just held the note out to him silently.

He took it, a puzzled frown on his face, and skimmed through it. When he finished reading and looked up at her, his face was so angry that she took a step backwards.

"Where did you get this?"

Victoria had told her what to say. The words came back to her like a script. "I heard them talking and I wrote it down."

"Who else knows?"

"Nobody."

Mr. Friedman crumpled the note into a ball and pitched it into the wastebasket. "Goddamned bitch," he said and Sharon wasn't sure if he was talking to her or not. He seemed to have forgotten her presence, because the next thing he did was grab his coat and stride out of the office without saying another word.

She could have cried. He wasn't happy at all. Victoria was still a meany.

Sharon knelt down beside the overflowing wastebasket and fished around until she found the crumpled ball of paper that had been the note. She smoothed it out and stuck it back in her pocket.

She was probably going to be in trouble for wandering around again, she thought dismally as she left Mr. Friedman's office. In the corridor, she bumped into Owen Knox.

He said, "Hello, Sharon," and kept walking.

She thought just a minute. Victoria had told her not to show the note to anyone else, but she hadn't said Sharon couldn't *tell* the note to anyone.

She ran to catch up with Owen.

"I know something," she bragged, and like always, he began to tease to get it out of her.

When he found out that Tina Sawyer was supposed to meet Nick Hanson at a motel on Sunset Boulevard that night at seven, he was so happy he patted her on the head and gave her a five dollar bill.

Best of all, he didn't ask her who else she had told. There was absolutely no way she could get in trouble.

"Nick," Owen said sternly. "I've heard some very distressing information about you. It's come to my attention that you're planning on meeting a certain female tonight at a motel on Sunset.''

Nick turned pasty white and for a startled moment Owen thought the older man was having a heart attack. "It was her idea," he blurted.

"I'm sure it was." That redheaded bitch! There was no one on the show she hadn't gotten to. No one except him. "But I think it would be a good idea if you didn't keep that little appointment, don't you?"

Nick agreed with such alacrity it was almost disappointing. You'd think he'd been caught with one of his jailbait girlfriends. "Don't worry about passing the message along to Tina," Nick said, rubbing it in.

"Tina?"

"I'll tell her myself that you won't be coming." Owen leered. 'No pun intended."

Nick looked as though he wanted to protest.

"Anything wrong?" Owen taunted, enjoying himself.

Whatever Nick intended to say, he thought better of it. He left Owen's office with his tail between his legs.

Tina was going to be one lonely lady this evening at that Sunset Boulevard motel. Owen would make sure she didn't have to wait alone for long.

Chapter Eight

Owen knocked lightly on the motel room door. When there was no response, he put his ear to the wood. He could hear the shower running inside.

He knocked louder.

The shower cut off. In a moment Tina opened the door, wearing an inadequate towel and a smile. The smile vanished when she saw Owen standing there. The blue eyes, so warm for everyone else, turned cold for him. He pushed inside before she could slam the door.

Tina retreated across the room. "What are you doing here?" She pulled the towel tighter, making her breasts swell above it.

"Expecting someone else?"

"Get out!"

"Why do you always treat me so badly, Tina?" It was a kid's whine, and it shamed Owen that it had escaped him.

She darted to the phone and lifted the receiver. "I'm calling Emery. He'll make you sorry you ever set foot in this room."

Owen grinned at her maliciously. "What about you? Who will you tell him you were here to meet? Does he have any idea what kind of a slut you are?"

Tina slammed down the receiver down. "I'm warning you, Owen. You better get out of here."

"We're going to have a good time. You're going to find out what you've been missing all these years."

He came closer and she backed up a few steps, toward the

bathroom. He rushed her then and she bolted inside the
bathroom, losing the towel. She tried to slam the door in his
face.

Owen put his shoulder to the door, forcing it open, and
sent her stumbling back against the toilet. She attempted
to push around him but she slipped on the wet tiles, falling to her knees. He grabbed her around the waist and
pulled her to her feet, trying to drag her out of the bathroom.
Tina fought him every step of the way, clutching the bathroom door frame, kicking at him.

Owen snatched a handful of her hair, yanking her head
back at a painful angle. She released the door frame to scratch
at his face with her nails, and he shoved her into the bedroom
toward the king-sized bed. When he forced her down on it,
Tina tried to scramble away. He fell on top of her heavily,
knocking the air out of her, so that she lay there stunned, the
blue eyes no longer cold, but wide with disbelief and fright.
Owen yanked his pants down, not even bothering to step out
of them, before he was on her like an animal, jabbing at her
with his penis.

God, he thought he was going to explode before he could
get it in her. She had recovered enough now to twist away,
keeping him from driving home, while her breasts bobbed
around wildly.

Jesus! All these years of waiting and he didn't want to
come on the sheets!

He drove his knee into her stomach, and when she went
slack beneath him, he rammed home in one continuous lunge
that must have taken him halfway to her tonsils.

Behind him, the door crashed open. "You whore!" Emery
Friedman screamed.

Tina shrieked, "Emery! Emery!"

Owen tried to disengage, to pull out, but she brought up
her legs to hold him and clawed at his face with her nails.

When Emery grabbed him around the waist and flung him
off Tina, Owen knew he was a dead man.

That whore!

Emery had dreamed of her like this, and the sight of her
now with another man, her damp hair curling wildly, her
creamy breasts mashed against his chest, her legs wrapped

around his hips, clinging to him as he bucked against her, was more than Emery's sanity could stand.

Emery flung the man off of her, not registering who it was through the red killing haze that possessed him. Even to the last the bitch clung to her lover, reaching out for the man's face with her hands, and that only increased Emery's fury.

His first blow caught her on the side of her face, and her shocked expression infuriated him even more. She wouldn't think it was wrong to fuck someone else. Anyone else. Everyone else.

"Slut!" he roared at her. "You slut! You whore!" His next blow caught her in the center of one of those ripe breasts and she squalled with pain.

Her lover leaped on Emery's back, trying futilely to pin his arms. Emery flung him off.

Tina, shrieking, tried to roll away. He followed her with hard, punishing blows to her body.

But it was her face that infuriated him, the false smile which promised it was only for him, though it was really for everyone. Anyone.

He hit her in the face, and she screamed.

He hit her in the face again.

And again.

And again.

And again.

She kept on screaming until he silenced her with a fist to her mouth. He felt her teeth go.

And he hit her again.

Owen scrambled from the room, zipping his pants as he ran. Tina's screams and Owen's curses followed him into the parking lot. He hesitated for a moment outside, and looked toward the motel office. He wasn't going to be the one who went back in there with a madman. But to call the police—

Tina's screams stopped abruptly.

"Hey," a fat woman in an open doorway two rooms down yelled at him in the sudden silence. "What's going on in there?"

Owen ducked his head and ran to his car. He climbed inside and fumbled in his pants for the key, praying it hadn't fallen out back there in the motel room. The fat woman hurried down to the open doorway and looked inside.

Owen found the car key and jammed it into the ignition finally. As the engine roared to life, the fat woman began to shriek. Owen burned out of the parking lot, praying that no one had gotten his license number.

On Sunset Boulevard a police car, its lights and sirens going, passed him, heading in the direction of the motel.

Owen pounded the steering wheel.

Friedman, you bastard! What have you done?

The news was all over the soundstage the next morning. The cast and crew clustered in little knots, exchanging their sparse information.

"Did you hear . . ?"

"The police report said . . ."

"No, it was . . ."

"Well, *I* heard . . ."

There was agreement on two points. Tina Sawyer, the producer's redheaded mistress, was hospitalized in critical condition. And Emery Friedman was in jail.

Owen Knox appeared, white and shaken, late in the morning. "I'm sure you all know by now that there's been an accident . . ."

"Cut the crap, Owen." That was Miranda Patton. "Are they going to can the show?"

"I don't know yet." He paused. "Things don't look good. For someone with that low standard of morals to be producing a show like this . . ."

Miranda snorted loudly.

"It's in all the papers," Owen went doggedly on. "No sponsor likes that kind of coverage."

She wasn't going to faint!

Victoria stood with her fists clenched, letting her fingernails bite into her palms, listening to Owen drone on. He had instructions from on high about dealing with the press on this. Rule number one was no interviews that weren't first cleared by the network and the sponsor.

"I heard Tina's face looked like raw hamburger," someone whispered behind Victoria, and a wave of nausea almost overwhelmed her.

What in the world had gone wrong? Why had Tina been beaten? The rumor flying around the set this morning was that Emery Friedman had found her in that motel room with another man, but no one had even mentioned Nick Hanson's name in connection with the incident. Nick himself walked around from group to group, listening to the gossip, and giving his own opinions in that calm, fatherly voice that belonged to Charlie Weston.

What had gone wrong? Why had Emery beaten Tina? From what everyone was saying this morning, Tina had been hurt much worse than Danny. That wasn't what she had intended.

Was it?

Or was she subconsciously hoping that Emery Friedman would react that violently? Had she been hoping that he would actually kill Nick Hanson? Had she allowed fantasy and reality to mix? Was she trying to punish her ''Father'' on the show for what her grandfather/father had done in real life?

Victoria had the most awful feeling that was exactly what she had done. And Tina was the one who had suffered for it.

She looked up. Nick Hanson glared at her from across the set.

He knew! She could tell he knew!

This time nausea got the better of her and she fled.

That vicious bitch, Nick thought, as he watched Victoria hurry away. He wanted to howl his outrage. She had tried to set him up. If she had succeeded, it would be him in that hospital bed instead of Tina Sawyer. Nick had no illusions about his ability to protect himself against a younger, angrier man. Emery Friedman would have beaten him to a pulp. Nick's classic face wouldn't be worth shit after that.

It was easy enough now to see why Victoria had done it. Just as looking back, he could see why she had cooperated so easily with her own seduction.

Sharon Bradford was the key.

Victoria had tried her best to keep him away from Sharon. Well, he had been toying with that tasty little morsel long enough. Time to sample it. And to let Miss Victoria Carr know after he did.

*   *   *

Sharon didn't understand why Nick was supposed to take her home instead of Marilyn—especially since Marilyn was right there—but she didn't care. She'd much rather be with Nick any old day than with dopey Marilyn.

Or with Inga.

She wondered if Marilyn would get in trouble with Inga over this.

Probably not, she decided, as she watched Marilyn pocket the bills Nick had handed her. Marilyn might be stupid about other things, but she was smart where money was concerned. Smart enough not to let Inga know she had it.

Too bad she didn't get an allowance, Sharon thought as she obediently followed Nick out to his car. It would be easy to get along with Marilyn if she had an allowance and could give the girl money like Nick had. Sharon had never seen Marilyn as happy as when Nick paid her.

When she saw Sharon's companion getting into her car alone, Victoria knew immediately what had happened. Across the lot, she could see Nick's car pulling out. Sharon's blond hair was visible through the passenger window.

Victoria looked around desperately for help.

When she saw Danny limping out of the soundstage, she ran toward him.

Danny hadn't believed what he heard when the words came tumbling out of Victoria, but he climbed into the Thunderbird with her anyway, easing his mended leg in carefully. If Victoria thought Sharon was in some kind of trouble, that was enough for him. Sharon was a cute kid and sometimes he found himself believing the eleven-year-old really was his little sister.

But that wasn't the reason he had climbed in beside Victoria without a moment's hesitation. The truth was he would do anything, go anywhere, just for the chance at a few moments alone with her.

Victoria wheeled through traffic like a stunt driver, keeping Nick Hanson's big Lincoln in sight ahead. When the Continental pulled into a motel, Victoria parked on the street.

Danny looked at the motel's sign with amazement. "That's the same motel where Tina . . ."

She nodded grimly. "Nick's favorite place." She got out of the T-Bird and walked swiftly toward the motel.

Danny followed her, trying hard to keep up. He still found it hard to put his full weight on his busted leg. "What's that got to do with it?" He had heard the rumors that Friedman caught Tina with someone. But Nick's name hadn't been mentioned.

"I tried to set Nick up so Mr. Friedman would catch him with Tina and beat him like he did you. I couldn't think of any other way to make him let Sharon alone." Nick's Continental was parked by the motel office. He came out, key in hand, and got back in. "I made sure Mr. Friedman knew Nick was meeting Tina here. Only something went wrong. Someone else must have showed up instead of Nick. I never meant for Tina to get hurt," she said over her shoulder. "I just wanted Nick to quit bothering Sharon."

Danny grabbed her arm and spun her around. "It was Nick last year, wasn't it?"

"Yes!" She pulled away and started to run. The Lincoln had pulled into a slot in front of a room. Nick got out and quickly hustled Sharon inside.

Danny limped after Victoria, fury building inside of him.

"Come over here, Sharon." Nick patted the bed beside him. She was a lovely little thing, he thought, as she crossed over to him. Eleven years old. Poised just on the edge of becoming a woman. A girl this age was so much purer than older girls. That was what Owen Knox had not been able to understand.

Nick had made a mistake with Victoria. She no longer possessed this wonderful purity. She had passed over into that mysterious land of womanhood. Nick found that terrifying. Give him an innocent girl-child like this one any day.

Sharon sat down on the bed beside him and looked up into his face with her trusting green eyes.

His penis was fully erect in his trousers.

"Give me your hand," Nick told her.

Victoria paused outside the door, uncertain what to do

next. Should they ask the manager to call the police? Surely someone would believe what Nick was up to now.

Before she could suggest that to Danny, Sharon's muffled exclamation came through the door.

Danny hit the door with his shoulder. Until that moment, Victoria hadn't realized how nearly grown he was. The door gave way before him, and he crashed into the room, sprawling on the carpet. Victoria rushed in behind him.

Nick sat on the bed holding Sharon in his arms. It looked like a scene from any *Charlie's Gang* script: Charlie Weston and JoJo.

Only Charlie Weston had his pants unzipped and his penis hanging out.

And JoJo was screaming in terror, trying to break free of his grasp.

"What the hell do you think you're doing?" Nick yelled at them. "Get out of here!" But there was none of Charlie Weston's authority in that order. Instead there was a thin quaver of fear.

He rose, still holding Sharon's arm. Danny stood up, favoring his mended leg, and advanced to meet him.

"Let go of her, Nick!" Victoria yelled at him.

Nick ignored her. "I told you to get out of here, Danny."

Danny swung at him, and his fist connected with Nick's jaw.

"Not in the face, you idiot!" Nick released Sharon, who shrank back against the wall, and raised both hands to protect his face. When he did, Danny brought his good knee up into the older man's crotch.

Nick screamed and fell forward, right into Danny's next punch, which sent him backwards, against the nightstand.

Nick slid down the carpet and lay there.

"Get up you son of a bitch," Danny raged at him. Nick remained immobile. Cautiously Danny bent over him. He felt for Nick's pulse.

After a moment, Danny stood up. He turned a pale, panic-stricken face to Victoria. "He's dead."

Sharon burst into noisy tears, and ran to Victoria, throwing her arms around Victoria's waist.

Victoria put her arms around Sharon automatically. "He

can't be! You didn't hit him that hard.'' The voice came from a long way off. It didn't sound like her own.

Danny sat down heavily on the side of the rumpled bed, staring at Nick's body. ''I think I'm going to throw up.'' He looked it.

Sharon clung to Victoria as though she would never let go. Victoria hugged her closer. Danny stared at her with frightened, vulnerable eyes, and Sharon's anxious face turned toward her, too. It was as though both of them were expecting *her* to do something, to make the decisions for the three of them.

Danny confirmed it. ''Should I call the police?''

Wouldn't the papers have a field day with it? She could just see the headlines: ''Bucky Kills Dad. Nan and JoJo Watch.'' And it wasn't even their fault! Would anyone believe them about Nick Hanson, about what kind of man he was? The police would question them, all three of them. They would dig into everyone's lives. They would ask her how she had known what Nick planned. Victoria's arms tightened convulsively around Sharon. ''We're not going to call the police,'' she said firmly. She knelt down in front of Sharon, so that they were face to face. ''Listen to me, Sharon. None of us want to go to jail.''

Sharon sobbed louder, and Victoria had to give her a shake to quieten her.

''What happened to Nick wasn't our fault,'' Victoria told her. ''You know it was an accident, don't you? Danny and I were trying to help you.''

Sharon nodded. ''He was bad, though,'' she said with sudden force. ''He tried to do bad things.''

''And we stopped him. But it's not right that we should get into trouble because he was bad, is it?''

Sharon shook her head.

''Then you have to help us.''

Some of the color had returned to Danny's face. ''What are you going to do?''

Victoria looked at Nick's body with distaste. ''Help me get him up on the bed.''

It took both of them tugging and pulling to get Nick's limp form back on the mattress. Sharon had retreated to the door and she hovered there, refusing to touch Nick's body. It was

Danny who performed the loathsome task of zipping Charlie Weston's trousers.

"Now what?" Danny asked her.

"Cigarettes and matches. We'll make it look like he was smoking in bed. He fell asleep with a lighted cigarette in his hand."

Danny took Nick's cigarettes from the bedside table and lit one. He puffed on it, until the end glowed. Then he paused and looked straight at Victoria.

She wavered for a moment, unable to say the words. The horror of what they were about to do was too strong. Then she thought of the police and reporters who would pry into her life—and what they would find—and she said, "Do it!"

Danny dropped the cigarette beside Nick's body. They waited just long enough to make sure it was smouldering against the sheet, and then the three of them ran out of the room.

"There's a pay phone across the street," Victoria told them as they cut across the parking lot. "We'll call the motel office from there when we're sure the fire is going. That way it won't get out of hand. No one will be hurt."

They piled into the Thunderbird and drove the few hundred feet to the phone. As soon as they were sure the fire was under control, they'd leave, Victoria told herself. Everything was going to be okay. There was no way anyone could connect the three of them with this. She knew that Nick would have gone out of his way when he registered to make sure that no one at the motel knew that Sharon was with him.

Victoria parked and rushed over to the phone booth. Of course, the directory had been stolen. She called information for the motel's phone number.

"Do you see any smoke yet?" she asked Danny and Sharon, standing outside the booth, their eyes fastened on the motel. "I'll call as soon as you do."

Sharon shook her head.

"Maybe you should go ahead and call," Danny said nervously. "What if . . . ?"

Whatever he had been about to say was lost when the door of the motel room burst open. A flaming figure ran from the building. The figure had run twenty feet before Victoria's stunned mind could comprehend what that horrible human torch was.

And then Nick Hanson screamed.

He kept running.

And screaming.

Half-way across the parking lot, he stumbled and fell, writhing in agony on the pavement. The screams went on and on.

And then they stopped.

People ran out of the other rooms. Someone threw a blanket over the burning man.

Victoria's vision was blocked by the gathering crowd.

Danny turned and threw up.

All the feeling had gone out of Victoria.

"He wasn't dead, Victoria," Sharon cried. "He wasn't dead. What are we going to do?"

Danny stopped retching. Still kneeling on the pavement, he stared up at her with sickened eyes.

If she let feeling come back, she would crumple to the sidewalk. And if that happened who would take care of Danny and Sharon?

They were her family, she thought. Her real family. Her only family. She wasn't going to let any harm come to them. She pushed sensation away. It was there waiting, and she might drown in it later, might sicken and die from it later, but for now Sharon and Danny were all that mattered.

No one had noticed them yet. There was still time to get away. "Get in the car," she ordered sharply. They obeyed immediately.

She pulled out from the curb and into the traffic. "What are we going to do?" Sharon wailed. Danny said nothing. He was looking over his shoulder at the traffic behind them like he expected a police car to pull them over at any minute.

"We're not going to do anything." Victoria couldn't believe how calm and mature her own voice sounded. "I'm going to take you and Danny home and none of us is going to say anything to anyone. Do you understand?"

"Why can't we tell?" Sharon protested. "Nick was bad. We didn't do anything wrong."

"We murdered him," Victoria said flatly. "If anyone finds out we'll go to jail. All three of us. Do you want that?"

Danny quit watching for the police and swung around to face her. "For God's sake, Victoria! It was an accident!"

"It was an accident until we lit the match. We killed him with that match the same as if we had shot him or stabbed him."

"Danny did it," Sharon said, pouting.

"We all did it," Victoria told her. "If you hadn't gone to the motel with Nick, Danny and I wouldn't have gone there either. We were only there to try and protect you because you're like our real sister. Danny knocked Nick down to save you from him. He lit the match, but I told him to do it. So we all did it." She felt so much older than both of them. "But we're safe. No one will ever know about this but the three of us."

She pulled over to the side of the road, with the motor still running, so that she could look at both of them. Sharon was still sulking. The full reality of what just happened hadn't really sunk in yet. Danny looked green, as though he might throw up at any moment. "Swear you won't say anything to anyone, Danny. No one ever has to know. Swear!" she said harshly when he hesitated.

"I swear," he said slowly.

"You, too, Sharon. Swear you won't tell anyone."

"You and Danny will get in trouble. It wasn't my fault," Sharon said, her chin lifted stubbornly.

"It was your fault for going to the motel with him. You knew you weren't supposed to do that."

"But—"

"Swear! You mustn't tell anyone on the show. Or the police. Or your parents. Or your nurse. Swear it."

Finally, she swore.

Victoria pulled back into the traffic. But burned into her vision, as if she'd stared too long into the afternoon sun, was an image of a fiery human figure writhing in pain.

She knew it would never go away.

Just shows you what a fast worker can do, Owen thought with great satisfaction as he sat down behind his desk with a pile of scripts. He'd gotten himself lined up to direct this new medical show for next season before the official announce-

ment that *Charlie's Gang* was cancelled even hit the trades.
And this show was going to be hot. A real winner.

He hadn't needed to see it in writing to realize *Charlie's
Gang* was finished. Over. Kaput. He'd watched Emery pound
it to death with his fists. When Tina's beating hit the papers,
the great American public was dismayed and outraged that
three sweet young children had been allowed to work with
such a terrible man.

The sponsor withdrew immediately; no sponsor, no show.
That was the way it went in TV land. Win some, lose some,
Owen thought. Medical shows were the coming thing, any-
way. Look how well *Dr. Kildare* and *Ben Casey* were doing.
This one would put both of those in the shade.

Too bad Nick wasn't around to star as the older doctor. He
would have been perfect for the part and since this wasn't
going to be a kiddy show, Owen wouldn't have had to worry
about Nick's extracurricular activities on this one.

No one had paid much attention to poor Nick's death. It
was an anticlimax. The show was already defunct. Hell of a
way for a man to end up. Burned blacker than a new bride's
toast. When the police told him Nick was dead, Owen had
braced himself for the rest of the bad news. He just knew that
Nick had been in that motel room with one of his underage
girlfriends. But no refugees from the cradle had surfaced.
Rumor had it that Nick was despondent over Tina Sawyer's
injuries. Just went to show how you could misjudge someone.

Stupid to smoke in bed like that. Owen had never been a
heavy smoker. After he identified Nick's body in the morgue,
he'd given it up entirely. He knew he couldn't count on too
much more luck in this life. He'd already used up his fair
share that night with Tina.

He'd waited and waited for Emery to point the finger at
him as the man who had been in that hotel room with Tina.
No chance Tina would. Too much brain damage from the
beating Owen had given her. Owen had even gone to visit the
bastard in jail, unable to stand the suspense any longer.

God, Emery had been a dismal sight. A broken man,
slobbering and weeping. Made you sick to your stomach to
look at him.

But the visit served a purpose.

He listened to Emery go through the whole sickening story

twice, and the one bright gleam in all that misery as far as Owen was concerned was that Emery had been too enraged, too single-minded in his fury, to remember the face of the man he'd caught screwing Tina.

So Owen was safe.

And his reputation was intact.

Actually, it was still increasing. Even though production of *Charlie's Gang* had ended, the reruns had started immediately and they were nearly as popular as the new episodes had been. A lot of people were giving Owen the credit for that and he wasn't one to deny it.

No doubt about it, that show had been one of a kind. The Weston family really got to people. All kinds of people.

Hell, sometimes he even watched the show himself.

BOOK TWO:
Victoria, Daniel, and Sharon

SCRIPT CHANGES FOR TV REUNION SPEC

Patton's Death To Be Followed
By Demise Of TV's Best Known Mom

The death of veteran actress Miranda Patton last week of lung cancer will necessitate changes in the *Charlie's Gang* TV reunion special script, announced Nayco Entertainment Group prexy Owen Knox. Although in ill health for several months, Patton was set to repeat her role as Mary Weston, TV's quintessential American Mom, in the TV special, *Whatever Happened to Charlie's Gang?* Knox, who was the director of the original *Charlie's Gang* series, said that the new script will begin with the gathering of the Weston children for the funeral of Mary Weston and will include remembrances of Patton, one of the original clean-the-house-in-high-heels-and-pearls Moms of the fifties' TV scene.

Knox refuted rumors that tragedy still dogs the cast of the classic fifties series, claiming no connection existed between the show and the unexplained suicide last year of

(Continued on Page 16, Column 3)

Chapter Nine

1962

"You've got to help me get out of here," Victoria told Joseph Moretti. "Otherwise I'll go crazy!" She looked anything but crazy silhouetted against the azure Pacific, the cool ocean breeze whipping her hair into a midnight black frenzy around her face.

"Here?" the lawyer said with a gentle smile. She was such a delight, so much like a woman on the outside while she remained the impetuous young Nan underneath. If only he were twenty instead of forty-four. "This doesn't seem to be such a bad place, Victoria." They stood a hundred feet above the ocean on a jagged palisade that afforded them a spectacular panoramic view of the seacoast and the secluded beach below. The paved area beneath their feet led back through a grove of slender Washington palms to Vincent Stanton's cavernous old house. Joseph knew that his client spent many hours here in his wheelchair, watching the breakers below, and he added, idly, "Your grandfather loves this spot."

Victoria made an impatient noise and turned her back to him. So much a child still, Joseph thought. Thank goodness the influence of that vile man who produced *Charlie's Gang* had not affected her in any way. But that stray thought helped

155

him to understand her restlessness. "I understand that you miss the show, but—"

"I don't miss the show at all!" she exclaimed as she swung around to face him. "It's time to get on with my life. I'm almost nineteen. I want to go to college this fall."

"I'm sure Vincent won't object . . ." On second thought, Joseph wasn't sure at all. His longtime client had shown amazing resistance to the idea of his granddaughter growing up or leaving home.

"Of course he won't object if I go to UCLA, but I don't want to! I want to go somewhere in the East."

"I know just the school for you." Joseph had just gotten his most prominent client's son into Harvard. That had been tricky considering the boy's grades and behavior. But Victoria would present no such problem. He hadn't realized until just now that the boy and Victoria were almost the same age. Perhaps something could be arranged between the two of them. "What would you say to Radcliffe?"

Victoria gasped with delight. "Oh, Joseph! Do you really think you could talk my grandparents into it?"

Joseph Moretti knew he would certainly try. Anything to hear her say his name again with that raising tone of elation.

"Yes, he's here," the detective said, holding the phone to his ear with his left shoulder, as he watched the sullen boy who sat on the other side of the desk. "Not in a cell, in my office." Although he would have much rather the boy had been in a cell. Danny Garrick smelled like a wino after a night in a Denver alley. The detective lit a cheap cigar to block the stench. "Tell her he's fine. A few scratches, that's all. Wait a minute." He held out the phone.

The boy made no move to take it.

"It's your mother, Garrick."

Danny Garrick shook his head. "I don't want to talk to her. She'll just cry."

She was crying now. It took several minutes to get her off the line and the LAPD back on. Good thing their department was picking up the tab for the call and not his, the detective thought as he took down the arrangements they had made to turn the boy back over to his mother. Real VIP treatment for the kid. The same as he had gotten here. Hell, everybody loved Bucky Weston. Even the patrolman Garrick had slugged last night when he was recognized and dragged out of the alley held no grudge. "The kid's got a solid punch," he had bragged like a proud father after he brought the boy in.

When the detective hung up the phone, he gave the boy a hard look. Danny Garrick was seventeen now, according to the LAPD, but he still looked like Bucky. A little older. A little harder, maybe. But that carefree kid was still visible underneath the dirt and blond stubble on that famous face. It would be a shame to see Bucky become a juvenile delinquent. Bad example for a lot of other kids who still watched the show in reruns. Time for a little father-to-son-type talk. The kind Charlie Weston had always used on Bucky. The kind, the detective thought with a small flash of shame, that he never found time to give his own three boys. "The LAPD said this is the second time you've run away in six months. You think that's fair to your mother, Garrick?"

The boy looked at him sullenly without replying.

"I used to watch you on television," the detective said abruptly.

The boy's head cocked, challengingly. "So?"

"So get hold of yourself." The detective played his trump card. "What would Charlie Weston think if he could see you now?"

The boy laughed.

He kept on laughing.

The detective wondered if the kid was on drugs.

Sharon hummed as she packed her clothes into the suitcases. It had been Inga who came and told her to get ready for a trip to Europe, but Mother and Father had arranged it. She and Andrew hardly went anywhere with Mother and Father. A month ago her parents had taken the twins and Inga and Marilyn up to their cabin in the mountains. Only it wasn't a cabin, it was a real house. And it wasn't any fun either. Inga wouldn't let her play with Andrew and Marilyn didn't want to go outside in the woods, so Sharon had gotten bored. That was why she had gotten spanked for playing with her mother's makeup case, and why she and Marilyn and Inga and Andrew had all come home early. Inga had been so mad at Marilyn that Marilyn had finally decided to quit two weeks ago. Sharon had been waiting and waiting to find out who her new nurse would be. But instead of a new nurse, she was getting a trip to Europe!

When she finished packing her own clothes, Sharon dragged a suitcase into Andrew's room and began to pack his things too. Inga hadn't said anything about going to Europe with them. Sharon had sneaked into her room early this morning and hadn't been able to find a suitcase anywhere. That was why she was so happy. It would be like old times with just her and Andrew. And no Inga.

Day after tomorrow would be their twelfth birthday and she would love nothing better than to spend it somewhere else. Inga had already told her that it was silly to have two birthday cakes and Sharon knew Andrew wouldn't like that: he loved having a birthday cake all his own.

Inga came in while Sharon was packing Andrew's things and stood there watching, her arms folded across her chest. It was strange but until Inga's birthday, Sharon hadn't realized Inga was the same age as Victoria, just nineteen. Somehow she seemed older. Besides Inga looked like a man with her stocky build and short blonde hair. The last time Sharon saw Victoria, she was even prettier than she had been when they were on the series.

Sharon and Victoria had been interviewed together after *Charlie's Gang* went off the air. Sharon hadn't enjoyed it much. Danny wasn't there, and Victoria answered most of the questions. She gave Sharon a quelling look whenever Nick Hanson's name came up. Not that Sharon wanted to talk about Nick anyway, especially to Victoria.

The thought of Victoria made her feel guilty. She had broken a promise to Victoria the night Nick Hanson died and she was deathly afraid Victoria might have found out. Otherwise, she was sure Victoria would have gotten in touch with her in the months since the interview. She missed Victoria and Danny so much she almost cried when she thought about it.

She missed Nan and Bucky and JoJo so much that sometimes she did cry about it.

And Charlie Weston.

She didn't miss Nick Hanson, not one little bit. But she missed JoJo's mom and dad and Miss Rand, JoJo's teacher, and even mean old Henry Kaiser, the boy next door who was always getting JoJo into terrible trouble.

She had tried to talk to her parents about doing another show like *Charlie's Gang,* but her mother had said, "No, no, no. Too much trouble." So now Sharon had to go to regular school with regular kids, and she hated it!

All the other kids had known each other forever and nobody wanted a new friend. Especially a chubby smart aleck who had been on television.

She was chubby, all right, but she didn't think she was a smart aleck just because she always knew the answers in class and had trouble waiting for her turn to say them.

Everyone else thought so, though, so she didn't have a single friend in the whole school, including teachers.

All she had left now was Andrew.

Inga never let her see him for more than a few minutes at a time, but at least he was there, and at night sometimes she could sneak into his room.

The news of the trip was the best thing that could have happened. Especially since Inga wasn't doing any packing.

She closed the suitcase full of Andrew's clothes and turned around to find Inga still standing there. But now Inga was smiling.

Sharon didn't like it when Inga smiled.

Bad things happened when Inga smiled.

All through dinner Vincent Stanton's eyes were on her. He knows I'm up to something, Victoria thought. Joseph Moretti dined with them occasionally, but this time it was at her request and not her grandfather's. Florence Stanton seemed to sense something was in the air, too, and she chattered nervously into any small silence.

Moretti himself was cool under fire, a charming dinner companion. So charming that occasionally Victoria found herself forgetting exactly why she had invited him there and relaxed enough to simply enjoy his company.

A dangerous thing to do, she reminded herself. When one wanted something as badly as she wanted to be free of her grandfather, it didn't pay to relax for a moment.

She had never realized just how much *Charlie's Gang* had really meant to her until the show ended so abruptly. At least heaven had been on their side. Nick Hanson's death was considered simply a tragic accident. The question of why Nick had been in that motel in the afternoon was deftly brushed aside. Besides, the damage had already been done by Tina's beating at the hands of Emery Friedman. The sponsor withdrew as soon as word of that reached the press and that was enough to force *Charlie's Gang* off the air. At first Victoria had been told it was only temporary, that the show would go back on the air as soon as a replacement was found for Nick. But the public was dismayed and outraged that the three sweet young children they saw each week on the small screen had been allowed to work with such terrible people. Thee wasn't a sponsor in the world willing to get mixed up in *that*. Everyone believed Victoria, Danny, and Sharon were the three innocent children they played on TV. No one saw behind the masks.

No one but us, Victoria thought.

Although production of the show stopped, reruns began immediately. She never went near the television set now. She was terrified she might flip it on and see Nick Hanson's face staring at her.

She had planned to wait until dinner was over to set off her bombshell, but suddenly she found she could not. The urge to see Vincent Stanton's eyes when he realized he had been outmaneuvered was too strong. She knew victory was certain. He would never refuse in front of Joseph Moretti to allow her to go off to school. Because wanting to leave home for college was a normal emotion, and above all, Vincent Stanton would want their relationship to appear normal.

Victoria waited until her grandmother had finished telling a story about her garden club to Joseph, waving her hands coquettishly.

"Grandfather, Grandmother," she said solemnly. "I asked Joseph to dinner tonight so that we could celebrate something he's helped me do." Vincent Stanton stirred and she was sure that it was her use of the lawyer's first name that upset him. "I've been admitted to Radcliffe!" At least she could still act. There wasn't the slightest suspicion in her voice that she expected anything but praise and admiration from her grandparents.

"You've got quite a girl here," Moretti said quickly. "I

can only tell you that Radcliffe is very eager to have her among its students.''

Florence Stanton turned to look at her husband. After a long moment she turned back to Victoria. ''We . . . we're so happy for you, dear.''

And that was that.

Victoria stared at her grandfather with a face fully as impassive as his own. I'm your daughter, after all, she thought triumphantly.

Vincent Stanton no longer looked so intimidating to her. He and Florence were really old, much older than she had realized before. They couldn't live forever. Someday they would be sick, incapacitated. Some day they would no longer be able to manage their finances. And on that day, she would be able to free herself of them finally, by taking control of them financially.

Beneath the table, Joseph Moretti squeezed her hand in congratulation, and she squeezed back.

It was at that moment Victoria decided she was going to marry him.

It was strange waking up in his own bed again after two weeks on the road. Strange being bathed and clean-shaven after living like an animal. Danny had slept naked. There was no Rosita in the house anymore to worry about her charge. Danny was surprised to find he missed the little brown woman. In many ways, she had been more like a mother to him than Beth. Maybe that was why Beth had let her go finally. Danny rolled out of bed, pulled on his swim trunks, and went down to swim laps.

Beth Garrick had picked him in Denver yesterday and raved at him all the way from the police station to the airport. ''Do you realize you could have been killed?'' she demanded. ''Where did you think you were going?''

When he told her New York, she was just as puzzled as if he had said the moon. The truth was that it didn't really matter where he went. If he'd been in New York, he'd have thumbed for Hollywood. Right now anyplace he was was the place he couldn't stand to be.

Every time he closed his eyes, he could see the flaming

torch that had been Nick Hanson running across that motel parking lot.

No one knew. No one had even questioned him about Nick's death.

Sometimes he thought that if he only had the luxury of confessing to someone, everything would be all right. But of course he couldn't.

It wasn't fear of what would happen to him that kept him silent, either. Punishment would have been a relief.

But he couldn't bear to implicate Victoria.

He dived into the Olympic-sized pool from the high board and then began to swim his laps. This was his ritual every morning when he was home. Sometimes, if he swum until he had exhausted himself enough, he could forget about Nick and Victoria and the whole mess. At least for a little while.

This morning it wasn't working. Danny gave up finally and pulled himself out of the pool. He went into the cabana to change from the wet swim trunks into cutoff jeans, not bothering with undershorts.

At the table beside the pool, orange juice was waiting. So were his mother and two of her female friends. New friends. Beth had gained a lot of new female friends since *Charlie's Gang* went off the air. All of whom wanted to meet Danny. He nodded and picked up a glass of juice.

The female friends were the real reason Beth was so frantic when he took off. She was afraid her newfound friends wouldn't hang around if her son wasn't home. "I could have you put in a juvenile home," she had threatened in Denver. But Danny knew how empty a threat that was.

She wouldn't dare send him away. Instead she would do anything she could to keep him from having a life of his own, from leaving her. She would never turn over his father's money to him, not until she was forced to. And she wouldn't give him control of his *Charlie's Gang* money, either. But even though she had passed along the safe deposit key Owen Knox had given her, she didn't know anything about the payoff he had received from Emery Friedman after his beating at Friedman's hands. That money tempted him, sitting untouched in the safe deposit box, but Daniel wasn't going to spend it. That payoff would make a big difference to him someday and he knew it. He'd paid for it with his blood; he ought to get some use out of it.

Anyway, Danny had discovered he didn't have to spend any money around these older female friends of his mother's. All he had to do was a mention a desire and it was satisfied.

Any desire.

He smiled at the thought, a bronze young god in skin-tight cutoffs.

All the ladies at the table smiled back.

Keith Bradford cursed beneath his breath as his wife dragged his screaming, sobbing daughter through LAX. Everyone they passed turned to stare. "Do something," he told his wife through clenched teeth.

Cynthia yanked her daughter's arm roughly, "Shut up, you little monster," she said in a low voice. Sharon kept screaming.

Keith and Cynthia Bradford had waited until they were at the airport to tell Sharon that Andrew wasn't going with her to Switzerland. At first she thought it was a joke. She had seen Andrew's suitcase put into the trunk with hers when the driver brought them to the airport. Andrew's suitcase, but none for Inga.

Inga had ridden with them in the car to the airport, though. Sharon had thought that was the reason Keith Bradford asked the driver to wait for a moment after the bags were unloaded —so Inga could get inside and go back home—but when she did, she pulled Andrew into the car with her.

Sharon shrieked in dismay as the car pulled away from the curb with Andrew inside. Keith Bradford grabbed his daughter by the back of her skirt to keep her from darting into the moving traffic after it.

Andrew was peering out the back window at her and Sharon could see the "o" of his mouth that told her that her twin was howling as loudly as she was.

Beside his face was Inga's. Smiling.

Cynthia Bradford yanked her daughter into an airport rest room and slapped cold water on her fevered face.

Sharon continued to scream.

"The room's fine," Victoria assured Joseph Moretti over the phone. "And my roommates are very nice." They were also very envious of her relationship with the handsome and distinguished older man whose photograph was on her study desk and who called her at least once a week from California. "And my classes are going well. But I want to hear what's happening in your life, Joseph."

She listened attentively, taking notes on the yellow legal-sized pad on her lap. Joseph had commented before on her excellent memory where his affairs were concerned. He had no idea she wrote down every scrap of information he told her about him and his law business and spent more time analyzing those notes than on any of her classes. He wouldn't tell her anything about his individual clients—even their names—but he talked to her for hours about points of law and court procedures.

Joseph might have thought she was majoring in Drama, but she planned two professions: actress and lawyer's wife. She spent a lot of dreary class time practicing her married name-to-be, Victoria Moretti, Mrs. Joseph Moretti, over and over in her graceful handwriting. Poor Joseph, she thought with a grin. The thought probably hadn't even entered his mind yet. He seemed to have the idea that he'd been cast for the role of kindly uncle.

The only disagreement they'd had was over her working while in school. She'd already had two modeling assignments and had been offered a part in a commercial, although she'd turned that last one down. So she made sure not to mention modeling and confined her acting to school productions. Once they were married, he'd go along with her plans to continue acting, so there was no use arguing about it now. She'd done enough arguing with her grandparents over it. Florence Stanton had told Victoria that Vincent Stanton would rather she didn't act anymore. "The moral atmosphere, you know," her grandmother said, and it was all Victoria could do to keep from shrieking with hysterical laughter.

She had two goals in life.

One was to free herself from her grandparents forever.

The other was to continue acting.

Joseph Moretti was going to be her means of achieving both of them.

Nora Trager put her hand on Danny's thigh.

Danny grinned down at her. He was reclining on a lounger by Nora's pool while Nora sunned herself on a mat beside him. Nora's husband was out of town so they had Nora's whole house to themselves.

"I've got something for you, Danny."

His grin widened. "And I've got something for you."

"No, really." Her pout would have been more effective if she hadn't moved her hand further up his thigh. "It's in the house." She stood up in one lithe, graceful motion and walked toward the house, swaying her bottom seductively.

You wouldn't know she was forty-seven, Danny mused, as he followed. He wouldn't have known it either if he hadn't sneaked a peak at her driver's license.

Upstairs, in one of the bedrooms, she opened a closet door. "Shirts," she told him. "You mentioned last week that you didn't have enough."

Twenty from L.A.'s best stores should help, he thought as he went through them. She had picked out just the right colors and styles, too. When he said so, she blushed.

"My . . . uh . . . nephew . . . is the same age you are."

Bullshit. It was her son who was the same age. He and Danny had been classmates in the seventh grade. Prudently, Danny didn't point that out. Instead he said, "Now all my pants will look out of date."

"We'll have to do something about that," she said, as she pulled down his swim trunks.

Afterwards, when they were lounging in the middle of her huge bed, she said, "You know, Danny, you need some money of your own."

"I have some money of my own," he said and was immediately sorry he had admitted it.

She rolled over on one elbow and studied his face. "And you don't want Beth to know about it. Don't worry. There's a lot of things we don't want Beth to know about."

She began stroking his chest with the palm of her hand. "Where is your money, Danny?"

As long as he had admitted he had it, it didn't seem like it would do any more damage to say where it was. "In a safe deposit box."

"That's a mistake, you know."

"No one can get it there. No one can take it away from me."

"But it won't grow either. You need to invest it." Her hand drifted lower, stroking. "How much are we talking about?"

"A hundred thousand dollars."

She sat up in bed. "That's criminal! Do you realize how much interest you're losing?"

He shook his head, amused at her vehemence.

She stopped stroking him and opened a drawer in the nightstand for a pencil and paper. When she had scribbled some figures on the paper, she showed them to him, and Danny was no longer amused.

"I can't put it in a bank. Mom will find out."

"Let me take care of it for you," Nora said. "In fact," she said, her hand cupping his balls again, "Let me take care of everything for you."

Sharon chewed on the end of her pen and tried to think of something pleasant to write.

She hated everything. Switzerland. The school. The other girls. But most of all she hated being separated from Andrew.

The one thing she lived for was the mail. Her letters to Andrew and her parents were never answered, but her letters to Danny and Victoria were.

Sometimes it seemed like Victoria and Danny were more like her parents than her real parents. Like they were the only ones who really cared what happened to her. She worked very hard to make her letters to both of them interesting enough so they would write back.

But it was hard. She didn't want to sound like a baby or a whiner, so she didn't write about the way the other girls ostracized her. She didn't write about the teachers who were so strict that they slapped you across the knuckles with a ruler for the smallest infraction of the endless rules.

So she made things up. And she copied lots of things from Victoria's letters and put them in her own letters to Danny. It was too bad that she couldn't do the same thing with Danny's letters when she wrote Victoria. But Danny wasn't a very good letter writer. Victoria sometimes forgot to answer Sharon's letters for a week or two, but she would make up for it by sending long, long letters, all about what she was doing and who she was seeing. Danny's letters were always short, sometimes not even a whole page long.

But he always wrote back right away.

Always.

The first thing Danny did when he came in was go through the mail on the table by the front door. He spotted the Swiss stamp immediately. He took the stairs two at a time, the envelope clutched in his hand.

He waited until he was upstairs, sprawled across his bed, to rip it open. Swiftly, he scanned through the pages in Sharon's round, childish scrawl, not bothering to read any of it until he came to the latest news about Victoria. That he read twice.

Then he pulled out a pen and paper and scrawled a reply to Sharon.

Too bad he didn't have the guts to write Victoria directly.

But thanks to Sharon, this was the next best thing.

Chapter Ten

1963

"Danny? Is that you?" Victoria sounded more shocked than surprised over the phone.

"I'm here. In Cambridge." Danny slumped back against the headboard of the hotel bed. "Can I see you tonight?" The pause was not encouraging. "I hitchhiked all the way from California."

"I already have a date tonight, Danny. What about tomorrow?"

"I wouldn't want to interrupt anything." Like hell, he wouldn't. "But I was really looking forward to seeing you tonight, Victoria. I have to leave tomorrow."

"Are you here on vacation?"

"No. I came to see you."

Another pause, longer this time. He felt like he was waiting for a death sentence. Then she said, "Would you like to come along with us? We're just going out to dinner."

No, I'd like for you to dump this bird whoever he is and spend some time with me. "I'd love to." Danny lied. "What time?"

When he hung up, he gave a huge sigh of relief, letting the tiredness seep through his bones. He'd crossed the country by thumb in less than a week, taking whatever rides he could get. He hadn't spent a single night in a bed.

He had cadged the money for the trip out of Nora and he still had almost all of it left. Enough for this hotel room tonight and a meal from room service. Enough to have the suit and tie he'd carried wadded into a ball in his knapsack all the way from California pressed. Enough to take Victoria out to dinner if he had the chance. Most important, the room was nice enough to bring her back to if the opportunity arose. He had skipped a lot of meals to make sure of that.

But it didn't look like that would happen. He hadn't even met her again yet, and already things were starting to get away from him.

He had thought it would be different now. In the two years since *Charlie's Gang* ended, he had learned to deal with women ten, twenty, even thirty years, his senior. So why should Victoria be different?

But he couldn't rid himself of the apprehension that she was something very different indeed.

Danny stood up and peeled off his shirt, and as he did he caught sight of the angry-looking scratch that began just below his left nipple and ran down across his belly. He wondered what Victoria would think if she knew he had almost killed a man on his little jaunt across the country to see her.

"But I didn't think you'd mind, Dom," Victoria said in a furious whisper. "He came all the way from California to see me. He's leaving tomorrow. The least you can do is be nice to him for one night." This wasn't going well, she thought. And where in the world was Danny? He was supposed to be here by now.

She and Dom Solari, Jr., stood on the steps of her dorm, arguing in the cold, wet winter wind, while they waited for Danny to appear. Actually she would have preferred not to have gone out with Dom in the first place. She had only dated him because Joseph Moretti asked her to. Anything Joseph asked, she did. "Dom's the son of a very good friend," the lawyer had told her. "Be nice to him."

So she had been, letting him drag her to school functions she didn't care about. Letting him use her as a decorative arm piece, even though Dom was so stuck up and pretentious that she was in danger of dying from boredom after ten minutes of his company.

Her roommates thought he was dreamy and swooned when he called her. He was okay, Victoria conceded, but not terrific. Six foot two of lean, lanky male with large brown eyes, he was just short of *too* handsome. His skin was smooth enough to be a girl's and his thin lips and delicately pointed chin had a decidedly feminine look.

It was his attitude more than his looks that left her unresponsive, though. He fairly bristled with his own self-importance. Not that some of it wasn't justified. He really was a Big Man On Campus. Almost everyone at Harvard and at Radcliffe knew who Dom Solari, Jr. was. But there was a coldness in Dom she found distasteful. He didn't give a darn about other people's feelings. All he cared about was appearances. She would bet that his anger at this moment had more to do with how it would look to be accompanied on a "date" with another male, than anything else.

"He's like my little brother, Dom. He played Bucky on *Charlie's Gang*."

"So what's he doing here?"

She wondered that herself.

When she looked up and saw Danny striding toward the campus toward them, she was confused. Because this was no longer Bucky, but a confident and very good-looking man, better looking than Dom and a couple of inches taller, with a ruggedly handsome face topped by the same thick, unruly gold hair she remembered so well. A man who made her heart leap when he looked at her.

But the next moment she remembered that he was just a kid, eighteen, and not even in college, while she was twenty, a woman, and she curbed the impulse to run to him, to hug him. Instead she extended her hand when he had bounded up the steps to greet her, and he took it solemnly.

When Danny saw Victoria standing in front of her dorm with the slick, sophisticated college man with the pretty boy face, he felt like a kid. Victoria's introduction only intensified that feeling. "Danny Garrick. We acted together on *Charlie's*

Gang. He's just like my little brother,'' she babbled to Dom Solari, Jr.

Christ, what a pretentious asshole Solari was, insisting on the "Jr." "My old man's rule. What he says, goes."

"My father was Leif Garrick," Danny blurted. "The movie star." He couldn't believe that was his voice. He had never bragged about his father like that before. "Everyone's heard of him."

Jr. hadn't. Unimpressed, he asked Victoria, "Shall we go?"

Solari loaded Victoria ceremoniously into the front seat of his brand new four-seater Ferrari, a 330 GT, and what in the hell was a college kid doing with a car like that? Danny wondered, crammed into the marginal rear seat. Jr. did everything he could to make Danny feel like an outsider, including ignoring Danny's existence by directing all his conversation to Victoria as they crossed the Charles River into Boston. Victoria made a few feeble attempts to include Danny, but Dom dismissed them before Danny could respond.

At the restaurant, it got worse. Jr. apologized to the waiter *twice* for the last minute addition to the party as if the fucking waiter cared. Danny wished he could stand up and walk out. But he couldn't. He had come all this way to see Victoria, and he meant to do just that. Even if he had to stare at her across the table while Jr. sat with his arm around her shoulders.

The waiter hesitated at Dom's order of champagne for the table, until he slipped the man a twenty. Danny grimaced at the elaborate ceremony Dom went through to assure the champagne was drinkable. Victoria frowned at him, but he didn't care. Dom was an asshole *and* a snob. When the waiter finally got around to pouring his glass, Danny downed it like a soft drink.

"A real man," Dom jeered.

"I do all right," Danny said.

"Smoke?" Dom held out a package of Camels.

"Sure."

Victoria shook her head when Dom held the pack out to her. Danny lit up and took a deep drag. Her worried expression and the harsh nicotine he inhaled suddenly combined to remind him of the night of her abortion. The smoke overwhelmed him. He choked and began to cough.

Dom made a production of leaning over to pound him on the back. When the second bottle of champagne arrived, Danny didn't want any more, but he knew he couldn't turn it down without Dom ridiculing him.

Too bad, because the alcohol loosened his tongue, and he kept talking on and on about himself. One tiny still-lucid corner of his brain was explaining to him that this was the first time in his life he had ever tried to be the aggressor where women were concerned. Always before, they had tried to seduce him. He had absolutely no idea how to proceed with Victoria. For some reason that reminded him of the blonde woman, Paula Nelson's friend, and the day when he was twelve that he had stumbled upon Paula and her friend in his mother's bedroom. The blonde had put her hand around his penis and said, "So this is the world-famous prick you inherited." That was his problem, he thought. Then *and* now. His famous prick.

"My famous prick," he said aloud, clearly. A dish clattered. He looked up.

The waiter removing the dishes of the second course had frozen in mid-motion. Victoria was watching him with the kind of involuntary fascination she might have reserved for anything that came crawling out from under a rock into the light of this very nice restaurant. Jr. grinned at him. "What did you say, Danny Boy?"

The 'Danny Boy' goaded him. "I said I have a world-famous prick. That's my problem. Inherited it from my father. Women can't leave it alone."

Victoria gasped. "Danny!"

Jr. poured him more champagne. "You don't expect us to believe that, do you, Danny Boy?"

" 'S true," Danny said earnestly, leaning forward. He had never told this to anyone before, especially Victoria. He was glad the champagne had unshackled his tongue. He *wanted* to tell her. He wanted her to know what had happened to him. "Older women. My mother's age. Started while we were on the show." He shook his head, and the room swam. "Couldn't get enough of me. Still can't."

He felt such a sense of relief at getting it off his chest after so many years. He had never told anyone, not even his mother, especially his mother, what went on with her friends.

Too late, staring bleary-eyed at Victoria, he realized she was furious.

He reached for his glass. She grabbed it first and moved it across the table, out of his reach.

"Come on, Victoria," Dom scolded. "Don't act like the kid's mother. What is he? Fifteen? Sixteen? He's old enough to drink."

"Not legally," Victoria snapped.

"Men don't always worry about legalities, Baby."

Victoria glared at him. "Is that another pithy little saying you learned from your father?"

". . . not a kid. I'm eighteen, now," Danny protested.

Victoria ignored him. "You ought to be ashamed of yourself," she told Dom. "You got him drunk on purpose."

" 'Scuse me," Danny said, and stood up abruptly. He stumbled off through the tables toward the men's room.

"Go after him, Dom," Victoria urged as she watched poor Danny lurch away.

Dom folded his arms and leaned back in his chair. "Why should I?"

"Because it's the gentlemanly thing to do. You are a gentleman, aren't you? Joseph Moretti told me you were." In their dates together she had learned that Joseph Moretti's name had a very strange effect on Dom Solari. She suspected that Joseph reported on Dom's behavior to his father. Whatever it was, it worked again. Dom went after Danny.

The waiter hovered again, and she waved him away, her cheeks still burning at what the man had overheard. *A world-famous prick!* What in the world had happened to Danny in the last two years? He had become a show-off, trying to impress everyone with how important his father used to be. A foul-mouthed kid. Really a kid, she thought, two years younger than she was. She had been so touched to find out that he had hitchhiked across the country to see her. Now she was mortified. It wasn't embarrassment that he had made a fool of himself in front of Dom and the waiter, either. No, it was something else. Something that she wouldn't dare admit to anyone. Dom with his pretty-boy good looks didn't excite her, but Danny certainly did. A kid. And that was more embarrassing to her than anything else that had happened tonight. She didn't intend to let Danny or anyone else know that.

Danny stumbled into the men's room and relieved himself. The room was still in motion so he crossed to the basin and leaned over it, splashing cold water on his face, until the spinning slowed.

When he straightened, he caught sight of Jr. in the mirror, lounging against the door, watching him. Slick, sophisticated Harvard man. How could he hope to compete with someone like that? Danny thought, as Dom took a long drag on his cigarette.

"Come on, Danny Boy, the lady's waiting. I've got to get you back to the nursery before my evening can get started."

"What does that mean?"

"It means that Victoria and I have some bedroom business to take care of." Dom leaned forward to stab Danny in the chest with his forefinger. "And no kindergardeners invited."

Danny took a clumsy swing at him.

Dom dodged the blow, laughing. He caught Danny's arm and twisted it up behind his back. "You think your old man's such hot shit? Let me tell you about my old man."

Danny struggled to free himself. He was a couple of inches taller than Dom, but he didn't have as much muscle as the Harvard man yet. That—and the champagne he had drunk— made the struggle in vain. "My father was a star," he gasped.

"Shut up and listen." Dom jerked Danny around until they were both facing the mirror. "My old man kills people. For real. Not like some fag actor. You do something Dominic Solari doesn't like, then you disappear. Permanently."

"Bullshit."

Dom pushed Danny's arm higher until the pain made beads of sweat break out on Danny's forehead. "You think it's bullshit. I'm the apple of my daddy's eye, Danny Boy. His favorite son. If I want you gone . . ." He pushed the arm higher, making Danny cry out. "You're gone!" He shoved Danny forward against the sink.

Danny hung there a moment. When he turned around he jerked his shirt up out of his belt, exposing the angry red line across his chest and belly. "You see that? Two days ago I almost killed a guy who tried to carve me up with a knife. I had him down on the ground with my knee in his throat and his own knife pointed in his ribs. He was puking and begging for mercy. You ever do anything like that yourself, Jr.? Or does Daddy do it all for you?''

Solari laughed. "Bullshit yourself, Danny Boy. I bet you did that with your fingernails." He grabbed Danny by the collar and jammed his shirt back in his pants. "Get a move on. My pecker's got business with the lady outside."

He dodged another wild swing by Danny, and grabbed his arm again, marching him out of the rest room.

"I just love a virgin," he whispered to Danny as Victoria spotted them, a worried frown on her face. "And tonight's the night."

"Is he all right?" she asked Dom, as though Danny were too young to answer for himself.

"He's fine, Baby. He just needs to get back to his hotel." Dom chuckled. "He's got to get himself a manicure."

Danny found himself thrust back in the rear seat of the Ferrari. He watched the silhouettes of Victoria and Jr. silhouetted against the oncoming lights through the car's windshield. This time Victoria didn't try to include Danny in the conversation. She chattered gaily to Dom without pause. When Dom stopped for a light, he leaned across the car and murmured in her ear. She laughed softly, in a way that made Danny want to kill Dom Solari, Jr., with his bare hands.

Dom straightened and glanced in the rearview mirror. "You feel like you're going to barf, you sing out, Danny Boy. Don't mess the carpet."

They rolled up in front of the hotel and Dom came around to open the door for Danny. Victoria leaned forward, so Danny could climb out of the back. On the sidewalk, he hesitated. Victoria extended her hand to him. "It was wonderful seeing you again, Danny," she said formally. Then Dom had him by the shoulder, yanking him away from the car.

They hadn't talked about anything, Danny thought dismally as Dom marched him up to the lobby door. "So long, Danny Boy," he said with a smirk. "You'll understand why we don't linger."

When he reached the Ferrari, Dom turned around and

called, "Don't forget to trim those fingernails." He got in
and pulled Victoria to him, planting a kiss on her upturned
lips.

Danny turned and plunged into the lobby.

As soon as they pulled away from the curb, Victoria said,
"Take me home, Dom."

"Don't cool off now, Babe," Dom protested. It was beginning to mist lightly. He switched on the windshield wipers.

"I have a test tomorrow. I really need to get back and
study."

"One more little drink," Dom insisted. "What will one
hurt?"

Victoria sighed. "Just one." The last one. She wasn't
going to date Mr. Self-centered Solari again. Joseph would
just have to understand. She stared out into the rainy winter
night and realized she missed California more than she had
ever thought possible.

Dom knew half the people in the bar. He pushed her
through the crowd ahead of him to a prominent table. Four
other couples joined them, jamming their chairs in tightly
around the table. Dom put his arm around Victoria's shoulders as they were shoved together. "Two Scotch and sodas,"
he ordered when the barmaid came by.

"I don't want Scotch," Victoria protested.

He leaned over and whispered in her ear, "It'll warm you
up, Babe. And then I'll warm you up some more."

She pulled back from him, but his arm around her shoulder
kept her from going far.

The five males talked about football, ignoring their dates.
Victoria made a half-hearted attempt to start a conversation
with the other girls, but they were too busy hanging on their
dates' every word.

When the drinks came, Dom immediately downed his and
ordered another round for himself and Victoria. This time she
didn't protest. She could see it would do no good.

Something brushed her thigh under the table and she shifted
away.

Immediately it was back, slipping beneath her skirt, caressing the soft flesh above her hose.

"Stop it, Dom!" she whispered, furious.

He gave no indication he had heard her, but his hand stayed where it was. She tried to push it away, without anyone realizing what was going on beneath the table, but she couldn't. Neither could she shift herself away from him since her chair was blocked by the fullback on the other side of her.

Now Dom's hand rose higher, caressing the crotch of her panties. She struggled beneath the table, but she couldn't dislodge his hand. Instead, he slipped his fingers inside the nylon, and into her.

"You bastard!" she said loudly. "Take your hand out of my panties! What kind of girl do you think I am?"

Dom jerked his hand back.

A silence fell over the bar.

Every eye in the bar was fastened on her. Dom stared at her with a sickly look of disbelief.

Victoria shoved back from the table and stood up. Her chair fell over with a crash. She picked up her untouched Scotch and soda and poured it down the front of his pants. "Don't you ever put your filthy hands on me again!"

She stepped over her fallen chair and walked out without looking back. The bar remained silent until she was almost at the entrance and then the applause started, building to a roar.

Victoria kept her expression calm, poised, and serene. But as she stepped back into the rainy winter night, she hoped there was enough money in her purse for a taxi.

Victoria walked into her dorm room and threw herself on her bed.

"Your boyfriend called," her roommate said, handing her a note.

Victoria crumpled it into a ball and tossed it in the wastebasket beside her desk. "I'll bet he did, that drip!"

"I thought you were crazy about him. Dreamy. Distinguished. An older man."

"Joseph!" she squealed. "Joseph called?" She rolled off the bed and dumped the wastebasket upside down, searching for the message she had balled up.

"Hooray!" she yelled when she found it. "He's coming with my grandparents in three weeks!"

"What happened tonight?"

"Nothing!" Victoria grinned. "And boy, was Dom Solari ever mad about that! I took a taxi home."

Then she forgot all about Dom. "What am I going to wear while Joseph's here?"

"Mom. I'm home," Danny called. Christ. He sounded like every family show from the fifties. He'd probably done that line five thousand times himself on *Charlie's Gang*.

This time no one answered.

A stack of mail waited on the table in the entry hall. Half of it was his: a thick bundle of letters from Sharon in Switzerland. He took the letters up to his room and tossed them in the middle of his bed. He took a shower and came back, a towel wrapped around his middle, and plopped down on the bed to read them.

He had the grace to feel ashamed of himself as he skimmed through the pages in Sharon's round, childish handwriting, looking for the parts about Victoria.

When he did, he was almost sorry he had. There were several pages about Victoria's boy friend. An "older man," so distinguished. He could just hear Victoria drooling over that stupid Jr.

He pulled his stationery out of the nightstand drawer and began to write a quick note to Sharon. Anything to keep her writing back. Anything to keep in touch with Victoria.

He finished it quickly and sealed the envelope. When he got up to lay it on his dresser, he caught sight of himself in the mirror. The scratch across his belly was nearly gone now. He couldn't believe he had been drunk enough that night to brag about it to Dom Solari.

He had been waiting beside a highway sign near a truck stop when the tramp came at him out of the darkness without a word. The knife slashed down through his jacket and t-shirt before he even realized it was there.

Danny brought his knee up into the man's balls, and then clenched both fists together and swung them into the tramp's windpipe.

The knife dropped from the man's hand as he fell backwards.

Filled with a bloody fury, Danny followed the man down, jamming his knee into the tramp's throat. He grabbed for the knife and stuck the point right against his attacker's ribs.

With the other hand, he grabbed the man's hair, jerking his head back so that he could see the tramp's face.

The man blubbered, begging for his life, spittle drooling down his chin. The stench of him was overwhelming.

Danny scrambled off of him, and to his feet.

The tramp continued to lie there, a wet stain spreading over the front of his pants. The words were indistinguishable now, like a baby's mewling.

Danny tossed the knife away into the night. He grabbed his knapsack and ran back toward the truck stop and light. A big eighteen-wheeler was just pulling out. It braked and the driver motioned him aboard. Danny jumped in and the guy took a good look at him in the light from the truck stop.

"You okay, kid? You're bleeding."

"Snagged myself on a fence back there," Danny said quickly. He could feel the wet stickiness of his blood now. He didn't dare look at it to see how bad it was. Instead he pressed the jacket against the cut to stop the bleeding and tried not to think of the human wreckage he had left back there in the darkness.

"And that was what you bragged to Jr. about," he told his reflection. "You're as big a drip as Solari."

"Danny! You're home!" his mother said from the bedroom doorway. She rushed forward and tried to hug him, but he stepped out of her grasp. "I was so worried about you, Danny."

He could hear Dom Solari's mocking "Danny Boy" as plainly as if Jr. was standing there. "Daniel, Mom. I want to be called Daniel now."

Beth rushed on without pause. "You should have let me know where you went. What you were doing."

"What's the matter? Didn't any of your good friends call when they found out I was gone?"

"That's not fair, Danny."

"Daniel! It's Daniel, Mother."

"All right. Daniel." She wrung her hands. Perfectly manicured as always, he noted scornfully. She always had plenty of time for herself. "You go off for weeks and I have no idea where you are . . . and when you finally come home—"

"Don't worry, Mother. Your friends are about to come flocking back."

"What are you talking about?"

"We'll make a deal. I won't be doing any hitching for a while. I'll lay around the house and be charming to all your friends."

"Of course you will. You were taught manners."

"I mean I'll be charming enough that those Hollywood bitches won't drop you again."

"Danny!"

"Don't you want to know how charming I'll be?"

She covered her ears with her hands.

He jerked them away.

"I'm going to fuck each and every one of them, Mother. That's what you want, isn't it?" Beth Garrick struggled to cover her ears again. "You want me to fuck them so you can be popular again, don't you, Mom? You just don't want me to admit that's what I'm doing."

"Danny, please, don't—"

"Daniel, Mother. Call me, Daniel. After all, I'm the man of the house now. I'm doing exactly what Dad did for you. Using my famous prick to make sure you have a little niche in Hollywood society. And in return you're going to do something for me. I'm going to go to college."

"What?"

He released her hands and she staggered backwards. "I'm going to UCLA. I'll start in January. Surely you can open the old purse strings enough for that."

"Well, of course, Dann—Daniel. But you were never interested in going to college before."

He thought of Dom Solari, Jr. Slick, sophisticated. A college man. "I'm interested now."

"Victoria? Aren't you Victoria Carr?"

Victoria slowed. She was on her way back to the dorm in the late evening mist. The boy in the car looked vaguely familiar.

"I saw you with Dom Solari last week. At the pub? Can I give you a lift to your dorm?"

Lightening crackled overhead. She ran for the car. "Thanks," she said as she climbed inside. "It's really rotten out—"

Someone grabbed her from the back seat. "Hello, Victoria," Dom said.

She lunged for the door, but the driver held on to her long enough for Dom and another boy to lift her over into the back seat with them. She kicked out as they did so, and her heel connected with the windshield.

"Hey!" the driver yelled. "She'll crack the windshield."

"Fuck your windshield!" Dom muttered, as he and the other boy pulled her down between them.

"Get in the front," he told the other boy as he put his arms around Victoria in a painful clench.

When the second pair of hands released her, she tried desperately to pull away, but Dom was too strong for her. He forced her back against the seat, until he was holding her down with his weight. He took her head between both of his hands and held it so that she couldn't look away. "Nobody treats a Solari like you treated me, Victoria. You're going to pay for that."

Lightening flickered followed by immediate thunder as rain began sheeting down. "Where to, Dom?" the driver shouted over the rain pounding the car.

"Here's as good as any place." He raised up enough to unbuckle his belt and unzip his pants.

Victoria brought her knee up. He twisted away so that it struck his thigh instead of his privates.

"Bitch!" he said and slapped her.

She jerked one hand free and slapped him back.

This time he balled his hand into a fist. The blow struck her on the side of the head. For a moment, her head swam and she lay there stunned.

Dom took advantage of that to rip her blouse open. He didn't bother to unhook her bra. He merely yanked it up roughly so that her breasts fell out of it.

"Wow!" the driver said.

"Turn around," Dom ordered. He bent down and took one of her nipples in his mouth.

Victoria raked her fingernails down his back.

The pain sent him into a frenzy. He struck her once, twice, three times, and then there was a wet sticky mess on her thigh. Premature ejaculation. The girls in the dorm had talked about it. "A real man," Victoria sneered. "Hit a woman and it makes you come. Does Daddy know *that* about his little boy?"

Dom roared with rage and struck her three more times with brutal force before the boys in the front seat were able to wrestle him away from her and slam him back against the door.

Victoria drew her legs up to her exposed chest, moaning.

"Get her out of here," Dom snarled. "Get her out before I kill her."

The two in the front seat piled out and pulled her out of the car. They carried her through the pouring rain the few steps to the grass and dumped her there.

The driver leaned over her while the other boy went back for her books. "He's president of his class," the boy whispered to her. "It won't do you any good to tell anyone. Nobody will believe you."

She could barely see the boy through the rain streaming down on her. One of her eyes was swelling shut.

"Just keep quiet," he urged.

The other boy dumped her books down beside her. Her notebook fell open. The two boys ran back to the car and it sped away into the storm.

Loose papers blew out of her notebook into the rain. One landed beside her face. As the water spattered down on it, the ink began to run on the page.

She closed her eyes.

"Holy Mother of God!" someone said nearby.

She didn't open her eyes.

She wasn't sure she ever wanted to open her eyes again.

"My God, Victoria!" Joseph Moretti exclaimed when he picked her up at the dorm.

"You should have seen me a week ago," she said ruefully.

"I can't believe the authorities would let something like this go unpunished!"

"It's as much my fault as theirs, Joseph. If I'd had enough sense to get the license plate of the car—"

"That's ridiculous! You've nothing to blame yourself for, nothing at all."

He had come full of apologies that her grandparents had not been able to make the trip after all. And while the school had notified her grandparents of the attempted rape, either the school had not emphasized the extent of Victoria's injuries, or her grandparents had not seen fit to pass that information on to Moretti.

She had come so close to giving the police Dom Solari's name. But her background as an actress had made her see the dramatic possibilities in withholding that information. If she gave them Dom's name, he and his father and some high-priced attorney like Joseph Moretti would attack her personally. It would be her word against theirs.

But this way the sympathy was all on her side. The unknown attackers had reaped nothing but scorn. There had been a series of editorials about the rape attempt in both the school and city papers.

She wondered how Mr. Dom Solari, Jr., felt about that!

In fact, she almost owed Dom her gratitude, she thought as Joseph Moretti fussed over her. He acted as though she were made of eggshells as he helped her into his car. They were supposed to be on their way to the football game, but he turned to her and said, "I don't want you among all those ruffians, Victoria. Let me take you back to my hotel. We can have lunch in the hotel dining room."

"Or champagne in your suite?" she teased.

"How did you know I have a suite?"

"Don't you always? Your clients expect it. That's what you told me last Christmas."

"You'll make some professional man a wonderful wife," he marveled. "Your memory is phenomenal."

"Only where you're concerned, Joseph."

He digested that in silence as they drove to the hotel, and Victoria fretted that she'd gone too far. But when they arrived at the hotel, he did indeed take her up to his suite.

Lunch arrived courtesy of room service along with a very good bottle of champagne. They sat and talked quietly. Rather, she talked and he listened. She told him amusing little stories of school, and dorm life. She even mentioned the occasional modeling jobs she had done, aware he wouldn't lecture her about that now in light of her injuries. "But no more of those for a while." She reached up to touch the largest bruise on her cheek and flinched. "Not until I heal."

Joseph came around the table and knelt beside her, laying his head in her lap. "What would I have done if something had happened to you?" he asked in a strangled voice.

"Joseph?"

He raised his head. Tears streaked his cheeks. "I love you, Victoria. I've loved you ever since I walked into that hospital room in Los Angeles. I know I'm too old for you, but—"

She silenced him by softly pressing her lips against his. When she drew back, she told him, "I love you, too, Joseph."

"Oh, Victoria!" He gathered her into his arms. This time he kissed her. "You will marry me?"

"Of course, Joseph."

"When you graduate. We'll tell your grandparents then."

And she would be free of their influence for the first time in her life.

Afterwards he made slow, tender love to her. So slow, so tender, that she wanted to scream at him, I'm a woman, not a china doll. I won't shatter!

But she didn't. Instead she lay there and thought about the way she had felt when she saw Danny striding across the campus toward her dorm.

When Joseph Moretti finally reached his own shuddering release, she was able to join him.

Chapter Eleven

1966

Sharon took her airmail stationery from her desk and carried it to the window seat. She curled up on the soft cushion, her feet tucked comfortably beneath her skirt, and stared out the window for a moment, seeing not snowy Gstaad but Danny Garrick's face. "Dear Danny," she wrote across the top of the page, and then sighed in exasperation. She crumpled that sheet in a ball and pulled out a fresh one. "Dear Daniel," she started again, and then chewed on the end of the pen, undecided as to how she should go on. Danny was no longer Danny, but Daniel. That was only one of the things that had changed since she'd been here.

The biggest change had been what happened last year when she was fifteen, and that was Danny . . . Daniel's fault. When she came to this Swiss school four years ago, she had been so lonely she thought she would die. The very worst thing had been being separated from Andrew, of course. But there were other things too. When she first arrived, she was overweight. That was bad enough, but then all the skiing and other sports combined with a spurt of growth to produce exactly the opposite effect for most of the past four years. She no longer resembled JoJo. Instead she was skinny, awkward, gawky-looking, a real scarecrow. No one liked her and she didn't even like herself very much. She had nothing to do but study, and that only made things worse. Her grades put her in the top of her class, and her teachers were always holding her up as an example to the other girls. The other students hated her for that and after a while, she began to hate herself.

That was the way it had been until Daniel came last year.

Most of the girls here were from other countries. But the ones from the United States wouldn't have recognized her as JoJo now, even if she'd made a big deal of it. But they all recognized Daniel.

Not for *Charlie's Gang,* but for his new movies. He was a real celebrity in the United States, and his fame had begun to spread in Europe, too. Once, just once, Sharon had mentioned to another girl that she knew Daniel Garrick, and she'd been labeled a liar on the spot. She didn't say anything else to anyone, but the word got around and the other students teased her about it.

Before, no one paid any attention to her letter writing. Now when she mailed off a letter, someone always commented on it, taunting her. They thought she was just another star-struck teenager.

Since Daniel's signature was an illegible scrawl and he never put his return address on the envelope, no one believed the notes she received were really from him.

The first Sharon knew about Daniel being in France to make a movie was when two of the older girls stopped her in the hall to tease her about it. "When is he coming to see you?" they pestered her. "Will he take you out on a date?" By the time she got away from them, she was in tears. She couldn't believe it. He hadn't even written her that he was going to be in Europe.

It was the talk of the whole school. Even the teachers made sly references to it in class. Sharon became so sick of it that she stole sheets from the laundry and hid them in her room, planning to lower herself out of her third story window one midnight and run away.

So no one was more surprised than she when the headmistress called Sharon to her office and said that a most irregular request had been made in Sharon's behalf, that she be permitted to have dinner with an unmarried male who was not a close relative. The school was very strict where its younger girls were concerned and normally this would not have been allowed, but because of the stature of Mr. Garrick, she would be given permission to go to dinner with him just this once.

The headmistress wrote her a note excusing her from class the rest of the day to get ready for her dinner engagement. Still not entirely sure that this was not some elaborate practical joke, Sharon had nevertheless dressed with care.

When Daniel arrived, she couldn't believe her eyes. He was all grown up, a man, not a boy. And so good looking with his unruly gold hair and golden brown eyes that even the headmistress swooned over him.

The dinner was a disaster.

He spent the whole evening pumping Sharon for information about Victoria. She wasn't a little kid anymore. She had realized at some point that the only reason he kept writing her was because he was interested in what she had to say about Victoria. That was why Sharon was always careful to sprinkle liberal amounts of information about Victoria through her letters. But in spite of that she still viewed Danny, or Daniel, as a brother of sorts. She had believed he felt the same way about her until that evening. Over dinner, she found out how mistaken she had been about their relationship. Daniel didn't care one little bit about her or her life. All he wanted to hear about was Victoria, Victoria, Victoria.

By the time the meal ended, Sharon was so furious that she was barely speaking to him. Not that he even noticed. He had already found out everything she knew about Victoria to date and he was silent as he drove her back to the school. He didn't even walk her to the door. He just let her off at the gate, saying, "Keep writing," and sped away.

As she trudged up the drive to the school, Sharon vowed that she would never write him another letter as long as she lived.

That resolve lasted until she pushed open the heavy front door and found a crowd of girls and teachers waiting for her in the hall. Not just waiting: avid for the details of her excursion.

She realized immediately what was going on, but she decided to use it for her own benefit. She was tired of being an outsider, and she blossomed from the attention she received that night. And afterwards.

Her amazing spurt of growth had finally leveled off at five foot nine a few months ago, giving her body a chance to catch up at long last. She had breasts and hips now and no longer had to safety-pin her skirts to her blouses to keep them from slipping off. Long hours with her new friends experimenting with makeup and eye shadow had taught her ways to make the green of her eyes even more brilliant. Now when she looked in the mirror above her washbasin each morning, it was herself she saw and not Andrew. Too bad she didn't have a photograph of the new her to send Daniel. Maybe then he'd be sorry he spent so much time that night talking about Victoria.

She stared down at the sheet in front of her for a moment and then crumpled it into a ball and tossed it across the window seat to join her first attempt.

"Sharon! Sharon!" Five girls bustled into her room at once. "Why are you sulking in here?" one demanded, and another reminded her, "We're supposed to go down to the cafe. You promised you would come."

She looked up at them, amused. They were the five most popular girls at the school. A year ago none of them knew her name. Now she was their leader. All thanks to that dinner with Daniel. "Give me ten minutes," she told them with firm authority, knowing they would wait an hour if she so commanded. "I have to write my letter."

She didn't have to say who she was writing. They all knew. Everyone knew now that the letters from America were from *him*.

That was why she had to be careful how she wrote this letter. She enjoyed being popular. She wasn't ready for it to end.

Sharon pulled out a new sheet of stationary. "Dear Daniel," she began again. "I've just had the most amazing news about Victoria."

"Someone stole my car!" Daniel complained to an audience of parked automobiles.

"That man is drunk!" a woman exclaimed to her escort who was holding open the door of a lavender Cadillac for her.

Daniel turned to stare at her rudely. "Are you talking to me, lady?"

Her companion, a pip-squeak, virtually shoved her into the Caddy and hurried around to the driver's side.

Daniel watched them pull out of the parking lot with a squeal of rubber and then took the time to relieve himself on the front tire of the Mercedes parked next to him before he started searching for his own car again. He had just bought the Tempest GTO in January, ordered it specially, with every power option a rising young Hollywood star might need. "And some son of a bitch stole it," he told the silent parking lot.

He had just about decided that the calamity of a stolen car called for another drink when he finally spotted the white hood of the GTO lurking beyond a gold Continental. He climbed behind the wheel and turned the key in the ignition. He had an overwhelming desire to give up and go to sleep right there. But when he slumped forward onto the wheel, he heard the crinkle of paper in his shirt pocket.

"Home, James," he said aloud.

He very nearly made it, too.

At Canon Drive and Sunset, he turned too sharply and ran the Pontiac up on the curb. He got out, looking for damage, but didn't see any. What he did see was the lights of a police cruiser reflecting off the pristine white surface of his car.

Daniel had done a cop show just last week, so he knew what to do. Before the patrolmen got out of their squad car, he had already spread-eagled himself against the Pontiac.

"Nice," said the older policeman. "Don't you wish all the drunks were this cooperative?"

The younger officer patted Daniel down, looking for an ID, and found the letter with the Swiss stamp in his pocket. "This addressed to you?" he asked. He squinted at the writing. "Daniel Garrick?"

"Naw!" said the older cop. Daniel was still spread-eagled on the car. The cop turned Daniel's head so that he could see Daniel's face. "Are you Leif Garrick's kid?"

Daniel nodded solemnly.

"He used to come down and bullshit with us when I was a rookie," the older cop said. "He was a great guy."

"The back of the car's full of suitcases," the younger cop said. He started back to the patrol car.

"Don't get on the radio," the older cop said. "This is Leif Garrick's kid."

"DWI," the younger cop said succinctly.

"No, the driver ran off. Didn't he, Daniel?"

"Son of a bitch ran away," Daniel agreed. He straightened up, staggered, and nearly fell over.

"No way," the younger cop said. "We could get canned over a thing like that. The kid's DWI. I don't care who his father is."

"Was," Daniel said.

The younger cop had his cuffs in his hand. "I beg your pardon?"

"My father's dead. Can I have my letter back now?"

The older cop took the letter from the other officer and handed it over to Daniel. "Get in the car, Daniel. I'll drive you home. You just follow me," he told the other cop. "And stay off the goddamned radio."

The younger cop stomped back to the patrol car, muttering under his breath about old farts.

"Woman trouble?" the older cop asked Daniel when they were both in the GTO.

Daniel nodded and patted the letter. "My girl's getting married."

"Dear John letter? Hell, Daniel, you're not a man until you've gotten one of those. I'll bet even Leif got his share. You just can't let it throw you like this. You think Leif would like to see his son in jail on a DWI?" The cop glanced at the rearview mirror. "I'll kill that little prick if he gets on the radio," he muttered.

"The little prick," Daniel echoed. "My girl's getting married to some little prick."

"What's with the suitcases?" the cop asked him.

"I was on my way to Cambridge to see her graduate. Was gonna leave at noon. But then the letter came. I'm twenty-one, making good money, have my own car. Going to UCLA. But I'm not sophisticated enough for her."

"Did you ask her to marry you?"

"Nope. Was gonna do that this weekend." He patted the letter. "But I found out she's getting married tomorrow."

The policeman sighed. "She probably got tired of waiting. You never know about women."

"Women," Daniel echoed, shaking his head sadly. He wished he had his bottle. He wondered what had happened to it.

When the police car pulled into the drive behind Daniel's car, lights flashing, Beth Garrick came rushing out of the house in her nightgown.

"Danny!" she screamed when he crawled out of the Pontiac. "Where were you?" She was all over him, crying hysterically, kissing him.

He pushed her away.

She turned to the policemen. "What are you doing to my little boy?" she demanded.

"No problem, Mrs. Garrick," the older policeman said. "We just brought him home." He looked right at Daniel and Daniel could see the scorn in his eyes. "You can tuck him into bed now."

Daniel wanted to say something to the man, to thank him, but his mother was pulling him into the house. When the door closed behind them, he shook her off. "I'm going to bed."

"I thought you had run away again!" Beth sobbed. "You can't keep doing this to me, Danny!"

"For God's sake, Mother! I'm twenty-one years old. If I want to drive my own fucking car to Massachusetts, it's not running away. What you're really afraid of is that I won't be around to service your women friends. We ought to put a sign on the front lawn. Daniel Garrick, Stud Service."

She covered her ears with her hands. "I won't listen to you when you talk like that."

"Just do it, don't talk about it, right?"

She started crying again.

Daniel went upstairs and passed out on his bed fully clothed.

He woke up at noon, showered, shaved, and went down to enlist in the army.

When he put his signature on the paper, he wondered if Victoria was married yet.

As Victoria started down the aisle, holding a bouquet of daisies, a rising sense of elation bubbled through her. She had outsmarted everyone. She was on top of the world. She would never be under anyone's thumb again.

It was a small wedding, with just a few of her college

friends in attendance. At first, Joseph had wanted to have a large wedding in Los Angeles. But she had talked him into this Cambridge wedding by hinting delicately that some of his clients might not find a big California wedding tasteful, considering the difference in their ages. To her annoyance, her grandparents had withheld their permission for the marriage at first. Not that Victoria needed it legally, but Joseph had no desire to strain his friendship with Vincent and Florence Stanton. Even after they finally agreed to the match, the Stantons flatly refused to fly to Massachusetts, giving Vincent Stanton's health as their excuse.

Victoria had spoken just once on the phone to her grandmother in the weeks since she and Joseph had announced their engagement. "He doesn't know why you were in the hospital that time," Florence Stanton told her. "He doesn't know you had an abortion."

I hadn't realized you knew that either, Victoria thought as she listened to the phone lines crackle between California and Cambridge. "Then he doesn't know I can't have children."

"Are you going to tell him?"

"I don't know," she said slowly, deliberately. "If I did, then I might have to tell him the reason why I'm so happy that I can't."

She heard Florence Stanton's sharp intake of breath before her grandmother slammed down the receiver. She wondered afterwards if that exchange was the real reason Florence and Vincent Stanton wouldn't be attending her wedding.

But to Joseph Moretti, her grandparents presented a different face. "It was just the difference in age that made them hesitate," he told her when he arrived in Cambridge. "I've talked to them both. Now they understand that I only want the best for you."

Victoria knew that the age difference wasn't the real reason they had balked at the wedding. It was their realization that once she married Joseph Moretti, she would no longer be their pawn! But she hadn't told him that.

As she joined Joseph at the front of the chapel, the moment was so perfect that she hardly dared breath for fear she would shatter it. This was what she had been working toward for so long. Today she had succeeded.

That knowledge left a smile on her lips that lingered even

after Joseph followed the pastor's instructions to kiss the bride.

It lingered until she caught sight of Dom Solari's mocking glance directed at her from the rear of the small crowd of well-wishers lining up to kiss the bride.

Victoria had an overwhelming urge to gather up her full skirt and flee from the chapel when she saw him standing there. She had avoided him for three years. Had never told a soul that it was he who attacked her. How could he have the nerve to appear now? As classmates and friends kissed her lightly and moved on, she tried to tell herself it was all a mistake, a figment of her imagination.

Dom, still smirking at her, began to push his way through the crowd straight toward her. As he approached, Victoria was very much afraid she was going to faint. Joseph stood by her side and she clasped his arm for support, then found herself being pulled forward.

Why was Joseph advancing toward her enemy, beaming, his hand extended in friendship? The two men shook hands and Joseph turned to his new bride. "Victoria, you know Dom, don't you? He's the son of my most important client. We'll be seeing a lot of him once get back to Los Angeles."

Dom moved forward, grinning down at her, "My turn to kiss the bride," he said. His cold lips came down on hers and Victoria wondered what in the world she had done.

Nora Trager leaned against Daniel's dresser, smoking a cigarette as she watched him pack a suitcase. "For God's sake, Daniel, don't you know there's a war on?"

"I've heard rumors."

"Your mother's having an emotional breakdown, you know."

"She'll get over it."

"And I'm horny as hell," Nora complained. "What will I do while you're off fighting?"

He patted the bed beside the suitcase.

"With Beth here?"

"You think she doesn't know what goes on between me and her friends?" Daniel said brutally.

Nora flushed. "If there's some kind of trouble with your deferment, my husband could help. He got my son's little problem ironed out.'' That was the first time she'd admitted she had a son his age.

"There was no problem at all. I enlisted."

"I didn't know you were that stupid."

"I wanted to see the world."

"You'll see a jungle in Southeast Asia! Look Daniel, if you want to hide out . . . go to Canada . . . . I can loan you the money. That little bundle I invested for you is growing nicely, you know. Pretty soon it won't matter whether Beth has your dad's money tied up or not."

"You just keep looking out for it and I'll be happy." He closed his suitcase.

"What about your career? You've been working hard and now it's starting to pay off."

That was true. Combining college and acting hadn't been easy, but he'd managed to do it these past three years. At first it was just a way to earn more money so that he could compete with Victoria's college man. Gradually he had come to realize that he actually loved acting, that he had a feeling for it. Just recently it had occurred to him that while he could be a more than competent actor, what he really wanted to be was a director. Eventually.

But in the meantime, his famous prick kept getting in the way. It kept him from being taken seriously. He had to fight for any attention careerwise, to start out against total resistance for every part he wanted. He knew that he had a growing sexual reputation in this town. That in combination with being his father's son presented him with twin stumbling blocks.

At least in the army he wouldn't have a problem with his famous prick.

He grinned at Nora. "I can't write you. Your husband might find out. So I guess this is good-bye for now. When I get back—"

"*If* you get back, your money will be waiting for you. And I'll be an old woman," she added with sudden bitterness.

There was no answer to that. "Good-bye, Nora," he said gently.

He wanted at least to kiss her but she gave him a long cool glance and left.

Daniel looked around the room one last time. His last letter from Sharon, the one announcing Victoria's wedding, lay crumpled in the wastebasket. He fished it out. Her return address was on the envelope. He stuck it in his pocket and left.

Joseph Moretti looked at his new bride across the breakfast table with something close to awe. The weeks they had spent in the Caribbean on their honeymoon had left her so fit and tanned that he wanted to eat her up.

Just having her at his side made him forget that he was an old man of forty-eight, twenty-five years older than his young wife. He had no doubt that she would prove to be a valuable asset to him in business also. All of his clients would love her.

Now that they were settled in their new home, it was time to accept a few invitations. "We're invited out to dinner tonight," he told her, and watched the quick smile light her face.

And fade just as rapidly, when he added, "With Dominic Solari."

"Why would Dom . . . ?"

"Not Dom. Dominic. His father. My most important client. He's a very influential man, Victoria. But you may not know that because he chooses to keep a low profile. It's quite an honor to receive an invitation to his home. He tries to keep his home life separate from his business. If this works out, and we're included in his circle of close friends . . . Well," he said expansively. "I just can't tell you where it might lead. If you're worried about having someone your own age to talk with, I'm sure Dom will be there too. He's working for his father now and living at home."

"But tonight . . . on such short notice . . . couldn't we put it off until . . . ?"

"Victoria! I thought you understood. When Dominic Solari beckons, any man in Los Angeles comes running. Including me."

He folded his napkin precisely and laid it on the table beside his plate. "I realize you might be shy about meeting such an important man, but I can tell you that if he likes you, there's no more steadfast friend than Dominic Solari." And what Solari's friendship meant to him each year in terms of dollars and cents was a staggering thought. "Be a good girl," he urged. "I'll see you tonight."

Joseph left the breakfast table, whistling.

Sharon and her friends were standing outside their favorite sidewalk cafe when the Frenchman approached. He ignored everyone but her. "Would you like to star in a movie?" he asked her, speaking in slow, careful English. "I have a part for an American girl."

"I'll bet you do! All five inches of it." Melissa Travers was the daughter of an English Duke and had the filthiest mind in the whole school. "That's the oldest line in the world," she told Sharon. "Let's go."

Sharon hesitated. Something about the Frenchman's thin intelligent face intrigued her. "How did you know I was an American?"

"He's been eavesdropping, obviously," Melissa said scornfully.

"From across the street? My card, Mademoiselle. Your green eyes would break a man's heart from the screen." His own eyes were wide-set, almond-shaped and brown. They focused on her so completely that none of the other girls existed.

Sharon looked down at the card to hide her blush. Philippe Tescier, Director, it said, with a Paris address. "Is this a legitimate movie, Monsieur Tescier? Because I'm a legitimate actress. I've been on American television."

"She knows Daniel Garrick," one of the other girls broke in.

Both Tescier and Sharon ignored the interruption, sizing each other up. "It is indeed legitimate, Mademoiselle. You are in school here?"

"You think we're in prison?" another of the girls asked sarcastically.

Sharon gave her a quelling look. "Yes, Monsieur," she replied politely.

"I will walk back to the school with you and speak with the headmistress. Your friends can accompany us so that your reputation will not be compromised. Your parents are in the United States?"

"Yes, Monsieur." She frowned at her friends and they

dropped back a good twenty feet, so that she and Tescier were strolling alone, and their conversation could no longer be overheard.

"You are underage, are you not?"

She was tempted to lie, but something about this man killed the impulse. "Sixteen, Monsieur."

"Then we must acquire your parents' permission for the project. But the pay would be sufficient to cover a year of your schooling. Not that someone of your class cares about details like that," he added with an underlying sharpness that made her wonder just what class he considered himself to be a part of. "You said you were on American television? What shows?"

"Just one, Monsieur Tescier, but it ran for five years. *Charlie's Gang.*"

He stopped and stared at her in amazement. "But it cannot be. You are the *enfant*? JoJo?"

When she nodded shyly, he said, "I knew you were an actress when I saw you."

"Thank you, Monsieur Tescier."

"Philippe. You must call me, Philippe, Little JoJo. What a beautiful movie we will make together!"

The other girls followed behind them, giggling and whispering like children. Sharon walked faster, hoping Monsieur Tescier would not notice how infantile they were.

"You have acted since *Charlie's Gang*?"

"No, Mon—Philippe."

"You miss it, the acting."

It was a statement of fact, needing no reply.

And entirely true, Sharon discovered to her great surprise.

Dominic Solari Senior was a shock.

Victoria had expected anything but the tall, powerfully-built man who strode across the palatial living room and took her two hands in his, nodding his head in approval. There was power in the thrust of Dominic Solari's square decisive chin, and passion in the full sensual lips beneath the classic Roman nose. He was younger than Joseph, only forty-two, but he looked younger still, with a dynamic quality about him that spoke of energy contained. He could have been Dom's older brother instead of his father. "Ah," he said in a warm baritone, "the lovely young wife of my good friend Joseph. Welcome to my home." He turned her hands palms upward, and kissed them both. His knife-sharp blue gaze seemed to pierce right through her. Victoria realized that for all his warmth and graciousness, Dominic Solari was judging her.

"Mr. Solari," she said warmly. "Thank you so much for inviting me." She heard Joseph's faint sigh of relief beside her and realized that he had been holding his breath, on edge about the meeting between his important client and his wife.

"Call me Dominic," he insisted and turned to introduce her to his wife, leaving Victoria with the feeling of having drunk champagne too fast.

In ten years, Giselle Solari would look like her husband's mother, but for now there was still a taut femininity to her roundness that hinted at the girl she had been. The delicately pointed chin that must have given her face a certain fragility when she was younger was almost lost now in her plump face. Giselle's soft brown eyes measured Victoria as if the younger woman were a rival for her husband's affections, and Victoria realized with a little start of surprise that she did find Dominic Solari attractive.

Joseph, more nervous and on edge than he had ever been before in all the years Victoria had known him, seemed almost physically terrified of the man whose approval he was trying so desperately to win. When he introduced her to the rest of the family—Dominic's two older sons and their wives—Joseph spoke a little too loudly, a little too heartily. When Dom Jr. appeared at last just as the family was about to go in for dinner, he seemed less menacing, a pale and not very accurate copy of his father. He acknowledged Joseph's greeting with a faint smile and turned away without speaking to Victoria. Observing Dom Jr. in this family setting, Victoria saw that he had only a superficial resemblance to Dominic Senior. The son had inherited Dominic Solari's height, but not his muscles. His father's nose dominated his lean face. But Dom Jr.'s eyes—wet and brown as a spaniel's—his thin lips, and his pointed chin were his mother's. He was not nearly as frightening to her now that Victoria had seen the original. Still, she could not miss the way that Dominic Solari beamed at his youngest son. Dom Jr. truly was his father's favorite.

But even Dom Jr.'s presence couldn't quell the sudden excitement meeting his father had generated. With the bubbles still racing through her blood, she found herself across from Dominic Solari at dinner. The men dominated the conversation. Victoria addressed a few remarks to plump and pregnant Alessandra, wife of Dominic's oldest son Cesare, who sat beside her, but the other woman made it clear the men's discussion should not be interrupted by idle female chatter.

After dinner the women rose to clear the table, while the men disappeared onto the terrace. Giselle chattered with her two daughters-in-law as they carried the dishes back to the kitchen and began the washing up. Victoria knew from the desperate glance Joseph had thrown her that she was not to join the men, so she drifted along behind the women, some silverware clutched in her hands. Pert Luisa, wife of the middle son, Nicolo, was talkative now that the men were gone. She snatched the silverware from Victoria and pushed her down into a kitchen chair to watch as the three Solari women washed and dried the dishes. There was considerable discussion of Dom Jr. and his current girlfriend. The women thought he should marry but apparently his father, satisfied with four grandchildren and two more on the way, was not putting any pressure on his third son just now.

Victoria found it difficult to believe as she listened to the chattering women that this was the same Dom Jr. she had known in Cambridge. She wondered what they would do if she suddenly stood and announced that he had tried to rape her and had instead ended up beating her so badly that she landed in the hospital.

The impulse to do so was so strong that she finally excused herself and went in search of the powder room. She lingered there, rearranging her hair, looking at herself in the mirror, and wishing the evening was over.

When she came out into the darkened hallway, someone grabbed her from behind. A hand over her mouth muffled her shriek of surprise.

"My father thinks you're charming," Dom Jr. whispered in her ear. "You and your husband will be frequent guests of the Solaris." He let his hand drift down the front of her dress and cup her breast. "How convenient for me." His fingers teased her nipple through the cloth and then drifted lower, across her belly, caressing her through her skirt.

Victoria lunged free of him and bolted back into the bathroom, slamming and locking the door behind him.

"Pretty Victoria," Dom Jr. said softly through the door. "Surely you have realized by now that I am my father's favorite son. It won't do you any good to complain to him. If I tell him I want you, I will have you. Your husband would sacrifice you in a moment if he thought you would lose him my father's friendship." Chuckling, he moved away from the door.

Victoria stared across the powder room at her reflection in the mirror. Dom's hand had smeared her lipstick into a red gash across her stark white face. Those chattering women in the kitchen would never believe her. And Joseph . . . Dom was right about Joseph. That was why she had never told Joseph about Dom Jr. She had realized instinctively it would do no good.

Now Victoria knew she was truly trapped.

Sharon's boots made soft crunching sounds in the snow as she ran through the silent night to the waiting Citroën. "I was afraid you hadn't gotten my message," she said when she clambered into the spacious interior. "Hurry up! Someone may come out to investigate."

Philippe Tescier sat there without starting the car. "I had another message today. One not so pleasant."

"My parents?"

He nodded.

She slumped back against the seat.

"Do you wish to go back to the school now?"

She couldn't read the expression in his eyes in the darkness, but the lack of emotion in his voice made her say rashly, "I still want to see your chalet."

He looked at her a moment longer, as though to be perfectly sure she meant what she said, and then started the Citroën's engine.

The chalet was alive with lights when they pulled up beside it. Inside it was warm and comfortably furnished. Sharon halted abruptly, startled to see that a couple lay entwined on the rug in front of the fireplace, the woman nude to the waist.

Philippe's hand behind her back urged her on past them and up the stairs.

In the bedroom, he took off his jacket and his sweater. When he reached for his belt buckle, Sharon said plaintively, "Aren't you going to kiss me?"

He came across to her and, his hand beneath her chin, tilted her face this way and that, looking at her eyes, the planes of her cheeks.

"Ahh," he said softly. His lips just grazed hers and then he walked out of the room. Sharon stood there, still in her jacket, not sure what to expect as she heard him clatter down the stairs.

Philippe returned in a few minutes with a bottle of champagne and two glasses. "Sometimes American girls are hard to judge," he said as he opened the bottle. "Your manner says one thing." The cork leaped out with a satisfying pop. "But your experience is something else entirely."

He poured them each a glass and raised his in a salute to her, before downing it. She followed suit. She had never drunk champagne before and she found she liked it. He watched with amusement as she finished her glass and held it out for more.

The second glass warmed her cheeks and she reached for the zipper on her jacket.

"Let me do that," Philippe said.

He opened the zipper slowly and helped her out of the jacket. When she raised her arms to brush her hair back into place, she realized he was staring at her full breasts beneath the sweater and she blushed.

"More champagne and you will not blush like that," he said as he took her in his arms. This time when his lips met hers, she kissed him back aggressively.

He pulled back and looked at her once more. "No, little Sharon. Don't pretend to be something else now. Let me lead you."

When he had undressed her and laid her back on the bed, he spent a long heavenly time covering her with kisses from the rosy tips of her breasts to the soft blond curls between her legs. In the midst of the rising heat of the passion he roused within her, she realized that it was the first time in her life that she had ever had the complete attention of any male besides Andrew.

That thought brought tears to her eyes, whether for herself or Andrew, she wasn't sure. But she was crying when Philippe entered her. As he captured her virginity, he leaned down and kissed each of her closed damp eyelids.

Her eyes fluttered open and she watched his face, the clenched jaw muscles, as he began to move within her. She ran her hands down the taut, quivering muscles of his arms, and then caressed his back, letting her hands move lower until she clasped his buttocks, pulling him closer to her, moving upwards in an effort to meet his thrusts.

It was over sooner than she expected.

He pulled out of her suddenly and groaned as his wet sticky seed spurted across her belly. He flopped over on his side and lay there panting for a moment. "So *enfant*," he said. "Today JoJo is a woman."

He drove her back to the school and she managed to sneak inside without being detected. When she climbed back into her bed and fell asleep, still in her clothes, there was only one clear thought in her brain.

It had been the most wonderful night of her life.

Joseph, in his robe and navy silk pajamas, sat down on the edge of the bed. "I know you're tired tonight," he said gently. "But you're so beautiful."

Tired wasn't the word for it, Victoria thought. Trapped was more like it. They had spent all evening at her grandparents, with her grandfather staring silently at her across the table and her grandmother chattering nonsensically. She had thought that by marrying Joseph she was freeing herself of her grandparents. Instead she saw them more often than ever.

Worse than that, though, was Joseph's preoccupation with Dominic Solari. The night before they had gone to Solari's home again, and although she had managed to avoid Dom Jr. by never being alone, he had let her know by his sly smile that he was just awaiting his chance at her.

If only she had told the truth back in Cambridge when he attacked her! Then someone might have believed her now.

Joseph leaned over and stroked her hair. He smelled of toothpaste and mouthwash, after-shave and deodorant. Like a perfect gentleman, he had showered, shaved, and deodorized himself before he came to her. Six months of marriage and she knew his routine by heart. Now he would ask her permission before he slipped the nightgown from her shoulders and began to make love to her in his slow, mannered way.

"Do you mind?" he said.

As he slipped the nightgown down, Victoria wondered what would he do if she said yes, she did indeed mind. That she wished he would just once proceed to the next step without asking her permission. That he was so much of a gentleman everywhere, including the bedroom, that he was driving her *wild* with boredom.

The thought of her career and getting back into it on a full time basis was all that kept her going. She had contacted her agent today, to let him know she was available again.

Predictably, Joseph murmured, "Do you mind?" one last time and entered her.

At least I have plenty of opportunity to practice my acting, she thought as she arched up to meet him.

Five unendurably long days passed before Sharon could sneak away from the school by herself and call Philippe's chalet from a phone in a tobacconist. When an unfamiliar male voice answered, she asked for Philippe.

"Will you stupid girls never stop calling!" the strange male voice exploded in rage. "Tescier has gone to Paris! He won't be back."

"But . . . this is Sharon. Sharon Bradford. Didn't he leave a message for me?"

"Sharon, Patricia, Julia, Marcie . . . calling at all hours of the day and night! I ask you, how can a man get any rest? God save me from you teenage sluts! There is no message for any of you!" He severed the connection.

Sharon hung up the phone and leaned back against the wall. The overpowering smell of tobacco made her head swim. She thought she might faint.

The shopkeeper said something as she bolted past him, but he might as well have been in another world. The bell on the door jangled wildly as she pushed through it and into the crisp air outside.

She paused, trying to decide what to do, and someone grabbed her from behind.

Sharon struggled wildly, but the shopkeeper's stout wife held her fast while she went through Sharon's pockets to see what she had shoplifted. When the woman found nothing, she released Sharon and went back in the shop, muttering to herself.

Sharon stood there a moment and then turned and followed her back inside the shop. "Do you have any American cigarettes?"

The woman stared at her sullenly.

"*Avez-vous des cigarettes—*"

"I understood you the first time," the woman said. "How many?"

"Two packs. And matches."

"The money?"

Sharon pulled a wad of francs from her jacket pocket. The woman took it, counted it, and then turned to get the cigarettes. She handed them back to Sharon with the change.

Outside once more, Sharon lit a cigarette defiantly, enjoying the scandalized glances that darted her way from passersby. She yanked off her cap and let her hair blow free, while she took another puff, scrupulously careful not to inhale.

She glanced back at the tobacconist. The shopkeeper's wife stared at her through the window.

Sharon laughed and waved and started back toward the school.

Every man she passed turned to give her a second glance.

"Absolutely not," Joseph said solemnly, as though he were standing before the jury in a court of law. "I've already discussed this with your grandparents, and the answer is no."

"You can't be serious!" Victoria screamed at him from across the breakfast table. "I'm a grown woman. I can do what I want. They have nothing to say about my life anymore."

"You're a married woman, Victoria. The wife of a lawyer. A very prominent lawyer," he added smugly. "It's not suitable for someone in your position to try and become an actress."

"I don't have to try and become an actress. I *am* an actress! My agent already has several—"

"No, Victoria. You're my wife. And that's all. It's all you need." Joseph dabbed his lips daintily with a napkin and stood up. "Oh, did I mention that we're dining with the Solaris again tonight."

When she didn't answer, he said sharply. "You realize how much of an honor it is to be included in Dominic Solari's inner circle, don't you, Victoria? I wouldn't want to see you throw any childish temper tantrums like this in front of Dominic." When she still didn't reply, he sighed. "Really, Victoria! You're acting like a child."

When he left, she remained sitting there, staring at her untouched breakfast. Everything was closing in on her. Joseph, Dom Jr., her grandparents. If she couldn't act, there was nothing left for her at all.

Why in the world had she ever thought that marriage to Joseph would be an escape?

Chapter Twelve

1968

Victoria's hand trembled as she raised the heavy brass knocker on the massive oak door and let it fall. This was going to be the most important interview of her life. And the most frightening.

When her agent called her yesterday with the news that he had a perfect part for her, he had also given her an ultimatum. If she failed to audition for it, he would drop her as a client. He refused to listen to her excuse that Joseph had forbidden her to act anymore and she needed time to accustom him to the idea. "Time is what you don't have, darling," Mel told her with brutal honesty. "You're twenty-five years old. Do you realize how many nineteen-year-olds are out there working their asses off while you sit on yours and whine about your hubby? You've kept me dangling for two years on this. I've lined up part after part you've refused to go after. It's time you made up your mind what you really want."

But last night when she told Joseph about the part and Mel's ultimatum, her husband merely said, "Good riddance to the man. I don't know why you bother to keep up the pretense of having an agent."

All her angry arguments had done nothing to change his mind. This morning he had gone cheerfully off to work, sure that everything was settled. That was when Victoria had finally realized what she must do.

She lifted the heavy brass knocker again. This time her anger at Joseph steadied her hand. When the door opened, it was Giselle Solari who stood there. "Dominic is expecting me," Victoria said.

Giselle nodded and led the way back to Dominic's study. She knocked on the closed door, frowning at Victoria as she did so, as though disturbing her husband was a terrible imposition.

When Dominic called, "Come in," Giselle stood aside for Victoria to enter and then closed the door behind her.

Dominic Solari sat at his desk, writing. Victoria was struck as always by how youthful he was compared to her own husband. Joseph looked every day of his fifty years. The muscular man behind the desk was only forty-four and could have passed for much younger. He looked up, and then rose to his feet, coming swiftly around the desk to take her hand in greeting. "What a pleasure to see you," he said, sounding as if he meant it. As always when Victoria was in Dominic's presence, the sheer energy of the man made her feel exhilarated.

How very dull my life with Joseph is, she thought suddenly.

Dominic pulled up a chair for her in front of his desk. When she had seated herself and he had returned to his own chair behind the desk, he said, "So, Victoria. How may I be of service?"

Victoria crossed her ankles and leaned forward. She spoke slowly, knowing exactly how her words might obligate her, "Dominic, I need your help."

Temple Jackson raised the tent flap and stepped inside to find a fight in progress. At least four grunts were rolling around on the filthy, beer-spattered floor of the tent, kicking, punching, cursing and raising holy hell. The big Texan watched for a minute, amazed that anyone could get mad enough to expend that much energy on a muggy gookville day like this bugger. Then he snagged a beer and sat back to watch. Temple loved nothing better than a good fight, as long as he wasn't in it.

It wasn't clear at first exactly who was licking who in the free-for-all. By the time Temple drained his first beer, he realized that the big, gold-haired man was kicking the shit out of the other three, but he still hadn't figured out what started the melee. Unless it was something to do with the three slant-eyed little mamas watching the brawl from the other corner of the tent and giggling for all they were worth.

By the time Temple drained his second beer, the big man had finished off the other three and left them groaning on the floor. The big man was all beat to hell and bloody, but that didn't stop him from staggering over to Temple and grabbing a beer himself.

"What was the fight about, son?" Temple asked idly.

The big man looked him straight in the eye and said, "It was because I have a famous prick." Then all the little oriental mamas came running over and threw their arms around the big man, yelling, "Daniel, Daniel."

By the time the big man loved his way through that covey of tail and fought his way through three more bars, Temple had found out that his name was Daniel Garrick. His daddy was the old-timey movie actor Leif Garrick, and he was that smart-ass little kid on *Charlie's Gang* that Temple had watched back home in Waco before he was fool enough to go and get himself drafted.

If there was one thing Mama Jackson's boy knew it was an opportunity when he saw one. Daniel Garrick was opportunity on the hoof and unbranded. Temple didn't know what the opportunity was just yet, but he was willing spend the rest of the night loving up Daniel's leftover bar girls, and see if it revealed itself.

Sometime just before dawn, Daniel got in a card game with three Marines. He won four straight hands, and then one of the Marines made a crack about Bucky Weston's manhood. Temple was beginning to understand that there wasn't a soul in Nam who wouldn't want to brag that he'd beat the crap out of either Leif Garrick's kid or Bucky Weston.

Daniel gathered up his winnings and stuffed all the money into Temple's hands. "Hold this for me," he said. "We'll count it after I clobber this guy."

Temple Jackson decided he had found himself a friend for life.

Sharon slammed her wine glass down on the table so hard

that the stem snapped. The Burgundy spilled out on the pristine table cloth, and Inga jumped up and came around the table to mop it up.

"Leave it, Inga," said Cynthia Bradford. "I'll ring for the maid."

"It will stain by the time that silly woman comes," Inga said calmly, as if she and her employer were social equals.

Sharon watched in astonishment. The fact that all of them—her parents, Inga, she, and Andrew—were eating dinner at the same table was unbelievable. That was the biggest change, but there were other, smaller changes in the six years she had been stuck in that finishing school in Switzerland, Sharon thought grimly. Her father's hair had gone from distinguished wisps of gray at the temples to totally white, a stark contrast to his tanned face. Her mother's face looked tighter, as though the skin had been stretched across her skull; Sharon had not realized until this morning that Cynthia Bradford must have had a face lift recently. Inga had changed too. Or maybe it was only her own perspective that had changed, Sharon mused. She was 5'9" now, and Inga, at five foot ten, no longer seemed to tower over her. All the Swedish woman's powerful muscles were still there, but now they were upholstered with a sleek layer of fat, which had also softened her hard cheekbones. Without those angular planes to her face, Inga's pale blue eyes no longer had the same frightening authority.

Or maybe it's just that I've finally grown up, Sharon thought.

But it was Andrew who had changed the most. The two of them were eighteen now, but Sharon no longer felt a kinship with her twin. She wasn't sure she would have recognized him if they had met on the street. He was taller than she, a man, not a boy, with wide muscled shoulders and a loose easy grin. He still didn't talk much. He shook her hand solemnly and said, "Hello, Sharon," when he came down for dinner, but that was the last thing he had said, to her or anyone else.

When Sharon tried to talk to him, Inga was there, between them, answering the questions before he could, and Sharon finally gave up. But her glance had strayed back to Andrew again and again. She couldn't believe how handsome he was. And how much of a stranger he had become.

Now as Inga mopped up the spilled wine, Andrew watched incuriously.

"I would have thought they'd teach you better manners than this in that fancy Swiss school," Keith Bradford told his daughter.

"Manners are not the point. I'm trying to discuss my future."

"We have discussed your future. Four years of college at a good American university and then—"

"Four more wasted years! I could have a film career in Europe right now. Do you realize how important a director Philippe Tescier is? He wanted *me* for the movie that won the Oscar for best foreign film last year! If you'd given your permission then—"

"You were too young then. You're still too young," her father told her.

"You need an education," Cynthia Bradford said. "Even if we did let you follow this wild plan of yours, who would stay with you? I certainly can't. Your father and I will be in New York for at least three months, and after that Rome, and after that—"

"We brought you back to enroll you in college and that is where you're going," Keith Bradford said.

Sharon shoved away from the table and stood up. "No, I'm not. I'm tired of everyone else deciding things for me. You sent me to Switzerland to get rid of me and now you're just trying to do the same thing all over again."

Cynthia Bradford gasped. "Why you ungrateful—"

"She could stay here with Andrew," Inga Lindholm offered with quiet authority. "I'll look after both of them."

"Oh, Inga," Cynthia Bradford said with a melting tone in her voice. "We couldn't possibly ask you to do that. Andrew is enough of a burden for you."

"Andrew is no burden." Inga reached over and patted him on the knee. "Sharon will not be either."

Sharon listened, dumb-struck. She couldn't believe that Inga whom she had always considered to be the enemy was actually offering to do something nice for her. Something wonderful for her. She held her breath as her parents looked at each other.

Then Inga spoke the magic words, the words that couldn't fail to convince them. "Besides, it will be good for Andrew."

Before Sharon could believe what was happening, they had agreed. It all seemed like a dream come true.

The best part was that she would be with Andrew again.

"My good friend, it's time we had a talk." Dominic Solari took out the box of fine cigars he kept in the lower drawer of his desk and offered one to Joseph Moretti.

Joseph shook his head. As Dominic went through the ceremony of lighting his cigar, Joseph studied him cautiously, trying to assess his mood. When he saw Victoria chattering with Dominic before dinner, he had been tempted again to tell her more about his client. If he could be sure she would hold her tongue he would warn her that the man who appeared so suave and urbane was actually the most dangerous man Joseph Moretti had ever known. Nothing could actually be traced to Solari—thanks in part to Joseph's own legal maneuvers—but the blood of many men was on Solari's hands. Whether Solari had performed the act of murder himself, Joseph was not sure. But he had given orders that had sent more men to their deaths than Joseph cared to think about. Now he was about to give another order, and Joseph quaked in his shoes. He had managed adroitly up until now to perform no illegal act himself. The hundreds of thousands of dollars that Solari had paid him over the years had allowed Joseph to live like a prince. Now he feared Solari would ask him to do something criminal in return for the gracious lifestyle he had enjoyed over the years. And Joseph knew he could not refuse.

"Victoria is unhappy," Solari said.

Joseph blinked. This was not what he had expected. "I'll ask her not to bother you with her problems, Dominic," he said quickly.

"No, no," Solari said expansively. "I like for my friends to confide in me. Sometimes it happens that I can do them a small service."

That stupid bitch! What had she told Solari? Joseph searched his mind frantically. He had been a fool not to warn her about this man. What could he have said that was about to be used against him? "Please, Dominic. Give me a chance to explain." He could feel the dampness in his armpits, of his palms, could smell the stink of his own fear. "She's only a girl, really. Twenty-five years old. She doesn't understand—"

"Victoria is a woman. A very passionate and gifted woman. She has a great talent, your wife. It's selfish to keep a treasure like that locked away, out of sight."

Now he began to understand. "The acting? Is that what she talked to you about? Her grandparents and I talked it over. It's really not a suitable—"

"Two old people. What do they know of youth's dreams?" Solari smiled at him. "But two men like ourselves . . . We're not old yet, Joseph. Not you and I. We remember what it was to be young, to have a dream, don't we?"

He didn't feel young. At the moment, he felt every one of his fifty years dragging him down. Joseph mopped his forehead nervously with his handkerchief. "She's not supposed to have that kind of dream," he said petulantly. "She's my wife. She's supposed to take care of my house, to entertain my guests, to . . ."

"To bear your children," Dominic finished gently. "But we both know, old friend, that bearing your children is an impossibility for her. If it were, I would not ask you to grant me this small favor."

How the hell did he know that? Joseph wondered. He had been meaning to talk to a physician about Victoria's inability to become pregnant. But he had feared it was his fault, not hers, and so he had put off investigating the problem. His anger—and his relief that his manhood was not in question—made him incautious. "Really, Dominic. This is my marriage, my life," he said more vehemently than he would have dared a moment before. "Surely you wouldn't ask me to do something I'm so strongly opposed to. Not when it doesn't affect you or your business."

"But it does effect me. It pains my heart to see that bright flame diminished. If you would grant me this one small favor, I would be in your debt."

Joseph knew it was true, knew that Solari was a man of his word. He licked his lips hungrily. To have Dominic Solari in his debt . . . "But her grandparents—"

Solari waved a hand. "Don't concern yourself with that. I'll speak with her grandfather."

"I . . ." Joseph grimaced helplessly. "All right, Dominic."

Solari rose. He leaned across the desk to shake Joseph's hand, catching Joseph's elbow with his other hand at the same time, making a brotherly embrace out of the gesture. "Thank you, my friend. I'm in your debt."

When Solari released his hand, Joseph rubbed his damp palms against his suit.

"Shall we join the others now?" Dominic asked. "I would like for my family to join in her happiness when you tell her that you have relented."

"Certainly, certainly," Joseph responded heartily. "If I could just . . ." He glanced at the door to Solari's private washroom, just off his study. Solari nodded, and Joseph darted through the door. His hands shook so hard, he could barely work the zipper of his trousers.

Dominic Solari watched the lawyer bolt into the washroom with a feeling of sadness. Joseph still had his uses as a front for some of Dominic's enterprises, but whether he realized it or not, he no longer handled Dominic's real law problems. Joseph had become a doddering old man. The thought of Moretti with young, vital Victoria disgusted Dominic. He could see why she longed for some release outside marriage. A shame she could not have children. He had seen the way his Dom looked at her. Now that would have been a match! To have grandchildren with that much fire and determination in their veins would have made him proud.

Dominic sighed and stood up as Joseph emerged, slightly shamefaced. At least it had not been necessary to take more drastic measures to assure Victoria's freedom. Joseph Moretti had been a good and faithful servant over the years.

It would have been a shame to have him killed.

Victoria looked up as Joseph and Dominic Solari came back into the room and the breath caught in her throat. Joseph looked positively ashen. Even stolid Giselle noticed and offered to fetch him a drink of water.

Dominic waved his wife away. "My dear friend Joseph has a little announcement for us," he told his assembled family.

"Ah, I just wanted you to know that my . . . that Victoria is going to be acting again."

"Joseph!" she squealed out and then blushed. "I . . . oh, thank you, Joseph. You know how much this means to me." She rushed across the room and hugged him.

"My old friend Dominic convinced me it was a good thing for you to do," he said.

There was no irony in his voice. Victoria aimed a sideways glance at her husband. Could it have happened this smoothly, with no recriminations? "Thank you, Dominic," she said, turning to Solari.

For just a moment, when she met Dominic Solari's ice blue gaze, she faltered. Someday there would be payment due for this favor. But not now. Not tonight.

Tonight she was ecstatic.

Even Dom Jr.'s baleful face could not kill her happiness tonight.

For the first time in her life she had everything she wanted. Everything!

1969

Temple Jackson laid back in the hammock and sighed contentedly. Cold beer in the cooler, a cute little mama with a fan half her size giving him a steady breeze to snooze by, and another one curled up in his bunk waiting his pleasure.

"War is hell," he told the little mama with the fan. She giggled and fanned faster, making her tiny little tits bounce to beat the band.

Man! This was the life.

And it was all thanks to Daniel Garrick.

Only if Daniel found that out, he would beat the shit out of his old friend Temple.

But it just hadn't seemed right to Mama Jackson's boy that an important man like Leif Garrick's son, who also happened to be a famous film star his ownself, should have to be out in the jungle trading insults with the gooks. Not when there was an oversupply of wetbacks and brothers to take care of that department.

So Temple had put out the word to a few people exactly who they were dealing with and turned up this cushy little assignment for the two of them.

They were *supposed* to be special advisors to a crew of Canadian bozos in Nam to film a documentary. Instead, he and Daniel spent their days sleeping and their nights boozing. And the little Oriental mamas were always on call.

Jeez, war was grand!

"Temple, you son of a bitch! Hit the deck."

Daniel's voice thundered over him as he was dumped out of the hammock and onto the ground. All the little mamas ran and hid, but he could hear them giggling like crazy somewhere in the house.

"What the fuck did you want to go and do that for?" Temple said, aggrieved. "I was trying to take a siesta."

"Tomorrow's the day you earn your pay again. The boys from Montreal finally got their shit together. We're going out on a helicopter in the morning and meet up with a patrol. We're going to give them the grand tour of the jungle."

"Oh, no! Oh, shit!"

Daniel smiled that big golden grin at him. "I knew you'd love it."

"So you finally decided to join us, Miss Carr," the director said loudly for the benefit of the crew.

"I was in makeup, Mr Pace," Victoria countered. *Where you sent me, you little bastard.* He was an inch shorter than her five foot seven inches, and that difference in height had began to gnaw on her like everything else about him.

"Primping!" Bernard Pace announced to everyone on the set, his dark suspicions about actresses obviously confirmed.

He was a pudgy little clown of a man with dark, curly hair that looked like he combed it with his fingers. Victoria had no idea how the laugh lines had become etched around his eyes and mouth because from the day they started this picture she had never seen him so much as smile. His clothes looked like he bought them at a garage sale and had a hobo sleep in them before he put them on in the morning. He didn't give a damn about anything or anyone except his movie. If he believed any stronger in the *auteur* theory, he would have actually signed his name to every frame of film. His only saving grace was that he was an absolute genius.

If not for that, Victoria would have walked off the set and the movie right there.

As it was, she waited a hour and a half before she suddenly turned and screamed at him, "I quit!"

"Oh, no, Miss Carr," Barney Pace screamed back. "You're fired!"

Barney Pace stalked off the set in one direction; Victoria, in another.

Victoria shut herself up in her trailer. Once inside, she grinned with wicked enjoyment as she stepped out of her shoes, because she knew something Mr. Genius Pace had forgotten in his rage. Too much of the film had already been shot. The studio couldn't afford to replace her. A director, though, that was an entirely different matter. She poured a small glass of Chablis and made herself comfortable.

He waited an hour.

When the knock came, Victoria set down her glass and took a deep breath. *You little bastard. Get ready to grovel!* She let a full minute elapse before she rose and went to answer the door. Bernard Pace stood on the ground beside the steps. She stared down at him coldly.

"All right, Victoria. I'm an ass." He smiled at her, and now it was obvious where all of those laugh lines had come from. Barney Pace smiled with his whole face. "Will you come back and make my movie?"

Victoria was totally disarmed. All the derogatory, insulting, sarcastic phrases she had been about to utter vanished from her consciousness. She found herself smiling back. "Well . . . since you ask so nicely."

But by the time her makeup was repaired and everyone was back in place, they had less than an hour of shooting time left.

They made the most off it. For the first time since shooting started, cast, crew, and director were in sync. When they finally called it quits for the day, Bernard Pace walked over and said, "When you get yourself out of all that goo, I'm taking you to dinner."

It never occurred to Victoria to say no.

This time he was headed home in a body bag for sure. Temple couldn't believe these damn civilians were dumb enough to get themselves out in the boonies where the gook assholes were firing live ammo. He'd made a practice of walking around life's little shitpiles. Even getting called up for service hadn't been too bad, because that had meant that little darling in Abilene had to take care of her own problems and not come after him as a daddy for her bundle of joy. He just didn't know what to make of grown men who had a choice between getting shot at and not getting shot at and chose the wrong one.

And look at Daniel, for Crissake. Enjoying every minute of it. You'd think he was making a goddamned movie.

Temple hunkered down further into his hole, watching morosely as Daniel fired occasional shots at the snipers with a borrowed rifle.

"Let the pros do it, son," he advised, when one shot came zinging too close to Daniel. "You're not being paid to get your hide punctured."

Daniel just grinned at him and popped another round into the trees.

Then one of the Canadians yelled that the chopper was about to go. Temple was first in line, dodging and weaving back toward the lovely bird that was going to take him out of all this crap.

Daniel came too, but slower, covering their rear, while the real soldiers kept peppering the trees like good little grunts.

Temple climbed aboard and yelled at Daniel to move his ass.

Those snipers kept letting off a good one now and then, and one caught the head Canadian right in the ear lobe, leaving him with a bloody bit of flesh dangling there.

Just then Daniel got one in the back and pitched forward into the mud, while that goddamned Canadian honcho started yelling at the pilot, "Take off. Take off."

"What about Daniel?" Temple yelled at him over the sound of the helicopter.

"Leave him. He's dead."

The way the snipers' fire was churning the mud around him, if he wasn't dead, he was sure gonna be.

Temple had ten thousand dollars in his account back in the States, money he had skimmed off of a lot of little scams, but mostly off of Daniel. If he could keep Daniel alive, that was only the beginning. Temple couldn't sit there and watch the best meal ticket of his life get punched.

The head Canadian was still squawking. Temple leaned over to the pilot. "You take off without me and you're dead meat, son."

The pilot nodded.

Temple piled out of the helicopter and ran back to Daniel. He grabbed him by the shoulders and started dragging him back to the copter. He could feel the mud splattering on his pants as the bullets hit the ground around him. One of the Canadians came running up and grabbed Daniel's feet, and together they carried him to the copter.

"Take off! Take off!" the Canadian honcho yelled as they tossed Daniel's dead weight inside.

"Do it, son," Temple shouted.

He stared down at Daniel's face as the copter lifted off at a crazy sideways angle and then tore out for home. He had just saved a man's life, Temple marveled. He never thought he'd be fool enough to do *that*.

He just hoped to God Daniel was gonna hang on long enough to be grateful.

In a Las Vegas motel room, Victoria learned that cuddling Bernard Pace in bed was like sleeping with a big overgrown teddy bear. A sexy teddy bear. They had flown to Nevada on separate planes Friday night. They had to be back on the set Monday morning. Even though this was only Saturday, Victoria was already thinking how quickly Monday morning would arrive. She sighed.

Barney pulled her closer. "Disappointed already? It took my wife a year to decide she couldn't stand me."

"I'm a married woman, Barney."

"I'm a divorced father of one."

"So what's the future for us when we leave this flashy paradise and go back to L.A? Absolutely zilch."

"Less than that," Barney said. "I love you dearly, but I can't take a chance on screwing up my kid. Laurel's only six years old. She's already gone through the abandoned-by-mommy shtik once. The kid was in analysis for two years. I swore never again."

"What's that supposed to mean?"

"It means you're not moving in with me."

"I don't remember asking to move in with you. You might not have enough bedrooms for me and my husband both."

"I'm serious, Victoria. You know we'll keep seeing each other. This flame's not going to burn out anytime soon. You'll be dumping Moretti, and then the next thing, you'll be wanting to play wife and mommy for me and Laurel."

She tried to roll away from him, out of bed.

He caught her around the waist. "You're crying!"

"You may be a hell of a director, Barney, but you're lousy with people! You know that's exactly what I want."

"We're two grown-ups, Victoria. We know things end, people change. Kids don't see it that way."

"All right, Barney."

"What's that supposed to mean," he asked suspiciously.

Victoria put her arms around him and hung on for dear life. "It means I'll take any little piece of you I can get."

Sharon hung up the phone and turned around to find Cynthia Bradford standing in the doorway to the living room, watching her. "Mother! I didn't know you and Father were back." Her parents had just spent six weeks in Turkey and were supposed to spend the next six in Rome.

"Keith went on to Italy without me. I had a few things to take care of here before I join him."

Sharon couldn't help wondering if those few things included a lover. She had never seen any overt evidence of her mother straying again after the interlude with Miranda's husband. If anything, her parents had seemed even closer after that. But watching her mother now, Sharon was almost certain that Cynthia Bradford had flown back to the States to meet someone. "Will you be here for dinner?"

"Not tonight," Cynthia said hastily, confirming Sharon's suspicions. "I have other plans."

Sharon expected her to rush away like she always did, but for once Cynthia lingered. "Inga tells me your career is going well."

Sharon shrugged. "It's doing okay. That was my agent on the phone just now. He has a pretty good part lined up for me." She had been getting a lot of small, but significant parts recently.

"That's good." Cynthia Bradford glanced down at her watch.

The gesture thrust Sharon back into her childhood so abruptly that she had no defense against the feelings that came rushing at her. She could remember so vividly all the times that she and Andrew had watched their glamorous mother who had no time for them hurrying off to some engagement. Determined

not to let those childhood memories get her down, she dropped
down on the sofa and picked up a magazine.

"Sharon?"

She looked up, surprised to find her mother still standing
there.

"I suppose I wasn't a very good mother," Cynthia Bradford said abruptly. "It wasn't you and Andrew, you know. I
just didn't like children. I still don't." She glanced at her
watch again, and Sharon realized suddenly that it was simply
a nervous habit, something her mother did when she couldn't
meet another person's eyes. "We were so relieved, your
father and I, when we found Inga. You just don't know how
. . ." Cynthia shook her head, as though Sharon had tried to
interject something. "I just wanted you to know that."

She hurried out of the room, leaving Sharon sitting there,
stunned. That was probably the longest conversation she'd
ever had with her mother, she thought. Too bad it was about
fifteen years too late.

And Inga as a surrogate mother was a laughable prospect.
At best there was an uneasy truce between her and Sharon.
As long as Sharon didn't try to be too intimate with Andrew,
to share anything with her twin that Inga wasn't a part of,
Inga stayed strictly out of Sharon's life.

Which was almost worth the price.

Something about Inga made Sharon uneasy. She had even
wondered if the woman might be a lesbian. God knows, she
looked like it, with her overdeveloped muscles and her close-
cropped hair. But if she was, she'd never made a pass at
Sharon.

Sharon stared down at the phone. That hadn't been a pretty
good part her agent had snagged for her; it was a great part.
There was a very good chance that her career was just about
to take off.

Now she had everything she had ever wanted, Sharon
realized. An acting career. Freedom from her parents. The
chance to see Andrew every day. And even an apology from
her mother for being such a crappy parent.

So why wasn't she happy?

Daniel woke to pitch darkness. "Temple?"

"I'm here, son." The Texan moved closer to Daniel's bed.

Daniel lay there, remembering.

"You all right, son? Want me to call the Doc?"

"How did I get back in the chopper, Temple?"

"Well, son, you don't think I'd just leave you lying there, do you? You don't treat a buddy that way."

Actually until Daniel woke up after the surgery, that was exactly what he would have thought of his buddy. Temple had never seemed the slightest bit altruistic. For Temple to risk his precious skin for somebody else was so far out of character for the man Daniel thought he knew, he realized he must not know Temple Jackson at all. Daniel grabbed Temple's hand and squeezed it. "I owe you, Temple."

"I know you do, son," Temple said as he squeezed back. "And I aim to collect."

Daniel chuckled. Now that was the Temple he knew.

But he still owed him.

"And this is your bedroom where you'll sleep with my daddy," Laurel Pace told Victoria with an air of pride.

Victoria met Barney's eyes over his daughter's head. Barney shrugged helplessly. He hadn't wanted to do this. Much as he loved Victoria, he didn't want to take a chance on what would happen to Laurel if their affair broke up. But his love for Victoria had overcome his scruples. She had moved so easily into his life and Laurel's that they had become a family in every way but this. In fact, it was Laurel who finally asked Barney when Victoria would come to stay with them for good.

He followed the two of them back downstairs and poured himself a drink. When he sat down in his favorite chair, the two females he loved best in the world were nestled side by side on the sofa, their heads bent over a storybook. They looked up and caught him watching them.

"Daddy?" Laurel squealed. "What are you smiling about?"

Barney gave a huge contented sigh. "Life," he told her.

Chapter Thirteen

1971

"Daniel? How long have you been in town? We've got to get together!" Sharon's voice was lower, sexier than he remembered it. For a moment Daniel regretted contacting her. She belonged to his childhood, a time he didn't want changed.

But then, as she went on, he was very glad he had let her know he was back. "We've got to get together, the three of us. You did know that Victoria's a big star now." They both were, but two vastly different kinds of stars. Sharon was the newest sexpot on the Hollywood scene. Daniel knew how it worked. She would glow like a supernova for a few months, a few years, and then flame out if she couldn't figure out some way to keep herself on top. Victoria was different: a serious, respected actress. Sharon knew that too. He could hear the self-consciousness in her voice.

When he hung up, he had a luncheon date for the first of the week with both of them. "A family reunion," Sharon had called it.

Daniel got a couple of cold beers out of the fridge and went out to join Temple by the pool.

Temple gave him a lazy smile as he took the brew and went back to watching the scenery. When they found this place two weeks ago, the Texan claimed the pool alone was worth the rent on the two bedroom apartment. It was an astonomical price to pay for the privilege of watching the bit players and extras flaunt their flesh, but still not quite high enough that a genuine Name would be found in one of the loungers. As soon as Daniel got some work, he planned to move on up, maybe to a beach pad. In the meantime, the rent was a drain.

Temple had been after him to call his mother, see if he could shake some of his dad's money out of her hands. But Daniel wasn't ready to let her know he was back in town yet. Nor had he told Temple about the money Nora Trager had invested for him. That must be quite a tidy little sum by now. It would be tempting to dip into it. But he wasn't going to. Someday he would have a use for that money and when he did, it would be there waiting.

He'd give both Nora and his mother a call next week. Better that than to let them read about his return in the trades. His agent had been ecstatic to see him back and in such good shape. Daniel was already up for at least two parts that looked solid.

It was a good life, he thought, as he stretched out in the lounger and closed his eyes, letting the sun warm his skin. A trusted buddy by his side, and lunch next week with the two top female stars in Hollywood.

And he knew at least one of the parts he was up for had his name on it.

That was all he needed. Just one big part.

And Victoria.

Temple frowned at his sleeping buddy. A year and a half of following Daniel around the country like a hound dog hadn't done a thing for Temple's bank balance. His pecker was a different story, though. Wherever Daniel went there were plenty of girls, more than even a stud like Daniel could handle.

Money was the problem. Temple had made quite a few good investments while he was still in Nam, some of them with money skimmed from Daniel, some of them with money acquired in other ways. Temple just had a natural born talent for acquiring cash and making it grow. And for spotting opportunity.

Daniel was still opportunity with a capital "O." As long as that happy state of affairs continued, Temple planned to stick to him like glue.

One of the bikini-clad girls climbed out of the pool and pulled the lower half of her suit up, outlining everything Mother Nature had given her for Temple's benefit. She wandered over and smiled down at him. "I've got something cold to drink up at my place."

Temple heaved himself up to follow her, leaving Daniel sleeping peacefully in the sunshine.

"But you've got to come, Victoria. It'll be just like a family reunion."

Victoria smiled to herself as she listened to Sharon bubble over the phone. When she talked like that, so fast and excited, she reminded Victoria of JoJo.

But that thought led directly to others Victoria had no desire to explore. "Sharon, really, I'm all—"

"Please, Victoria. I know it's a lot to ask on such short notice, but please."

Now she *really* sounded like JoJo and Victoria could hear the "Nan" creeping back into her own voice, when she gave in. It would be interesting to see if Daniel still retained any of Bucky in his makeup, she thought as she put down the phone. Now all she had to do was explain to Barney why she couldn't meet him for lunch on Monday.

She paused at the door of the family room, enjoying the scene. Barney and eight-year-old Laurel had their dark curly heads bent over the monopoly board. They were a family in every way but one. She was still married to Joseph Moretti, and Joseph refused to even discuss the possibility of a divorce.

Barney and Laurel glanced up at the same time and smiled identical father-daughter smiles when she came on into the room.

For a crazy moment, Victoria was so happy she wanted to weep.

Sharon arrived first and waited impatiently for the others, so nervous she feared she might throw up. *Stage fright. After all these years I finally have stage fright!*

The intimate little restaurant was so "in" it had barely

been discovered yet. That was why she had chosen it over Daniel's suggestion of the Polo Lounge. It will give us more privacy, she had told him. But the real reason was that at the Polo Lounge, Victoria would have gotten the lion's share of attention from everyone from actors to busboys. Here Sharon might be on almost equal terms with her. Sharon had even toyed with the idea of not inviting Victoria at all, or else telling Daniel she had, but that Victoria couldn't come. She felt thoroughly ashamed of that impulse. She really *did* want to see Victoria.

Besides, if Victoria didn't come, she wasn't sure Daniel would either.

Sharon spotted him from across the restaurant. She rose and hurried toward him as the headwaiter brought him over, hugging him in delight.

Daniel hugged her back and then held her out to really look at her. None of the still photos he had seen had prepared him for the reality of Sharon's brilliant green eyes in that perfect face and her breathtaking figure. Photographs didn't come close to doing her justice. Where had little JoJo gone? Was this glamorous woman with the gleaming platinum hair who he had been corresponding with all these years? It couldn't be!

The throb of his manhood embarrassed him. It was almost like getting an erection watching your mother for Christ's sake. She had been his little sister on the show and somehow, although she was far from that now, it was still how he thought of her. His physical attraction to her made him uneasy.

Then, behind her, he saw Victoria at the table, smiling fondly at both of them, and he hurried Sharon across the room toward her.

Sharon looked from one to the other of them. For one wild minute she felt as though she were ten years old and back on the set of *Charlie's Gang*. They were the adults and she was the child. And as always, the adults were ignoring her.

Twice she tried to join into the conversation. Twice they ignored her conversational gambits, chatting on, looking deep into each other's eyes. She didn't know what exactly she had expected out of today, but it certainly wasn't this.

And who were they actually?

Daniel was a former teen star trying to get back in the swing. Victoria was the darling of the critics. But she, Sharon, was hot at the box office, and that was what really counted.

Still she couldn't damp down the rage building inside her. She felt the same way she did the few times she had gone out to dinner with her parents as a child. Keith and Cynthia Bradford had been too caught up in each other to even notice or talk to her then. That was what was happening now.

"I'm surprised you didn't bring your boyfriend," Sharon said suddenly, spitefully, to Victoria. "Or didn't you want Daniel to know?"

"Know what?" Daniel asked gamely.

"Wouldn't all the people who used to watch us on *Charlie's Gang* be surprised to find out Nan was married to one man and sleeping with another?"

Victoria frowned at her. "That's hardly a secret, Sharon. Barney and I have been together for over two years now."

But it was obviously news to Daniel, Sharon noted with relish.

"Barney?" he asked.

"Bernard Pace. The director." Victoria glanced down at her watch. "And he's a stickler for punctuality. I'm supposed to take his little girl to the zoo this afternoon."

Daniel watched her go. It wasn't until the big black Mercedes had pulled away from the curb that he realized he hadn't told her his big news, why he was late. He had gotten not one, but both the parts he was up for and filming on the two features would be juggled to accommodate *his* schedule.

Only now, it didn't seem like such a big coup. Directors were the important ones in Hollywood, not actors. Men like Bernard Pace wielded the real power.

Daniel found that intriguing.

1972

The phone rang in the middle of the night. Victoria grabbed it before it could ring again and said, "Hello," softly.

"Your grandmother died tonight," Joseph Moretti said without preliminaries. Her grandfather was already dead from a massive heart attack three months ago, just after her reunion with Daniel and Sharon. Victoria had hoped her grandmother might blossom since she was finally out of Vincent Stanton's grasp, but instead Florence had simply withered away.

Joseph let her know that he had already taken care of the funeral arrangements.

"I'll close the house," Victoria told him. She was the sole beneficiary under her grandmother's will. "I'll want to go through everything before I put it on the market."

"I'll be glad to help you, Victoria."

"No, I want to do it myself," she said quickly. If any secrets of her past still lurked in that house, she wanted to be the one to find them.

"Victoria, don't you think it's time you stopped acting like a whore and came back to me?" Joseph asked plaintively.

She hung up the phone without replying. Barney was stretched out beside her, sleeping soundly. The phone had not roused him. Victoria longed to wake him up and tell him that for the first time in her life she was completely happy.

The past was finally dead.

Barney was the future.

Victoria turned the key in the front door of the Stanton house for the last time. To bad she couldn't do something as final about her marriage, she thought, staring up at the huge old house.

Joseph had been at her grandmother's funeral as he had been at her grandfather's. At least she had kept Barney out of it. He had wanted to come to the funeral and so had Laurel. But where Laurel was concerned, Victoria had absolutely put her foot down. She didn't think a nine-year-old belonged at a funeral unless she had to be there. Laurel had already gone through enough pain in her young life. No need to bring her more. Laurel was abnormally sensitive to Victoria being gone for any reason—afraid, as Barney had pointed out before, that her "mommy" would desert her again—and this time was no exception. In fact, Victoria had gone to great lengths to minimize being separated from her new family for Laurel's sake, even though her career was going so well that the pressure on her to travel more was intense.

Victoria had brushed Joseph off at the funeral and driven

back to her grandparents' house alone. The cleaning and sorting would be left to a hired crew. Victoria was looking for only one thing: her mother's diaries. It took her three whole days to go through the house from top to bottom. Three totally exhausting days. She could not sleep at night for the creaks and groans of the huge old house. Laurel had phoned at least six times a day, asking, "Aren't you through *yet*?" Even, Barney, wonderful, wonderful, Barney, was beginning to complain.

She hadn't dared tell Barney what she was looking for. She didn't want him to ever find out the sordid truth about her grandfather, her mother, her.

But after three days of intensive search, she had not been able to find Thea's diaries. Her grandmother must have burned them as she had wanted to so long ago. So this morning Victoria had placed a call to Joseph's office and left a message for him that she was through with the house and to go ahead and hire someone to clean it out and sell the furnishings. She wanted nothing of what was here for herself.

Victoria knelt to slip the key under the mat for the real estate agent. When she rose, the sound of an automobile made her turn. Joseph's car was pulling into the drive.

As he got out of the car, she was struck again as she had been at the funeral by how elderly he looked. He was fifty-four now, but he looked ten years older. In fact, he looked old enough to be Barney's father. The thought of Barney at home waiting for her, made her ask sharply, "What do you want, Joseph?" when he reached her.

"You broke your grandparents' hearts by abandoning your marriage, Victoria. It's time you came home." He shook his head sadly. "They were good decent people. They couldn't understand why you've acted the way you have."

Decent! If he only knew! "I'm not coming back, Joseph. It's time you got used to the idea."

Victoria started around him to her own car, and he grabbed at her clumsily. She sidestepped him easily and put her Mercedes between them.

Joseph was panting. "I can make things very awkward for Pace," he gasped. "You'll see. He has custody of that little girl, doesn't he? I'm sure the courts wouldn't think he's exposing her to the proper environment by living with a woman like you. A woman who has abandoned her husband."

"You can go to hell, Joseph." The coolness of her own voice astounded Victoria. "I want a divorce. I'm going to marry Barney Pace."

"You'll get a divorce over my dead body, Victoria."

When Victoria got home, Laurel ran to her and hugged her. Barney was out and the child clung to her, not letting Victoria make two steps on her own.

This was a ridiculous situation, Victoria realized. It was only making things worse for Laurel, and she had promised Barney she wouldn't do that.

Joseph had to be forced to go along with a quiet divorce. But there was only one person in the world who could do that.

Victoria shivered at the thought.

Instead of Giselle Solari who opened the door for her, this time it was Dom Jr., with his hot eyes. "Your father is expecting me," Victoria said quickly, before he could try anything.

Dom chuckled, a low vicious sound like an animal's growl. "I know. I'm to show you right in. Right in."

There was an awkward moment after Dom Jr. opened the door to his father's study when she thought he might stay and listen in, but he left, closing the door behind him.

"How may I be of service, Victoria?" Dominic Solari greeted her, and she knew everything would be all right.

"Barney! Barney!" Victoria called as she hurried through the house, searching for him.

She found him in the kitchen, cooking. He was a wonderful cook and this was his form of relaxation. And Victoria's too, since she didn't have to worry about preparing evening meals. "What's the uproar, woman?"

"Barney, will you marry me?"

"Of course I would, if you were free. You know that."

"Joseph is going to give me a divorce."

"Really?"

"Really!"

He dropped the spatula and grabbed her around the waist, whirling her about.

Laurel ran in from the family room. "Daddy! Daddy! The eggs are burning."

Barney released Victoria and grabbed the skillet, dumping it and its contents in the sink. Then he picked up Laurel and hugged her tightly. "How would you like to be a bridesmaid at Victoria's wedding?"

Laurel's face drew into a pout and for a moment Victoria thought her heart would stop beating. She knew that if Laurel disapproved, then Barney and she could never marry, no matter how much they loved each other. "Who's Victoria going to marry?" Laurel demanded.

"Me, dummy," Barney said.

Laurel shrieked with delight.

Victoria felt the sun come out.

The eggs smouldered in the sink.

Victoria was the first one off the plane from Reno, almost tripping in her eagerness to get down the ramp. She was a new woman, a free woman. And as quickly as they could set things up, she would be Mrs. Barney Pace.

She had expected Barney to meet her but instead a tall man in a dark suit collected her and her luggage. "Mr. Pace is tied up at the studio. He asked me to pick you up," the man said. "And since you can't see Mr. Pace right away, Mr. Solari asked that you stop by his house before going home."

She wanted very badly to refuse. Laurel would be waiting. Although Victoria had talked to her every single night on the phone while she was in Reno for the divorce, she knew that the little girl wouldn't be satisfied until she saw Victoria in person again. One of her suitcases held a gorgeous two-foot-tall doll in a satin wedding dress for Laurel. Victoria couldn't wait to see her stepdaughter-to-be's face when Laurel opened the box.

But she didn't dare refuse a direct invitation from Dominic Solari. Not after all she owed him.

Only after she had climbed into the long black limousine did Victoria realize that it had not been an invitation but a summons.

She expected him to greet her with the same phrase when she entered his study. But instead of "How may I be of service?'' Dominic Solari said, ''We are old friends now, and friends sometimes owe each other debts of gratitude.''

She nodded cautiously, unsure where this might be leading. She had heard through the grapevine that Dom Jr. was getting involved in the Hollywood scene as a producer. Was Dominic going to ask her to star in one of his son's pictures? If so, the answer was no. She wouldn't risk her career, even for a debt like the one she owed Dominic.

''I'm a proud father, Victoria. I have three fine sons. Two of them have wives, families. But the third, the youngest, the dearest to my heart, does not.''

Victoria nodded again. Perhaps he was going to ask her advice on Dom Jr. He wouldn't like what she longed to tell him. That Dom should have been drowned at birth. She gazed at Dominic steadily, not letting a flicker of what she felt show on her face.

''You're a strong, spirited woman, Victoria. You have been wasted for years on an old man. Now you are free at last. And I had a small part in making that happen,'' he said modestly.

For the life of her Victoria couldn't figure out what was going on. Was he propositioning her? There was a spark between them, no doubt about that. And at forty-seven, Dominic was certainly no old man. She loved Barney and had never been tempted to stray since they had been together. Not until now. Dominic Solari's dynamic personality seemed to fill the room. Victoria shifted uncomfortably. ''What is it you're asking me, Dominic?''

He frowned at her bluntness. ''The return of a favor, Victoria. That's all. My son is in love with you. Marry him.''

For a moment she couldn't believe she had actually heard the words. ''In the first place I wouldn't marry Dom if he were the last person on earth. Did you know he tried to rape me once?''

Dominic Solari ignored her outburst, continuing on in the same steady voice, ''He needs a strong woman like you, Victoria. He's too rash, too impulsive.''

''That's your problem, not mine. In case it slipped your mind, I wanted this divorce so that I could marry the man I've been living with for two years. I'm going to be Barney Pace's wife and the mother of his daughter.''

"No."

That was the most deadly word she had ever heard.

"This is ridiculous, Dominic. You can't force me to marry Dom."

"I don't want to force you to do anything, Victoria." He spread his hands out wide. "I want you to grant me this small favor in return for the favors I've done for you."

"This isn't a small favor! This is my life!" Victoria stood up. "I won't do it, Dominic."

She grabbed her purse and started for the door. Before she reached it, she heard something hit the top of Dominic's desk with a thud. Without turning, she knew what it was.

"If you refuse me this request, this box will be delivered to Bernard Pace tomorrow morning. Also, since I am now a majority owner in the studio which employs Mr. Pace, I can tell you that I am sad to learn that his services will no longer be required on his current picture. Also, I believe the former Mrs. Pace could be located and dried out. It may be that she relinquished custody of her daughter hastily. She may reconsider that decision and try to get the child back. Courts tend to favor the mother in cases like this. Even when the mother has a record like hers."

Victoria turned and walked back to his desk. Inside the box were the diaries she had searched her grandparents' house for in vain. All of them, filled with the damning truth in her mother's handwriting.

"You know what's in these?" she asked him.

"I do."

"Then why do you want me in your family?" she asked bitterly.

Dominic Solari rose and came around the desk. He took her hands and looked down into her eyes. "I am not judging you with this, Victoria. You are judging yourself. You have put a tighter noose around your own neck than any I could fashion. You will marry Dom rather than let Bernard Pace know this about you."

She knew he spoke the truth. "What about Dom? Does he know?"

"Not unless you tell him yourself."

She jerked her hands away. "Are you crazy?"

"I know that you will never truly love until you find the man who loves you knowing everything about you."

"What about you?"

Now it was his turn to be startled. "What do you mean?"

"Does Giselle know the truth about you? That you're a mobster? That you have people killed?"

She expected him to deny it. Instead he said, "No. She is my wife. The mother of my children. She knows I'm a good provider. That's all she needs to know." He sighed heavily. "It is also all she wants to know."

For the first time she wondered what it must be like to be him. To be unable to share himself with the woman he loved.

They took each other's measure.

"I have to tell Barney myself."

"There is no need. He has already been told."

That was like a physical blow. "And Laurel?"

"She is no longer any concern of yours, Victoria."

She thought about the doll in her luggage. She thought about Laurel, clinging to her waist. Another mommy had abandoned her today.

"I've had a room prepared for you," Dominic Solari said. "The wedding will be this weekend. I'll ring for the maid to show you upstairs."

He watched Victoria leave his study like a sleepwalker. For the first time in his life, he envied someone else. His youngest son was the apple of his eye, but Dom Jr. was no match for a woman like this one. Too bad she could not have children. To see grandchildren with his blood and hers mingled, that would be a triumph.

Dominic Solari found himself speculating on what it would be like to have a woman of such beauty, such intelligence, and sensuality at his side. Giselle was his wife and there was no lack of bed partners. But to have this woman would be something else. Something better.

Joseph had been too old to ignite the fires of her passion, and Bernard Pace too much of an intellectual. For a moment, Dominic allowed himself to imagine her body bucking up beneath him, her dark eyes staring into his as they made love.

He sighed. If it had not been for his son, Dominic would have taken her for himself long ago.

Victoria's luggage had already been unpacked. All of her

clothes hung neatly in the closet. All of her personal things were in the bureau or else in the adjoining bathroom.

But the bride doll had vanished.

It was part malice and part something else that led Sharon to make the call. "Daniel? I'd been meaning to get in touch. How's the new movie going?"

Sharon really had meant to contact him in the weeks following their "reunion" lunch, but she just couldn't bring herself to do it. She wasn't sure exactly what she had expected from that meeting. But whatever it was, it hadn't occurred.

She was twenty-one now, and making plenty of money. Yet she was still lonely. Still unsatisfied. Living here in her parents' home with Andrew and Inga only made her feel more alone. The sensible thing to do was move out of this house and into a place of her own.

Sharon knew she wouldn't, and her own lack of initiative disgusted her.

And now this. When she got the news this morning, she felt like a ten-year-old again. She still couldn't believe Victoria hadn't let her know. Sharon broke in on what Daniel was saying, "I was really surprised to hear about Victoria, weren't you?"

"To hear what?" Daniel asked sharply, and Sharon was momentarily elated to realize that he was as much an outsider in Victoria's life as she was. Then the gloomy feeling that had enveloped her this morning when she heard the new swept back over her again.

"You knew she was getting a quiet divorce in Reno, didn't you?"

He mumbled something she didn't catch.

"Well, everyone thought she was going to marry Barney Pace when it came through. But she didn't. She married someone else."

"She's remarried?"

Sharon wondered if she had his full attention. "I just told you that."

"Who did she marry?"

"Dom Solari, Jr. His father—Daniel? Daniel? Are you there?" Sharon stared at the phone in disbelief.

Daniel had hung up on her.

Dom Solari, Jr.

The slick, sophisticated college man.

Daniel had heard the rumors that Victoria was getting a divorce, that she and Barney Pace would finally wed. He was almost reconciled to that. Pace was a man Daniel respected and admired.

But Jr.!

The loudmouth.

The know-it-all.

The pretentious asshole.

The murderer's son.

My old man kills people . . . You do something Dominic Solari doesn't like, then you disappear. Permanently.

That was the family into which Victoria had married.

Nothing ever changed, Daniel thought. He was always too young, the kid brother. She had never taken him seriously.

And now it was too late.

Chapter Fourteen

1973

A picture window at one end of the gym in the immense Solari home overlooked a garden of lush Peace rosebushes, the landscaper's gift to the daughters-in-law of the family, although none of them but Victoria ever ventured there. The gym held enough exercise equipment for a spa: two exercise bicycles, a rowing machine, exercise tables, rollers, belts, push-up weights, and more. Victoria finished her warmup and moved to the free weights to begin the rigorous set of exercises her coach had designed for her.

The body was perfect and it was going to stay that way. Thirty was a dangerous age, her coach had warned Victoria yesterday. After thirty-five, the abdomen and upper thighs went. If she let herself slip now, she might never reach the peak again.

And Victoria was definitely at the peak. She had her choice of roles to choose from, and she chose carefully. Even though every moment away from Dominic Solari's mansion was a release, she refused to accept just any role. Only the ones that would keep her star on the rise.

Sometimes she thought that if only she and Dom were living somewhere else, she would be able to make it.

Sometimes she thought that if she and Dom lived anywhere else, she would fall apart.

God, the world was crazy and she was going insane!

Why in the world had Dom ever wanted to marry her? He had made love to her halfheartedly a few times since their marriage. Now and again every few months he would remember she was his for the taking. But the rest of the time he ignored her. He certainly gave no indication of the great passion he had indicated to his father.

She suspected more than anything else, he had simply wanted to punish her for that long ago humiliation in Cambridge.

More and more she found herself wondering if he might be a homosexual. As his interest in her faded, and their sexual encounters became fewer and fewer, they also became more brutal.

Sometimes she could barely walk the next day.

Sometimes she thought about Baney, sweet, tender Barney, and such an empty ache filled her that she thought she would die.

Sometimes she wondered if she had been strong enough to tell Dom the truth about herself, about the incest in her family, would he have left her alone? Would he have let her go ahead and marry Barney instead? But the chance that he might have told Barney was too great. She couldn't bear to see that knowledge in Barney's eyes.

So she suffered Dom's assaults and his verbal abuse. But only when they were alone. When they were with his family, he either ignored her completely or treated her with such scrupulous politeness that her sister-in-laws remarked on it enviously. Her mother-in-law never commented. Victoria suspected those soft brown eyes of Giselle's saw the truth about her youngest son.

Then there was Dominic Solari himself. The master of this house. The father of her husband. The ruler over a criminal mob, if all the stories about him were true.

The man who excited her as no one else ever had.

She knew Dominic felt it too: the electrical sexual attraction between the two of them.

But he did nothing.

She was so unfulfilled now. The last time she had enjoyed

making love was long ago with Barney, the night before she left for Reno. There had been no enjoyment with Dom since then. He didn't care whether Victoria achieved release or not.

She wondered what kind of lover Dominic Solari would be. He had fathered three sons on placid Giselle, but there were rumors that he had mistresses.

She hefted the weights and the muscles above her breasts tightened. Her hair clung to her face in damp wisps.

"You are magnificent," a male voice said behind her.

She turned.

Dominic Solari stood there, devouring her with his eyes. She could feel the different parts of her body warming with the heat of passion as his glance slid over her.

Carefully, he took the weights from her and set them down. She was drenched in unladylike sweat, but somehow she knew it made no difference to this man.

He stepped closer to her, until their bodies were almost touching. "You know I want to take you to bed?" he asked her softly.

"Yes." Her voice was husky, colored by her passion.

They stood there, separated by only an inch or two of air between them. Her breasts heaved behind the leotard with the extent of her exercise, with the knowledge of his desire, barely missing contact with his chest.

When they touched each other, it would be like a spontaneous combustion. Victoria was halfway to a climax, already warm and wet, just thinking about it.

"Get dressed," he said abruptly. "You have a lot of work to do." He started for the door of the gym.

"Dominic? What are you talking about?"

He paused. Without turning around, he said, "You and Dom are moving into a house of your own."

"But, Dominic . . . us? What about us?"

"There is no us," he said cruelly. "You are the wife of my son."

He left, slamming the door of the gym behind him, as if he were trying to put that moment of almost passion behind him.

And put her behind him as well.

"I love young men. But then a lot of women in this town do." Kyna Hensley pronounced "women" as though it began with a "v." It was the last trace of Europe in her sultry voice. "That must make you very popular." She twisted slightly, so that she could see Daniel's lazy smile above her.

He straddled her trim body as she lay face down on the satin sheets of the king-sized bed, massaging her bare buttocks, her strong almost unfeminine shoulders. There wasn't an ounce of extra flesh on her anywhere. Only the lines on her face betrayed the fact that she was forty-eight. When she turned her face to the pillow once more, the body became that of a twenty-eight-year-old.

"Young men are so wonderfully self-absorbed," Kyna went on conversationally, as though she were unaware of his maleness rubbing against her back. "You don't have to worry about them falling messily in love. They save that for younger women."

Daniel moved further back and lifted her up on her knees, entering the soft warmth of her from behind. She sighed with pleasure.

"But with you I think there will be none of that, Daniel," she went on as he began to move inside her with firm strokes. "You are not ready for love yet. The musician is more concerned with his instrument than with his audience."

To prove her wrong, he brought her to a shuddering climax, before he took his own release.

Afterwards they lay entwined on the huge bed, her head on his chest, her dark hair spilling everywhere like silk. "Now do you think I'm more interested in myself than you?"

"You make love well, Daniel. But you are not in love. When that happens, you will know the difference."

He thought about Victoria. "I've been in love."

"And what happened?"

"The lady married someone else."

Kyna raised up on one elbow and looked down into his face. "Is it really love or is it a phantom?"

He didn't want to think about Victoria now. He took Kyna's hand and guided it down between his legs. "This is no phantom."

Kyna squeezed his firmness and chuckled. "Thank God for young men!"

"Sharon, this is Philippe Tescier."

This was her night, her party. She was the important one here, the star. He might be well-known in France but he certainly hadn't made his mark in the U.S. yet. If she snubbed him tonight, half of Hollywood would do the same tomorrow. Considering how he had dumped her in Switzerland, she was sorely tempted. She almost turned and walked away. It was the cynical gleam in his almond-shaped eyes, expecting just that action on her part, which held her there. Sharon extended her hand. "Why, Philippe!" she said graciously. "It's so wonderful to see you again."

"You two know each other?" the hostess asked.

"Why, we're old friends, aren't we, Philippe?" Sharon slipped her arm through his and leaned her head against his shoulder.

"Old friends," Philippe agreed, amused.

Later, in bed, she gouged his ribs with a fingernail. "Old friend," she taunted. "Why didn't you ever try to get in touch with me again?"

"For what purpose?" he asked with French practicality. "Your parents refused permission for the film. You had used me for your sexual experimentation. Our business was done for that time."

"And now?"

"And now, *enfant*, I think I will let you move into my apartment with me. We will amuse each other for the next six months. Until I return to France."

"Don't be silly. Why would I want to do that?"

"Why, indeed?" Philippe murmured as he slid back into her.

Daniel got up in the early dawn hours, leaving Kyna slumbering alone in the big bed, and took a shower. For the third time that week, he worked off his beard with her delicate feminine razor. He ought to start leaving an electric shaver here, he mused as he wrapped a towel around his middle and went downstairs to see if there was anything to eat in Kyna's kitchen.

He was scrambling himself some eggs when he realized he wasn't alone in the big kitchen. He whirled around, skillet in one hand, spatula in the other.

A little girl, twelve or thirteen, dressed in a thin cotton

nightgown, stood just inside the doorway watching him with
large eyes that slanted slightly upwards like a cat's, giving
her an exotic, vaguely oriental look. Her skin was ivory,
almost dead white, and her hair a stark black with a striking
widow's peak that added to the oddity of her thin face.

"Want some breakfast?" Daniel asked her.

"Are you my father?" she asked with a serious frown.

To his credit, Daniel didn't even crack a grin. "Nope."

"Then will you marry me when I grow up?"

"Good grief!" Kyna exclaimed from the kitchen doorway.
"He will think you are an imbecile, Caro! Get back to your
room and get ready for school."

The cat-like eyes flickered toward Kyna and the little girl
darted out of the kitchen without another word.

Daniel dished the eggs into two plates, the miniscule portion Kyna insisted upon and the rest for himself. "Your
daughter?"

"Yes, and for that she hates me." Kyna set the table.

"You'd be tough competition for an adolescent," Daniel
said as she leaned against him to place a napkin in his lap.
"Or any other woman for that matter."

She patted his cheek. "You're a darling boy. So was
Caro's father. Jack Chen. The cinematographer. Perhaps you
know him."

"I've met him." A cold, cynical bastard, but talented.

"He was the cinematographer on my last film. He made
sure every frame was perfect. Absolutely flawless. And of
course, that ended my career."

"I don't understand."

"Oh, Daniel!" Kyna pushed her plate aside. "You are a
beautiful young male animal! Of course you don't understand. You see, thanks to Jack, I was at the peak of my
beauty. I finished the picture in a blaze of glory." She waved
her hands expansively. "I was at the height of my fame."

"So?"

"Dear Daniel," she said with a sad shake of her head.
"Many years from now you will learn that from the peak of
the mountain, every road leads down."

"That's bullshit."

She raised one elegant eyebrow. "You haven't lived long
enough to have an opinion on this subject, Darling. Be-

sides . . . by the time the film ended, I was pregnant with Caro.''

''You didn't marry him, though.''

''His infatuation with me ended when the film did. He needed a new challenge. As for the child he fathered . . . '' She shrugged. ''He's never even asked to see her.'' She frowned. ''It wasn't that he doubted she was his daughter. It was simply that there was no place in his calculations for a child.'' Kyna brightened. ''But perhaps you'll be good for her, darling.''

Daniel wondered.

1974

''Goddamned lush,'' Dom Solari raged. He struck out at Victoria. She lurched away, still clutching her glass, but leaving a moist trail of vodka across the deep white pile of the carpet. ''They're going to be here in five minutes,'' he bellowed at her. ''Drink some coffee and fix your makeup!''

Victoria hurried down the hall and slammed the door of the master bedroom behind her. Last year, she wouldn't have dreamed of drinking in the afternoon. Last year, she wouldn't have been clever enough to hide a bottle of vodka in a shoe box in her closet.

One more little drink, she told herself, as she filled her glass. Otherwise she wouldn't be able to make it through this meeting. She carried the glass with her into the bathroom and began to repair her face.

It was bad enough being married to Dom, but since the first of the year, he had been managing her career. He fired the agent she had, dependable, brutally honest Mel, and from that moment on she had lost all control over her own life. He had chosen her new agent, her directors, her roles, even her wardrobe.

They were all equally bad.

Victoria couldn't decide whether he wanted to humiliate her or if he simply had no taste at all.

She had heard rumors he used his studio connections to launder mob money. Other people had heard those same rumors, and combined with Dom's lousy taste in every choice he made for her, the hints of mob involvement had been enough to make her career nosedive.

She had considered appealing to Dominic once more, but this time she knew it would do no good. He wouldn't take action against his own son. Even if he did, no legitimate director would touch her now.

Victoria took a good long look at herself in the mirror, forcing herself not to flinch away from the puffy, drinker's face that confronted her. *Oh, Barney. It would have been so different if we were together.*

"Victoria," Dom Jr. bellowed from the living room. "Get your ass in here!"

She forgot about Barney, her fading looks, and everything else. All that mattered was getting another stiff drink down herself before Dom dragged her out there to talk to his sleazy director about the next rotten movie he had signed her to make.

"It was bad enough that you moved out of this house without a word to your parents or anyone and moved in with this man. But this!" Inga raged. "It's just too much!"

Sharon stared at her icily. "You're not my keeper. I'm not asking your permission for anything. I simply want to tell my brother good-bye."

"You want him to know you are acting like a whore?"

"Don't be ridiculous. I love Philippe. He loves me. I'm going back to France with him. That's certainly not acting like a whore."

"Are you married? No. Then you are a whore!"

Inga spoke so loudly that Sharon was afraid her voice might carry out to Philippe waiting in the car in the drive. He wouldn't wait long, either. He had seen no need for this good-bye meeting to begin with.

"Please let me in, Inga," she pleaded. "I only have a few minutes." She knew she would never be able to force her way past the other woman. Beneath her sleek flesh, Inga had more muscles than Philippe.

Inga shook her head. "I will not have Andrew upset by your wicked ways."

A car horn sounded from the drive.

"You bitch," Sharon said.

"Whore," Inga countered.

The horn sounded again.

And that was that, Sharon thought as she raced down the steps toward the waiting car.

Good-bye Andrew. I love you.

1975

The newest of the two Oscars gleaming on Daniel's bookshelf drew Temple's eye. He gestured at it sheepishly. "I guess you're gonna rub that in."

"It means more to me than the other one," Daniel said, ignoring the conversational bait. He had known immediately that he had the perfect vehicle for his directing debut in *Sunshine Man*. And with Kyna coming out of retirement to star in it, how could it lose? Only nobody was willing to put any money in it. Temple had told him flatly to forget it. There was no way he could come up with the money on his own.

That was when Daniel had sprung the surprise of the nest egg Nora Trager had invested for him so many years ago. The sum it had grown to was enough to lure in other investors. However, Temple had still been against the project. Possibly becáuse Daniel had refused to reveal where the money had come from. Daniel plunged ahead anyway, and *Sunshine Man* had been a low budget, high profit winner.

The beating he had taken from Emery Friedman had finally turned out to be worth something, Daniel thought cynically. That reminded him of Victoria and he wondered what she was doing now. After her marriage to the College Man, her career kamikazed. Rumor had it that if she did get work now, she was unreliable. A boozer.

"You're really hot now, son," Temple said proudly. "Anything you want, you got. Money's no problem with those two little gold guys on the shelf." He dropped a pile of scripts on the coffee table. "You just pick one of those and make us and a whole lot of other folks real well off."

Daniel picked up the first one, opened it up to the title page and then dropped it back on the pile with a sigh. "I'll go through them tonight."

Temple frowned, but he didn't say anything aloud. He'd been after Daniel for a week to settle on his next project. He didn't know that Daniel was searching for something special: a role a thirty-two-year-old actress could really get her teeth into. A come-back for Victoria.

Solari might have gone to Harvard, but his judgement wasn't worth shit. He had picked one bomb after another for his wife.

Daniel knew there was only one way to an actress's heart. Once he found that role, she would drop Solari cold. That thought was enough to get him started on the tedious task of script reading. He picked the top one up again, and began to read.

Temple beamed.

1976

It was only ten o'clock in the morning and Victoria had already finished half the last bottle of vodka in the house. She was still alert enough to wonder what she would do the rest of the day if she didn't get some more booze delivered.

Naturally the phone book had vanished. She tried calling information, but she couldn't get the operator to look up the number of the liquor store for her.

As a last resort she lurched into Dom's office and began pawing through his desk, looking for one of the bills, the ever increasing bills, from the liquor store, knowing that it would have the telephone number. She took the bottle with her.

But that, too, proved frustrating. There were bills for everything from flowers to furs in his drawer, none of them marked paid, but not a scrap of paper from the liquor store.

Angry and frustrated, she yanked the center desk drawer out too far and it fell to the carpet. Victoria got down on her hands and knees and began to pick up the scattered contents, dumping them back into the drawer haphazardly. She saw the little green notebook taped to the back of the drawer the same instant that Dom himself came storming into the office.

"You stupid drunken bitch!" He gave her a slap that sent her reeling, and stuck the drawer back into the desk. Then he manhandled her back upstairs and into her bedroom.

"Stay here until you sober up," he ordered.

And she did.

She intended to be completely sober when she investigated the contents of that little green notebook.

Dominic Solari was startled by the appearance of the woman on the other side of his desk. For the past four years, since her marriage to his son, he had watched Victoria slide downhill. Now she was the woman who had stood in the same spot and demanded that he speak to her husband about her acting career.

Poor Joseph Moretti, Dominic thought. He was no match for a woman like this, a woman with the guts to go after whatever she wanted. "How may I be of service?"

Victoria smiled mockingly. "No, Dominic. This time I can be of service to you." She leaned forward, and the mockery fled. "I know that I owe you a great debt for your help in the past. I'm ready to pay that debt in full. I have a piece of information that would be worth a great deal to you." She settled back, smiling. "More, possibly, than the debt I owe."

"So you want something further in exchange for it?" Dominic asked, amused.

"A divorce."

He got up and poured them both a brandy. It had been a mistake, that marriage to Dom. He saw that now. But he had hoped that her fire would make more of his son. Instead, Dom had almost put that wonderful fire out. Now, looking at her, trim and vibrant again, Dominic almost hated his son for that. The decision he made then went against his instincts, but nevertheless there was a debt here to be settled. Dominic owed *her* for his misjudgment. He handed one of the brandies to Victoria. "If the information you have is correct, the divorce will be arranged."

For just a moment, that supreme self-confidence wavered. "He won't agree to it."

"Don't trouble yourself. It will be taken care of."

Uncertainty still flickered in her eyes, but she opened her purse and took out a sheaf of papers. "Dom is cheating you," she said baldly. "I copied these figures from a book that he has hidden in his office at home. They're accounts that he's set up to channel your money into. Also there's a list of names and payments in the back of the book. I thought you might be interested in those too.''

Silently, he flipped through the pages. The amount of money Dom was siphoning off was phenomenal. Dominic could feel the rage building up inside him. He was generous with all of his sons. They had only to ask and anything he had was theirs. Dom would be sorry he had tried to go behind his father's back.

Then Dominic flipped to the last page and read the list of names there.

The names of his enemies.

The amounts his enemies had paid his son for unspecified services.

But looking at those names and dates, Dominic could name each service Dom had performed.

''Dominic? Are you all right?''

''I'm fine, Victoria. It's not every day that a father finds out that his son is . . . cheating him. Perhaps I should have given him a larger allowance when he was a boy.'' The hollow joke fell flat between them. ''Everything will be taken care of. Say nothing to Dom. I'll phone you when the matter is settled.''

''You'll see that he gives me the divorce.''

''You will be free to remarry, Victoria. I promise you that.''

Daniel stroked the sleek nude body of the young actress in bed beside him. ''Do you remember my name?'' he asked her. He had forgotten hers.

''Of course, Mr. Garrick,'' she said seriously. The ''Mr.'' struck him as comical, considering they were both naked.

''Mr. Garrick was my father,'' he told her. ''I'm Daniel when we're like this.''

''I'm Cindy,'' she said, snuggling closer.

''Are you here because of my father?'' When that popped out he knew he was drunker than he had realized.

''Who's your father?''

''Leif Garrick.''

''Is he a director too?''

''You don't know who my father was?''

''No, Mr. Gar—Daniel.''

"Then why are you in here with me?"

She looked startled. "Who would turn down a chance to be with you? Especially," she began to stroke him between the legs, her hand caressing higher and higher, "especially when there just might be a part in your new movie for me."

Now he remembered her name. And the part she wanted. It, like the lead in his last movie, had been tailored especially for Victoria. Only he hadn't even contacted Victoria's agent. One mention of her name and the money people had threatened to bolt. He hadn't realized that Victoria's College Man was a mobster, and the son of a mobster. Daniel might be hot, but not hot enough to make up for that. Nobody wanted to tangle with the mob.

But every young actress in town wanted to go to bed with a hot young director.

Why not? The only woman he really loved was Victoria and she was married to a scum gangster.

He rolled over on the girl and entered her so swiftly that she squealed in delight.

Caro Hensley watched the doorway of the bedroom. She had seen Daniel stagger into the room earlier with one of the women from the party. Her mother still circulated downstairs, performing her hostess duties. Later on, Daniel would fall into Kyna's bed dead drunk.

Caro continued to watch until Daniel and the woman came out of the room. It was obvious to Caro that he wouldn't even remember the woman's name or face in the morning. She wondered if he would even remember who Kyna was by the time he fell into her bed.

Caro went back downstairs only enough to steal a bottle of champagne. She could have stayed and mingled with the party guests. Even though she was only sixteen, she could pass for one of the starlets in the dress she had borrowed from Kyna's closet which revealed her small firm breasts and her slim, supple figure.

Unless someone looked in her eyes, she thought as she climbed the stairs again. There was a little too much intelligence there, too much cynicism. Too much of her father, the human calculator.

In her room, Caro opened the champagne and poured

herself a glass before she turned off the light. Then she lit a cigarette from the pack she had taken from a purse downstairs. Grass would have been better, but the champagne made it almost all right.

She sat there in the dark, watching the glowing red tip of her cigarette and wondered when Daniel would get around to fucking her.

"The new stationery you ordered, Miss Lindholm," Corrie, Inga's petite red-haired young assistant, said as she laid a sample on Inga's desk.

Inga caressed the heavy bond, her fingers lingering on the engraved letterhead: Inga Lindholm, Talent Agent. "How wonderfully expensive it feels." She grinned up at the girl. "Just like your skin."

The girl blushed, making her freckles more prominent, and Inga chuckled. She found it amusing that a girl who saw nothing wrong with indulging a man's every sexual appetite with gusto could still be embarrassed by discovering it was possible to attain equal—if not better—ecstasy with her own sex. Corrie had only been working for the agency six weeks, and Inga had conspired to make them pleasurable ones. "Don't forget Andrew and I are expecting you tonight," she reminded Corrie. "And tell him I'd like to see him when he has a moment."

The girl retreated to her own desk, still blushing, but Inga had no doubt she would be at the Bradfords' that night. Inga had considered moving to a place of her own, but there was really no need. The Bradfords were seldom in Los Angeles these days, and the house was Inga's to do with as she wished, all expenses paid. It would continue to be so long as she fulfilled her part of the bargain.

She stroked the creamy bond again. The main lesson she had learned from her association with the Bradfords over the years was that rich people can do anything they please. Being rich had allowed the Bradfords to whisk a seventeen-year-old Swedish au pair girl back to America with them and eventually secure her citizenship. Being rich had allowed them to shift the burden of a troublesome son onto that same au pair's wide and capable shoulders. When Inga asked that a second nurse be hired to assist her so that she could go to college, the

Bradfords did not hesitate to hire Inga's choice, freeing her days for study. They didn't even question her about her choice of courses. Nothing mattered except that they be free of the burden of Andrew.

Last year Inga had gone to the Bradfords with her plan to open a talent agency, along with the promise that she would continue to shoulder the burden of Andrew. The Bradfords had suffered no financial strain in seeing her dream become a reality. Small wonder, then, that Inga wanted so badly to be rich herself.

The lean times before she secured employment with the Bradfords, the times with red, chapped hands and too little to eat, working herself into an early grave for that filthy English family who thought au pair was simply another word for slave, had been worth it. It had been through gossip overheard there that she had learned of Keith and Cynthia Bradford's search for a strong, capable caretaker for their child.

It was only after they arrived in the United States that the Bradfords told her the truth about Andrew. A problem with his brain, they said, stemming from an accident caused by a careless nurse.

Of course that was untrue. Anyone could see that Andrew's brain was perfectly normal; it was the lack of a true mother which had warped him. Cynthia Bradford had no maternal instincts at all. Because of that, her son was an emotional cripple. But Andrew was almost normal now. The medication he took daily, and the doctor he visited on a regular basis, kept him on an even keel emotionally. As long as Inga presented him with a strong, loving, female figure, she had no difficulties with him. She had given him a mixture of punishment and love in the exact proportions he craved, a mixture which had become punishment and sex as he matured. Now Andrew's parents no longer needed her to be his watchdog. But still they wanted to be free of him emotionally, free of any guilt that would bind them to him. Financing her talent agency had seemed to them a small price to pay for that freedom.

Andrew had become Inga's partner in the agency and her constant escort, accompanying her to dinners, to parties. He never strayed from her when they were out, hovering over her like a doting lover. No one realized he was terrified of speaking to strangers. And to Andrew, everyone was a stranger.

But with the face of a young male angel, he had no need to speak. Lovely young women clustered around him everywhere, and she and Andrew had her pick of them.

"Inga?"

She looked up.

He was so handsome it made her breath catch in her throat, a male version of Sharon, tall and blond with those same incredibly green eyes. "I have a book for you, Andrew." She handed it across. "Robert Frost."

"More poetry?" he said happily. She had introduced him to Sandburg and Eliot recently, but it was Eliot he loved the best. He could quote long passages from "The Waste Land" and "The Hollow Men." He sat down and began to flip through the book.

"We made a great deal of money this month, Andrew." Through her association with his twin during Sharon's stay in Hollywood, Inga had gotten her foot in the door. Now through her own sexual excursions, she had made many more useful contacts. "Your parents will be pleased."

He glanced up, hopeful. "Will they?"

"I'm sure they will. In fact, your mother will probably send you a present." Inga had already picked out a new television set. It would be delivered to Andrew later in the week with his mother's name on the card accompanying it. Inga walked over to him and bent down to place a kiss on his hair. "Corrie's coming tonight," she said softly. "You'll enjoy that, won't you?"

He frowned. Sometimes he objected to her little games. But he always went along. Eventually.

"It will be fun, I promise you," Inga assured him. But not as fun as it could be, she thought as he went back to the Frost. Little girls like Corrie were amusing, but every time she looked at Andrew, she saw Sharon—and it was Sharon she wanted.

The maid brought Victoria the phone out by the pool. "It's Mr. Solari," she said.

"I don't want to talk to him," Victoria told her, and flipped over on her stomach. They'd had a rousing fight before Dom left this morning. He had another ridiculous piece of trash he wanted to call a movie and she had refused to read the so-called script. If his father's driver hadn't arrived to pick him up, the fight would still be going on. "Why are you still standing there?" she asked the maid irritably.

"It's Mr. Dominic Senior, ma'am." the girl said shyly.

"Why didn't you say so?" Victoria snatched the phone from her hands. "Hello? Dominic?"

"Victoria?"

For a moment, she didn't recognize the voice on the other end of the line. "Dominic? Is that you?"

"That little matter we talked about is taken care of, Victoria. Your debt is paid in full."

"He agreed?" She had never expected that. It had been weeks since she'd talked to Dominic and she'd been watching Dom ever since. She couldn't see any indication that Dominic had done anything. This morning when Dom left for the meeting with his father about the financing of that awful new movie, he'd been so happy he was humming. "I hope you're right, Dominic, because I'm not making that movie. If you think that I'm—"

"He's dead, Victoria."

She stared at the aquamarine waters of the pool. "Dom's dead?" The little maid, halfway back to the house now, stopped in mid-stride. One of Dom's little entertainments, Victoria realized as the girl turned a stricken face toward her. "An accident?"

Then Dominic said, "The police say someone executed him," and she forgot the little maid, and everything else.

"Someone . . . " Her whole body began to shake as though she had a terrible fever. "Someone . . . Dominic, you—"

"You need a rest, Victoria. I think you should get out of the country for a while."

"You didn't—"

"I'm sending my car for you. You have a passport, don't you?"

"Yes, but—"

"I've made reservations to Paris for you. Don't bother packing. You can pick up whatever you need there."

"But Dominic—"

"Good-bye, Victoria."

Her hands were trembling so badly it took her three tries to get the receiver back into the cradle. The little maid looked at Victoria strangely as she bolted past her into the house.

Victoria locked herself in the bedroom and stripped out of her swimsuit. She dressed rapidly and took only a moment extra to stuff a few things into her big purse. When she caught sight of her face in the mirror, she didn't recognize herself. That woman in the mirror, her eyes wide with terror, could not be her.

Victoria jammed on her sunglasses and ran downstairs. The horn sounded outside as she reached the bottom of the staircase.

She had never expected Dominic to kill his own son!

Jr.'s face stared at Daniel out of the morning paper. "Producer Brutally Murdered," the headline read. "Mob Ties Suspected."

He stood up abruptly.

"What's wrong, Daniel?" Kyna asked. Caro watched without comment.

"I have to make a phone call," he said and hurried to the room that had become his office. Swiftly, he dialed Victoria's number.

The maid answered. "I'm sorry, sir. Mrs. Solari is out of the country."

Daniel hung up slowly.

Too late. He was always too late.

Chapter Fifteen

1978

Daniel wondered what in the hell he was doing in this empty hospital corridor at three in the morning. He and Beth hadn't even been in the same room since he got back from Viet Nam. Their only communication had been a few desultory phone calls. Once he started the proceedings to wrest control of his father's money out of her hands, their only contact had been through the lawyers. Perhaps Leif Garrick had an intimation that his son would turn out to be as worthless a profligate as himself. In any case, he had tied up Daniel's trust so completely that Daniel would be an old man before he could get it turned over to him.

Or Beth would have to die.

Christ! Now that her death was a possibility, the money no longer seemed as important.

It had been his mother's lawyer who tracked him down at Kyna's earlier this evening and informed him that his mother was dying. Daniel hadn't told Kyna where he was going when he left for the hospital. That was the beauty of their relationship, he thought without humor. He acted like a complete shit, and Kyna accepted whatever he did and whomever he slept with. Several times she had asked him to move in

with her, but he always refused. He came and went as though
her home was a hot sheet motel.

And she let him.

The lawyer came out of the room.

"Well? Can I go in now?"

It didn't seem possible that the stuffed shirt's face could
grow more somber, but it did. "I'm sorry, Mr. Garrick. She
refuses to see you."

"What the hell do you mean? You said she asked me to
come."

"She did indeed." The lawyer was visibly upset. "I'm
afraid it's all my fault, Mr. Garrick. I should never have
mentioned where I located you."

"She knows I'm a big boy," Daniel said harshly. "She
knows I sleep with women."

"But not that woman."

"Kyna?"

"Mrs. Garrick has a special dislike for Miss Hensley," the
lawyer said pompously. "Surely you knew that."

"If I kept up with all the cat fights my mother has gotten
into over the years, I wouldn't have time for anything else."

"Miss Hensley was your father's mistress at the time of his
death."

The nurse came out and said, "She's asking for you, Mr.
Holmes."

"Excuse me," the lawyer said and went inside.

Daniel waited almost fifteen minutes before the lawyer
came out once more. He had come close to turning on his
heel and walking away during that quarter hour. He really
wasn't sure what held him there.

"I'm sorry, Mr. Garrick," the lawyer said somberly. "She's
gone. I tried to get her to allow you in, but she refused."

He didn't feel anything. Someone else's voice said, "May
I go in now?"

The lawyer stepped aside.

The woman in the bed was a stranger. She looked so small,
almost childlike beneath the sheets. How could he have come
into the world from a body that small?

Daniel walked closer.

One of her hands lay palm up on the sheet. He reached

down and took it. He felt absolutely nothing inside as he gazed down at the perfect ovals of her coral pink nails.

Daniel lay the hand back down on the sheet. He turned and started out of the room.

The lawyer stopped him at the door. "Here, Mr. Garrick," he said, extending his handkerchief.

Daniel wondered how long he had been crying.

Kyna's face was pale porcelain against the shadowy charcoal of her hair. She looked like the dark, sultry villainess she had played so successfully in dozens of films. Beneath the sheets she was naked.

Daniel sat down on the edge of the mattress. "Kyna?" He touched her shoulder.

She woke as she always did, swiftly, completely, and smiled up at him.

The smile faltered and faded when it was not returned. "Something is wrong, Daniel?"

"Why didn't you tell me that you were my father's mistress?"

She frowned at him. "I was one of your father's lovers," she said slowly, "But then a lot of women in this town may say that." She chuckled bitterly. "It was not an exclusive club."

"You were his last mistress."

"Perhaps. Beth thought so. Only Leif knew for sure."

"My mother hated you, didn't she?"

She shrugged. "She hated all the women he took to bed. But she never hated him. None of us did."

"Tell me about it."

"Why?"

"Tell me."

She scowled at his tone, but she obeyed. "I was a girl, twenty-two, when I met him. We were lovers for five years. If he had not died, he would have broken my heart. As it was, he broke Beth's instead." Kyna sat up, wrapping the sheet around herself. "Beth has never forgiven me because she was a nobody after Leif died. I was not. I had my career."

"Your career and her husband."

Anger flashed in Kyna's eyes. "If you want to hash this

over, go to your mother. Why am I the villainess? It was she
who could not keep her husband from straying.''

''My mother is dead.''

''Oh, Daniel.'' She would have put her arms around him,
but he moved away and stood up.

''So,'' she said. ''That will be that, I suppose.''

''Yes.''

He paused at the door and looked back at her. She was
fifty-three now. His mother's age. He had been two years old
when his father first took Kyna to bed. She could have been
his mother. Nausea threatened to overwhelm him.

He slammed the door behind him and stumbled down the
stairs.

''Daniel!''

Caro stood at the top of the stairs. She wore nothing but a
long t-shirt. He could see her nipples and the dark public
triangle through the thin white cotton. ''Where are you going,
Daniel?''

''Good-bye, Caro.''

He plunged on out of the house and into his car. For a
moment, he rested his forehead against the steering wheel.
Then he started the engine and drove down the drive. He
paused at the end of the drive and glanced in the rearview
mirror.

Caro had come outside. She couldn't possibly tell that he
was looking at her in the rearview mirror, but she waved
anyway.

Daniel gunned the engine and roared out into the street.

In a flowing white extravaganza of satin and lace, Inga
Lindholm entered the living room of the Bradford's mansion
with Keith Bradford as her escort. Her short mannish cap of
blonde hair was hidden beneath yards and yards of veiling. So
was the satisfied smile on her face as Andrew's father left her
with Andrew in front of the minister and went to join his
wife.

Andrew gazed at her with a mixture of love and terror. She
reached across to take his hand and gave it a firm squeeze as
the ceremony began. The minister was old and frail with a
weak voice that crackled like paper. Inga's voice was louder
than his and much deeper as she responded with her ''I do,''

and then waited impatiently for Andrew to say the same
words. That was all that stood between her and complete
success now. The years of nursing Andrew, of going to
college, had finally paid off. Her agency had some of the
most sought after clients in Hollywood. Andrew's parents
trusted her completely. Even though she was thirty-five now
and Andrew only twenty-eight, they had agreed immediately
when she spoke to them about the marriage. To Cynthia and
Keith Bradford, Inga's marriage to their son represented a
permanent solution to their problem.

Inga wondered if they realized it was the solution to hers as
well. She still gave Andrew a mixture of punishment and
love. But sometimes she felt more release in administering
the discipline rather than the sex, and there was always the
chance of discovery. It was remote, since the Bradfords spent
very little time in Los Angeles these days. But after the
wedding, and the deeding of this house to Andrew and herself
as a wedding present, even that distant chance would vanish.

"I do," said Andrew in a firm, masculine voice that gave
no hint of the child that sometimes lurked behind those green
eyes.

"I now pronounce you man and wife. You may kiss the
bride," the pastor said, and when that was accomplished,
chastely, the small group in the living room came up to offer
their congratulations.

Inga Lindholm Bradford watched them with cynical amusement. Cynthia and Keith Bradford beamed, delighted to be
free at long last of their unwanted burden. Philippe Tescier,
petulant at having been dragged from France to attend the
wedding of his lover's brother, had already strode across the
room and was urging the caterer to open the champagne.

And Sharon.

Beautiful, beautiful Sharon, with her full, pouting lips.
Inga knew she would dream about those lips tonight. Sharon's eyes were wide and vulnerable as they fixed on her
twin's face. There was a tie between Sharon and Andrew so
strong that nothing could sever it.

Not the sulky Frenchman.

Not Inga herself.

Inga smiled, as Sharon and Andrew embraced.

That tie between the twins was what she counted on. She

was a patient spider, spinning and spinning her web for years. One day she would yank a single thread and the fly would be hers.

1979

Victoria circulated through the crowd on the terrace of the Hotel Carlton, listening with heady excitement to the whispers that followed her through the black tie crowd. Her latest film, *Morning's Madness,* had screened last night. Today everyone in Cannes was talking about it.

She had been so terrified about the film's fate that she had only decided to come to the Cannes Film Festival at the last minute. It had been too late to get a suite anywhere along the Croisette. Yesterday she had found that irritating; this evening, she didn't care.

Last night, she had bolted from the screening just before the end of *Morning's Madness,* not wanting to share her delight with anyone. Slipping off her heels and hose, she walked barefoot along the palm-tree-lined promenade, swinging her shoes by their delicate straps. Passersby must have thought she was truly drunk!

This evening she still felt inebriated with success, even though she'd had only a single glass of wine earlier. She was meeting a Swedish producer later for dinner at *La Côte* and she wanted a clear head in case his project turned out to be of interest.

An American distributor stopped her. "When are you coming back to the States, Miss Carr?"

"Maybe when they stop banning my movies."

Everyone around them laughed. It seemed ludicrous now that *The Four Lovers,* the first movie she made after arriving in France, had been considered pornographic in the U.S. and banned in several American cities. Especially since it had gone on to win the Oscar for Best Foreign Film that year.

When she arrived in Europe, fleeing from Dom's death, and the terrible knowledge of what she'd forced Dominic to do to his own son, her career had been the furthermost thing from her mind. The time finally came, though, when she roused herself to think about her career once more. It was then Victoria decided to recreate herself, to go back to playing the kind of roles Barney would have chosen for her. Just the thought of Barney, even now, made her want to weep. She would give anything if she could make him understand why she had done what she had done.

However, that was yesterday's water under the bridge. Now she had only herself to worry about. And a revitalized career. The notoriety following Dom's death and then the furor over the banning of *The Four Lovers* had made her an instant star again in the States, but now she was wary. Instant stars had a way of winking out suddenly. She wanted to go back in such a burst of glory that there was no way anyone could ignore her.

That was why she was at the Carlton. Fishing. Trolling for the part, the director that would bring her back to the U.S. on a wave of critical acclaim. Or notoriety. It didn't matter which. Only that it worked.

"Victoria!"

She turned and found herself being hugged by Sharon. A changed Sharon. In Hollywood, her long blonde hair had been straight, platinum. Now it was a more natural blonde, and tousled wildly, as though Sharon had combed it with her fingers. Sharon had put on pounds too. Not enough to hurt her in person, but Victoria's experienced eye told her that the gain would show on the screen. She was surprised that a professional like Sharon would let herself go like that. Or that Sharon's famous film director lover would allow it. Perhaps they were no longer together. "It's so good to see you," Victoria told her, and was surprised to realize it was true. "I can't believe how we've kept missing each other since I've been in Europe."

"Me either," Sharon said quickly.

Victoria noted cynically that neither of them wanted to acknowledge the fact that unless they were equals careerwise, they had no intention of searching each other out these days. And now that they had met again, they were both at a loss for words. "I miss your letters," Victoria said into the silence that had fallen between them.

"It's been years since I've written you or Daniel," Sharon protested, clearly startled.

"They meant a lot to me, though," Victoria confessed.

"Maybe I didn't realize how much at the time. I wasn't always very good about answering them, was I?"

Sharon looked pleased. "But you wrote such nice letters back when you did answer. Daniel's were. . . ." She frowned as though something about Daniel's letters had been unpleasant.

"He never wrote me." Only now did it occur to her to wonder why not. "I suppose you two were a lot closer than he and I."

Now Sharon really looked surprised, but before she could say anything else, a lean and intense-looking man walked over and put his arm around her, smiling at Victoria as he did so. "To see two such beautiful women together is a delight to the eye."

Victoria recognized Philippe Tescier from his photographs and from Sharon's longing glance turned his way. "And to hear such extravagant praise is to recognize a Frenchman is present," she countered, laughing.

"Sharon has been talking about you and your long friendship with each other," the director said gravely. "You must come and stay with us for a weekend. We have a little farm outside Paris. Surely searching for a new vehicle for your talent is too arduous a task to carry on without respite."

"Am I that obvious?" Victoria asked ruefully.

"Only to a director like myself who knows that talent such as yours must continually search for the perfect outlet."

While Philippe waxed poetic, Sharon's face assumed that pouty look which always reminded Victoria of JoJo. Although she might be interested in renewing her friendship with Victoria, Sharon was obviously not interested in doing so with Philippe about.

"How kind of you to offer a haven," Victoria said smoothly. "We really must get together some time, Sharon."

And then the Swedish producer swooped down on the three of them. "Victoria! Precious! You haven't forgotten our dinner engagement!"

Too bad Tescier's invitation would never be extended for real, Victoria thought as the producer ushered her inside the Carlton. A prominent director like Philippe Tescier might just have the part she needed to send her home in style.

They quarrelled all the way back to the farm. Or rather, Sharon quarrelled and Philippe drove in silence.

"You just asked me to introduce you to her. You didn't tell me you were going to invite her to the farm." That, to Sharon, was the ultimate sin. Philippe might have his other women—she *knew* he had his other women—but never at the farm. At the farm he was hers alone.

Last year when she and Philippe went back to the States for Andrew's wedding, they had barely settled into the hotel before he was phoning around, setting up meetings, talking deals, and then disappearing for long stretches of time. When he came back to the hotel, he would have the satisfied tomcat grin on his face that drove her wild with jealousy.

He couldn't understand why she was so upset about her brother's wedding. That Inga was thirty-five and Andrew only twenty-eight made no difference to him. He could not fathom why her parents' elation over the match distressed her so. Sharon knew that Inga's talent agency was a huge success. Inga no longer needed the Bradfords' money. Apparently they had been afraid Inga would dump Andrew back into their laps. As far as they were concerned, his marriage to her would prevent that unthinkable eventuality.

Not that Andrew was a problem. He was so sweet, so childlike, so incredibly handsome. Looking into his face was, for Sharon, like seeing a masculine version of her own beauty. Philippe, the bastard, had intimated that Sharon had incestuous designs on her own brother and that was why she was so upset about the wedding!

But that wasn't it at all. Taking care of Andrew had once been her prime purpose in life. A thing like that wasn't easy to give up. And she knew, *knew*, that Inga was bad for him.

But her parents wouldn't listen. When she complained too much to Philippe during that L.A. trip, he had simply gone out again.

She wasn't sure exactly how she had known that sexual sparks flew between Philippe and Victoria back there at the Carlton, but she knew. The thought that he wanted to invite Victoria to their home enraged her beyond the caution she normally used in dealing with Philippe's mercurial temperament. "If you want to have an affair with Victoria, you can go to Paris to do it. I won't have her under my roof!"

"You are acting like a child," Philippe said.

Sharon's gasp of indignation turned into a gasp of terror as he passed a car with less than a millimeter to spare. "Why do you have to drive like that? We have all the time in the world!"

"Why do you always complain about my driving? I am an excellent driver." He was a good driver, she supposed. He took ridiculous chances, but he had an uncanny ability to make the right move at the last second with deadly calm. But that sort of cold-blooded skill belonged on the race track, not the public highway.

However, she refused to be baited by the subject of his driving. Sharon knew from experience that this was just a ploy to distract her. If she got off on *that*, she would never get back on the real subject which was Victoria and his obvious infatuation with her.

If she allowed him to sidetrack her tonight, then would come the long lunches in Paris and "The meeting broke up too late for me to drive back" excuses that meant he was fucking someone new.

Well, not this time. Not at the farm.

So when he said, as he pulled into the courtyard, "Call Victoria tomorrow and invite her down next weekend," Sharon said, "No."

She opened her door and paused.

He had not cut off the motor.

"Do you think I'm a complete fool? I know what you're planning!"

He put the car into gear and looked over at her.

Sharon slammed the door closed.

Philippe drove without comment back to the village they had shot through earlier at grand prix speed. When he reached a certain house, he pulled in front of it and parked.

Sharon sat in the car looking straight ahead, her cheeks burning with indignation.

Philippe got out and started up to the door. He had reached it, had his hand, in fact on the knob, when she called his name.

He turned, slowly.

"All right," she said sullenly. "I'll invite her."

"Good," Philippe said. He reached for the knob again.

"Philippe!"

He went inside.

"You son of a bitch!"

Her voice echoed down the empty street. Sharon shrank
down in the seat. The last thing she wanted was to be spotted
waiting outside a whorehouse at 2 a.m.

She checked the ignition. He had taken the keys. It was a
ten mile hike back to the house. She sat there, waiting, until
he emerged forty-five minutes later with that feline look of
satisfaction on his face that made her dig her fingernails into
the armrest.

After five years of living together, she had Philippe's
routine down cold. He would go straight to bed and sleep till
noon.

Then he would wake up randy as a goat and expect her to
be there, warm, loving, available.

He turned the key in the ignition.

Sharon opened the door on her side.

The temptation was so strong to just leap out and walk
away.

Philippe switched off the ignition and turned to face her.
"Would you like to go inside with me, *enfant*?" In the
sudden silence, his voice was sinister. He leaned closer. "We
could share the same whore."

Sharon looked at him, afraid to speak, her door still open.
She never knew when he was joking and when he was not.

Philippe raised an eyebrow. When she remained silent, he
reached for his own door latch.

A frisson of terror ran up her back.

"No," she said, slamming the door. "Take me home."

Philippe laughed.

But he started the car and drove her home.

"And as you see, Victoria, we have dogs." Philippe
shrugged helplessly as the pack of hounds surrounded him,
demanding his attention. "We raise more dogs than crops on
this farm, thanks to Sharon's tender heart."

Sharon didn't look that tenderhearted at the moment, Victoria observed. It was obvious from her petulant expression as
she trailed after them while her lover showed Victoria the
farm that Sharon's invitation to Victoria to visit this weekend
had come at Philippe's insistence.

But you know how to play the game, Sharon. I don't intend

to sleep with him. But I can't turn down an invitation from a director of Tescier's statue when he might have the part that would take me back to the States in style. Aloud, Victoria said, "This is a wonderful place, Sharon. I can see why you and Philippe enjoy it so much."

Sharon turned a poisonous look her way and strolled off without replying. But she didn't wander so far away that she couldn't keep an eye on Philippe, Victoria noted wryly. Not that he had made a single move toward her. Still Sharon, resembling a ripe young farm girl in her peasant blouse and full skirt, leaned against a fence railing and watched them.

Philippe seemed unaware of Sharon's baleful scrutiny or her obvious charms. He took Victoria's arm and, as they strolled toward the house, he spoke the words she had traveled to his farm this weekend to hear. "Let me tell you about my new project."

As soon as he started to outline the film, Victoria's heart began pounding with excitement. She knew she had been right to accept this invitation in spite of Sharon's animosity.

This was the part, all right. *Her* part.

"You gave that part to *Victoria*!" Sharon could not control the rising shrill of dismay in her voice.

They were eating brunch in the farm's dining room. Honest peasant food, Philippe called it. What did he care how fattening it was? He could eat pounds of the greasy meats and cheeses the cook served up and not gain an ounce anywhere on his lean frame. He cut himself another generous helping of sausage now, and complained, "You sound like a fishwife."

"You knew I wanted that part, Philippe. I star in your movies."

"And is there a contract between us which binds us? I have no recollection of one. Besides, you are not right for the part."

That stung. "I can act circles around Victoria any day."

"You are a fat drunken cow." He said it calmly, like he drove, with no heat, no passion.

"And *you* are a son of a bitch."

Ah, a little flicker of anger there, Sharon noticed. "My mother was married," he said stiffly. "This does not excuse the fact that you are becoming an overweight alcoholic. If you still had your looks, I would put you in the film. A bit part, perhaps," he added cruelly. "You would be a footnote in film books in years to come."

Sharon shoved away from the table and ran upstairs, slamming the door of the bedroom behind her. Cursing to herself, she paced back and forth across the room, very much wanting a drink. Perhaps she was drinking more these days. So what? Look at the stress she had been under! Who wouldn't drink?

She couldn't believe that Philippe had gone through that entire weekend without laying a finger on Victoria, but she knew it was true. She spied on them everywhere they went, never leaving them alone or unwatched for a moment.

When Victoria finally left, Sharon had been so relieved that she could have cheered.

Now she found out that Philippe had offered Victoria the lead in his new movie! And worse, this afternoon he was on his way to Paris to sign the contract with her.

A soft knock sounded on the bedroom door. Sharon flung it open.

"Would Mademoiselle like me to bring her brunch in?" the maid asked. She held out the tray with Sharon's plate on it.

The disgusting sausages floated in an ocean of their own fat. "No," Sharon told her. But before the maid could leave, she changed her mind. "Wait a minute," she told the girl.

Sharon peered out the bedroom window. Philippe was outside in the courtyard, fiddling with the motor on his car.

She leaned out the window. "Philippe? Darling?" she called sweetly. "I've decided you're right. I'm going on a diet today."

Sharon drew back inside and snatched the plate from the maid. She shooed the girl from the room and then threw open the door to Philippe's closet. Working swiftly, she gathered up his favorite suits, three of them, and piled them in the middle of the floor. She scraped her plate into the center of them and then grabbed the sausages, using them as fat brushes to paint the suits with bold strokes of grease.

She rocked back on her heels, admiring her artistry with a satisfied grin. Then she tied the whole mess in a loose bundle and took it over to the window.

"Philippe?"

He looked up from the motor.

"Give my regards to Victoria."

She dumped the whole mess out the window. The hounds ran to investigate. Immediately, they began to growl and fight over the bundle, shredding the fine cloth as they competed for the sausages inside.

Philippe slammed the hood of his car. The look in his eyes reminded Sharon of the night he had made that obscene proposition to her in front of the whorehouse. She ducked her head back inside the window. She was relieved when she heard the sound of his car leaving.

She poured herself a glass of brandy from the bottle on Philippe's dresser and then stripped out of her clothes and examined herself, nude, in front of the mirror.

A fat, drunken cow, he had called her.

Well, she wasn't drunk at the moment, not even pleasantly high. But fat . . . perhaps. She had gained at least five pounds the past month. Alcohol had a way of adding the weight. In another year she would be thirty.

Sharon twisted and turned, trying to see if her fanny had started to droop, or her breasts betray her to gravity.

Not yet. But soon.

How did Victoria stay so perfect looking? she wondered dismally.

She picked up one of Philippe's shirts that had dribbled to the floor as she snatched his suits from the closet, slipped it on, and went down to the kitchen. "I will have only a small piece of broiled chicken for dinner," she told the cook, "and a green salad, no dressing."

"Mademoiselle is dieting?" the cook asked slyly. All the servants had heard the uproar this morning.

"Yes, Mademoiselle is dieting. And if Mademoiselle doesn't lose five pounds by the end of the month, Mademoiselle will find a cook who cuts calories better than the present one."

Sharon started out of the kitchen and then came back. "Oh, and have someone take what's left of Monsieur Tescier's suits to be cleaned."

" 'You are so beautiful.' " Philippe Tescier leaned closer to Victoria on the sofa. The words were from the script in his hand, but there was an electric excitement in the air between them. It had started on the set, that first day, when he was explaining Victoria's role to all of them.

It had continued to build for the past three weeks. When he told her today that he was coming to her suite tonight to help her with her lines, Victoria hadn't said yes or no. It was already beyond that. The way Philippe worshipped her with his eyes was transforming her for the camera. It was as though the camera was seeing her with *his* eyes. It was all there in the dailies.

She had tried desperately not to let this happen, to think of Sharon. But Sharon herself was making that impossible. Puffy-faced, petulant, whining and clinging. You didn't treat a man like Philippe Tescier that way and hope to hold him. Still the thought of Sharon made Victoria put up her hand in a vague, half-protest. "Philippe. . . "

He pushed aside the neck of her blouse and kissed her in the valley between her breasts. He lifted his head and looked directly into her eyes. "You are a goddess," he told her softly in French. "And I am your consort. I worship you with my body."

In any other language it would have been laughable. In French, it was the absolute truth.

The next day's rushes were the best ever.

Sharon drove herself to the set. She knew she had never looked better. By dieting and working out every day, she had lost fifteen pounds. Her body was as slim and taut as it had been when she was fifteen, the first time Philippe made love to her. At this point she would settle for even the footnote part that he had taunted her with the morning he left the farm. He had not been back. Eight long weeks of his absence had nearly driven Sharon up the wall.

There was a bit of trouble getting admitted, "a closed set," the man kept yammering in French, but Sharon went right past him.

The first thing she saw was Victoria in naked splendor on a bed with the camera pointed at her. Philippe was looking down into the face of a wizened man who was gesturing in Sharon's direction. The attention of everyone else on the set, the camera operator and assistant, the sound technician,

When he finally came upstairs, he had a bottle of wine in one hand and two glasses in the other. He sat down beside her on the bed and solemnly poured each of them a glass. She could tell it was not his first that day.

Philippe drained his glass before she could lift hers the first time and poured himself another. He sat there silently, staring moodily into the Burgundy as he swirled it around.

"What's wrong?" Sharon asked timidly, when he remained silent.

"Your friend has returned to America."

She couldn't help the little gasp of elation that escaped.

"You are pleased? Let me tell you that she has wrecked the financing for my next film by her action." He drained that glass and poured another. " 'It's over, Philippe,' " he mimicked savagely. " 'I'm going home.' "

Wary now, Sharon tried to move away. He grabbed her by the wrist, almost crushing the bones. "Philippe!"

"She decided that I could do no more for her. She has received offers because of my film, but she will have nothing more to do with me."

"You've received offers to go to America, too," Sharon reminded him. She had wanted him to accept, but he had refused.

He ignored that. "I decide when things end." He drained that glass too and turned to look at her. "*Merde!* Can't you even keep yourself up?"

She pushed the wisps of her hair back from her face. "I didn't know you were coming. I—"

"Shut up!" he said savagely. "Take off those rags!"

She put the wine down and stood up, no longer worried. Her hair might be unwashed and she might have no makeup on her face, but her body was still all right. She had vowed when she came back from Paris—when he threw her out of Paris—that she would never let the body go again. She pulled the peasant blouse over her head with one graceful motion, letting her breasts fall out, firm and magnificent. With tantalizing slowness, she slipped the skirt down over her hips. She wore nothing beneath it.

Philippe dropped the wine glass. She heard it shatter as he shoved her back onto the bed, fumbling with his pants, and then he thrust into her. Half a dozen strokes and he came, falling heavily on top of her as he did so.

He never came inside her. Never. Not even the very first time in Gstaad. He was too worried about making her pregnant. She wondered if he had intended to this time. More likely he was just too drunk to pull out in time. He continued to lay on top of her, a dead weight crushing against her.

"Philippe?"

He answered with a noisy snore.

She pushed him off of her. He rolled over on his back, one arm falling loosely off the bed, and lay there snoring.

Sharon raised herself on one elbow and studied him intently. Philippe's pants were half way down his thighs, his spent penis curled to nothingness, his mouth open. He hadn't bothered to shave, and there was a raw place on the side of her neck where his day-old beard had rubbed. She could feel the wet stickiness of him between her thighs, and the ache there from the rough way he had taken her.

Oh, well. At least he was back.

And Victoria was gone.

1980

"Look at this!" Philippe found Sharon in the farm's dining room and thrust a Paris newspaper article at her. "Your friend has prostituted herself."

Sharon scanned it quickly. "It's only television, for God's sake. That's where we both started. Victoria's looking for a sure thing. After all," she added maliciously, "she's not getting any younger."

"Americans are stupid about women. All they care about are teenagers!" He raged around the room. "In France she could be a film star of the first magnitude. There she is a has-been."

"Right, Frenchmen are so enlightened," Sharon said bitterly.

Philippe swung around to stare at her and she retreated a step. "What is that supposed to mean?"

"I'm pregnant, Philippe. I want to get married." This wasn't the way she had wanted to tell him, but once the words were out, she was glad.

"And who is the lucky groom?"

"Philippe?"

"No."

"I won't have this baby out of wedlock," she said defiantly.

"Don't."

"You want me to marry someone else? You really want that?"

He strode forward and caught her face in his hands, staring down in her eyes. "Kill it."

"I . . . I can't do that." Her knees threatened to give way. She reached behind her for a chair and sat down. "You have to understand that—"

"Kill it or leave."

He walked out.

In a moment Sharon heard his car start. When it had roared from the courtyard, the cook stuck her head through the kitchen doorway, a foxy grin on her fat face. "Mademoiselle will be dining alone tonight?"

Sharon lay on the table in the cramped little clinic Philippe had sent her to, letting them scrape the life from her insides.

She couldn't feel the knives, not with all the drugs they had pumped into her. But she could feel a hollow growing inside her as they worked, growing larger and larger, a huge empty space pressing outward.

There was a stir where the doctor stood between her thighs and the nurse at her head asked a question.

Dreamily, she heard the answer and that was when she knew the true meaning of emptiness.

"Twins," the doctor had said.

Chapter Sixteen

1981

Victoria stood in the producer's outer office, examining the sketches for her wardrobe on *The Clan* for the new season. She had won the role of glamorous "bitch" on this prime-time soap last year and she *loved* everything about it: the fantastic costumes, the jewels, the melodramatic overacting. The character she played was bigger than life and Victoria interpreted that character with such flair for the television audience that the whole country had ended the show's first season locked into a love-hate relationship with her. Her life was definitely on the upswing since she had returned from Europe. She was back in control and loving it.

"Disgusting!"

Victoria looked up and the sketches slid from her hand.

Barney Pace stood there. "Another sell out," he said bitterly. "You were a fine actress, Victoria. How could you pervert your talent like this?"

He knelt to rescue the sketches and shoved them into her hand. Then he stormed out of the office without giving her a chance to say anything.

Victoria felt so weak she had to sit down. She hadn't seen Barney since she'd had that disastrous interview with Dominic Solari.

Now she realized all over again how very much she loved Barney and how extremely remote the possibility that he would ever forgive her for the hurt she'd inflicted on him—but especially on Laurel—by marrying Dom.

"Are you all right, Victoria?" the designer asked, coming back into the office.

"Fine, Kenny," Victoria lied, and forced herself to go through the sketches again.

It wasn't until later that night as she roamed restlessly through the house she had bought when she signed to do *The Clan*, that she thought to wonder what in the world Barney had been doing there today in the producer's office.

A dozen roses arrived at her home the next morning. Two dozen more were waiting for her when she reached the studio. Everyone asked her who had sent them. Victoria could only shake her head in bewilderment. When three dozen more arrived an hour later, she closed herself up in her dressing room and tried to fight down the panicky feeling building inside her.

No card was enclosed with the roses, and she had a terrible fear that they might be from Dominic Solari.

She hadn't contacted him or spoken with him since the day Dom was murdered. But Dominic had smoothed the way for her, she knew. Her finances had been transferred to Europe without a hitch. She had no problem with any of the legalities concerning Dom's death. Dominic took care of everything.

Victoria was terrified that she might put herself in Dominic's debt again. Dom's death had released her; she had no desire to imprison herself once more.

When the knock came at the door, she almost didn't open it. When she did, the marvelous arrangement of four dozen red roses dwarfed the delivery person behind it.

"Come in and put them down," Victoria said. "Is there a card?"

The roses were lowered and Victoria gasped when she caught sight of Barney's face behind them. "No card. Just a personal apology," he told her.

"You?"

"I'm sorry for what I said yesterday," he said soberly. "Since we'll be working together—"

"What?"

"I've sold out too. I'll be directing several episodes of *The Clan* this season."

Victoria could only stare at him and then she burst into noisy tears.

"Victoria? I said I was sorry." When she continued to bawl, Barney gathered her into his arms and began kissing her.

She kissed him back, but the tears continued to roll down her face.

"You're tearing me apart," he complained. "I told you I was sorry."

"That's not it, Barney." She tried to stop the tears, but she couldn't. "I look at you and I think of all the wonderful years I've missed. I still love you, Barney."

He held her closer.

"I want to tell you what happened," she murmured into his shoulder.

"You don't have to. I figured it out. That asshole Solari made some kind of threat against me with the studio so you'd marry him, didn't he? And you believed him."

This was the time to tell him the truth. That it had been Dominic and not his son who threatened her. And to explain the hold over her Dominic had with the knowledge of her secret. Not even Dom had known that.

But she couldn't bring herself to tell Barney the truth. Instead, she let him hold her, comfort her. And when he said, "I know now that you did what you did to save me," Victoria remained silent, trying not to wonder what Barney would have thought if she had replied, "And myself."

Hot damn, this was a wonderful night!

Warren Neville had already pocketed over two hundred dollars tonight in tips parking cars for the big party at Kyna Hensley's home. Now he was ready to make some real bucks.

It was hell what an actor had to do to survive, Warren commiserated with himself as he ducked into the bushes to trade his valet's uniform for a tux. For the sake of his career, he had even changed his name. Not that it was a particular hardship; he loved the name he had picked for himself.

Sometimes he just muttered it over and over and letting the syllables roll off his tongue. Perfection!

As he climbed up and over a window sill, Warren promised himself, not for the first time, that one day he'd have one of these mansions himself. He'd been hanging around on the fringes of Hollywood society for years, drifting, waiting to be discovered, waiting for his big break to happen.

"Someday" was his motto. He had a criminal record under both his real name and his stage name. The offenses under his stage name were minor: theft, drugs, assault and battery. Just enough to make him interesting to the tabloids when he really hit it big, he congratulated himself.

The problem was his real name. Elmore Smith was wanted for the Big One back in Missouri: murder. But who'd connect an eighteen-year-old hayseed with a top star like Warren Neville was going to be? Not a chance, he assured himself, as he made his way across the dark room and eased open the doorway into the hall.

When he stepped out into the corridor, Warren looked like all the other invited guests. His timing was perfect, as always. Party goers were still arriving in enough numbers that he had no trouble spotting the room where the guests dropped off their purses and furs before heading for the goodies.

Warren snagged himself a drink off of a passing waiter and mingled, careful not to be spotted by the hostess herself, until the flow of incoming guests trickled to a halt. Then he made his way to the treasure room.

Sure enough in the faint light from the window he could see purses and furs heaped on the bed. Bonanza!

He pawed through the purses, stuffing his pockets with money, credit cards, anything of value, and tossing the stripped bags aside.

A faint whiff of cigarette smoke floated past his nostrils. Warren whirled around. A red tip glowed in the darkness behind him.

"I was just looking for my wife's purse," he said placatingly to whoever stood there. "You know these dames. They change purses so much you never know which one they've got with them."

The tip glowed redder as the unknown watcher took a deeper drag, then was crushed out.

Warren never carried a gun. He was good enough with his fists that he didn't need to. He was poised, ready to deal with the watcher.

The woman who emerged from the darkness into the faint light was in her early twenties. She was a little thing, no more than five foot six, with long black hair and—rarer than a true blonde in this town—skin as white as paper.

Warren relaxed. Even if this dame knew judo there was no way someone her size could stop him. He could be out the window before anyone else realized he had been there. The plastic in his pocket meant the night had been a profitable one already. Only he knew how to make it even more profitable still. A little bit of nookie would go good just about now, with his adrenaline still high. She was such a little thing, it wouldn't be any trouble at all to grab her and fuck her. All he had to do was get close enough to belt her before she could scream. He could feel his prick hardening.

He took one step forward and she raised a hand, like a policeman stopping traffic. There wasn't a bit of expression on her face. She had strange eyes, this one. They slanted like a chink's. Her hair was odd too, a widow's peak. You didn't see many of those.

"It's okay, baby," he said soothingly. A couple of inches closer and she didn't have a prayer of getting away.

"Hurry up and finish what you were doing." Her voice was low and husky enough to be a man's. It made shivers go up his spine.

But he didn't need a second invitation. He hated to walk off and leave that much cash and credit cards just laying there. He finished stuffing his pockets and stood up.

If she had hoped to trap him with that much more evidence on his person, she had a big surprise coming. A *big* surprise, he thought with pleasurable anticipation. He shifted his weight, ready to strike her right on the point of her chin as soon as he could get close enough.

She raised her hands and fumbled with something behind her neck. At first he thought she was taking off the necklace, and he had no quibbles about adding that to the night's haul, although usually he let the jewelry alone. Too much trouble to fence.

She moved her hands and the dress slid down her body, leaving her totally naked.

Warren stared at her, open mouthed. He didn't even try to grab her tits as she walked past him to the bed, wearing only her high heels. They were nice ones too, hard little apples that would just fit his palms. She shoved the purses aside and spread a sable coat out over the other furs.

"Have you ever fucked on sable before?" she asked him as she lay down on the bed and spread her legs.

"Who the hell are you?" he demanded, but he stripped out of his clothes.

"Caro Hensley, the daughter of the house. Who the hell are you?"

He hesitated, but only for a moment. "Warren Neville," he said as he crawled up on the bed. The feel of sable against his knees nearly made him come right there. He plunged right into her and she reared her ass up to meet him.

It was a good fuck, one of the best. When he pulled out of her, she wiped his dick off on the sable. Then they both got dressed. She helped him lower his loot out the window and carry it back to his car.

After that she insisted on dragging him back to where the guests' cars were parked. When the police finally showed up, they were balling again in the back of the car and she swore they had been there all night.

She even told his boss that he deserved a bonus for his valet work.

For services rendered.

"I was humiliated!"

"Because the fuzz caught your daughter screwing the hired help?" Caro threw open the curtains and let the sunlight come flooding into Kyna's bedroom. "You look like a corpse," she told her mother with cheerful malice. "No wonder there aren't any sleepovers up here this morning."

Actually Kyna looked damned good for a old lady of fifty-six, but Caro could never resist the impulse to stick in the knife and give it a twist.

Caro moved over to the mirror to examine her own face. If Daniel Garrick had stuck around, would he still be balling her mother or would he have finally turned to her? She hadn't seen him in the flesh since he broke up with her mother. She had no idea why she missed him so much. Kyna would never talk about why he left, which only made Caro more angry with her.

Sometimes she thought she had been born angry with her mother.

"I was terrified you would be charged with something. I don't care how wild and reckless you are elsewhere, just don't bring your wildness here. Or your drugs," Kyna added.

The old lady had finally caught on to the fact that her daughter was dealing. Not much, and not because she needed the money, but Caro didn't intend to give it up, no matter how Kyna bitched. Caro enjoyed the power too much, the control it gave her over other people. "Your friends like it," she taunted. "They prefer knowing they can get their little pleasures from someone they trust."

"Then they are fools! You're just like your father. No one can trust you!"

Caro took one step toward the bed. Just one.

Kyna cowered back against the headboard.

Caro laughed.

She was still chuckling to herself as she went downstairs. She wondered if Warren Neville was up yet, and hoped he wasn't. She had gotten his address from the valet people, and it would be nice to catch him in bed this morning.

She had understood immediately what a useful person Warren could be to her. She had learned a great deal about him before he finally left last night. Including the fact that he made a fair amount of money doing little semi-legal jobs for some of Hollywood's shadier elements. He was free to continue that as far as Caro was concerned, as long as he was available to do her errands when she needed him and to satisfy her sexually when she needed that.

But as for the out-and-out illegal things, she'd have to insist he clear those with her first. She wouldn't want her newfound friend ending up in jail.

Not before she was tired of him, anyway.

1982

When the call from America came, Sharon sat on the railing of her hotel room balcony, staring down at the quiet Paris side street below. She wasn't planning on jumping. Not really. It just seemed so wonderful symbolic to be balancing on the edge of the balcony just as she felt that she was balancing on the edge of her life.

Inside the room, Philippe was meeting with some money men. She and Philippe were still together, but only because Philippe found her occasionally useful. As a bed partner. Or as an inducement for an investor who wasn't willing to invest in Philippe for his brilliance alone.

Sharon didn't care anymore. The empty space had remained inside her after the abortion. She knew it could never be refilled.

A *gendarme* strolled across the street and disappeared into the hotel before she could count his gold buttons. Sharon swayed back and forth on the balcony. "*Pardon, Monsieur l'agent?*" she asked the night breeze. "Should I jump?" She felt so light tonight that she would drift down to the pavement like an autumn leaf.

Should she?

Shouldn't she?

Should she?

She leaned out into the breeze.

The phone began to ring.

"Sharon!" Philippe called angrily from inside. "Get that!"

She lost a shoe over the railing when she scrambled back. It made a wonderful splat on the canopy below before it tumbled on into the street.

Perhaps not tonight, Sharon thought dreamily as she wandered toward the phone. But soon.

She picked up the phone. "A call for Miss Bradford from America," the hotel operator said, and she waited an interminable length of time for it to be put through.

At first she didn't recognize the soft liquid sound of despair on the other end of the phone. Then it resolved itself into what she remembered best from her childhood: Andrew weeping.

"Andrew? Andrew!"

An ocean away someone replaced a receiver and the connection was severed.

In the dining room, Laurel Pace was methodically smashing crystal goblets.

"She'll get tired eventually," Barney assured Victoria. The two of them sat a discreet two feet apart on the sofa in Barney's living room. "More champagne?"

Victoria held out her glass. The way things were going this glass and Barney's would be the only two pieces of crystal left in the house in an hour's time. Laurel had started her destruction spree by smashing her own glass against the wall earlier when Barney asked her to join them in a glass of champagne. She had never forgiven Victoria for "abandoning" her when Victoria was forced to marry Dom Jr. She totally rejected Barney's effort to explain the circumstances. When Victoria attempted to intervene between father and daughter, Laurel exploded. There was a huge wet stain on the delicate wallpaper just behind Barney's head. Laurel had moved on from there to the glasses at the wet bar. She finished those off in short order and had been in the dining room for almost fifteen minutes. "You don't think she'll forget about the ones in the kitchen, do you?"

Barney shook his head. "She's got a wonderful memory," he said, an inappropriate note of pride in his voice.

"Just because that child psychiatrist told you she should act out her aggressions at five, doesn't mean he would say the same thing now that she's nineteen."

"It will be all right," Barney said calmly. "She'll get it out of her system tonight and be in a wonderful mood tomorrow."

He rose and put on a record. When he came back, the two of them sat quietly listening to the muted sound of jazz through the tinkle of crystal, thinking their own private thoughts.

Black humor, was Victoria's conclusion. If this only were someone else's life she would be laughing hysterically. How in the world could she love Barney so much and still manage to cause him nothing but pain where his daughter was concerned?

They had succeeded in keeping their affair a secret for

almost a year, but a blind item appeared in one of the columns this morning. When she saw it, Victoria knew it was only a matter of time before - Laurel found out they were seeing each other again. For Barney's sake she had been willing to call it off right there. Instead he insisted they tell Laurel together, tonight. "Laurel's a big girl," Barney told her this morning. "She'll understand."

Now, into a sudden and ominous silence, he said, "I think she's calming down, don't you?"

Victoria was very much afraid Laurel had only run out of crystal.

When Sharon landed at LAX, Inga was there to meet her. They did not speak. There was nothing more to be said. They had talked on the phone while Sharon waited at Kennedy for her flight to L.A., and the terms were clear. All she had to do was be Inga's slave and Andrew wouldn't be tortured anymore.

Inga drove with swift sure movements.

Sharon watched the city blur by from behind her dark glasses and thought about the terms.

When they reached the house, Sharon said, "I want to see Andrew."

"Not yet, pet. First we make it legal."

Inga sat beside her, thigh touching thigh, as Sharon called her agent and fired him. He hung up threatening lawsuits.

"If my parents knew what you're doing to Andrew . . . " she said when she hung up the phone.

"Your parents enjoy the freedom they have now. They have no more worries where your twin is concerned. They think I am wonderful with him. And I am. Just as I will be wonderful with you, pet."

Inga leaned forward and kissed her on the mouth.

Sharon sat there, letting the woman's lips slide against hers, keeping her own mouth closed.

Inga leaned back. "I thought everything was clear between us, Sharon. You make me happy; I make Andrew happy. If you do not make me happy . . . "

This time when Inga leaned forward, Sharon opened her mouth.

*   *   *

Daniel was so drunk he couldn't figure out what it was about this house he was supposed to remember. Nor why the slender woman helping him up the stairs sounded so familiar.

"I've never seen you like this," she said, as she helped him into a bedroom, and dumped him unceremoniously on the bed.

"I've never seen you at all," he told her, shielding his eyes from the brightness of the light overhead. "Turn that damned thing off."

"Not until you take a good look at me, Daniel."

She performed some sort of magic trick with her dress and then she stood there with nothing on, her small firm breasts pointing his way. No tan lines, he noticed, and skin white as a vampire's.

"That's a good trick," he said. "I like that." He wanted to roll over and go to sleep, but she tugged his pants and underwear off. Then she bent over him and urged him back to consciousness with her mouth. When the results pleased her, she mounted him in one graceful motion, fitting him neatly between her legs and brought him to a quick, competent climax.

"My billfold's in my pants," Daniel told her. "Take twice whatever you usually charge. You earned it."

She laughed. "You really don't remember me, do you?"

Her hair made a funny peak on her forehead. There was something about hair like that he was supposed to remember, but he was too damn drunk. He shook his head groggily.

"Cute little Caro?" she prompted. "Your aging girlfriend's daughter?"

"Jesus Christ!"

"Now's a good time to say 'My how you've grown,' " she said sardonically as she dressed.

"Remind me to say it in the morning," Daniel said, and then he turned over and passed out.

In the morning, she was there with orange juice and coffee when he woke. "My," he said, "how you've grown."

"You remembered."

"How could I forget?"

"Any special reason to party so much last night?"

"Maybe I was looking for just what happened." He took a

sip and was pleased to find that she had fortified the orange juice with vodka.

"One more drink and you wouldn't have been able to play."

"Then you came into my life at the perfect moment." He finished the screwdriver and pulled her into the bed beside him, kissing her to stop her questions. He didn't want to talk to her or anyone about the blind item in the gossip column about Victoria and Barney Pace. He had really thought he wasn't vulnerable to Victoria anymore. That little paragraph had proved him wrong.

Caro didn't leave him any free time to ponder what had started last night's drunk. She swarmed all over him, using her hands and her mouth to rouse him, and then taking her pleasure exuberantly. "Do you know how long I've been waiting to fuck you?" she asked him when he had rolled off of her. "Ever since I was thirteen."

Daniel grimaced. "I hope after all that time I managed to meet your expectations."

"More than. In fact, you deserve a reward." She disappeared for a few minutes and came back with a little silver box. "Have some?"

"Just what the doctor ordered," Daniel said as he took a pinch of the cocaine. "You're a lady of many talents."

"Daniel, this is Kyna Hensley."

Daniel shifted the phone to his other ear, and looked at the woman asleep beside him in the bed. "Yes," he said noncommittally.

"I know you've been seeing my daughter, Daniel."

"I never thought you were a prude. Or a hypocrite. The lady in question is over twenty-one."

"She's twenty-two. And it's not the 'lady' I'm worried about. It's you."

"What's that supposed to mean?"

"A mother shouldn't have to say these things about her daughter, but I'm frightened for you with Caro. She's strong-willed and dangerous. She is involved in drug-dealing, did you know that? She knows strange and unwholesome people."

"You wouldn't be jealous of her, would you?"

"Don't be stupid, Daniel. I'm terrified of her. If you had any sense, you would be too."

The connection was broken.

He hung up the phone.

Caro stretched and yawned. "Who was that?"

"An admirer of yours. Warning me about your fatal charms."

The hazel eyes grew cold. "My mother?"

"The same. She thinks you're bad for me."

"She's right."

She reached for him under the covers, but he caught her wrist. They had made love earlier in the evening and now all he wanted to do was go back to sleep.

"Run along home, now," he told her, "like a good little girl." He turned over, his broad back to her, and drifted off to sleep.

By ten the next morning, Caro was back. Temple Jackson was already there, going over business affairs with Daniel in the big teak-paneled family room. She could see the amused look in his eyes when she arrived. Everyone knew Daniel refused to let his women stay the night at his place, and the Texan derived a wicked pleasure from Caro's discomfiture. She ignored Temple and went in to fix Daniel's breakfast.

"That's one hard-eyed little mama," Temple told Daniel as Daniel's new bitch girlfriend breezed by them on her way back to the kitchen. "Must be like striking flint when you get into her."

"Lay off, Temple," Daniel pleaded. "I've got a hangover you wouldn't believe."

"Sure, son. Just sign these papers and I'll be on my way."

He watched as Daniel scrawled his signature on page after page without bothering to read all the fine print. Not that he'd find anything today. But some days . . . Temple gazed out the big glass wall that covered one end of the room, not seeing the tropical greenery outside. He was making a real fine living off what he was skimming from Daniel's business affairs. He sure wouldn't want anything to queer it.

1984

Thank God it was a private wedding, Victoria thought when she saw Laurel. Even Barney's limitless patience with his daughter stretched nearly to breaking when he caught sight of her in black dress, black hose, and black shoes coming down the stairs to Victoria's living room where the small party waited.

"She forgot the black band for her arm," Victoria whispered to him, letting him know with the small attempt at a joke that she didn't mind.

She had picked out a pearl gray suit for herself and as the ceremony meandered on, she realized how closely it matched Barney's complexion. She shouldn't have put him off for so long about marrying, she scolded herself. But she had known what a pain Laurel would be, even if Barney had steadfastly refused to face facts.

When the ceremony ended, they adjourned to the garden for champagne and wedding cake. Victoria looked at Laurel's face and wondered if she should have had plastic glasses instead of crystal.

However, Laurel restrained herself admirably. She even went so far as to raise her glass in a mocking salute to Victoria when the toasts were offered. The revolt seemed to have ended with Laurel's notion of the proper color for wedding guests' attire.

But when Victoria went up later to change out of her wedding suit, she discovered why Laurel had done nothing else. She had already struck before the ceremony.

Victoria and Barney had planned to spend a few days alone in Hawaii, flying out later this afternoon. Her suitcases, neatly packed earlier this morning, were open and all the clothing in them had been shredded into rags.

When she came back downstairs, still in her wedding suit, Barney said, "I thought you were going to change."

She could see the triumphant smile on Laurel's face as she waited for Victoria to tell Barney what she had done. Victoria leaned close to Barney and said, "I've decided to be romantic and buy whatever we need in Hawaii. Let's just leave."

Barney looked at her a little doubtfully, "Are you sure?"

"You say they always loose your luggage. Besides, we won't be wearing a lot of clothes, anyway." Barney brightened at that.

The bridal couple started toward the front door. The few guests in attendance followed them. Barney stopped in front of Laurel, kissed her goodbye gently, and took Victoria's arm once more.

Laurel's smile wavered and faded like a child who has been promised a birthday party and then finds there will be none as Victoria and Barney departed in a confusion of good wishes.

Victoria wondered grimly how much of her wardrobe would still be intact when she returned.

Sharon sat naked in the middle of the hotel bed reading *Daily Variety*. The item about Victoria's wedding was on the same page as the review of Sharon's new movie. Sharon didn't bother to read her review. She knew it would be good. They were always good now.

Professionally Inga was the best thing that had ever happened to Sharon. She had put Sharon into one serious role after another, building her from a star into an actress. And if she couldn't get the parts she wanted for Sharon one way, she could always get them another.

The short fat man washing himself so painstakingly in the bathroom was a very important studio executive who would make the final decision about an absolutely wonderful part. A part that would make some actress's career.

Sharon's name was on the short list and after today, it would be at the top.

Her reputation alone might have been enough to put it there, but Inga missed no chances. And no opportunities to make sure Sharon was at her beck and call.

If she didn't do exactly what Inga said, Andrew was the one who paid for her disobedience.

Her orders for today were to make sure the little fat man had a good time.

And she would. Because it was Andrew who would suffer if he didn't.

Caro and Temple found Daniel in the worst dive on Sunset. He had already been in at least one fight tonight. Blood was caked along his right eyebrow where someone's ring had gouged a line and there was a purple lump on the right side of his jaw. He was still drinking, and the weak little bartender hadn't had the nerve to cut him off, even though it was obvious he was too drunk to walk, let alone drive.

For once, Caro was glad the big Texan was around. She could never have gotten Daniel out of that place alone without Temple's help. Temple loaded him into her car and then followed her back to Daniel's in his Ferrari.

When they arrived, he carried Daniel upstairs and dumped him on his bed. Then he announced, "I'm no goddamned nursemaid," and went downstairs to mix himself a drink.

Caro was undressing Daniel when she found the clipping in his pocket, and item from *Daily Variety* about the wedding of Victoria Carr and Bernard Pace, the director. She read it over twice and then stuffed it back in his pocket.

A lot of things were clear now.

Daniel woke in a foul mood. It didn't lift his spirits any when he came downstairs and found Temple hovering around with his ever-present papers to sign. He fixed himself a drink and scrawled his signature carelessly across each one, not bothering to read them.

Caro came in just after he finished, thank God. She would have nagged him to read everything like she always did, and his head was already coming apart at the seams.

But instead of saying something about the paperwork, she hoisted the little paper bag she carried. "Surprise!"

"What's that?"

"Dr. Feelgood's Pharmacy."

She emptied the colored pills out on the bar and picked out two. "Dr. Feelgood suggests these for a hangover."

Dr. Feelgood turned out to be right.

Chapter Seventeen

1987

With a sigh, Victoria sat down at her dressing table and began to comb the night tangles from her hair. Rising was a problem. Her role on *The Clan* meant she had to get up early every morning. She tried to dress with a minimum amount of noise so that she wouldn't wake Barney. If she did, he'd never go back to sleep and she would feel guilty the rest of the day. The gray of exhaustion was always in his face now.

It would be easier all around if she and Barney had separate bedrooms, but Barney wouldn't hear of it.

Victoria didn't feel like insisting. Seeing the smirk of triumph on Laurel's face if her father moved out of Victoria's bedroom would be too much to bear, even if she and Barney knew the truth. So Victoria rose long before dawn and stumbled around the darkened bedroom in silence, preparing for the drive to the studio.

She never switched on a light until she was in the dressing room with the door angled so no glare would fall on Barney's face. In spite of the care she took not to disturb him, this was her favorite time of the morning. As she ran the comb through her hair, she could just see the line of Barney's shoulder beneath the sheet, moving slightly with the regular rise and fall of his breathing. That soft sound in her bedroom was the most wonderful thing she could imagine. It made up for all the other little irritants life continued to toss her way, the biggest of which was Laurel.

If she didn't love Barney so much, she would hate his daughter. Snide and sarcastic, making every bit of their living together a supreme strain for the three of them, Laurel was a jewel, all right.

Poor Barney would listen to her complain about Laurel for hours on end and never mention that it was at least partially Victoria's fault that Laurel had turned out to be such a mess. If only Dominic Solari had not stepped in and forced her to marry his son. If only Laurel had not been abandoned by her own mother.

If only, if only . . .

Life was full of regrets; the biggest of which was that she had wasted so many years away from Barney.

Barney stirred restlessly in his sleep, and Victoria grinned at herself in the mirror. Poor Barney! He had to listen to just as much bitching and complaining from Laurel about *her*. But he never passed a single word of that on.

Just as she was sure he never told Laurel that Victoria thought it high time a woman of twenty-four was out on her own and not still living with Daddy. But hard as it was for Barney to have the two women he loved best in the world living in the same house and hating each other, that was what he insisted on and that was how it was.

Barney stirred again and she wondered if he was having a bad dream. In a moment she would slip on her dress and tiptoe through the bedroom on her way downstairs to wait for the car to be brought around. But for right now, she just wanted to sit here, safe and secure. Ratings were down this season on *The Clan* and the writers were coming up with all sorts of crazy things for the characters to do in an attempt to boost popularity again. None of them would work, of course, but by the time everyone figured that out, *The Clan* would have lost a large part of its audience. Victoria wished she could talk to Barney about it, but she hated to bring up the subject. It would only remind him how long it had been since his last opportunity to direct.

She stood up with a sigh and began to slip on her clothes.

When she emerged, dressed, her hair hidden by a scarf and her face masked by dark glasses, Victoria paused.

Something in the bedroom had changed.

She took one uncertain step forward, and then another, before she realized what it was.

The soft whisper of sound that was the center of her universe had ceased.

Barney was no longer breathing.

"What could be so terrifying about pieces of silk?" Inga asked reasonably. She looked like an overweight motorcyclist in her black leather pants and vest, her arms rippling with muscles.

Sharon stood beside the bed, nude, her arms clutched tightly to her chest. She could still leave, she comforted herself. Even now, she could walk away. Nothing held her here. Nothing except the soft sound of Andrew's tears, muffled by the closed closet door.

"A fragile little piece of cloth," Inga soothed as she tied a scarf to Sharon's right wrist. "You could rip it with your fingernails." She tied another to Sharon's left wrist. "It's not the thing itself, you understand. The cloth is only a symbol."

The ribbons of silk were like soft caresses against Sharon's bare thighs. She could feel her nipples coming erect. Inga knelt at her feet with two more scarves. "I don't want to do this, Inga."

Inga paused. "Would you like Andrew to take your place?"

Would you like a cup of coffee? There was no more emotion in the flat words than if she had asked that. Sharon wanted to scream: *Yes! Take him! Not me!* The memory of the bright lines of blood the whip had left across his buttocks kept her silent.

As if she had spoken aloud, Inga nodded. "Very well, then." She tied a scarf to each of Sharon's ankles.

When Inga stood up, Sharon saw the last piece of silk she held in her hands and took an involuntary step backwards. "No!"

"Just another piece of silk. And of such fine quality, too. I got this one especially for you." Inga rubbed the shimmering black cloth against her own cheek. "So soft. So smooth. Just like your skin."

Sharon shook her head. "Not that, Inga."

"On the bed," Inga directed as though Sharon hadn't spoken.

Slowly Sharon sat down on the bed, the scarves trailing from her limbs.

"In the middle, Sharon." When she complied, Inga tied the scarf on Sharon's right wrist to the bedpost.

Sharon whimpered.

"That's not so bad," Inga scolded, the voice of the eternal nanny. She went on efficiently tying the knots until Sharon was bound to all four bedposts. "Not bad at all," she said as she leaned forward and touched her lips to Sharon's softly.

Then Inga took the last piece of silk, the shimmering black hood, and slipped it over Sharon's head, cutting off every vestige of light.

That was bad.

It was past midnight, but there were still three lines of cocaine on the table in front of Daniel. He had forgotten everything about the two men across from him, everything except that someone had pointed them out as looking for a project to invest in.

He was giving them the pitch he had honed with such perfection over the past two years. He had it down so well that sometimes he gave it to Caro as they were balling.

She didn't think that was funny.

He did, though. He thought a lot of things were funny. Particularly the way these two were hanging on his every word. Then he really got into the meat of the idea and he started to believe his own bullshit. Making this movie would mean a lot to him. Daniel took another snort, and waved to them to do the same. They declined and waited.

He wasn't sure that they understood the depth of this picture, what he really was talking about.

"This is the kind of film Barney Pace makes," he said.

The two exchanged glances.

Daniel could see that he was losing them. "As a matter of fact, I could bump myself up to producer on this baby, and bring Pace in as director. He's not doing much these days."

"He's not doing shit these days, Man," one of the two said. "Come on," he told his partner.

"What's wrong?" Daniel asked him. "Pace would be perfect for this." And maybe, just maybe, he could lure Victoria off that piece-of-shit TV show to star in it too. "He's just a little old, that's all."

"He's just a little dead, that's all," the first man said.

"You're fried," said the other one, starting to rise.

Daniel grabbed him by the lapel. "Wait a minute! Barney Pace is dead? When?"

"Are you shitting me? Six or eight months ago, man. The whole town went to the funeral."

He yanked himself free of Daniel's hand and the two of the walked away.

Daniel sat there, staring down at the coke. Barney had been dead for six months and he hadn't even realized it.

Even then he didn't comprehend the total significance of what he had learned. It was two days before he realized that he had one more opportunity with Victoria.

He wasn't going to blow it this time.

That was the morning he flushed three thousand dollars worth of cocaine down the toilet while Caro cursed.

1988

"It's insurance," Warren Neville told Inga Bradford as he showed her how to operate the hidden video camera. "You never know what might happen in this crazy business. This way you're prepared." The hefty lesbian wasn't one of his favorite people, but her money spent just like everyone else's.

As wily as Inga was, he was surprised she hadn't come up with this little moneymaking scheme herself. Videos of Sharon Bradford—even with an overweight dyke—would bring top dollar. Hell, he'd even shell out for that himself.

What he'd *really* like was a go at that luscious piece of ass himself, but no way would that happen while Inga was around.

One of these days, though . . .

"You are sure this will work?" Inga asked him. "There will be enough light?"

He patted her beefy shoulder. "Not to worry. You'll see every hair on her pussy with this baby. These films will be money in the bank. In fact, if you need someone to peddle them for you, just let me know. I've got connections.''

Inga's pale blue gaze turned hard. "You keep this to yourself, Warren.''

"Sure, Inga. You know you can trust me.''

Inga snorted. "Show me again the control in the bedroom.''

Owen Knox tapped the memo on his desk idly and stared into space. Talk of a *Charlie's Gang* reunion special had surfaced every few years, but nothing had ever come of it. The three child stars of *Charlie's Gang* had grown up to be very important people: a famous television star, a top Hollywood actress, and an Academy-award winning actor/director. It was considered extremely unlikely that any of the three would agree to film a special. But Daniel Garrick had let a few key people know that he might be available for the project, and that meant a whole new ball game.

Owen rubbed his shiny pink scalp thoughtfully. He had been small potatoes when *Charlie's Gang* went off the air in 1961, but now things were different. He had developed an eye for trends over the years that served him well on his climb to the top. Since taking over as President of Nayco Entertainment Group ten years ago, he had turned it into one of the major suppliers of fast-food entertainment in the business. He knew what worked and what would not. When the biggest network was committed to you for two pilots a year with at least one guaranteed to go series, that proved you had one of the top track records in the industry.

Owen's hobby was still information gathering and he had learned of Daniel's interest in a reunion special almost immediately. Owen knew if he could manage to get the three stars of *Charlie's Gang* to return for a two-hour prime time network reunion movie, it would be a professional coup. He already had a title in mind: *Whatever Happened to Charlie's Gang?*

Selling the project would be no problem. *Whatever Happened to Charlie's Gang?* had the two things network executives love best in a one-shot TV movie: promotability and stars, in this case, three of them.

There was an old Hollywood adage that people want to fuck movie stars and hug TV stars. As far as Owen was

concerned that meant the cast of the *Charlie's Gang* special
had the chance of drawing the TV *and* movie audiences; a
real blockbuster event! Those three famous faces would be on
the cover of *TV Guide, People,* and half-a-dozen other
magazines.

The project had winner written all over it.

All he had to do was sign the two women and get a
halfway decent script. Hell, if he got the three stars, it didn't
matter if the script was sheer crap.

But the script would be good; Owen would see to that.

These days he left nothing to chance.

". . . persistent rumors that Victoria Carr, Sharon Bradford, and Daniel Garrick might be considering a return to
television in a reunion special based on the *Charlie's Gang*
series which originally aired in the late fifties. However,
sources close to these top stars refused to comment on—"

Inga pointed her remote control at the television and the
female announcer's voice cut off in mid sentence. "No way
will I let you do that crap!" she told Sharon, slumped in an
armchair beside her. "I turned them down flat."

Andrew moved across to sit directly in front of the television, his glance riveted to the screen as clips from *Charlie's
Gang* began to run. For so many years, those three children
were the only reality in his life. The volume was so low he
could only hear whispers of the dialogue, but that was all
right. He moved his lips with the Weston children, knowing
the words as well as he knew his own name, even without the
sound.

A string of commercials replaced the clips, and depression
hit him like a physical blow. He slumped forward, his elbows
resting on his knees, his hands supporting his chin, and stared
at the screen. If wishes worked, he would be on the other side
of the glass with Bucky, and Nan, and JoJo, instead of here
with Inga.

Behind him there was the sharp sound of flesh striking
flesh. Andrew turned.

Inga and Sharon stood facing each other. Sharon was stripped
to the waist and Andrew longed to turn his eyes away from
her nakedness. Inga had taken off her skirt and wore nothing
at all from the waist down, but that was different because

Inga was his wife. Sharon was his sister and it wasn't right to look at your sister when she wasn't wearing any clothes. Some long-ago nurse had told him that, and he knew it was the truth. But the terror in Sharon's face made it impossible for him to look away.

Inga had her hands on Sharon's shoulders, pushing down, but Sharon refused to kneel until Inga slapped her face again.

With agonizing slowness, Sharon gave way to the pressure Inga applied, sinking to her knees on the carpet, her face level with Inga's crotch. Now Inga was pulling, instead of pushing, pulling Sharon's tear-streaked face toward the blonde mat of hair at the top of her legs.

Andrew, trembling, turned back to the screen, but the clips of *Charlie's Gang* weren't there anymore. He hugged his arms around himself, rocking back and forth in front of the television.

He wished the volume were on again so he wouldn't have to listen to the noises behind him. He put his hands to his ears, but he couldn't block the sound of another slap and Sharon's loud sob.

Andrew scrambled to his feet. The two women stopped their struggle for a moment, staring at him with angry blue eyes and terrified green ones.

"Go to your room, Andrew," Inga ordered. She raised her hand to Sharon again.

Andrew picked up the panty hose that Inga had dropped beside her chair and looped the legs around Inga's neck.

Inga released Sharon, who scrambled a few feet away, still sobbing. Inga's face was as ugly as a Halloween mask as she turned to face him. "I told you to go to bed." She smiled in the way that always meant he was going to feel pain. "If you want to play, I'll take care of you later. Now it is Sharon's turn."

She reached up to yank the hose from her neck, and Andrew jerked it tighter.

"Andrew!" she warned.

He pulled the loop tighter still.

The pressure against her windpipe transformed Inga's face. Now she had the same look of terror in those pale blue eyes that had been in Sharon's glance earlier.

She clawed at the hose, trying to free herself.

Andrew pulled tighter.

Tighter.

Tighter.

The slap was so unexpected that he released the hose and cradled his cheek with his hand.

Inga sat down heavily, yanking the hose from her neck, and panted for breath.

Bewildered, he met his twin's eyes. "What did you do that for?" he asked her.

Sharon put her arms around him, pressing her bare breasts against his shirt. He remembered what the long-ago nurse had said. If looking was bad, touching was ten times worse. He tried to shy away, but Sharon clung to him. The wetness of her tears soaked through his shirt front.

"Oh, Andrew," she said softly. "You mustn't do that. Bad things will happen to you if you kill Inga. You don't want to be punished."

He wondered what she meant by that.

Inga punished him every day.

Why did they have to bring that up again!

Didn't they realize he had served his time in prison?

The newscast had gone from clips of the old *Charlie's Gang* show to still photos of himself and Tina Sawyer. Emery Friedman grimaced at the TV. He hated to watch those old photos of Tina. It hurt too much to see the beauty his hands had destroyed.

Tina recovered to some extent from the beating, but he had been told she never regained her looks. Rumor had it she ended up as a common streetwalker. Emery had no idea whether that was true. By the time he emerged from prison, she had dropped from sight completely, presumed dead. He lost all contact with his wife and children, with all his old friends.

He rose to cut off the TV just as the female newscaster came back on the screen. "Here's a message for the three stars Hollywood is calling 'The Glitter Gang,'" she said, simpering at the camera. "Think of your fans. Nan . . . Bucky . . . JoJo . . . We want you back. And . . ." she added with a slow, conspiratorial wink, "the word *is* from Owen Knox, President of Nayco Entertainment Group, the money is good enough even to lure Hollywood's 'Golden Boy' back to the small screen.''

Emery switched off the set and picked up the phone. "Warren?'' he said, when Neville answered on the second ring. "I have three little jobs for you.''

"Legal or illegal?'' Warren Neville asked.

"Since when did you care?'' Emery Friedman replied.

"How can you watch that trash?'' Giselle Solari screamed at her husband. "That woman killed our son.''

Dominic Solari sighed and switched off the VCR. He had taped all of Victoria's performances on *The Clan*, so he could watch them days later without upsetting his wife. He'd had no idea she'd return from shopping so quickly this afternoon or he would never have indulged himself. It was not his wish to cause Giselle any more pain. The years had not treated Giselle kindly since her youngest son's death. She was a broken old woman. Still he could not help protesting mildly, "Victoria is a good actress. The show is—''

"She is a murderess!'' Giselle screeched. "A murderess who killed my boy!''

"You don't know what you're talking about.''

"A mother knows,'' she muttered darkly.

His wife left the study finally, still muttering to herself, and Dominic could not resist the temptation to turn the VCR on once more. What would Giselle have said if he told her a woman like that had been wasted on a treacherous little thief like her son? A woman like Victoria Carr deserved better than the man Dom Jr. had turned out to be.

The camera moved in for a close-up, and Dominic hit the pause button. He stared at Victoria's lovely face, filling the screen.

He had always been fascinated by Victoria Carr, Dominic admitted to himself. Now he realized that he was in love with her.

Squad cars blocked the drive of the Bradford mansion.

Sharon bolted from her car, not bothering to cut the engine, and raced into the house. A policeman started to block her way, and then recognizing that famous face, stepped aside and let her enter.

Voices came from upstairs, from Inga's bedroom. Sharon hurried up the stairs. A crowd of men, in police uniforms and plainclothes, were clustered by the door. A flashbulb went off in the interior of the bedroom.

Sharon shoved through the men. "Stop her!" a man in a suit yelled, but it was already too late. She was inside the room, her glance fixed as everyone else's was on the nude body, neck at an awkward angle, that hung by a rope from the light fixture.

The police photographer moved in for a close-up.

"My God!" Sharon screamed as the flash went off. "What happened?"

"Someone get her out of here," a policeman ordered.

Sharon was hustled out of the bedroom and down the stairs. "Sit here, Miss Bradford," someone said, leading her to the sofa.

Someone else placed a glass in her hand and ordered, "Drink this."

She drank the brandy like water, coughing and sputtering after she swallowed, until someone else pounded her on the back.

"Miss Bradford? Are you all right? Should we call a doctor?"

"What happened?" Her voice was calm, deliberate; her hand was shaking so hard the remaining brandy in the glass came close to sloshing out.

A man in a suit knelt down in front of her and took the glass from her hand. "Your sister-in-law is dead, Miss Bradford. I'm sorry."

"How . . ?" She remembered Andrew with the hose looped around Inga's neck. Her stomach rolled queasily. "How did—"

"It's not official yet . . ."

"Tell me," Sharon shrieked suddenly.

The man in the suit exchanged glances with another man in a suit. "Who's your doctor, Miss Bradford?"

It was an effort, but she made her voice calm once more. "I just want to know what happened."

"She killed herself."

Sharon blinked at him. "Inga?"

"Had you noticed if she was depressed recently? If she—"

"You think Inga. . ." Her teeth chattered as though she

had a chill. *Please God! Let Inga have killed herself. Don't let Andrew have murdered her. Please!*

"I'm sorry Miss Bradford. Sometimes it happens. There was an overturned chair at her feet. She just . . ." He looked at her face and fell silent.

After a moment, Sharon said, "Where's Andrew?"

"He's safe, Miss Bradford." The officer patted her hand. "Your parents have been contacted, and they sent someone to pick him up. You have nothing to worry about. We tried to get in touch with you, but the studio had no idea how to—"

"Andrew's with my parents?"

"Yes, Miss Bradford," the policeman said slowly, as though he were speaking to a child. "Would you like for this officer to contact someone for you?"

"I want to talk to my parents."

"Mike," the officer called across the room. "Give Miss Bradford the number where you reached her father."

Sharon waited impatiently for the man to find the number among his notes and then rushed into the study, closing the door behind her. She sat down behind the desk and dialed the number.

It rang.

And rang.

And rang.

Where was Andrew?

She dialed the number again.

It rang, and at the same time there was a soft knock on the door. "Come in," she said impatiently.

The phone kept ringing.

A policeman entered. "We'd rather you weren't alone just now, Miss Bradford."

The phone kept ringing.

Ringing.

She slammed down the receiver.

Where was Andrew?

Who the hell was his buddy? Owen Knox wondered as he paced around his office. Someone was going all out to ensure that nothing stood in Nayco's way on this *Whatever Happened to Charlie's Gang?* project.

Owen's grapevine had reported back some *very* interesting

snippets of information about the former stars of *Charlie's Gang*. Until now, Owen had thought he'd spent enough years in this town not to be surprised by *anything*. As a matter of fact, he *wasn't* surprised; he was stunned.

The word was out that Victoria Carr had received advance warning that her contract on the very popular night-time drama, *The Clan*, would not be renewed for next season. It was common knowledge that her lifestyle, which included the support of Barney Pace's daughter, made it imperative that she have more work as soon as possible to pay the bills. There was no way in the world she'd turn down the reunion special.

If Daniel Garrick hadn't already indicated an interest, getting him now would be no problem. Not after his portion of the financing of an upcoming movie had been mysteriously blocked, making the rest of the backers withdraw from the deal temporarily. The scuttlebutt around town was that the movie was so important to Garrick that he would do anything, even appear on a TV special, to get the project going again.

But today's news had been the kicker. Just when Sharon Bradford's agent appeared to be the only stumbling block to the project, the woman had committed suicide. With her gone, Sharon was a cinch to sign for the reunion special.

It was just too good to be true.

Not that the police had a shred of evidence Inga Bradford's death was anything but a suicide. Owen had already checked on that. But the agent's death had made Owen realize finally that someone was maneuvering the three former child stars into taking part in the special whether they wanted to or not. God or Fate, it made no difference. Owen would be the one who benefitted.

Alone in the office, he grinned suddenly.

Nothing would stop the special now.

BOOK THREE:
The Burning Man

The Hollywood Reporter
August 17, 1989

THREE DEAD AT NAYCO EXEC'S HOME

Three as yet unidentified bodies were discovered by fireman in the aftermath of Tuesday night's fire on the grounds of Nayco Entertainment Group President Owen Knox's Bel Air home. Authorities suspect arson in the fire which threatened several multimillion dollar homes in the area before fire fighters succeeded in bringing the blaze
—continued on page 21

Chapter Eighteen

1989

Long-legged, high-breasted, small-waisted, glistening with sweat on the large expanses of skin bared by the minimal lycra suits of peach and pearl, the two women followed the taped workout routine with identical grace. The mirrored walls of the exercise room doubled and redoubled the arrogantly slim and youthful bodies with no visible sign of the twenty years' difference in age between them.

"How long are we going to stay here?" Laurel Pace whined as the tape died away with a sigh and a click. She hated the whine in her voice, hated the Palm Springs house, hated the early morning workouts, hated her stepmother. *My wicked stepmother*, she thought as she caught Victoria Carr's surreptitious glance at herself in the nearest of the mirrors.

Now that the sweat of exercising had washed away the concealing mask of makeup, the difference between a twenty-six-year-old face and a forty-six-year-old face, even surgically improved, was dramatically obvious in the cold silver reflection. The surgeons with all their skills and the cosmeticians with all their potions could not replace the lost dew of youthful skin once it was gone. So why, then, were everyone's eyes always drawn to the older woman's face, as

Laurel's were now, ignoring her own fresh beauty for the brunette masterpiece beside her?

But masterpiece or not, the face was aging and Victoria saw it too, although the tiny frown line that appeared between the perfectly-arched brows was quickly smoothed away. Victoria had paid too much for that face to let a tiny thing like the truth mar it, Laurel thought savagely. "Why can't we go back to Los Angeles today instead of waiting until next week?" she demanded.

Victoria took her towel from the bar and patted her face delicately. "You know why," she replied with exaggerated patience as if the woman beside her were six instead of twenty-six. "I have to get in shape for the *Charlie's Gang* special."

"Why bother? No one's going to believe you anyway. TV's greatest bitch become Goody-Two-Shoes again for a couple of hours? What do you think that will prove?" Laurel swiped her own towel across her face, mopped the valley between her breasts, and then slung it back at the bar. It hit the mirror instead, leaving a damp parenthesis on the silvery surface before it slipped to the floor. "It's a little late to try and convince anyone you're really an actress, isn't it?"

"It will convince them I'm a star, darling, and that's something else entirely. It will prove to those bastards at the network that my fans watch *me*, Victoria Carr, not the character I play on *The Clan*."

Laurel listened idly, more interested in the incipient cellulite the high-cut suit exposed on her lean flanks than in Victoria's machinations. Sometimes the poor senile dear seemed to be having trouble remembering she was just a has-been who had lucked into a last refuge on a prime-time soap. Lately she seemed to be suffering from the delusion that she actually *was* the brilliant, conniving bitch she played to perfection each week on *The Clan*. Laurel smiled at the curve of her thigh. That would make a nice speculation for the manuscript she was working on in secret, the book she had fondly titled, *Stepmommy Dearest*. "Why do you even care what they think, Victoria?"

"I care and you'd better care, too . . . if you want to go on sponging off me. We live a little too well, you know. Neither of us has ever had to economize. We could regret that."

Laurel looked up at her stepmother and smiled sweetly. "Why should we when they keep paying you such fabulous sums for being a nasty but glamorous old hag?"

The look in Victoria's eyes made Laurel think she had finally succeeded in actually wounding her stepmother; then Victoria's next words wiped the delighted smile from Laurel's face. "They may not renew me for next season on *The Clan*."

All Laurel could think of was that the piles and piles of manuscript pages in her bedroom wouldn't be worth shit if Victoria Carr fell off the top of the bitch heap before she could get them published. "You can't let them do that," she said, the childish whine back in her voice.

"I'm not sure I can stop them," Victoria said softly, as much to herself as to Laurel. "Whatever I do has to be done before it's general knowledge that I won't be offered a new contract. Once word leaks out, no one will touch me. That's why I was in such a rush to sign up for the *Charlie's Gang* special. It's like fate or the network or someone was making sure I didn't have any choice." She shrugged helplessly, looking lost and vulnerable for the first time in the twenty years Laurel had known her. "And I don't. No choice at all. We're going to need that money very badly, I'm afraid."

Laurel stared at her blankly. "How could you let this happen?" she screamed suddenly.

Victoria reached for her, but Laurel backed away, glancing around wildly. She snatched up a leg weight and threw it overhanded across the room. It smashed into the mirrored wall and glass exploded everywhere. As if that were a signal the maid began to scream somewhere in the house.

Victoria reached down and picked up another leg weight. "Here," she said, tossing it to Laurel. "Do it again if it makes you feel any better. But it won't change things. You'll still have to grow up one of these days."

The maid began to screech on a different key . . . something about fire . . . the police . . .

Victoria turned and hurried out of the room.

Laurel tossed the leg weight aside and followed, her tantrum forgotten for the moment. She found Victoria and the maid standing in the entry hall, staring at a scorched spot on the oriental rug. The maid had the presence of mind to douse the little blaze with the atrium hose before the smoldering carpet could burst into flames. "Someone threw it in here, *Senora*," she cried. "You call the police, yes?"

Victoria stared down at the obscene little wire figure that the flames had liberated, her face ashen.

"You call the police, Miz Carr," the maid demanded. "You call now?"

"Oh. My. God." Victoria sank to her knees beside the scorched spot on the rug.

"Victoria?" Laurel said hesitantly. "What is it, Victoria?"

"Miz Carr?" the maid asked. "You want me to call the police?"

Victoria paid no attention to either one of them. She wrapped her arms around herself as though she were unbearably cold, and began to rock back and forth as the sobs came.

"Victoria!" Laurel cried, outraged. "You can't do this!"

The tears came faster, twisting Victoria's beautiful face, racking her body, making her ugly. Ugly!

"Don't you do this," Laurel screamed at her stepmother. "You can't do this, Victoria!" She fell forward on Victoria, knocking her to the floor, and began to pummel Victoria's defenseless body with her fists.

"Miz Pace! Miz Pace!" the maid screamed.

Beyond hearing, Laurel struck the weeping woman beneath her. She was sobbing herself when the squat maid finally managed to pull her off of her stepmother's helpless form.

"You're supposed to take care of me!" Laurel screamed at the huddled figure on the floor. "You're supposed to take care of me, you bitch!"

"What the fuck is going on?"

Temple Jackson grinned at the big angry man pacing in front of the glass-walled view of lush California greenery at the other end of the huge teak-paneled family room. There was nothing sweeter than hearing a maverick squall when the hot iron hit its ass, the Texan thought. Not unless it was watching an expert turn one of the little fuckers into a steer, and it looked like that day wasn't too far off either. "Somebody just doesn't want you to make that movie. Nothing to get so excited about. Have a drink. Send for some blow. Fuck my new secretary." His grin widened. "Now there's an idea,

Daniel. That little mama's been hot for you ever since the day I hired her. Want me to give her a call?''

Daniel wasn't listening. "Christ, Temple! Do you realize how much of my own fucking cash I have invested in *Night Time*?''

"Mistake Number Two," Temple said calmly. That the financing for *Night Time* was all crapped up was just one more sign that Mama Jackson's boy better be winding up his little stint as Daniel Garrick's business manager and moving on to greener pastures. The hefty amounts Temple had managed to siphon off from Daniel's money as it passed through his hands had given him ample traveling funds, and the indications that someone was getting ready to nail Daniel's ass to the barn door said, Make your reservations *today*, Son. But the rawboned Texan was surprised to find he was enjoying himself too much to miss whatever was about to happen next. Temple loved the way life's little shitpiles tended to even things out between the tortoises and the hares. Nobody loved a Golden Boy forever and Daniel Garrick had been too lucky too long. It was going to be downright soul-satisfying to see him have to bend over and join the rest of the poor, sore-assed bastards for a change. "You forgot the prime rule of business, Son. O. P. M. Other People's Money."

"Which leads to N. F. A. C.," Daniel snapped.

"What's that?"

"No Fucking Artistic Control. I didn't spend all these years getting to where I am just so that some asshole can grab me by the balls."

Temple shrugged. "He didn't grab them. You handed them to him on a big silver platter. Now he's got 'em on a sharp stick over a slow fire."

Daniel stopped his pacing beside the massive stone fireplace. With that golden tan and the golden hair and all that golden sunshine gilding him, he looked like a real Golden Boy, Temple thought. Like the two Oscars on the mantel behind him. It was going to be *damned* satisfying to see Daniel Garrick take his tumble.

"Mistake Number Two?" Daniel said suddenly. "So what was Mistake Number One?"

Temple shoved his mind firmly back on track. It didn't do to let your attention wander around Daniel or you'd find your own ass nailed to the barn. "Fucking," he pronounced. "Isn't that always your first mistake, son? That goddamned Pearson's too tight-assed for this to be a simple business deal. Who were you playing around with? His wife or his daughter? Or did you stick it to his mistress?"

Daniel smiled for the first time since Temple had shown up at his royal command and all the charm that made him so dangerous came flooding out into the room. Temple had to fight his own instinctive response to it. "I'm innocent," Daniel told him.

Temple snorted. "Bullshit! No one tries to shave your balls off with this much delight if you haven't been fucking someone near and dear to them, Daniel."

The smile faded. "You're right. But I haven't. So find out why the razor's out. And in the meantime—"

"In the meantime, we have what's known as negative cash flow, son. All you have going for you is this What-happened-to-Charlie's-Gang-piece-of-shit. Don't blow that one, Daniel. We need the money."

"Sure," Daniel promised easily, the smile lighting up again.

"Don't pull that crap with me," Temple said fiercely. "You gotta do that show whether it makes you lose your lunch or not."

"Nothing's going to keep me from doing it, Temple. I promise you that."

There was so much conviction in Daniel's voice that it made the Texan nervous. He'd been expecting Daniel to reject doing the remake of the kiddy show ever since the project first came up. So why wasn't he? Temple liked knowing why Daniel did what he did. It was safer that way. And to do this piece of kiddy shit was out of character for the man who was fighting tooth and nail for artistic control over *Night Time*. But then so was weaning himself off the blow. If there had been one nice thing about Daniel's bitch girl friend, Caro Hensley, it was that she had kept Daniel so blitzed on cocaine he hadn't known or cared about his financial condition. He had left everything to Temple, and Mama Jackson's boy had done just fine.

Now everything had changed.

Daniel was clean and sharp for the first time in years and

that was dangerous for Temple. But whoever had Daniel by the balls had the Golden Boy's complete attention at the moment.

Go or stay? That was the question. Should he leave while the getting was good? Or stay and take one more slice off the top?

Before the financing of *Night Time* went sour, Temple had his mouth all set for a piece of the *Charlie's Gang* action. Now he was beginning to suspect someone else did, too. Daniel hadn't realized it yet, but it looked like someone was trying to make sure he didn't have any choice but to sign for the reunion show. And Mama Jackson's boy knew for a dead solid fact that nobody did nothing except for cash. So the real question was that with an unknown partner in the game, was there gonna be enough gravy left for everybody to sop the plate? He would to have to spend a little time refiguring the odds on this one. Temple strolled over to the bar and poured himself a calming slug of Scotch. "Look, Daniel," he began. "Why don't we—"

A tiny popping sound from somewhere outside interrupted him, and suddenly Daniel wasn't looking or listening. He barrelled past Temple and through the French doors, slamming them against the walls with such violence that they rebounded in a shower of shattered glass.

The Texan followed slowly, picking his way through the broken glass as he stepped between the ruined doors. He had an awful feeling that one of life's little shitpiles might be laying right ahead of him, and he was going to do his goddamnedest not to step right in it.

Outside, Temple hesitated, giving himself plenty of time to look around before he stepped out into the open, away from the shelter of the house. Too fucking much cover, he thought with that churning feeling in his lower intestines he'd had so often in Nam. The sniper could be anywhere.

At the far end of the patio, Daniel knelt over the huge, apricot-colored mastiff sprawled on the flagstones like a toy that had lost its stuffings. His arms were around the beast, his broad back exposed, unprotected.

Temple waited for a long slow count of ten. When Daniel still knelt there unbloodied, Temple forced himself to walk

across the flat, paved expanse, praying he wouldn't crap his
pants on the way.

It was only thirty feet to where the big man knelt; it seemed
like a mile. The Texan's armpits stunk with sweat by the time
he reached him. "Daniel?"

"Some son of a bitch shot my dog," Daniel said hoarsely,
still cradling the massive head and shoulders.

Beyond Daniel, by the pool's edge, a small blaze merrily
scorched the flagstone beneath it. "He left you a present."

Daniel followed Temple's gaze. "What the fuck is that?" He
lowered the dog's huge head gently to the flagstones and went
to investigate. Hoping like hell their sniper had simply offed
the dog and run, Temple followed Daniel to the side of the pool.

By the time they reached it, the small fire was already out.
Clearly visible through the last of the smoke was the glowing
red wire shape of a man.

Temple nudged the strange little figure with his shoe.
"Holy shit! Talk about your fucking wishful thinking. Look
at the prong on that guy!"

Daniel stared down at the object without speaking.

"This shithole town is full of more crazies than Houston
and that's going some." Temple glanced around nervously.
"I'll call the cops."

Daniel caught Temple's arm before he could start back to
the house. Temple was only a couple of inches shorter than
Daniel. Back in Nam they'd been on almost equal terms. But
Daniel had remained all steel-hard muscle beneath that golden
skin and Temple knew that these days he had the soft ass and
slack belly of a pencil pusher. With a calculator and columns
of figures was the only way he could take Daniel Garrick
now. The thought of just how much more he could take the
other man for before he cut out for high ground kept Temple
standing quietly while Daniel's fingers bit into his arm. Daniel continued to stare at the crazy little wire figure with the
enormous cock until the red glow of wire dulled to gray.

Daniel let go of Temple so suddenly that the Texan staggered. "We're not calling anyone. Help me bury this goddamned dog."

A walled garden sheltered the graceful cedar and stained
glass front of the low-slung home from intruders, but the rear

of the house was open to the beach and Malibu's celebrity parade. Wearing only his red swim briefs, Warren Neville strode along the priciest sand in the world just as though he belonged there with all the other beautiful bodies.

As he approached the house, Warren waved and nodded and smiled with just the right amount of disdain and disinterest to convince even the most glittering of the stars on the sand this evening that he had as much right to his space in the fast lane as any of them. Who would think he did not? Star quality? He had it. Rippling muscles and magnetic eyes? He had those, too.

When he reached the wooden stairs to the deck, Warren went up them without even so much as a casual glance over his shoulder to see if he was observed. It made no difference. The woman inside the house was his now, whether she knew it or not. All that remained were the formalities. Inside the tight swim briefs, his cock stirred at the thought; he'd had a hard-on for two days just thinking about the formalities. He didn't let the drawn curtains behind the sliding door to the deck deter him. He knew that inside Sharon Bradford waited for him. Warren rapped on the glass sharply.

The curtain moved and the most beautiful face in Hollywood stared through the glass at him. Tousled blonde hair and unbelievable green eyes in a perfect oval face; Sharon Bradford was even more lovely in person than on the screen. More beautiful from a foot away then she had been across a crowded restaurant or a studio parking lot. She gazed at him blankly and let the curtain fall shut.

Warren had expected that. He rapped on the glass again, more sharply than before. For a brief moment there was no response, and he glanced around the deck for something to heave through the glass. Then the door shot open along its track, taking him by surprise, and Sharon Bradford herself half-stumbled, half-fell against him, so that he held her priceless ass in his hands.

"What the hell do you want?" she demanded, shoving his hands away. She was drunk, which he had expected. On champagne, judging by the crystal flute in her right hand, and that he would not have guessed. But he was thankful for small favors; he hated the second-hand taste of gin in a woman's mouth.

Warren moved swiftly, countering her fumbling attempts to push away from him. To anyone on the beach below, his movement would make it seem as though she were hugging him in greeting and ushering him inside, when actually he was half-dragging, half-carrying her off the deck and back into the room behind her. Once inside, Warren allowed her to push him away. He shut the sliding door and closed the curtains before he allowed himself the luxury of looking at what his hands had just explored.

Sharon Bradford wore a simple white cotton sundress, only nothing on that body could ever be simple. Her nipples stuck out hard and straight like little thumbs beneath the sheer cotton, and he had a difficult time lifting his eyes to her face. When he did, Warren saw that she wasn't alarmed, not yet. She was drunk and confused and a little angry, but not alarmed. "I don't know you," she complained. "Who are you?"

"I'm Warren. Warren Neville." Suddenly his palms were damp. "Inga wanted us to work together."

Sharon shook her head. "Inga's dead."

His nervousness vanished. He stepped closer. "Inga was worried about you. She said she couldn't feel the heat anymore. She said you were cold."

"She's the one who's cold! She killed herself, you stupid bastard!" Sharon pushed past him, heading for the open champagne bottle on the table behind him.

Warren leaned over and grabbed it before she could and held it just out of her reach. "Last year you were on the 'A' list, Sharon. Right up there at the top. Now you're on the 'D' list and going down. Inga would never have let you do anything as stupid as turning down that *Charlie's Gang* special. She said to me, 'Warren, if something happens to me, you take care of Sharon. Help her make the right decisions.' She said to me, 'Warren, you can make her hot again. One picture with you and she's on top again.' " That last wasn't part of his deal with Emery Friedman, but Warren had no intention of letting an opportunity like this get away from him. 'Someday' was finally here.

"I told you Inga's dead." Sharon set the crystal flute down with exaggerated care and ran her fingers through the tousled blonde mane. "I'm between agents right now, but I won't be for long. I'm going to get a male agent this time. Men make all the decisions in this town anyway.'' She seemed to have forgotten Warren stood there. "I'm tired of having a woman agent.''

"No top agent will touch you now, Sharon. You're cold. Inga knew I could bring back the heat. She knew I'd be good for you. The chemistry—''

"What are you, thirty-one? Thirty-two? They want kids now.''

His face hardened. What did she think she was at thirty-nine? "I'm twenty-seven," he lied.

"I'm sure you'll get your big break, Warner—''

"Warren!''

She focused on him with an effort. "Warren. But it will be with someone besides me. Now you have to go." She leaned forward, steadying herself with both hands on the tabletop, her tits pointed straight at him. If a man weren't careful those hard little thumbs would poke his eyes out. "I'm waiting for someone.''

"I know you're waiting for someone, Sharon. Me." He gave her the smoldering look he practiced in his mirror a dozen times a day.

"That's a good line," she told him. "Try it on someone in your own league.''

"I am in your league, Sharon." Warren wasn't daunted. He had known it would take time to convince her. He decided not to mention the six video casettes, Inga's private films of Sharon. Not yet. He would give her time to get used to him before he let her know what he planned for the two of them. That was the best way. "Your new agent will be contacting you tomorrow about the *Charlie's Gang* special. You just sign the contract like a good girl.''

"I don't know what you're talking about. You'll have to leave." Sharon straightened up, smoothing the white cotton dress across her thighs. Thinking of what lay between them, Warren almost came. "Someone will be here in a few minutes with something very important to me. You'll have to—''

"With news about your brother," he said flatly. "Here I am.''

Sharon looked at him doubtfully. "I don't think you're the one.''

''I talked to him yesterday. He's fine. He sends his love.''

The look that leaped into those green eyes made his cock twitch, and then she was all over him, beating at him with her fists. ''Where is he? Where the hell is he? You've got to tell me where he is!'' she yelled, while her tits bounced and rubbed against his bare chest.

Warren grabbed her and slammed her down onto the white leather sofa. She scrambled away, screaming, and he grabbed her again, careful not to bruise that delicate skin as he reached up under her skirt and ripped her panties away. For all the magnificent tits and ass, she was really a scrawny little thing once he had her down on the sofa, firmly impaled on his swollen shaft. He thrust into her furiously and came almost at once with such force that he thought his balls were exploding.

Warren lay on her limp form heavily until he caught his breath. ''God, baby! You could make a man lose his mind with something like that.'' He rolled off and stood up, pulling his swim briefs back up, and smiled down at her. That was how he liked to see his women, freshly ploughed. The tears on her cheeks didn't bother him; he knew they wouldn't last for long, just until she got used to him. But her eyes were still squeezed shut and he wanted to see that vibrant green one more time before he left. He reached over and stroked the soft curve of her cheek. ''Come on, baby. Give us a smile,'' he coaxed.

Her eyelids fluttered open and green ice stared back at him. ''You don't even know my brother!''

''Oh yes I do, Sharon. Inga and Andrew and I got to know each other very well. We talked about you a lot.''

Whatever she was about to say died on her lips.

''We're going to get along fine,'' he assured her. ''When your new agent calls tomorrow, you just sign the reunion special contract like a good girl.''

''Where's Andrew?'' she whispered.

''I'll keep in touch,'' Warren told her. He had convinced her like Friedman wanted. Now he was anxious to get away and start things moving for himself. This was it. The big one. Warren Neville and Sharon Bradford. They'd be legends, like Tracy and Hepburn.

He paused, his hand on the closed curtain, and looked back at her. She was standing now, and except for the tear tracks on her cheeks and the ruined panties on the floor beside the sofa, there wasn't a hint in the room of what had just happened.

Warren smiled and jerked his hand back as something crashed against the other side of the door. "Shit!" he yelped. "What was that?"

Sharon shook her head numbly.

Warren shoved back the curtain. The wooden deck was empty except for a small blazing object laying just outside the glass. He slid the door open and stared down at it for a moment before he crossed the room for the open bottle of champagne. The blaze had blackened the timbers beneath it by the time he returned. Warren released a generous splash of champagne over the flames and they died in a sputter of protest.

Sharon came up behind him as he stared down at the crazy little wire figure with the king-sized cock. "What is this?" he asked her. "Some kind of party favor?"

Sharon Bradford threw back her head and began to laugh.

Warren's palm itched with the urge to slap her out of her hysteria. But he was no fool and marking that face would be a truly foolish thing to do. He upended the bottle of champagne instead, drenching her hair with the rest of it.

She shut up abruptly.

Warren slung the empty bottle back into the room behind her. It bounced and rolled across the hardwood floor. "I'll be in touch," he told her and took the stairs to the beach two at a time.

As he jogged along the sand, he smiled at all the beautiful bodies wrapped in the warm glow of sunset.

He really did belong.

The burning figures had not worked. The three on the flickering black and white screen still ignored him. They had forgotten the burning man.

Together Again, the advertisements said. *Nan, Bucky, and JoJo. A September Special. Wait for It.*

But he had already waited for almost thirty years.

He wasn't waiting anymore.

Chapter Nineteen

Daniel sat in his armchair, reading through the script of the reunion special. Caro, sprawled on the sofa across the room, regarded him warily. He looked different, older, more mature, with his reading glasses on, and that bothered her almost as much as the script in his hands. She just didn't know how to take him recently. He seemed to be slipping out of her control. He didn't indulge in anything these days from cocaine to sex—at least not with her, she thought bitterly.

Victoria Carr was the reason.

Daniel had become a different person since the subject of the *Whatever Happened to Charlie's Gang?* special came up. Caro knew it was because he still had a thing for Victoria Carr. Soon he would spend three weeks shooting the TV movie, three weeks from morning to night with Victoria Carr while he shut Caro out of his life. What was she going to do when that happened? Caro wondered.

Watching him frown with concentration as he read the script made her angry. But almost immediately that anger froze into icy purpose, a legacy from her father. She knew it wold be fatal to bring Victoria's name into the conversation; she attacked obliquely. "You're not seriously thinking about doing that piece of crap, are you? Nobody with credentials like yours does shit like that."

"So you're an expert on careers now," Daniel said without looking up from the script. "How do you find time with all your extracurricular activities?"

Ever since he had cleaned up himself, he'd been after her

to drop her casual drug dealing. And she had for the most part, only keeping it up where she could gain some personal advantage from the transaction. Like the services of Warren Neville.

She got up and came across the room to sit on the arm of his chair. "That hurts, Daniel. You know I care what happens to you." She laid her hand on his arm and he looked at it as though it were a spider that had dropped there from the ceiling.

"Come off it. You are the coldest, most self-contained bitch I've ever met, Caro. It's your main charm."

He had told her that before and usually she laughed at him, but this time she found she couldn't. This time it really hurt. Was it her fault that her illustrious parents had gone out of their way to make her an emotionless bloodsucker? She jumped up and walked over the glass wall at the other end of the room.

Daniel continued to read the script. When she didn't reply, he looked up.

The reflection of her face in the glass made him rise and come to stand beside her. "We're really not that good for each other, Caro. You know that."

"You're good for me," she insisted stubbornly.

"You know that's not true."

She refused to reply and he went back to his armchair, to the script, to Victoria Carr.

Why was it that everyone you ever loved never loved you? Caro wondered.

After a moment she went over and sat down on the carpet at Daniel's feet. "Here," she said, slipping the script from his hands. "I'll help you learn your lines."

Victoria sat in a lounger by the pool, a floppy straw hat shielding her face as she read the script for the reunion special. A faint breeze stirred the pages and she was struck by the sensation of *déjà vu*, reminded of the first time she had leafed through the script of *Charlie's Gang* on the beach at her grandparents' house.

So much had depended on that script.

So very much depended on this one.

Thank God she had left Laurel in Palm Springs. And thank

God there had been no further sign that someone knew the secret of Nick Hanson's death. Whoever had delivered the wire figures to herself, Daniel, and Sharon had not resurfaced or sent any demands.

As Victoria leafed through the script, she had the most terrifying feeling that she was fighting for her life these days. Without her part in *The Clan*, she had nothing. She should have pushed Laurel out on her own after Barney died, but she couldn't. Her lingering loyalty to Barney prevented it. So did the knowledge of what her own desertion had done to the girl. But she knew they were not good for each other. And if Laurel ever found out the truth about Victoria, about Victoria's family, she would destroy Victoria with it. She wouldn't be smart enough to understand that Victoria was the only thing that stood between her and poverty.

Perhaps smart wasn't the right word. Emotionally mature was the real term. All Barney's attempts to shelter and protect Laurel had only made her supremely dependent.

God, how she missed him!

It had been so hard watching his career slide. She wondered if Laurel realized that it was Victoria's money and not Barney's which had kept them going ever since she and Barney married. Laurel had protested violently when Barney let his own house go to move in with Victoria, not realizing he had only leased it over the years. Victoria had bought the Palm Springs house after Barney died, hoping that staying there for part of the year would help both her and Laurel to recover their equilibrium. All it had done was drain the coffers even further.

Victoria turned to the script again. It was extremely well written and she had been delighted to see that the scriptwriter had given her an unexpected bonus. Daniel's character, Bucky, was a divorced, single parent of two boys, poised on the brink of marriage to the divorced, single parent of two girls. Sharon's character, JoJo, had become an independent, unmarried business woman, owner of a chain of aerobic studios. But Victoria's character, Nan, was the matriarch of a large family of her own.

Victoria's instincts told her there was a powerful television series in that concept. The reprise of the Nan character could give her career a new turn. To go from being the ultimate

prime-time bitch she played on *The Clan* to the "good woman"
who headed up an entire family: the promotional possibilities
alone would get the series off to the kind of start that would
guarantee its success.

But there was more to it than that. The character she played
on *The Clan* was basically immoral, as were most of the other
characters on the evening melodrama. Their family unit was
the source of endless plot turns and twists, with its strife and
backbiting.

Maybe, just maybe, America was ready for a new view of
the family. A family that loved each other and worked to help
each other achieve their goals.

Betrayal, greed, and lust were the distinguishing characteristics of the family on *The Clan*. But there could be a
different kind of family on evening television next season,
one whose hallmarks were love, hope, and laughter.

Nan's family.

Victoria desperately wanted to play the woman Nan had
become.

So she couldn't afford to mess up on this role. She had to
put everything else out of her mind, including Laurel, and the
delivery of the mysterious little burning figure.

But could she play that good woman? Victoria felt almost
as helpless as when she first confronted the problem of playing
Nan on the original *Charlie's Gang*. The difficulty of making
someone believe that she came from a happy family. That
Victoria Carr could indeed be someone's favorite.

Involuntarily she thought of Dominic Solari. He was the
only person who still knew her secret. She had called him
from Palm Springs the day the burning man was tossed into
her house. She had been crying hysterically, and he had
not recognized her voice at first. He talked to her for
over an hour, gradually calming her down until she could
describe the little wire figure. But when it came to telling him
why she had been so terrified by the symbol of the burning
man, she balked.

When reason finally intruded, she was careful to ask him
for nothing. She assured him that it had been enough to talk
to him, to dispel her fears. She had not given him the
opportunity to ask how he could be of service. She wanted no
more debts owed to Dominic Solari.

And yet there was a connection between them anyway, something neither of them could deny.

After she returned to Los Angeles, he had fallen into the habit of calling her once or twice a week, near midnight. She lay in bed with the lights out and the phone at her ear, and his deep voice was her entire world. They talked about her day, about how the special was progressing. They never spoke of him, of his life, of what he was doing.

He had been in the paper a few weeks ago. She had been leafing through the *L.A. Times*, and Dominic's eyes had suddenly stared into hers. He had been embroiled in some kind of investigation, but the news story had been careful not to put any labels on him. Like mobster. Or Mafia.

Victoria wondered if Dominic's wife had seen the article. If Giselle had seen it, would she have read it?

Each time the phone rang near midnight and she picked it up, Victoria realized she was treading a dangerous tightrope. Dominic was a fascinating, exciting, and deadly man; one slip and she would be in his debt again. She didn't understand why, but the thought of that made her feel alive again, for the first time since Barney's death.

It was strange but Dominic was the only man in the world who knew what she was. Just as she knew what he was.

However close he might be to Giselle, Victoria was certain his wife did not know that he had their son murdered.

Victoria shivered in the warm California sun and went back to the script.

Every time the door to the makeup trailer opened, Sharon gave a nervous start, twisting around in the high, canvas-backed chair to see who had entered.

"Do you want me to bar everyone until we finish?" Gerald Parks, the makeup man, asked nastily. He was afraid they would hold up shooting again today while he worked on her and he would be blamed once more.

Sharon tried to smile, but it came out more like a grimace. "Sorry, Gerry," she murmured. Victoria had her own makeup artist and Daniel had already come and gone. But it was taking the makeup man longer and longer each day to erase the dark circles under Sharon's eyes with his sponges and brushes. She realized her squirming didn't help. "I'll try to be still."

"Do that!" he snapped, not mollified at all.

Sharon was a basket case and she knew it. She couldn't believe what was happening to her! She hadn't been able to get in touch with Andrew since Inga's death. The police told her he was with her parents. But she hadn't been able to contact her parents either, and no one seemed to have any idea where they might be staying. Neither they nor Andrew had come to Inga's funeral. The only reason Sharon had gone was the vain hope that her twin might be there.

She was glad Inga was dead!

But she couldn't rid herself of the terrifying fear that Andrew had murdered his wife. That was why she hadn't filed a missing persons report with the police. The authorities still believed Inga had committed suicide, but Sharon knew her torturer well enough to know that Inga would never have killed herself.

Inga loved to give pain, not to receive it. She would never have put that rope around her own neck. She didn't believe in ropes. A silk scarf, the mere symbol of bondage, was enough for Inga. She didn't need the reality of rope or chain. And especially not around *her* neck. Always someone else's. Sharon rubbed her own neck with a trembling hand.

Where was Andrew?

She couldn't believe how quickly her father's influence had gotten Andrew whisked away after Inga's death. Whatever hush-hush thing her father did for the government still gave him more power than ordinary mortals, even after all these years. But what had he done with Andrew? Had he and Mother hidden her twin away somewhere? Or worse: had they finally had Andrew committed?

And then there was Warren Neville.

She wouldn't think about the rape. If she started thinking about that, she would go crazy!

The makeup man reached for a new brush. Ignoring the no smoking sign, Sharon took advantage of the pause to light a cigarette, a new habit she'd picked up since Inga's death.

"Sharon!"

She took three quick puffs, inhaling deeply with each one,

and then snubbed it out. Gerald made a production of fanning
the smoke away with a magazine.

So far she had managed to avoid Neville again. But to do
so, she had given in to his demand and signed with the new
agent. First the reunion special, the agent had told her, and
then a movie with Neville. She had nodded, her teeth clenched
together to keep them from chattering, but she wasn't going
to do any movie with Neville. She would kill the son of a
bitch before she let him get near her again. If it weren't for
Andrew she would have had him arrested. But if he knew
anything about Andrew at all she couldn't risk it. She *had*
gone to the police and tried to get a gun permit, but they had
refused to issue one to her.

Beyond that brief stolen moment together at the press
conference, she and Daniel and Victoria hadn't discussed the
tiny burning men that had been delivered to each of their
doors. No one had come forward to blackmail them. But it
couldn't be coincidence. Someone knew what had happened
on that long ago day.

This afternoon she had another meeting with the publicist.
More prying and poking. He was looking for any angle to
publicize the reunion special. She was doing her best not to
give him anything.

One more thing, Sharon thought grimly. Just one more
thing and she would go stark, raving mad.

"Sharon! For heaven's sake, be still! Do you want to hide
out in here all day?"

"Sorry, Gerry," she murmured, but that was exactly what
she did want. To hide here, or else on the set, back in the
fantasy world of *Charlie's Gang*.

Only even that was starting to change. Something was
happening to her as they worked through the script. It was as
though the grown-up JoJo was beginning to have an effect on
Sharon Bradford the actress.

Sharon wondered if Daniel and Victoria felt that way, too.

She reached for her cigarettes.

"Sharon!"

Bucky leaned over and took JoJo's hand in his. "Don't you
see? That time is gone. I can't go through the rest of my life
being called a kid's name like Bucky. I'm a grown man now.

I've got children of my own now. I'm Charles, not Bucky. And you're Joan, not JoJo.''

"I don't want to be Joan," JoJo said forlornly, that pathetic little catch still in her voice after all those years. "I don't want to let that time go, Bucky!"

Charles "Bucky" Weston leaned over and put his arm around his sister. "It's already gone, Joan. The only thing we can do is try to recreate it for our own kids.''

The tears came tricking down Sharon's face right on cue, and Daniel almost felt like crying himself. When the director approached, Daniel saw that his eyes were suspiciously moist. Half the people on the set were bawling.

"I grew up with that goddamned show," the director said and walked away swiftly, dabbing at his eyes.

Daniel gave Sharon a hug that wasn't in the script, and she looked up at him with surprise, the tears still running down her cheeks. "We did it, Sis!" he said exuberantly. "There won't be a dry eye in America when they play that one."

Victoria had walked on to the set and now she crossed over and put her arms around them. "Both of you were great. You just stole the whole show right there."

"You've got some good scenes, too," Daniel said magnanimously, but he wasn't so sure she hadn't spoken the truth just now.

Sharon started to edge away and Daniel grabbed her by the shoulder once more. "Oh no you don't, Sis," he said, "I'm taking both of you lovelies out to dinner. This has been too good a day not to celebrate!"

"Oh, Daniel, I can't," Victoria said contritely. "I'm meeting my stepdaughter later. She just got in from Palm Springs. It's something I really can't get out of."

They were alone now, the three of them, with no one else in earshot. "Have either of you been bothered again by our little dollmaker?" Daniel asked in a low voice.

"Nothing," Victoria said. "It's so strange. I thought someone would at least demand money."

"We'll keep our fingers crossed," he told her.

Victoria left and Sharon said, in a small voice, "I'd better be going, too."

"You won't go to dinner with me?"

She looked at him in astonishment, obviously thinking he'd only meant to invite her if Victoria was there.

"I'm not that self-absorbed kid who came to see you in Switzerland," he said gently. "Believe it or not, I, like Bucky, have finally started to grow up." He started to add "Sis" but suddenly that didn't sound right anymore.

The woman who stood there was no longer simply a part of his childhood. No longer a means of keeping tabs on Victoria. Not a surrogate little sister.

Exactly what she *was*, he didn't know yet.

But he had the strangest feeling he would enjoy finding out.

Caro Hensley was waiting in the dark living room when Daniel got home. It had always infuriated her that Daniel refused to let her move in with him. Even in the heat of their affair, he refused to let her stay overnight or leave any of her clothes there. But she could see by the expression on his face when he switched on the light and found her sitting there, that now was not the time to bring up that old argument. "I thought you might take me to dinner," she said quickly. "You can tell me all about today."

"It's after eleven. I've already had my dinner."

"Who was the lucky woman? Victoria?" She hadn't meant to let that name slip out.

Daniel looked at her in surprise. "What's that supposed to mean?"

Normally Caro was calm and controlled. Now there was something in her that yearned to rage out of control, to cause a scene, to throw things, to rend her clothes. She had the feeling that if she just gave free rein to her emotions she would be cleansed of all her negative thoughts. "You've craved after the delicious Miss Carr for years. You think I don't know that?" That last sentence turned into a shout.

Daniel stared at her as though she were some sort of alien creature which had suddenly plopped down in the middle of the room.

Caro sat down abruptly. "Were you with her?"

"I don't owe you any explanations."

"It was her." She jumped up and began to pace around the room. "Do you have anything here?"

"Anything what? Some of your nose candy?"

"I need it, Daniel!"

"Then go talk to your friends. I don't do that anymore."

"Did you screw her tonight? You've been waiting all these years to do it. Was it worth the wait?" She plucked aimlessly at her dress, snagging the silk with her nails.

Daniel caught her hands. "Calm down, okay? I wasn't with Victoria. I was with someone else."

"Who?"

"Look, Caro, I don't—"

"Who?" she screamed it.

Daniel dropped her hands and said, "I'm going to tell you and then you're going to leave. You and I are through, Caro. You already knew that."

"If you don't tell me immediately, I'm going to kill myself right here!" Caro wasn't joking. She was so far out of control that seemed like the only salvation.

"Sharon Bradford. Now I want you out of here."

She let him bundle her out of the door and down the drive to her car. She just sat there in the dark until he went back inside.

Sharon Bradford.

That was the name of the other actress on *Charlie's Gang*, the one Daniel had never paid much attention to. It was also the name Warren Neville had mentioned to her a few nights ago. Someone had hired him to terrorize Sharon Bradford in order to force her to take the part in the reunion special, but Warren had his own plans for the actress. He had asked for Caro's help then, but she refused. Warren had been angry. He knew he needed Caro's cool logic working in his behalf.

Caro clenched the wheel, making herself take deep breaths until her hands stopped shaking and her heart stopped pounding.

"All right, Warren," she said aloud in the empty car.

Now she would help him do anything he wanted to the Bradford woman.

She would do anything to get Daniel back. Anything to forget how she had felt when she was out of control a few minutes ago.

Anything.

*   *   *

When Owen got a call from one of the security guards at the studio, he almost didn't respond. "I caught him trying to get on the set of the *Charlie's Gang* reunion special. You might want to see this guy before I turn him over to the police," was all the man would say over the phone.

The temptation was great to turn over and go back to sleep. But there were enough weird happenings connected with this special to keep Owen from sleeping soundly. He had never figured out who stacked the deck so that his three stars would have to take the parts. Grateful as he was to that unknown someone, Owen didn't like things to happen that he couldn't control.

So he got dressed again, told tonight's companion to lock up when she left, and drove back to the studio. Years ago, he had briefly had and discarded a wife, but this was a much more convenient arrangement. On nights like tonight, he was quite happy that there were no questions to answer.

However, he was a little peevish by the time he finally reached the studio. This had better be worth his while coming down here, he decided. When the guard asked him if he wanted a cup of coffee or a beer, Owen told him stiffly that what he really wanted was back home in bed and to just get on with it.

"He's in here," the guard said. "I didn't want anyone else to get a look at him before you."

The guard led the way to an unused office and unlocked the door. A man sat in the middle of the room in a straight-backed chair.

The guard turned and locked the door from the inside.

The man looked up.

"I'll be damned," Owen said.

"I saw it too," the guard said eagerly. "Right away."

Owen walked closer.

"Be careful, Mr. Knox. He was a little wild when I picked him up. He might be on something."

Owen studied the face. The eyes were an exact copy, that trademark green. Something was missing from this set, though. "Who are you?"

The man frowned at the guard. "He hit me. Here." He pointed to his jaw.

"I had to, Mr. Knox. He would have gotten away otherwise."

"Why were you here?" Owen asked him.

"Where's Bucky? I found his room, but no one was there. Can I have a cold drink?" He sounded like a child.

Owen studied him thoughtfully for a moment. "Go get him something," he told the guard. "Don't hurry back."

When the door closed behind him, Owen said, "Are you related to Sharon Bradford?"

"I'm her brother."

Owen snorted in disgust. Sharon's brother had been married to that agent who just died. He had to have had more on the ball than this. What was his name? "Andrew," he said aloud.

"That's me," the man said happily. "Do you have my medicine? Inga used to give me medicine. She read poetry to me."

He had to be the one all right. "Does Sharon know you're here?" Maybe he could gain a few points with her by handing her brother over without any publicity.

"I don't love Sharon any more. She always promised to take me to see Bucky and JoJo and Nan, but she never did. Do you know where they live now?"

"Ah . . . do you have a doctor? Someone I'm supposed to call?"

The sullen expression reminded Owen of Sharon when she was a little girl. "I don't like doctors."

"I think you probably need one, don't you?"

"I kept the secret all these years for them," he said petulantly.

Owen's heart gave a little bounce. "What secret was that?"

"I gave them each a burning man."

Owen shook his head in disgust. This wasn't making any sense at all. Let Sharon Bradford handle this looney. He had his hand on the door, when Andrew said, "I hated them for killing Charlie Weston. If they hadn't burned him up, then I could have gone to play with Bucky and JoJo and Nan. Sharon promised me I could. But then they killed Charlie Weston and I never got to go."

Owen turned around slowly. "Nick Hanson died in an accident. He was smoking in bed."

Andrew shook his head. "Daniel hit him and thought he was dead and then they set the mattress on fire. It wasn't Sharon's fault, though. She told me it wasn't."

Jesus! It could have been like that!

There was a soft knock at the door. The guard came in with a cold drink in a can. "Here you go," he said heartily.

Andrew took it and slurped it down.

"Shall I call the police now, Mr. Knox?" the guard asked quietly.

"No need for that," Owen told him. "The poor fellow is just a little confused. I'll take him home with me. Have my car brought around." He took out his billfold and peeled off two hundred dollar bills. "Oh, and don't say anything to anyone about this, all right? We wouldn't want any negative publicity before the special comes out."

"Looks like all these big shots have a *National Enquirer* story hidden somewhere." The guard pocketed the bills and went to see about the car.

"Andrew, I'm going to take you home with me," Owen said.

"Do you know Bucky and Nan and JoJo?"

"I sure do," Owen said heartily. "I'll fix it so you can see their show all day long if you want."

"I want to see *them*."

"Maybe I can fix that, too," Owen said swiftly. "But right now you have to be very quiet. Don't talk to any one until we get home, all right?"

"Do you have ice cream at home?"

"I'll get you all the ice cream you can eat," Owen promised. It looked like it might be worth it.

An old man in a hunting cap, flannel shirt, and corduroy pants sat in a rocker on the front porch of the caretaker's cabin when Sharon pulled up in front of it.

"You're all grown up," he called to her when she got out of the car. "But I recognize you from your movies, Miss Bradford. There wasn't no use in you driving all the way up here. I told you on the phone that there ain't nobody up at the cabin."

"Did you actually go up and check?"

"Didn't have to. There wasn't any fresh tracks up the trail. No fresh tracks; nobody up there."

Sharon was dressed for a hike in jeans and boots. "Can I get the car all the way up the trail?"

He looked at the big Mercedes and spat thoughtfully. "Not one that big. You need a little Jeep to get up that trail. You'll have to walk it. Want me to go with you?"

She didn't like the leer on his face. Ever since Warren Neville had broken into the beach house, she had been terrified of being alone with anyone she didn't know. "I'll go by myself," she told him.

When she started off on foot, she could feel him watching her. She turned around and stared coldly, but it did no good. He lifted his hunting cap in a mock salute and continued to stare. He watched her until a bend in the road took her out of sight.

It was hard going up the trail. Her father kept a four-wheel-drive vehicle for this steep climb. Not that they came up here all that often, since Cynthia hated the outdoors. Keith Bradford had used the cabin as a place to entertain business associates. Sharon had only been up there once in her entire life, right before she went to school in Switzerland. There was nothing in the world to indicate that she might find Andrew or her parents here. Nothing but the fact that she had tried everywhere else and they just seemed to have vanished off the face of the earth.

By the time she reached the cabin, she was sorry she had come. A wild goose chase she thought, and then she saw her father's four-wheel-drive vehicle sitting behind the cabin half-hidden in the bushes.

"Mother! Father!" Sharon called to the cabin. "Are you there?"

The woods were silent.

The door was partly ajar.

Sharon walked up to the cabin slowly. "Mother? Father?" she called again. When there was no answer, she pushed the door open and went inside.

Animals had been there first. Things were scattered around the cabin. Sheets had been ripped up. Andrew's clothes were in one of the bedrooms. When she saw them, she almost cried with relief. But she couldn't find anyone in the house.

In the master bedroom where her father's clothes hung beside her mother's, there were rusty red stains on the wood floor.

When she saw those, Sharon retreated back outside. The woods were still silent. The keys were in the jeep, but it was almost out of gas. When they had come up before, her father brought extra gas in a jerry can on the back of the jeep. There wasn't one there now.

The overpowering silence got the best of her and she plunged back down the trail. She was halfway back to the old man's cabin, when she heard the sound of something behind her in the woods.

She froze in terror.

When the small fawn came rushing out of the undergrowth and hurtled past her, she felt no sense of relief.

Something was terribly wrong back there at the cabin.

Where was Andrew?

Owen switched off the VCR and leaned back in his chair. In all his years of information gathering, this was the culmination for him: the biggest and most valuable piece of information he had ever come across. It would place three of Hollywood's hottest properties under his thumb for the rest of their lives. He had over two hours of Andrew's rambling, disjointed story on tape. No one could look at those green eyes and doubt the family connection. No one could listen to that clear, childlike voice and doubt Andrew's tale.

Owen took the video cassette out of the recorder and put it back in his safe. Then he went in search of Andrew. Owen found him driving a golf cart around and around the swimming pool. The gardener shrugged his shoulders helplessly when he saw Owen. "Hope you don't mind, Mr. Knox. The boy really wanted to play with it."

Boy was the right term, Owen thought as he watched Andrew. Sharon's twin was thirty-nine, but his face was the unlined, carefree face of a young boy. "Let him do anything within reason," Owen told the gardener. "Just don't let him leave the grounds."

Andrew caught sight of Owen and waved, laughing with pleasure as he took the far turn around the pool.

Owen laughed and waved back.

What a perfect day, Owen thought. He was planning a very special wrap party for the three stars of *Whatever Happened to Charlie's Gang?* Today was the day he would issue the invitation.

Andrew drove the golf cart around and around in the sunshine. He liked driving, but no one had ever let him drive this much before. He had wanted to drive his father's jeep away from the mountain cabin, but he had been afraid to take it without permission. He had hated being there in the cabin. Hated being with his parents.

They didn't care about him. All they cared about was Inga. They asked him over and over what had happened to her. When he explained that he didn't know, they called him a liar.

Andrew could see the front gates open as Owen Knox's big black car went through them. When the gates closed again, the gardener dropped down in one of the loungers by the pool and pulled his hat down over his face. Andrew kept going around and around the pool, giving the lounger a wide berth.

He had thought Sharon would come and get him by now. She had always promised to look after him. Since before Inga died. He wondered if Sharon was mad at him because of the little wire man. Or maybe because of what happened to Mother and Father.

Andrew pulled the golf cart to a stop on the far side of the pool with the motor still running. When Inga died, he had been confused. He had hated Inga so much for the way she had treated Sharon that he thought he would be glad when she died.

Instead he had cried. He had been sitting on the floor beside Inga's overturned chair, sitting there and crying when the police came. The police told the man his father sent to get him about that. That was why his parents thought he had been the one who hurt her.

But he hadn't.

He had wanted to. He had tried to the night that Inga hurt Sharon. But Sharon made him promise he wouldn't do anything like that to Inga again, and he hadn't.

He wondered who had.

Andrew squinted at the gardener. The man's face was

hidden by the hat, but his chest was rising and falling with an even rhythm.

Sharon hadn't made him promise anything about their parents, but Andrew was afraid she was going to be mad about that anyway. That was why he had dragged them so far into the woods. Maybe no one would find them there.

Why did everyone always have to be so mean to him?

Inga had been mean and his parents had been mean. Sharon was being mean right now by not coming for him. If only he could find Bucky and JoJo and Nan. *They* wouldn't be mean. They would be his friends.

When he was little, he used to confuse Sharon with JoJo, but now he knew that they were not the same at all. Sharon was different now. She looked like a woman. JoJo was still the same.

Then was when he remembered the burning man.

Andrew drove the cart away from the pool slowly, glancing over his shoulder to see if the gardener would rouse from his nap. When the man didn't sit up or yell, Andrew speeded up, heading down the hill toward the big garage.

Ever since the night Sharon had told him about the burning man, Andrew had seen him so clearly in his dreams that he sometimes thought he had been there too.

When Sharon had described the scene to him, she had cried. But when Andrew thought about the burning man, he didn't feel like crying. He felt happy instead. He could see a glorious flaming figure striding across the earth. Everyone got out of his way, and no one was mean to him.

Andrew would like to be like that.

The night of the burning man had been the night everything changed. After that, Sharon couldn't be JoJo anymore. After that, JoJo stayed the same and Sharon was the one who changed.

Andrew parked the golf cart by the garage and cut off the engine. There were five cars in Owen Knox's garage and every one of them was full of gasoline.

Andrew searched through the garage until he found a long piece of tubing and several cans. He siphoned the gasoline very carefully, just a little from each car, so that no one would know it had been taken. When the cans were full, he put them in the golf cart and drove them to a place on the grounds he had discovered this morning before anyone else was up.

Then he drove the golf cart back to the pool. When the gardener woke up, Andrew was still driving the cart around and around the pool.

And thinking about the burning man.

Chapter Twenty

"Giselle was a virgin when I married her." Dominic's rich, full voice flowed out of the phone.

Lying on her bed in the darkened bedroom, Victoria felt that she and Dominic were the only two people awake in this huge city, with the telephone the only connection between them. The thought pleased her. "You expected that. You would not have married her otherwise."

"Of course not. It was an arrangement. Between my family and hers. Part of the specifications were that she be a virgin." He sighed. "She was so pure, Victoria. So untouched by the world. I could not help but keep her that way."

It was a plea for understanding. "But that kept you from loving her."

"She gave me three sons."

And you murdered one of them, Victoria thought, but they never spoke of that.

Dominic sighed again. "You know that and forgive me for it," he said in answer to her unspoken thought. "She would not."

"I don't forgive it or accept it, Dominic. I simply know it. As you know what you know about me."

"I remember that day I found you in the gym and I told you that you and Dom would leave my house. I should have made love to you then."

"I wanted you to," she said.

336

Victoria heard the sudden intake of breath on the other end of the phone as desire struck him like a physical blow.

Gently, oh, so gently, she hung up the phone.

A dangerous game.

One misstep and she was lost.

"I have another job for you," Emery Friedman told Warren Neville, and then paused, his glance fixed on something further away than the grimy wallpaper of the cramped apartment.

Warren shifted uncomfortably. "What's the deal?" he asked as Friedman continued to stare into space without speaking.

Friedman's gaze shifted to Warren, and Warren almost regretted speaking. But the rage that lurked behind the old man's watery eyes was not for him. "There is a rumor that Owen Knox has a very interesting houseguest these days," Friedman said. "Find out who it is."

"Sure thing," Warren said, relieved. He had been worried Friedman might have found out about his plans for Sharon Bradford and himself. He had carried out all three jobs Friedman had given to him. Sharon had been the toughest, but she had finally signed with the agent Friedman had wanted her to take. There were other things, though, that Warren wanted her to do for himself. However, since their little beach party, he hadn't been able to get close enough to her to influence her again. Caro had promised to help him, but she was a quirky broad. Who knew when she would get around to applying herself to Warren's problem? Meanwhile there were scripts going to waste, scripts for movies that would earn megabucks with the names of Warren Neville and Sharon Bradford attached to the package. "No sooner said than done," he promised.

"I don't want Owen Knox to know he's being watched," Friedman said.

"No problem. I'll get right on it." Warren practically fell all over himself in his urge to get away. There was a bad smell in Friedman's apartment, something he couldn't quite identify. It had been here the last time too, a fetid, physical smell. He wondered if the old man had cancer.

But in the late afternoon sunshine, he forgot about Friedman. He would take care of this new assignment, but not until tomorrow. Right now, he had something much more to his liking.

Sharon Bradford had moved out of her parents' old place after Inga's death. Now she had moved back in. It was time he paid her a visit.

Emery scarcely noticed when Warren Neville left. He was too consumed by his anger to function for a few minutes. He had to be very careful when he thought about Owen Knox. Otherwise the red killing haze swept over him blotting out everything else.

It was the prison psychiatrist who had helped Emery to remember what really happened when he broke into that motel room. Only the shrink hadn't realized it.

He had labored for months to help Emery deal with his emotions. Suddenly one day, right out of the blue, Emery had remembered a significant detail about the man he had found fucking Tina.

A bald spot on the back of the man's head.

Just that bald spot, nothing else.

The psychiatrist had come up with all sorts of interesting theories about what that bald spot indicated about Emery's psychological state. The doctor had been fond of the theory that it meant Emery thought he had found his father fucking his mother. He was so fond of his conclusions that he told Emery he was going to write a paper on the subject.

He didn't realize that the image of that bald spot had given Emery a name and a face.

And a reason to live.

A year ago a doctor had told Emery he had six more months. But here he was, still alive.

Still hungry for revenge.

When the doorbell rang, Sharon went downstairs to answer it herself. When she moved back to her parents' old home hoping this would be the place Andrew would return to, she had kept on only the barest minimum of staff, a maid and a cook, both of whom were off this evening. She wished she dared to go to the police about Andrew's disappearance. Her lingering suspicion that Inga's death had not been suicide, but murder, kept her from it.

Before the incident at the beach house, she would have thrown the door open without a second thought, hoping that it would be Andrew standing there. Now more cautious, she put her eye to the peephole.

It was Warren Neville's face she saw through the tiny opening.

For a moment, she thought her imagination was simply playing tricks on her, feeding her fears. Then he called her name through the door.

Sharon backed away from the door, and then turned and fled up the stairs. At the top of the staircase, she paused, trying to think.

The doorbell rang again and again. Neville began beating on the door, shouting her name through the wood.

The Beverly Hills patrol could be here in five minutes if she called, only she didn't dare summon them. That man had claimed to know something about Andrew. If he was telling the truth she didn't dare have him questioned by the authorities.

Abruptly the pounding on the door stopped. In the sudden silence, Sharon heard a scraping sound at one of the living room windows.

She bolted down the hall to her bedroom, locking the door behind her.

There was a phone on the nightstand beside the bed. She stared at it as she listened to the sounds of Neville trying to break in below.

The sounds stopped, but she knew he was still out there, waiting. She didn't dare go outside. And if she just waited, sooner or later he would break in.

If only there were someone she could call!

Warren was hot to have her again, but not so much that he forgot his usual caution. He could wait until dark. It would be better after dark. She would have time to think about what he was going to give her. And so would he.

He drifted back into the shrubs and hunkered down to smoke a couple of joints while he watched evening turn into night. When the light came on in her bedroom, he figured he had waited long enough. He made his way around to the back of the house where he had a favorite window he had used before.

It went up as smoothly as the last time he'd used this particular entry. He waited a moment before he boosted himself inside. He was cautious still, even though he wasn't expecting a burglar alarm. He'd already learned that Sharon Bradford seldom activated her alarm system. Not when that nutty brother of hers was on the loose. He wasn't worried about any cops showing up for the same reason.

Inside the darkened den, he was reminded of the night he'd done dear old Inga. He'd left enough clues around her corpse that anyone with half a brain would nail the brother for the job, but so far the police seemed uninterested in calling it anything but suicide. Probably old man Bradford had taken care of someone.

Ain't money grand!

He'd really hated to snuff old Inga. She was much easier to work with than Caro. Not as much fun to screw, though, he thought, as he walked cautiously through the dark dining room. Old Inga just tolerated men; it was women she really liked. Warren had even picked her up a few, for a tidy sum, of course. But it was Sharon Bradford who had really turned Inga on.

That was the reason Warren had to kill her.

Inga hit the roof when she found out he'd been hired to deliver Sharon to a new agent. He'd offered to split the money, but no go. She didn't want the money. She wanted Sharon in the sack.

He couldn't blame her, Warren thought. That was just what he wanted himself.

He knew his way to the bedrooms upstairs. The first two he tried were empty. When he paused before the third one, he could feel in his very gut that this was the right one. He stood outside the door, rubbing himself through his trousers, enjoying the sensation of knowing that Sharon was on the other side and his.

"Sharon," he said softly. "Let me in."

The door opened and something exploded outward with such force that he was slammed against the wall on the other side of the hall. A fist came near to taking the side of his head off and a knee jolted upward into his balls, making him scream with pain. A forearm jammed against his throat made spots dance before his eyes. Through the haze, he could see Daniel Garrick's face shoved into his.

"You're going to get out of this house, slime, and you're never again to bother this lady again."

Warren tried to yank free of the giant's grasp. He was rammed back against the wall again so hard that he thought he might have a concussion.

"You're not coming back again, are you, slime? Promise the lady."

The pressure against his throat was released just enough for him to croak, "Promise."

"That's not good enough. If you ever get within two blocks of Sharon again, I'll kill you. Understand that?" The forearm jammed into his throat again until he gagged for air.

He just managed to nod before the blackness took him.

"Tell me about him," Daniel said.

Sharon's head was against his chest. He could feel her shoulders trembling. She told him everything. Not just about Warren Neville, but about Inga and Andrew, and her fears.

As she talked, he could feel the rage building inside him. Along with something else.

He wasn't sure what this new feeling was. He only knew that it made him want to hold her close, as though she were dearest treasure in the world. It made him cover her face with tender kisses. It made him take her there in her bedroom, possessing her with his body for the first time, but differently than he'd had any other woman in his life.

For the first time, he was more worried about her than himself. Her pleasure than his. And when he brought her to a tender climax, his own was more powerful than it had ever been before.

He wanted her again, immediately. But he made himself wait. "Get some clothes together," he told her. "You're coming to my place."

. She looked tentative. For a moment he thought she had heard the stories about him, that he didn't like his women to stay with him overnight. That as he had with Kyna and Caro, he either stayed with them, or kicked them out each night. But instead of mentioning that, she said, "What about Andrew? He might look for me here."

"I'll help you find him," he promised. "One more day until the party at Owen's and then we're free of this. We'll hire a private detective to find Andrew, but you and I will leave town."

He held her close. He was in unknown territory here. He had never felt the desire to look after anyone else except Victoria.

But somehow this new feeling was different from that. Victoria had never needed him in this way. Sharon did.

When Warren Neville came to, he had been dumped unceremoniously in front of the Bradfords' big driveway like so much refuse. He had barely staggered to his feet before Daniel Garrick's Ferrari came barreling down the drive. There were two people in the Testarossa, and Warren knew one of them was Sharon Bradford.

He knew, too, that he would have to take care of Daniel Garrick. Permanently.

Sharon Bradford was his property and he didn't appreciate Garrick horning in. This was one time he wasn't going to wait for Caro to come up with something. He could take care of this little matter himself.

He was prepared to stake out Garrick's home and wait there all night and all day if necessary, but it wasn't. By the time he got his poor battered body over there, Garrick's Ferrari was parked in front of the house, unattended.

Brake lines were Warren's specialty. Poor Garrick would just lose his brakes all at once. The way the son of a bitch drove, that would be it.

Warren left Garrick's happy and went to take care of that little spy job for Emery Friedman.

Sharon was still asleep upstairs.

Daniel took off the glasses he had begun wearing this last year for reading and rubbed his eyes wearily. He had been looking over these figures last night when Sharon called. He hadn't wanted to believe what he suspected was true. But the figures didn't lie. Temple Jackson was stealing him blind. He wondered how many years it had been going on.

He had been looking for the source of the glitch in the

financing for *Night Time*. What he found was Temple's big paw in the honey jar.

Daniel picked up the phone and dialed Temple's number. He was surprised his voice was so calm as he asked Temple to come by the house.

"At this hour of the morning?" the Texan grumbled. "Son, you're crazy!" But he finally agreed.

Daniel went to the kitchen and brewed himself a pot of coffee while he waited. He carried a cup outside and stood looking at the morning.

He missed the dog. He'd gotten the big mastiff last year after he finally managed to kick the cocaine. They liked to watch the morning together while Daniel drank his coffee. There hadn't been another sign of the bastard that shot him.

Daniel thought about the little burning man and Sharon safely asleep upstairs. After the party at Owen's tonight, they would get out of town for a while. Maybe drive up the coast.

Someone came out of the house behind him. Daniel turned, a smile on his face, but it was Temple.

"I don't know what the fuck you wanted at this hour that couldn't wait," the Texan grumbled. He looked at the coffee cup in Daniel's hand. "You gonna offer me some of that?"

"I've been going over some of my finances."

Nothing changed in the morning, but suddenly there was a wide awake alertness about Temple that hadn't been there a moment before. "Glory hallelujah," he said. "I've been after you for years to look at figures and you finally decide to do it on the one morning I'm sleeping in."

"The game's up, Temple."

"What are you talking about, son?"

"I owe you something. You saved my life in Nam so I won't call the cops in on this. But we're through."

He had expected Temple to bluster and deny the charges. Instead, the Texan just looked at him contemptuously and walked back into the house.

Daniel wondered if he had made a mistake, sacrificed a friendship over a few vague suspicions. He'd been half crazy these past few weeks. Maybe he should call Temple back and apologize to him.

*   *   *

Temple hurried through the house, trying not to run. He'd been afraid Daniel would beat the shit out of him. That was still a distinct possibility. Because no way had Mr. Garrick discovered the extent of Temple's plundering in one quick go through.

But because he knew Daniel would not prosecute him, regardless of the amount, he paused in front of Daniel's Ferrari.

Of course, the golden boy had left his keys inside. The Testarossa was worth three times what Temple's heap was worth.

It didn't take Temple two shakes to make up his mind.

Daniel heard the familiar sound of the Testarossa's engine and cursed. By the time he made it to the front of the house, Temple and the Ferrari were gone.

"Daniel?"

Sharon stood on the stair behind him. She wore one of his shirts and nothing else.

"Is anything wrong?" she asked him.

"Not anymore," he told her.

Victoria went down the line of figures again. Even with the money from the special, there was no way she could survive with the kind of expenses Laurel was running up. There had to be a limit somewhere. Surely even Barney wouldn't have expected her to keep paying and paying. But then again, knowing the endless patience he'd had with his daughter, and the never-ending guilt he felt, maybe he would.

She sighed wearily and went down to breakfast. Laurel was there before her. Her stepdaughter didn't return Victoria's morning greeting. Laurel had shown up the first of the week, refusing to stay in Palm Springs one day more. For Barney's sake Victoria would try to stand it, at least for another week or two, and then they would have to work out something else. It wasn't right for a woman of twenty-six not to be out on her own.

The maid set a plate of fresh fruit in front of Victoria, the only breakfast she allowed herself these days. Surely *someone* would see the series potential of Nan's character. She intended to be in fighting trim when they did.

"Who called you so late last night?" Laurel asked suddenly.

Victoria felt her heart flutter painfully. She hadn't given a thought to Laurel being in the house last night. She forced herself to spear a bite of melon before she answered calmly, "A friend."

"A man?"

"What makes you say that?"

"You look different, you know." Laurel studied her stepmother critically. "I'd almost think you're having an affair with someone."

"And if I was?"

"Father wouldn't like that."

"Barney's dead," Victoria said softly. "If I did have an affair, it would be my business. Not yours. You're too old to need mothering anymore."

"I'm glad you finally see that," Laurel said, but there was a tremor in her voice as if she could sense what was coming next.

"I think it's time you were out on your own, Laurel. Do you still want to be living with me when you're thirty?"

"Only with your checkbook."

"Thank you. That's the first honest thing you've said to me. It makes everything easier for me."

"Then I wish I hadn't said it. The last thing in the world I want is to make things easier for you."

"You can't still hate me after all these years?"

Laurel shoved back her chair. For a moment, remembering Palm Springs, Victoria felt a flash of physical fear. Laurel saw that and chuckled. "I'll always hate you, Victoria. You destroyed my life."

"I didn't mean to. There were things you didn't understand at the time. Things—"

"Do you realize how long I waited for you to come back?" Laurel screamed it at her.

"I'm here now."

"It's too late."

The two women stared at each other across the table.

The only thing we have in common is our love for a dead man, Victoria thought. "I'm cutting the umbilical cord, Laurel. You're going to have to find a place of your own. Start looking today."

"Because you don't want me to find out who your new boyfriend is?"

"Because it's time for you to grow up and act like a woman instead of a spoiled child."

"You don't know how much of a spoiled child I can be," Laurel told her with the sound of vicious promise in her voice. "I know a lot of things about you that you wouldn't want anyone else to know."

Victoria put her coffee cup down, carefully so that it would not rattle in the saucer. "Are you threatening me, Laurel?"

"Daddy said you were supposed to take care of me." Now it was a child's voice petulant, whiny.

Victoria stood. "He should have asked me to see that you grow up." She glanced down at her plate, but her appetite had vanished. After she left the dining room, she could hear the sounds of crockery being smashed.

Damn it, Barney! You were such a wonderful man. How could you have been such a lousy parent?

Caro called Daniel's house. Her hands were trembling so badly that she misdialed twice. When the phone finally rang, it was Sharon Bradford who answered it.

By the time Daniel came on the line, Caro's terror had changed to anger. "What's she doing there?" she screamed at him. "Did you let her spend the night?"

"That's none of your business," Daniel said calmly.

Immediately she steadied herself. "I just heard the news on the radio. What happened?"

"Temple was driving my car. The brakes went out. He's dead."

She didn't give a shit about Temple Jackson. "The radio said the brakes had been tampered with."

"The police are looking into it. I don't think there's anything to that. No one's got it in for me and there's no way in the world anyone else would have known that Temple would be driving my car."

She could tell by his voice there was more to it than that. She wondered if he and Temple had finally had a blow up. "Daniel, can I come over when she leaves? I want to talk to you. Just talk."

"She's not leaving, Caro."

He hung up and she just stood there holding the phone until her mother's voice broke the spell. "Is he all right?"

"Who?" Caro replaced the receiver in its cradle.

"Daniel. Wasn't that who you were calling?"

She turned around and glared at her mother and Kyna took a step backwards. "Don't spy on me old woman," she said coldly. "I told you before that I don't like it."

Kyna shuffled out of the room and Caro wondered what Daniel would have thought if he could see his lover now. She wondered why it didn't give her more pleasure than this to have her mother under her thumb. She wondered why nothing at all gave her pleasure.

She dialed Warren Neville's number. "Warren? You and I have to have a little talk."

From his vantage point overlooking part of Owen Knox's estate, Emery Friedman watched the grounds all through the long afternoon. Warren Neville's report about the houseguest who looked amazingly like Sharon Bradford's missing brother had piqued his interest, as did anything concerning *Charlie's Gang*. Or Owen.

But he couldn't afford to think about Owen. Not yet.

A small caterer's van arrived midway through the afternoon. Emery wondered who the party guests would be. When the cars arrived at seven, and he picked out the three attendees, Emery hoped that Owen had ordered enough supplies so that one more guest wouldn't overload it.

He patted the revolver in his pocket.

This was one party he definitely planned to attend.

Victoria wondered why she had even bothered to come tonight. She had checked with her agent earlier in the day and there hadn't been the slightest bit of interest in her proposal about the new series. Even her agent was treating it like a joke.

But Victoria knew, with an experience born of working in the industry since she was a child, that even if she managed to hang on to her role in *The Clan* this year, that would do it for her. One more season and the series would probably be axed; one more season and she would never be able to shake that role of superbitch. Her career would be over. There was only one thing that could help her now: a complete change of direction.

When she accepted Owen's invitation, she had assumed this would be the kind of big Hollywood party where mingling just might pay off with a new part. Instead, she found there were three guests instead of two hundred.

Victoria sipped her drink, listening to Owen Knox simper and preen, and wished she were a million miles away.

The light went out of the world this afternoon. It had been bad enough to learn that Temple was a thief, had in fact been a thief all the years Daniel had known him. And then to have him die like that, in an accident that just might have had Daniel's name on it.

But even worse, sometime this afternoon things had changed between himself and Sharon. She insisted on going home to dress for tonight. Then she had shooed him out of the Bradford house, telling him that she would take her own car to the event at Owen's. It was as though she were trying to kill what had sprung up between them last night.

Now Daniel sat between her and Victoria.

Between the woman he had loved from afar for so many years, and the woman he had loved with all his heart since last night.

Neither of them seemed to be aware of his existence.

She had known what to expect, Sharon thought. It was a repeat of all the years the three of them had known each other. She had realized this afternoon what would happen. She might be enough for Daniel when Victoria wasn't around; but when Victoria was there . . .

So Sharon had tried to prepare herself for this evening by leaving him before he could start ignoring her again.

Only it wasn't working.

Owen rubbed his hands in glee. The special was in the can and after tonight these three superstars would be under his complete control. He could afford to play with them a bit. Let them grow slightly bored. Let them wonder why he had called them here. Let them wonder why he had insisted that it be just the three of them and no one else.

But now it was time. "Shall we adjourn to the screening room?" he asked them. "I've arranged a private showing just for the three of you. The last of the original cast."

That startled them.

"But Owen," Victoria protested, "What about Rudy Haynes and—"

"Oh, they were in the original cast of *Charlie's Gang,*" Owen admitted, as he ushered them through the house. "But not in the little drama I'm talking about."

He saw the flicker of exchanged glances between them and chuckled softly to himself. He had managed to reduce them to the level of children again and he found that amusing.

In the screening room, hors d'oeuvres and champagne had already been set out. "Enjoy yourself," Owen said expansively. "Kick off your heels, girls. Take off your jacket and tie, Daniel. I've gotten rid of the hired help tonight. We're all alone."

"What are you going to show us?" Sharon demanded as Daniel took Owen at his word and loosened his tie. "A stag film?"

"Better than that," Owen promised. "This is a copy of the reunion special that the public will never see. I had it put together just for the four of us."

He dimmed the lights.

On the large television screen at the end of the room, clips from the original show began to run. "We were too cute to be believable," Daniel said in the gloom.

"You'd never know what we were really like," Sharon said softly.

Victoria gripped the arm of her chair and said nothing.

Gradually shots of the actors as adults were interspersed with the kids they had been. Now it was easy to see in those childish faces the attractive grown-ups they would become. It was the introduction to the special.

"We've seen this, Owen. Over and over." Victoria rose. "I'm sorry, I've had a long day. I don't want to be rude, but I really must—"

"You haven't seen this," Owen said sharply.

Andrew Bradford's face jumped out at them.

Sharon gasped.

Andrew stared straight into the camera. "When can I see Bucky and JoJo and Nan?"

"Later," Owen's voice came from off-camera. "Right now, I want you to tell the camera just what you told me earlier. Then you'll be on television just like the Weston children."

Andrew smiled happily and began to talk about the burning man.

"But how did he know?" Victoria whispered. "We swore we wouldn't tell anyone."

"I told him," Sharon said. "I told him everything that ever happened to me. I told him everything that happened that night." She glared at Knox. "Where is he?"

"He's safe."

Daniel gestured at the screen. "No doubt that's a copy?"

"The original is locked safely away, yes. I wouldn't be foolish enough to do anything else."

"What do you want out of this?" That was Victoria.

"You. The three of you. From now on I have you in my pocket."

"You were the one who delivered the little figures," Victoria accused suddenly.

Owen looked confused. "What figures?"

Another exchange of glances between the three of them. Owen ignored it. He had them now. "I assume we understand each other."

Exchanged glances again.

"Now what?" Daniel asked. "Money?"

"Oh, no. Nothing as crude as that. I have plenty of money."

"Then *what*?" Sharon demanded.

"Power. You work when I say you work. You turn down projects when I tell you to. You tell me little tidbits that I can use to manipulate other people. In return I don't tell anyone about you."

"It wasn't our fault," Sharon said suddenly. "It was an accident. We're not responsible."

Victoria and Daniel looked her way, surprised. That was the first time since Nick Hanson's death that she had absolved the other two of any blame.

"No, I don't suppose it was your fault," Owen said slowly. "If anyone's, I guess it was mine. I should never have put someone with Nick's proclivities on that show. But you see when the talk about Friedman's new series first started, I knew there wasn't a chance in a million that I would be connected with it. That self-important bastard didn't even know I was alive. And I hated his guts.''

Victoria stared at him, horrified. "You *knew*? You knew what kind of man Nick Hanson was and you let him work with children?''

Owen grinned wryly at the cosmic joke he had played on himself. "I didn't just *let* him. I went out of my way to make sure he would get the role. I campaigned harder for Nick than his own agent. Not that he wasn't perfect for it, you understand. He was a fine actor. He played Charlie Weston to perfection. But I knew about Nick's taste for young girls. I was counting on that. I figured that if his sexual leanings didn't come out, I would start a few rumors. Can you see what the headlines would have been? *Child Molester Stars on Family Show*. Friedman would never have worked on TV again, no matter who his father-in-law was. But then I was offered the chance to direct the show. I couldn't turn it down, and it was too late to get Nick dropped.''

"You're sick!" Victoria accused.

"No," Owen said solemnly. "I was ambitious and stupid. I outsmarted myself, you see. But I wasn't a murderer. You three are.''

"You son of a bitch!" It was a new voice from the back of the room. Thin and reedy with rage.

"Who the hell . . .?" Owen switched on the lights.

An old man stood there, his face contorted with anger, a .38 revolver in his hand.

"You son of a bitch!" he said again.

"Emery?" Owen said hesitantly, eying the revolver. "My, God! Is that you, Emery? I thought you were dead!''

"I remembered, Owen. I remembered you with Tina that night!''

"Now, Emery . . . Don't—''

"You son of a bitch!" Emery Friedman pulled the trigger.

The bullet went wild, striking the big screen behind Owen. "Emery, don't! Let me ex—''

Friedman fired again.

Owen bolted from the projection room and out into the night.

Friedman went after him, gun in hand.

Victoria had never felt so calm in her life. She walked over to the VCR and slipped the cassette into her purse.

"What good will that do?" Daniel asked. "He said he had another one."

"We'll have to get it too."

"We should call the police," Sharon said. "But if we do, I'm afraid they'll arrest Andrew, too."

"We can't call the police. We can't let anyone find out about us and Nick," Daniel said.

There was another gunshot outside in the night.

Victoria looked at the other two. "We have to go after them. We have to try and stop Friedman."

"I'll go," Daniel said. "You two stay here."

"We're all going," Victoria said firmly. "We're all in this together."

But for all her brave words, she and Sharon found it impossible to keep up with Daniel once they left the paved area near the pool and plunged into the darkness beyond the house lights. Hampered by their heels, they fell far behind him.

"What are we going to do when we catch up with them?" Sharon gasped as they made their way across the estate.

"Whatever it takes to stop Friedman," Victoria said grimly. "If he kills Owen, everything will come out."

Andrew remained sitting in the little room with the peephole where Owen had put him before the party started. For the first time in years, the filmy curtains that were always closed between himself and reality had opened.

When he watched the tape, he had finally grasped that the Weston kids had grown up and that JoJo was now Sharon, Nan was now Victoria, and Bucky, his best friend, Bucky, was Daniel Garrick.

And he had grasped one thing more.

Owen Knox, the man who had brought him here, who had promised to be his friend and let him play with the Weston children, was trying to hurt them.

Trying to hurt Andrew's family.

Now Andrew realized why he had dreamed over and over about the burning man.

He went to get the gasoline.

Owen ran across the grounds. He was fleeing in no particular direction, except away from that madman Friedman. He couldn't forget what Friedman's fists had done to Tina Sawyer's face. That was thirty years ago and the man who followed him was old and frail now, but the rage behind that act, that deadly rage, was fully capable of murder with the revolver Friedman carried.

Owen's heart pounded in his chest, but he didn't dare stop to catch his breath. He had tried to count up the shots Emery had fired, and then he realized Emery could have easily reloaded the gun. There was no way he could tell how many shells remained. Nothing he could do but flee for his life before that wild man.

He was trying to make a large circle and wind his way back to the garage. The keys were usually left in one or more of the cars. If he could just get to the garage, he could get off the grounds. He had been a fool to dismiss everyone, even the security guards, tonight. But he hadn't wanted witnesses when he blackmailed his victims. Who could have known that Emery was still alive?

Owen came upon the cliff, suddenly and without warning.

It was a sheer drop near the back of his estate and he had never paid the slightest bit of attention to it in the daylight. Now, in the darkness, it loomed before him like a bottomless chasm.

He almost went over. He only had time to realize, draw back, and then Emery was on him, beating at him with the butt of the revolver.

Owen grabbed Friedman's arm, clutching at the gun. In the back of his mind was the thought of how ludicrous this would look to an outsider. Two old men struggling for control of the revolver.

And then the .38 was in his hands. "Let go, Emery," he said through clenched teeth.

Friedman continued to struggle.

Until the gun went off.

The roar was so close and so deafening, Owen had no idea what had happened for a moment. Then he saw the look of utter astonishment on Emery's time-ravaged face.

"I wasn't even touching the trigger!" Owen said desperately. "You did it, Emery! You pulled the trigger yourself!"

Friedman straightened up slowly, releasing his hold on the gun. His hands dropped down to clutch his stomach and he took one step backwards. And another.

Then Friedman disappeared, and Owen realized that he had gone over the cliff.

He heard the sickening thud when Friedman hit.

Still clutching the gun, Owen took two steps, to the very edge of the drop, and peered down into the darkness. Was the son of a bitch still alive? Or was he just faking, hoping that—

The sound behind him was so sudden and unexpected that Owen turned and fired without thinking at the big shape that loomed up out of the night at him.

"Christ, Owen!" Daniel sat down heavily on the ground, clutching his chest.

Victoria could feel the thousands of places her skin had been lacerated as they fought their way through the shrubs and bushes. It was a good thing they weren't filming tomorrow. There wasn't enough makeup in the world to cover what she and Sharon were doing to themselves. But neither one of them had suggested they turn back.

When she pushed out into the small space on the cliff's edge and saw Owen standing there and someone sitting on the ground, clutching himself, she thought it was all over. Friedman had been subdued.

Then Sharon gasped behind her and Victoria realized it was Daniel who had been shot.

Then started forward, and Owen swung the gun around their way. "No closer, ladies," he said. "I'm trying to decide what to do."

"For Christ's sake, Owen, call an ambulance," Daniel said weakly. "Otherwise, you're going to have another corpse on your hands."

"I'm very much afraid I'm going to have more than that."

"What do you mean, Owen?" Victoria asked slowly.

"I don't see that I have any choice, Victoria. I was on top

of the world a few minutes ago. Now Emery is dead and Daniel is dying. I can't very well let you two live, can I? You're the witnesses after all.''

"He's not dead yet," Sharon said desperately. "Let me call an ambulance.''

The gun swung her way. "No. Come over by Daniel, so that I can see you better. You, too, Victoria.''

"You don't have to do this, Owen," Victoria pleaded. "We'll stand by any story you want. Only let us get help for Daniel.''

"The story is the only logical one under the circumstances. Emery Friedman couldn't stand the thought of the remake after all these years. He killed the three of you and then committed suicide.''

"No one will believe that, Owen." Daniel's voice was weaker. Sharon dropped down beside him.

"They'll believe it," Owen predicted confidently. "And think of the ratings.''

He raised the gun, pointing it at Victoria. Sharon screamed, "No!''

And the burning man came out of the night.

Chapter Twenty-one

Owen shrieked and fired.

The burning man kept coming. Aflame in the night, he looked seven feet tall. He came directly toward Owen whose back was to the cliff.

Then the burning man opened his arms and clasped Owen to him in a fiery grip.

Owen flamed up, a second human torch, as the two of them stumbled backward and over the edge of the cliff.

"Oh, my God!" Sharon screamed. "That was Andrew! That was Andrew!"

Victoria caught her before she could plunge after them and held her tightly. "Listen to me," she said fiercely. "Daniel will die if we don't get him help." She gave Sharon a shake. "Do you understand?"

Sharon's eyes were dull with pain, but she whispered, "I understand."

Flames were crackling below the cliff. Victoria ripped away part of her skirt and tried to stem the flow of Daniel's blood from the chest wound. By the time she managed to slow it, she could see Daniel's face in the light from the spreading fire and he didn't look good.

Sharon knelt beside Daniel, but she was looking at the edge of the cliff, where Andrew had gone over. "We've got to hurry," Victoria told her. They could feel the heat from the flames now.

Working together, she and Sharon managed to get Daniel to his feet. But he was so weak from the loss of blood, he could barely walk. It was only by half-carrying, half dragging him, that they were able to get him as far as the garage.

He was still conscious when they loaded him into the back of a Mercedes. Victoria got behind the wheel. "No," he protested when he saw Victoria pick up the cellular phone. "You call an ambulance or take me anywhere yourselves and the whole story comes out."

"It's all right, Daniel," Victoria assured him. "I know what to do."

Dominic Solari answered on the second ring, and he listened in silence as she gasped out the barest sketch of what had happened.

"All right," Dominic told her. "This is what you do," and he explained where she should drive.

"Thank you," she said when he had finished.

"Don't worry," he told her and she knew there was no longer a reason to do so.

When she broke the connection, she realized that she had put herself into his power once more.

And how badly she had wanted to do so.

"Who was that?" Sharon demanded.

"A friend. He's going to see to it that we get help for Daniel without getting any of us in trouble."

Sharon put her arms around Daniel. "What about Friedman and Owen? And the tape of Andrew?"

"He'll take care of everything." Victoria eased the car carefully down the drive.

The red glow of the spreading flames fire grew larger behind them. Even with the Mercedes's windows up, they could hear the distant wail of fire engines.

Two miles away, Victoria stopped and cut the lights.

Five long minutes passed with nothing happening. Sharon grew frantic. "We can't just sit here! He's bleeding to death."

"They'll be here," Victoria said confidently.

They were. Five men in three separate cars. One of them was in charge. Quickly, he explained to the three of them what was happening while another man administered first aid to Daniel.

"None of you were at Knox's place tonight. We're working on alibis for the ladies. Garrick, you were experimenting with Tony here on a bit of business for a new movie. Tony's a quick-draw artist. He'll say he accidentally shot you." He turned to Tony. "Ready to drive him to the hospital."

Tony nodded.

"It'll play hell with your reputation," Daniel muttered.

"Best paying gig I ever took," Tony assured him.

Then had just a moment, the three of them, to clasp hands, a family for the last time.

They they were each loaded into a separate car and driven off in three different directions.

Kyna Hensley went into her daughter's bedroom reluctantly. But she was more afraid of what would happen if she didn't tell Caro what she had heard on the news, than if she did.

She opened the drapes, letting the afternoon sun into the room.

"What are you doing?" Caro demanded.

"It's almost three. I thought—"

"Get out of here."

"Caro . . ."

"Out, I said."

"On the news, they said . . . Daniel has been shot."

Caro sat up in bed. "Is he dead?"

"They think he'll live."

"Get out."

Warren Neville broke all the speed limits getting to the dock for the late night rendezvous with Caro. When she called this afternoon and said that she had a bidder for the video tapes of Sharon and Inga, he couldn't believe his good fortune. Especially since she had chewed him out so thoroughly the day before. He hadn't wanted to admit to Caro that his little plan to do in Daniel Garrick had gone astray, and taken out Garrick's business manager instead, but Caro knew how good he was with brake lines. She'd even had him do a couple of magic tricks with brake lines for her when someone rubbed her the wrong way. But *brother*, had she been pissed over this one.

Warren knew that Caro had been Daniel's girlfriend for years, but it didn't occur to him that Caro might have any tender feelings where Garrick was concerned. Caro didn't have tender feelings for anyone.

She didn't like sloppiness, though, and taking out the wrong man had definitely been sloppy.

But good old Caro. She wasn't going to hold a grudge. Not when he had video tapes of Sharon Bradford that were worth a bundle.

When he heard that Garrick was in the hospital today because a quick draw had gone wrong, Warren had checked around, trying to locate Sharon, and found that the lovely Miss Bradford was not in evidence anywhere. That was definitely odd.

The news was that there had been a fire on the grounds of Owen Knox's estate last night. Three charred stiffs had turned up after the fireman finally got the blaze under control. Warren wondered if the fire had anything to do with the information he'd passed along to Emery Friedman. Probably so, which meant he should have charged the old fart extra. Warren was starting to get a funny feeling. Like maybe it was time to pack up and move on for a while.

But first things first.

Caro was waiting on board a trim little boat and she had her whole drugstore of goodies with her. "We don't meet the buyer's boat for a couple of hours," she told Warren. "There's no reason we have to be bored while we wait."

"Want to watch these?" he asked, hoisting the briefcase.

"Why don't we make one of our own?" she asked him.

Sex with Caro was like nothing else Warren ever experienced. She was so aggressive that it was almost like trying to ball another man. There was never any of this bullshit about using her. Caro Hensley used everyone else and threw them away when she was through.

After a good fuck and a generous helping of Caro's pretty pills, Warren was totally relaxed. He lay back on the bunk and let the motion of the boat lull him as it shot through the water.

It was half an hour before Caro shut down the engine and threw out the anchor. "It's almost time." She passed him another handful of pills. "These will help you deal. Don't settle for less than half a million for the tapes."

Warren brightened. This was sounding better by the minute. "You really think we can get that much?" He gulped down the pills, and chased them with the vodka she offered.

"Maybe more if you're sharp. It's all up to you, Warren. This is your big break."

He felt good about that as he went topside. He was proud Caro had finally recognized his talent.

On deck, it was a clear dark night with the stars dancing around like a fireworks' display. He held on to the rail and looked around, but he couldn't spot the lights of the other boat yet among all the other points of light.

"There he is." Caro pointed to starboard. "You'll have to swim over. It's nothing for someone like you," she told him.

Warren was still basking in the glow of that when he started down the rope ladder into the water, the briefcase slung over his shoulder. He hesitated just before he went in the water. He couldn't seem to spot the buyer's boat among all the other dancing points of light. But he never suspected a thing, not until Caro's strong hand on his shoulder knocked him clear of the boat and out of reach of the ladder.

Even then he thought it was an accident as he plummeted like a rock into the depths. He grasped frantically at the briefcase, trying to yank the strap free of his shoulder.

Just when his lungs were about to burst, he managed to jerk it off. Half a million worth of video tape went one way; Warren went the other. He shot for the surface, and broke out into the air gasping and coughing.

Frantically, he paddled around, trying to spot Caro's boat or the buyer's.

That was when he realized there was no other boat and Caro's craft was receding rapidly into the night.

He was a strong swimmer. He could have dog paddled and floated for hours. Only now he was beginning to realize that the last handful of pills Caro treated him to had not been uppers. He could feel his muscles loosening gradually and his brain beginning to shut down.

Warren paddled and shouted and screamed. Then he floated and splashed and mumbled.

And after that, he followed the briefcase down into the cold Pacific depths.

*   *   *

Caro watched with the binoculars until Warren Neville went down for the last time.

"That's for trying to kill Daniel," she told the night wind. She had warned Warren when Daniel's brakes failed. Oh, she knew his working methods all right. Knew that had been his method of rubbing someone out. She had warned him then not to try anything else. Daniel was off limits.

She started the motor and headed back to shore. After she docked, she stopped at a pay phone to call the hospital and learned that Daniel's condition was improved. She felt almost lighthearted as she drove home.

When she got there, she saw that every light in the house was on. She couldn't believe that her mother was having a party tonight.

Then she realized there were no cars outside.

Caro went inside slowly. One of the maids met her, sobbing. "What is it?" she asked harshly.

"Oh, Miss Hensley . . . your mother . . . she's dead. Sleeping pills."

Somewhere inside her, so deep inside that Caro hadn't even been aware of its existence, a door had been ajar. Now it slammed shut.

She would never be able to cry again.

A box was delivered to Victoria two days after the fire at Owen Knox's estate. She did not recognize the man who brought it, who insisted on putting it directly into her hands, but he had the look of the men Dominic Solari had sent to spirit her and Daniel and Sharon away that night.

Victoria clutched the box and hurried upstairs to her bedroom, to open it in private. Inside she found the original tape Owen had made of Andrew and also the volumes of her mother's diaries.

Victoria knew what that meant. If she came to him, it would be of her own free will. Because she wanted to, not because he had forced her.

She carried the box outside. It took her over half an hour to burn it and its contents. When she had finished, Victoria sat and looked at the ashes for a long time.

This was the most frightening thing Dominic had ever done.

*   *   *

It was a strange feeling to have come closer to dying in Los Angeles than in Viet Nam, Daniel thought as he left Kyna Hensley's retrospective. This was the first affair he had attended since he got out of the hospital and he found the normal social chatter astonishing. How could people forget how slender a thread their life hung from?

He had wanted to turn down this invitation. But as Kyna's only living director, it would not have looked right if he failed to attend.

He had seen Caro across the room, but he had not made the effort to cross over and say anything to her. Nor had she turned his way. Studying her profile covertly, he could see there was more of her mother in Caro's face now: a stolid self-containment that reminded him of Kyna.

The face he wanted to see had not been there. Not that there was any reason that it should have. Sharon had never been connected with any of Kyna Hensley's films. Neither Victoria nor Sharon had contacted him after that night when he ended up in the hospital. He had not expected it of Victoria, but he found that he missed hearing from Sharon very much. She had become a very important part of his life over the years, and he had only lately come to realize that. He knew she had been in seclusion following the discovery of the murder of her parents at the hands of person or persons unknown. He had tried to call her several times, but he never got through. He wondered if his messages had been passed on to her. He was very much afraid that they had and she had chosen not to respond.

He remembered all the times he had skimmed through her letters looking for news of Victoria, passing up what was right in front of him.

What a damned fool he had been!

Everyone thought he was the luckiest man in Hollywood, a "Golden Boy." The truth was, he had no luck at all. He had blown his chance for happiness by loving the wrong woman for all these years.

The steps hurrying up behind him made him turn. Caro stood there. Behind her the lights from the building glowed so brightly he could not see what expression was on her face.

"You never loved either one of us," Caro said.

"Us?"

"My mother or myself." Precisely articulated so that there could be no mistake.

He might have lied, but there was a terrible urgency in her posture. "No."

"Have you ever loved anyone, Daniel?"

"Yes."

"But you're still alone?"

"Yes."

"Good," Caro said with a vicious pleasure. "I want you to feel it, too."

She hurried back into the light, into the crowd.

"Your limousine, Mr. Garrick?" the valet said.

"Thank you."

But before the valet could raise his hand, a Mercedes cut in front of another limousine and stopped right in front of him.

The door opened. "Daniel?"

Sharon was there, a vision in silver.

He climbed in beside her.

The valet shook his head.

The Mercedes cut into the line of moving traffic and was gone.

The telephone rang at five a.m.

Victoria roused enough to answer it.

"Miss Carr? Miss Victoria Carr?" It was a young woman's voice, soft and tremulous, with more than a trace of New York accent. "Is that you?"

"This is Victoria Carr." She resisted the urge to say, Can't you East Coasters ever remember the time difference?

"You don't know me, but I'm one of your biggest fans . . . and . . . I just think it's terrible!"

"What's terrible?" Victoria raised up on one elbow and switched on the lamp beside her bed. "Who is this?"

"I can't give you my name. My boss would have my skin. I . . . I work in a publishing office and I've seen the manuscript. There's a good chance we'll publish it, but I thought you would want to know ahead of time. So that . . . so that it wouldn't catch you completely by surprise."

"What manuscript?"

"It's by your stepdaughter, Laurel Pace. She's calling it,

Stepmommy Dearest. And it's just terrible, Miss Carr. The most vicious attack. I couldn't believe half of it was true, even though you played that terrible woman on *The Clan*. But then, last night, after I saw *Whatever Happened to Charlie's Gang*, I knew I had to tell you about it. You were so wonderful in that, Miss Carr. Nan was so brave, taking charge of her own life like that. You know, I grew up with *Charlie's Gang* . . .'' The girl faltered. "I have to hang up now, but I just couldn't let something like that happen to Nan. Not without warning her. Good-bye, Miss Carr.''

Victoria hung up the phone. She lay there for a long time looking at the other half of the bed. Barney had lain there, eons ago.

She got up and went to the window, staring out at the faint light of dawn. She had never felt so alone in her entire life.

"Really, Miss Carr, are you sure you shouldn't consult with your financial advisors before you do something quite this . . . benevolent.''

The lawyer had been a guest at Victoria Carr's wedding to Barney Pace. He still remembered the black outfit Barney's daughter had worn.

"I think this is what Barney would have wanted.''

"But this kind of settlement . . . Your own finances aren't . . .''

"My own finances are quite adequate for my personal needs, and I'm hoping to start on a new project soon. I'll be selling the house here. It's too big for just one person. I'm thinking about an apartment.''

"Miss Pace won't be living with you anymore?''

"I think Barney would have wanted it this way, don't you? He'd think it was time his little girl finally grew up.''

"High time,'' the lawyer said violently and then apologized for being unprofessional. "But Miss Pace is quite . . . opinionated. What if she prefers your house here to the one in Palm Springs?''

"I'm afraid she has no choice. You see, both houses are in my name. Mr. Pace was somewhat short of funds when we married and then his career went . . .'' She stopped. "I had to pay for everything you see. But I wouldn't want that to get out,'' she added hastily.

"Of course not."

"Laurel has been like my own daughter, you understand. But now, like any mother, I have to nudge her out of the nest. I couldn't think of a better way to do it."

"Miss Carr, you are a woman in a million," the lawyer said. "I'll take care of every detail for you. If you'll wait just a moment, I'll have my secretary make that one small change."

And that should take care of Laurel, Victoria thought as she signed the papers with a flourish. Thank God for the early morning call that alerted her. And to think the woman had called because of Nan. Would her character on *The Clan* have inspired that kind of loyalty?

Laurel could try to incite the public against her by claiming she was a cruel stepmother, but the size of the trust fund Victoria had set up for her this morning and the deed to the house in Palm Springs should convince the public otherwise.

Especially when there was no reason in the world for Victoria to take those steps. No one would know about the phone call from New York. No one would suspect that she had known what Laurel was planning.

Ingenious how the lawyer had set up the trust fund. So that Laurel had just enough to support herself in the Palm Springs house.

Too bad Laurel hated Palm Springs.

Victoria had no idea what Laurel had actually said in the book, but whatever it was, no one would believe her now. Just as America did not guess the truth behind those three perfect children so long ago on the television screen. Just as no one knew the truth behind the three imperfect adults they had become.

"Thank you, Miss Carr," the lawyer said as she handed over the papers. "I'll have this taken care of right away. And may I say how very much I enjoyed the *Whatever Happened to Charlie's Gang* special last night. Nan is an amazing woman. You know, I grew up with *Charlie's Gang*."

Victoria reached over and patted his hand. "We all did," she said.

EPILOGUE

ON THE COVER 102
Is the real Nan lonely, and longing for remarriage? Returning to television as America's Premier Mom on the new hit series *Nan's Bunch*, VICTORIA CARR reacts to rumors about her life offstage, telling the world she loves being single
People Magazine, October 15, 1990

VICTORIA CARR
An accomplished actress, Carr, 47, has seen her career go through many upheavals. But the most abrupt switch came this year when she traded her niche as TV's top villainess for a more satisfying role as the wise and gently witty mother of *Nan's Bunch*. "It's very gratifying to finally play a character that I don't mind women using as a role model," she says.

From "America's 100 Most Important Women,"
Ladies' Home Journal, October, 1990

CHARLIE'S GANG CURSE KEEPS REAL-LIFE NAN A WIDOW:
Why Victoria Carr Will Never Remarry.

Headline, *National Enquirer*, October 23, 1990

1990

Noticeably pregnant in her miniscule yellow bikini, Sharon sat cross-legged on the foredeck, trying to ignore the crowded, noisy waterfront behind her as she leafed through a month-old copy of *Daily Variety*. The Mediterranean mooring—bow anchored toward the harbor's center by a buoy and the stern tied to the quay—put the length of the chartered yacht between her and the staring foot traffic, but the port racket was inescapable. There was no way to anchor clear of the hubbub and still stay in sheltered water, and Sharon found herself longing for the tranquil sea of yesterday. In the privacy of the cobalt-blue waters of the open Mediterranean, she would have discarded the tiny bikini and sunned all over.

Still, there were compensations for being in port, she thought, exchanging the *Daily Variety* for a *Hollywood Reporter*. Daniel had brought back a huge stack of back issues of the trades when he went to pick up the mail this morning and now she was catching up on news and gossip. An interesting tidbit caught her eye, and she glanced over at Daniel.

Reclining on the mat beside hers, he was skimming through the equally large stack of scripts that had shown up in the mail, reading only the lines of dialogue in a determined effort to finish the whole batch before they left port tomorrow morning.

"Victoria's show is getting great ratings," she told him.

"Umm," he said.

Sharon grinned to herself. That had been his answer to every item she'd read aloud to him the last half-hour. She leaned back, enjoyed the gentle breeze against her skin. Her miniature diver must have enjoyed it too, because he turned a long, lazy flip in her belly.

"Your son just did a somersault," she told Daniel, expecting the same inattentiveness all her other conversational gambits had received.

"Ummmmm," Daniel said, right beside her ear, as he leaned over to kiss her. He moved over to her mat and pulled her close. They stayed like that, looking out across the harbor.

"It's almost perfect," Sharon said softly, after a long time had passed.

Daniel stroked her belly. "We'll make an early start tomorrow," he promised. He knew how much she was looking forward to their remaining two weeks aboard the yacht.

"It's not that. I wish Victoria weren't still alone."

Daniel nuzzled her ear. "You mustn't worry about Victoria. She's not like us. She doesn't really need anyone else."

Sharon wondered if that was true.

But when Daniel pulled her even closer, and the baby turned another slow flip, she was too happy to worry any longer.

Victoria sat at her dressing table in her ivory satin robe, removing the last of her makeup. The face that emerged from behind the cosmetic mask looked remarkably fresh in spite of the chaos she had just gone through.

Year before last at the Emmys ceremonies she was still the prime-time bitch everyone loved to hate in a shimmering sheath of black satin with a strapless top only a millimeter away from indecency. The paparazzi had swung in her direction like piranhas with Nikons, hoping to snap a photograph that would belie the ones released from her publicist, while the crowd of onlookers hurled verbal stones at the character she played.

Tonight when her limo arrived outside the auditorium, the only thing shocking about her organza gown sedately covered with a sequined tuxedo jacket was its shade of pink. Nevertheless, there had been a momentary hush in the cordon of the press when she stepped out, and a corresponding lull in the crowd noise. Then, as the electronic flashes began to flicker like lightning, the mob behind the police barriers surged forward calling her name and Nan's. For a few tense moments, it looked as though that ocean of onlookers might come surging past the barriers before Victoria could be hustled into the auditorium.

What did it matter if she wasn't up for anything this year? At the party afterwards, it was her and not the winners the interviewers sought out. So many people had grabbed her by the arm tonight that when she slipped back the loose sleeves of the robe, she could see the faint imprint of fingers already darkening into bruises on both forearms.

Victoria grimaced wryly into the mirror. Part of the price of fame.

And the other part, of course, was the incessant question from *everyone*, not just reporters: when will there be another man in your life?

No one, it seemed, could bear the thought of Nan Weston/Victoria Carr without a mate or at least a steady boyfriend.

She sighed as she stood up. After a lifetime in the spotlight, she should be used to it by now.

"*Nan's Bunch* has been picked up for the 'back nine,' " she said as she entered the apartment's bedroom. "We'll have a full season of twenty-two programs. Usually the network waits until November or December to make that decision."

"They made a wise choice." Dominic Solari, already in his pajamas, leaned back against the headboard of the king-sized bed, watching a tape of *Nan's Bunch* on the television across the room. "Would you like more champagne?"

When she nodded, he used his remote control to freeze the video tape. He rose and poured two glasses from the bottle of Dom Perignon they had toasted with earlier and presented one to her with a flourish. "We'll toast America's darling."

"And yours?"

"Most assuredly," he said and kissed her.

Victoria followed him back to the comfort of the bed, leaning against his shoulder. But when he reached for the remote control to restart the tape, she caught his hand.

The frozen image of her face filled the whole television screen. She studied it as she sipped her champagne.

"What do you see there?" Dominic asked her gently.

"I understand how people can look at the face of someone on television and feel as though they know the person behind it," she told him. "They believe wholeheartedly in Nan. She is the perfect mother. Just as Nan, Bucky, and JoJo were the perfect children. No one suspected the truth about us then; no one suspects the truth about my life now."

"Are you sorry?"

"That the wholesome matriarch is in reality the mistress of a Mafioso?" Victoria laughed when he flinched. "I thought we had agreed to be perfectly honest with each other, Dominic."

"Honest," he protested. "Not brutal. You are really a remarkable woman, Victoria."

"A woman who loves you very much." She slipped off the robe and came to him, naked and unashamed.